THE RED MOUNTAIN

Douglas McArthur

D1073573

Running Boar Media

I

ISBN 978 1 8382 1800 3

Published by
Running Boar Media
Abergavenny, Wales

www.runningboarmedia.com

Grateful thanks to Lu, with love.

To Frank Olding, my Welsh and Roman history mentor

To Paul RG Haley, who photographed the Legio VIII Augusta on a memorable day at Vindolanda, just below Hadrian's Wall.

The lads and lasses of the Legio VIII Augusta Living History Society who could not have been more helpful.

Corinthus Civilis on the front cover - Batavian Auxiliary, Miles Gaius Valerius Crispus on the spine - Legio VIII Augusta, and Tessararius Falco on the back cover.

PLACE NAMES

Alesia	Alise-Sainte-Reine
Armorica	Region of Gaul including Brittany Peninsula
Bravonium	Leintwardine, Hereford
Burrium	Usk
Caletum	Calais
Camulodunum	Colchester
Cantiaci	Province based on Kent
Corinium Dobunorum	Cirencester
Cornoviorum Viroconium	Settlement of the Cornovii, Wroxeter
Deva Victrix	Chester
Durobrivae	Water Newton, Cambridgeshire, where Ermine Street crossed the River Nene
Durovigutum	Godmanchester, Huntingdonshire
Eboracum	York
Gallia Lugdunensis	Central province of France between Lyon and the Loire. At its centre is Lutetia Parisiorum or Paris
Gesoscribate	Brest
Glevum	Gloucester
Gobannion	Abergavenny
Isle of Mona	Anglesey
Levobrinta	Forden Gaer (at the conflux of the Severn and Afon Rhiw)
Lindum	Lincoln
Londinium	London
Luguvalium	Carlisle
Mediolanum	Milan
Mynydd-Bach	Near Shirenewton, Chepstow
Pennocrucium	Near Stretton Bridge, Staffordshire
Portus Dubris	Dover
Uriconium	Wroxeter
Venta Silurum	Caerwent
Verulamium	St Albans

Rivers

Tamesis	Thames
Sabrina	Severn (Roman)
Hafren	Severn (Celt)
Wysg	Usk

EBORACUM

MONA

DEVA

LEVOBRINTA

R Hafren

R Sabrina

GOBANNION

R Wysg

BURRIUM

VENTA SILURUM

ISCA

MYNYDD BACH

CAMULODUNUM

R Tamesis

LONDINIUM

PORTUS DUBRIS

CALETUM

CHAPTER I

First light came cold and sharp for the slaves rousted from their rough shelters. After a meagre breakfast of hard bread and warm barley gruel, they were released from their shackles and drew tools from the supply wagon before trudging listlessly to work.

A watery sun filtered through the clouds but there was no sign of rain on the meadow, surrounded by forest in sparsely populated eastern Britannia. A cold wind blew in off the Oceanus Germanicus many miles away.

Lenc of Alesia, an immunis, a chosen man in the Auxiliary Cohort III Gallorum, attached to the XX Valeria, one of Rome's elite legions, sipped his warmed wine as he watched the scarecrow prisoners reluctantly prepare for their day of toil.

He was a Gaul but had been in the service of Rome since his father had sold him into the Legion when he became one mouth too many for their small farm to support. He had the dark curly hair and slightly swarthy complexion of the Celt, which not even the seemingly constant, insidious rain on this island could wash away. Not a handsome man, there was something about him that made women look twice and men suck their stomachs in.

His arms carried several tattoos, the running boar of the XX Valeria and the spread-winged stork of the III Gallorum, his Auxiliary Cohort, which, in less complicated times he had joined as a boy soldier. There was a message to Antenociticus, the soldier's god, and harking back to an earlier time the crossed hammer and axe of Toutatis, an older god of war. Several scars

1

criss-crossed his torso, a particularly vicious one about six inches long stood out in a livid weal on his right forearm. He had a black-bearded Goth in Northern Germany to thank for that one.

He was sitting on a stool outside the leather tent where Optio Pluvius, his immediate boss and mentor, was studying designs for the bridge they were building over a sizeable stream. Hundreds of slave teams were driving a new road from Londinium to Eboracum, the start of what would be called Ermine Street, a stone highway driven almost the length of this god-forsaken country, allowing the Legion swift access to subdue unruly locals. The route had been surveyed and mapped and slaves were building separate sections, camping by the roadside, laying hardcore and clinker before square stones were laid by army engineers with the precision and skill needed to support the weight of a marching legion, eight men abreast, horses, even siege engines. The locals, more used to mud tracks, had never seen anything like it.

Lenc's team was building a bridge in a pleasant little valley half-way between Durovigutum and Durobrivae, two days' march from Camulodunum, a seemingly safe area, but even so the road builders knew better than to drop their vigilance.

A legionary guard, posted on the bank, stiffened when he saw two slaves square up to each other. They had the same whirling tribal tattoos and both looked angry. The guard, not unduly alarmed, let his whip dangle from a loop round his wrist. "Get back to work you fuckwits," he shouted. "Save your arguments for your own time."

One of the slaves, wild of beard and eye, brandished a mattock, a tool with a flat digging blade on one side and a heavy pointed chisel on the other. The other looked round for a weapon and picked up a fist-sized stone.

The guard whistled and caught the attention of a cavalry auxiliary, who wheeled his horse and cantered over. He was about to order them to get back to work when the slave with the stone hurled it violently at the horse's head, making the animal rear up in pain and fright. The auxiliary fought to control his beast as the other guards, attracted by the noise, hurriedly drew their swords.

Then, from out of the ground, twin apparitions covered in grass and clods of earth reared up behind the panicking horse. One slashed the animal across the hind leg hamstrings, and screaming, it fell back, eyes rolling and wide, snorting in pain and terror.

The rider twisted and turned in his now very real danger. The all-powerful cavalryman, his horse disabled, was about to be slaughtered by mud and grass-caked apparitions that sprang from the ground.

As the horse went down, the rider had the presence of mind to kick free, but slipped on the damp ground and in a flash the second apparition was on him, wielding a vicious blade. The auxiliary was still trying to tug his own weapon free as the mud-caked Briton steadied himself, and with a wild cry plunged his long knife into the soldier's neck. The attacker didn't need to check whether his victim was dead. A half-severed neck testified to that.

The guards stared in disbelief as the ground came alive across the entire building site. The auxiliary cavalry, supposedly their defence against the hated Britons were targeted and stopped in their tracks by more grass and shrub-covered apparitions which sprang up from the earth. There must have been about 50 of them, and looking round, grimly selected their targets.

Surprise was complete as the warriors worked quickly in pairs to attack horse and rider. The front man went for the horse, grabbing at the reins close to the head to either bring it down or at least distract it, while the other went for the rider, who was desperately occupied, trying to control his terrified beast. If the rider managed to draw his sword, the rear man went for the back legs of the horse, slashing tendons and hamstrings, bringing it down in agony. Then, it was an easy matter to unseat the rider and with one slash open his throat. The attacks were lethally effective as almost in seconds the much vaunted cavalry were cut to pieces.

Lenc threw his horn beaker to the ground and pulled his sword, while behind him, Optio Pluvius sprang up in bewilderment as the camp erupted. Finally the legionaries pulled themselves together to fight for their lives against the mud-caked Britons.

The Senior Optio Guard Commander bellowed his orders, but his men were in dire straits. Half of them were cut down before they could recover from their surprise and gather themselves for defence.

Most of the slaves stared in surprise as the apparitions attacked their masters. They were as wild haired and filthy as the attackers, and watched in fascinated terror as they saw the Romans getting the worst of the fight. Some of them, including the pair who had caused the distraction, were obviously in the know and joined the fight using their tools as weapons, or snatched up discarded swords to help complete the rout of their captors.

As the cavalry was swiftly and efficiently disposed of, so it became the turn of the infantry guards. Even as they snaked out whips and drew swords, the sheer weight of slaves forced to work in drudgery for an enemy they despised, fell on them.

Two slaves clad only in loincloths, and carrying mattocks rushed at Lenc, screaming in triumph. He stepped to one side as the first brought his weighted pick whistling down, just where his head had been a heartbeat before. Lenc stepped forward, raising his short sword and swung down and through the slave's exposed neck. He wrenched his blade free as the other slave stepped back, eyes wide with fear. The man hurriedly dropped his weapon and held his arms out in supplication, mutely pleading for his life. Lenc took a step forward, holding his sword down at waist height and pointing up at his assailant. Even as the slave opened his mouth to call for help, his breath was strangled to a groan as Lenc's blade stabbed violently up and through his chin. A gout of blood coursed from the tear as he slumped to the ground.

In the centre of the camp, the Guard Commander tried to take control. Initially horrified when the attack started, after a second of terror, he gulped and shouted to his men to rally round him. He realised the warriors must have quietly infiltrated during the night then gone to ground, expertly covering themselves with turf and grass, after persuading two of the slaves to create a diversion.

A swift glance showed what was left of his command were fighting individually for their lives, so pulling them into a defensive position was going to be hopeless. He collected himself and ran towards one of his men, who was screaming obscenities and fighting off three demons armed with rusty swords.

He slashed violently at the nearest as he came within reach, catching him high on the arm, almost severing it. The warrior shrieked and sank to the ground as his sword splashed into the stream. Now that the odds were even, the other two looked undecided who to attack, but the Guard Commander made up their minds for them by snarling and surging forward, swinging his sword. Again he slashed, his sword ringing as it connected with his opponent's weapon, knocking it from his hand. He stepped back and stabbed deep into the warrior's chest, then twisted and pulled the blade from the still-standing corpse with an ugly sucking noise.

The last man tried to defend himself and stepped back, his sword raised, looking desperately from one to the other as they moved carefully towards him. Then with a wild cry he sprang forward at the Commander, opening himself up to the other soldier who stabbed him under the armpit, straight into his heart. The two stood for a few seconds, panting. The soldier squinted round uncertainly, and nervously wiped his clammy sword hand on the short tunic under his body armour. They seemed to be the last ones standing.

The Guard Commander also looked round, registered Lenc, the engineer, quietly disappearing into his tent and warily whispered, "No place for us here lad, think we should make ourselves scarce."

The soldier nodded, his mouth dry. Carefully they stepped away from the stream, behind the foundations of the new bridge. The stonework gave them some protection, shielding them from the enemy, and they might have made it except for one slave who had merely sat at the edge of the fight and watched, saw them and shouted. The Romans jumped to their feet and started to scramble up the bank but with a sinking certainty knew it was too late.

Two of the attackers, mounted on fine Roman horses, savagely wheeled and galloped after the fleeing soldiers, and within a few strides they were headed off and forced to stop. Their chests heaving, both from fear and exhaustion, they stood back to back as the triumphant warriors slowly circled them.

One of the riders gestured to the nearest slaves who were busily stripping the dead soldiers of their weapons and armour. They paused for a moment and stepped hesitantly towards the last two Romans, who hefted their swords and crouched defensively. Both knew there would be no mercy, their last task to take a few of the enemy with them, before their inevitable end.

"Come on then you bastards, let's see what you're made of," growled the Commander. His feet shifted to get a better grip on the grass as he mentally prepared himself for his last glorious charge in the service of the empire. He raised his sword, but before he could launch himself into the advancing slaves, a shower of stone rained down. Together, they both sagged unconscious as the rocks pulverised their bodies, and with a triumphant shout the slaves surged forward to wreak their vengeance on the still bodies. They seemed not to know or care that the men were already dead, jostling and pushing each other in their desperate need to get in close and beat the inert bodies with rocks, slash with swords, even kick with bare feet, releasing their pent-up rage and frustration on the inert corpses. Finally the mad frenzy died away and the slaves just stood there, breathing heavily as they started to wonder about their fate.

They looked round at the attackers, who were checking the fallen soldiers, unceremoniously dispatching those still breathing. They collected weapons, armour, even clothing and food. Some of the slaves had found the Roman mess tent and were digging into a cauldron of stew still bubbling over the fire. They yelped as the hot meat and gravy burned their fingers, but they didn't care, just gulped it down, jostling each other to get their share before it was gone. Their own food, hard bread, cheese and the barley from which gruel was made was piled in sacks. There would be time enough to eat that shit once the decent stuff was gone.

Lenc backed into the tent pulling Pluvius in with him.

"What's happening?" asked the wild eyed optio querulously. "Why don't we go out and fight?" he demanded.

Lenc faced him. "Because it's too late," he hissed furiously. "We're the last standing, we can only save ourselves." From the fragile security of their tent, Lenc watched the last of the guard detail savagely cut down. If they were not careful, they would be next.

"Come," he said to Pluvius who seemed unable to grasp the mortal danger they were in. Carefully, Lenc teased open the flaps to the rear of the tent and looked out. He could see the tree-line but no warriors.

"We're going to have to move as fast as possible, but whatever happens, don't stop. We've got just one chance to get away. If one of us goes down, the other must keep going, have you got that?" Lenc tried to impress his urgency on the older Optio, who licked his lips and nodded distractedly.

Lenc smiled. "Now draw your sword, you remember how to use it, do you?"

Finally Pluvius seemed to realise what was happening. "I was fighting barbarians while you were still at the breast, don't worry about me, I know what to do."

"Good man," said Lenc. "Time to go."

Crouching, the two scurried away from the tent, and after making a wide circle, dropped down into the stream bed which afforded some cover upstream from the bridge works.

Lenc risked a glance over the bank towards the camp, but so far they seemed to have got away undetected.

The new road was being cut through a forest, and the first task, in case of ambush, was to clear the trees for an arrow's distance either side.

He pointed to the tree-line. "That's where we'll go. If we can make the trees we should be fine."

Pluvius swallowed and nodded. "Come on then."

The banks gave some protection until the stream widened and the land fell away to flat meadow. Lenc looked round, they still had some way to go.

Lenc grimaced, "We're going to have to run for it."

Pluvius nodded, and they both stood, hefting their swords. As they started running, Lenc estimated they had about 200 paces to go. He had never felt so nakedly exposed but as they got closer to the sanctuary of the trees, he began to hope they would make it. Until Pluvius stopped, holding his side. "I can't go on," he groaned. "You go, save yourself."

"Do you think I'm leaving you here, you silly old fool, if you want to live, come on." The trees were getting closer as Lenc dragged the protesting Optio along when suddenly there was a shout from the camp. Lenc looked behind and saw warriors climbing up into the saddle, then to his horror, two archers stepped out, readying arrows to fire.

"Come on Pluvius," he yelled desperately, "One last effort, we have to outrun those archers."

This new threat seemed to give Pluvius a surge of energy, and he started running by himself. Lenc was aware of arrows thudding into the ground round them and knew it would not be long before they got the range. At least it stops the horsemen from getting too close, he thought desperately.

The dense canopy was almost in touching distance when the inevitable happened, a heavy, iron tipped arrow slammed into Pluvius' lower back, knocking him violently forward, almost into the treeline. Lenc stopped and without a thought, grabbed his mentor and hauled him into the cool sanctuary of the forest. He looked down at the ashen-faced Pluvius, slumped on the forest floor. "I'm finished," he said. "You only have one chance. Run man, run. If nothing else, you must get back and report. Go now. I don't have long anyway."

And with a sigh, the older man sagged, eyes sightless.

Lenc choked back the emotions that welled up inside him, and collected himself. He could hear the horsemen galloping towards the woods, and knew time was short. He touched his friend's forehead one last time, turned and ran into the woods.

Afterwards he could not say how long he ran, but enough to shake off his pursuers. When he finally felt safe enough to stop and catch his breath, he sank down onto a fallen log and looked round.

According to the sun, he was travelling east, which was good, because if he changed direction to the south, he should come across the new road, and from there, if he managed to avoid his pursuers, would eventually run into a patrol. He wondered if he was the only survivor. Probably, he thought morosely.

After a short rest he set off again, navigating by carefully watching glimpses of the sun's movement across the sky. He moved quickly, pausing only to listen for alien sounds in the depths of the forest. Visibility in the trees was poor and he was only too aware that there might be enemy parties out searching for him. The thought of being captured alive made him swallow nervously.

Only after it was obvious the raid was a success, a small party of riders left the cover of a copse of trees and rode slowly towards the scene of carnage. The slaves looked uncertainly at each other, as the riders trotted nearer.

The front rider had the bearing of a leader, a big man with blond curly hair, swept back and held by a band tight to his forehead. He wore a torc of woven strands of gold, a bright rope around his neck hanging below his dense beard trimmed to just beneath his chin. His drab cloak, gathered at the neck, trailed across his horse's flanks, and he rode high in the saddle with an imperious air.

On his approach, the slaves instinctively huddled together, some were clearly fearful of this latest turn of events, others looked defiant.

His gaze rested thoughtfully on the emaciated, filthy slaves, then at last he spoke. "If you don't understand me, get one of the others to translate. Some of you have been slaves for a long time, but at last your future is up to you. How many of you fought the Romans at Medway?"

At least half held up a hand.

"Some of you may recognise me. I am Caratacus and I fought with the Catuvellauni on that terrible day. We outnumbered them, and we were brave and good fighters. But the bastards beat us because they fought in a way we had never experienced before.

"I am still of the Catuvellauni, but I am of Britannia as well. When we drive the Romans back into the sea it won't be a victory for any one tribe, but for the tribe of Britannia. Join me and you can be part of that. Even if you are from the mainland, you can be part of our fight against the march of Rome." He nodded at a small group who, by their tattoos were marked as Goths from Germania, and leaned forward on his horse's pommel. "Some of you have come a long way to these shores, but if you want to fight Romans, does it matter where you came from? Join us and your home can be here. When we have won, you can return to your native land, taking with you the lessons learned." His eyes blazed.

"How to fight them, and defeat them. You can stay here and

wait for the Romans, or you can run but, if you are caught you will be crucified, you are carrying the slave mark of Rome."

Some of the slaves unconsciously fingered their brand, high on the forearm. "If a Roman sees that you are done for. If you make it home, even your countrymen may be tempted to turn you in for the reward."

He paused and looked meaningfully at the slaves. "Or you can fight the bastards with me. I promise you nothing but pain and hardship but also the chance to drive the invaders back into the sea. Come with us and be men again, take your chances by yourself or stay here and await your masters' pleasure, it's up to you."

With that, Caratacus wheeled his horse, and followed by his mounted entourage rode slowly back towards the trees. Behind him, his warriors, who had taken part in the raid, some still wearing their soil caked camouflage sacking moved in behind, yelling their fierce war cries. The slaves stood apprehensively. Some had been in captivity for many years. Some were from the mainland. At least with the Romans, the work might be tough but they usually got fed and they were still alive.

"Fuck it," exclaimed a heavily tattooed Goth. "I've been a slave three winters I have no family, they saw to that, and I have been treated like an animal. I am Visgar, son of Visgarda of Alamani. I don't care about this place, but I care about freedom. I shall fight. You can have my sword arm until we defeat the Romans, then I go home."

Caratacus heard him and half turned in the saddle. He gestured a wave that said 'follow me' and turned to the wood again.

The big Goth stripped a Roman body of sword belt and cloak and ran to catch the war party. As he did so, other slaves followed his lead, snatching up weapons and clothing the raiding party had missed, and hurried after them in a motley gaggle.

A handful of men from nearby tribes scattered in different directions and ran alone, hoping their salvation lay with their kin. A small group just sat down among the dead looking wistfully at the retreating backs of the raiders and their newly freed slave brothers.

As they approached the treeline, Caratacus motioned to one of his lieutenants, "How many are following?"

The young warrior looked behind him. "About 40 I suppose."

"Good, they will make fine killers of Romans."

With the tree line in easy reach, Caratacus wheeled and waited for his raiders. He hailed the front runner of the small band.

"Orventus, your men have done well this day. You have made the Romans think twice about building their damned roads. Did any get away?"

"Aye lord, two made it to the forest, one got no further, but I am afraid the other disappeared into the trees." Orventus shrugged. "We won't be able to repeat this raid, Lord, for they will be in strength next time."

"You speak wisely," conceded Caratacus, "and I agree with you. The Romans are maddened by our pin-pricks and will surely soon lash out. We are gathering men and weapons, but only when we have enough will we be able to take them on again in open combat."

Both men remembered the gut wrenching fear of their flight from the terrible battles on the banks of the Medway and Tamesis. The Britons outnumbered the Romans four to one and were on home ground, yet these warriors used to large raiding parties had no answer against the discipline of the battle-hardened Legions. They had thrown men and chariots at the unflinching shield wall, then when their shattered remnants pulled back to regroup, the mighty Roman machine tramped forward, moving inexorably toward them, stepping over dead and dying bodies. The wild men of Britannia had never encountered such a way of fighting before and it had taken a lot of their army to die before they realised they could not win that day. Almost as one, the survivors turned and fled, harassed and cut down by disciplined auxiliary cavalry who completed the rout.

Caratacus at least realised that the old tactics, if tactics they could be called, would not work against this military machine, the like of which he had never seen before. So with a heavy heart, he left the field to the victorious enemy, leaving many hundreds of dead and as many again as slaves. With his head bowed, he vowed he would never again fight the Romans on their own ground and to their rules until he rode at the head of an army that could match Rome in skill, discipline and tactics.

CHAPTER II

That night, Lenc slept fitfully under the forest canopy. He had stumbled across the new road in the late afternoon but could not take the risk that there were still barbarians around. Rather than step out onto the bare arrow-break and walk along the road, he decided to wait in the shadows until the morning, and a Roman patrol came along, which it had to soon.

Then as darkness fell, he realised he was in for a chilly and hungry night. He had no cloak or blankets and daren't light a fire. All he could do was gather twigs and leaves and try to burrow under them for some semblance of warmth. It didn't work.

Several times during the night he wriggled out of his hide to try and get warm by moving around. His fear of discovery had abated as, on his own, he was far likelier to hear the enemy trampling through the undergrowth than they would hear him blowing on his cupped hands or stamping his feet.

Thankfully, after an eternity of shivering, he finally became aware of the night steadily turning into day, a patina of frost glistening on the undergrowth in the weak early sun.

He stayed under the canopy till the sun was high in the sky, at last feeling more human in the sunshine but ravenously hungry. He put the thought of food from his mind as he rested his head on his arms, a patrol must turn up soon he promised himself. But it was some hours before he was finally jerked into consciousness by the steady tramp of Roman marching. He peered out of the undergrowth and there was the sight he longed for, a column of 80 Roman soldiers in full battle gear.

He emerged from the tree cover and walked towards the Century, his arms up high and palms open. On seeing this lone dishevelled figure suddenly appear, the centurion called for 'all round defence'. Instantly the column shook out and established a shield wall either side of the new stone highway. The centurion noted the gashed uniform and bloodstains on Lenc's face and uniform. "Report, soldier," he ordered grimly.

Lenc snapped to attention, "Sir, Immunis Lenculus, engineer attached to XX Valeria, our bridge building camp is just ahead. Yesterday morning we were attacked, I think I must be the only survivor. There were about 50 of them, who managed to infiltrate our camp during darkness and conceal themselves in the ground until we started work, then they jumped out completely surprising us. I managed to escape with my optio, but he took an arrow as we made it to the treeline."

The centurion nodded, "Go to the supply wagons at the rear and get some food and water. You will come with us to the camp where I will need a full report."

Lenc saluted as the centurion waved the column forward. Then he breathed a huge sigh of relief as he realised that in the marching column he was finally safe. After wolfing dried meat and bread, washed down with brackish water, he looked round and started to take an interest in his surroundings. They could not be too far from the camp, and noted that the officer had thrown scouts out to the edge of the trees and well ahead.

Suddenly the lead scout sank to one knee, holding his clenched fist up high, then pointed up ahead. As the column approached he ran back to the centurion and reported that the camp was just ahead, although he could see no sign of life.

The officer nodded and looked round for his senior optio, a primus pilus who ran forward when he saw the scout signalling. "Tell the men to keep their eyes open," he said grimly to the optio. "The raiders could well be watching us and waiting to take us on as well. Take two sections forward to investigate the camp, at the first sign of trouble, double back to the column. Slow and easy, no heroics."

The optio nodded and the scout ran back to his position.

Lenc had moved forward and overheard this conversation. The centurion saw him and beckoned. "Is there anything I should know of this camp," he asked.

"Well sir, we were building a bridge over a brook with quite steep banks, which could hide enemy. That's how we managed to get clear without being seen. Apart from that there is no cover."

The century nodded. "Good, stay up with me and keep your eyes peeled."

The column, fully alert, moved carefully forward along the stone road until the camp came into sight. Suddenly the scout once again dropped to one knee and made a chopping motion with one hand, indicating he had seen something.

"Optio," ordered the centurion, "take your men forward." Instantly the detailed sections trotted towards the camp in an extended line. Lenc turned to the officer, "Sir, could I go forward as well, I may be able to help."

The centurion gestured assent, Lenc nodded his thanks and trotted after the advance party. He caught them up at the edge of the camp where they paused, uncertain where to start. Lenc whispered to the optio the layout of the camp. "There's the bridge we were building. The guard camp is on the higher ground with the horse pickets, and downstream are the shelters for the slaves. Most of the fighting was up around our tents and the bridge itself."

The optio nodded. "We'll all stay together until we're sure they've cleared off," he said. "We'll make for the army tents first."

He gripped his spear and moved out, his men following at the crouch. They were just taking their first tentative steps into the tent area when suddenly there was a keening cry of desperation and six filthy and emaciated figures stood up, jabbering and wailing.

16

"God's blood, it's the slaves," Lenc said in amazement.

The slaves walked towards the soldiers, holding their arms out in entreaty. The optio watched them for a second or so, then dismissed them.

"You," he said, pointing at Lenc. "Stay with me. Two end men go and sort those slaves out. Get them sat down and for the gods' sake shut 'em up. Rest of you, we're going to clear this camp at speed. When we get to the other side, go to ground and we'll call up the column. I want this done quickly. Any enemy you see on the ground, make sure they're dead. We'll sort out our own when we're sure the enemy has all fucked off. Right," he glanced round, "ready to move? MOVE."

As one, the legionaries jumped up, ready for the grim business ahead. Bodies were checked to confirm any life, and in minutes the small camp had been covered and the soldiers sank down on the perimeter, spears outwards. Only then did the optio stand to signal the main party, which immediately moved forward. The slaves huddled together, whispering fearfully.

The optio called Lenc over. "Can you see anything of interest, anything that will help us?"

Lenc had already been studying the ground, and reached down, picking up a long piece of sacking, covered in mud and clods of grass. "This is how they were concealed," he said. "They infiltrated the camp in the dark, contacted the slaves and got a couple of them to start the diversion just after they started work. The sacking was a good enough disguise at dawn. Not perfect but good enough."

"Good enough indeed," said the centurion, who had just arrived. "And even if they were discovered before the diversion there would still have been enough of a surprise for the bastards to do a lot of damage.

"We'll take the slaves back to camp where the intelligence boys can have a word. In the meantime, a funeral pyre for our people. Once that's done we'll head back to report."

"Sir what about the Briton dead? Do we bury them?"

The centurion looked round at the scene of the short but savage battle. "Fuck 'em," he said tersely. "Let them rot where they are."

Chief Inquisitor Marcus Relis watched impatiently as the six surviving slaves stumbled through the now complete West Gate of Camulodunum. Their hands were tied and they were shackled together by neck restraints. He could smell their fear as, when told to stop, they sank exhausted to the cobbled road.

He took a deep breath and shouted in outrage at the officer in charge. "Optio," he blazed. "Why are these men treated in this way? They have shown their loyalty to Rome and should be treated as allies and friends, not enemy. Release them at once."

The optio snapped to attention and stared fixedly to his front, his face ashen.

"When you have untied them, feed and clean them."

Then as he turned away, he whispered, "keep a close eye on the snivelling bastards, let them speak to no-one till I interview them."

Suddenly the optio understood, but let no trace of recognition show. Instead he banged his right fist to his breast-plate in salute. Hurriedly he shouted to his men, "Release the prisoners, er…" he hesitated, "the friends of Rome."

Once released, the puzzled slaves were led to an annexe of the gate guard house. The room was bare, but clean, whitewashed walls and a stone floor. The only windows were high up, too high to see out of, or more importantly for any curious person to see in.

Still the prisoners huddled together defensively. Some of the small number began to wonder if they had done the right thing in putting their trust in the devil they knew. They had expected to be delivered back to the slave pens, ready for more back-breaking toil, yet here they were, being treated like real human beings.

Their nervous mutterings choked off as legionaries crashed open the door and staggered in with wooden pails of steaming water. Strangely, the soldiers were smiling. The slaves looked on aghast, what was coming now?

The guard commander, a rictus smile stapled on his face, put down his knobbly vine cane and mimicked washing his face with the water. Somehow, he managed to mime the action of washing while keeping his big smile going.

Reluctantly the slaves shuffled forward. There were brushes in the water and hesitantly, one of the bolder reached in for one, looking for approval from the guard.

"Good, good," encouraged the guard and the slave, a wiry Gaul, soaked the brush and applied the water liberally to his sweaty and mud-stained body. With the guards willing them on, all six men gathered round the buckets and soaked themselves. Rags of clothing fell to the ground as the slaves capered in the unaccustomed luxury, scrubbing hard at the ingrained dirt which had become their lot.

Nodding approval, the guards, still smiling, backed out of the room, ostentatiously leaving the solid oak door unlatched. As they entered the clean air of the guard compound the commander let go his breath.

"Dirty bastards," he muttered. "Let's hope this farce will be worth it."

With the water finally cooling, the door once again swung open for cooks to enter with steaming pots of food, bread, and even some wine. The guards motioned to the slaves to empty the water buckets outside and stack them tidily, then indicated that they could eat.

Not knowing when this bounty would end, the slaves hastily snatched bowls, wooden spoons and mugs, afraid they would be spirited away as mysteriously as they had arrived.

The main cauldron contained a bean stew, which, wonder of wonders even contained some meat. It was good and wholesome, and apart from what they had snatched at the bridge camp, quite the best food these deprived men had eaten since their capture.

They hurriedly devoured the stew, dunking bread in the wine, reluctant to lose a drop. As they were coming to the end, Marcus Relis walked in, with the now customary big smile stitched on his face. His teeth were white and even, but somehow with the predatory look of a wolf, and the smile did nothing to reassure the apprehensive slaves. He stood in front of them in the centre of the room, legs apart and thumbs hooked in his sword belt, bare-headed but wearing his armour. He gazed at them for a second or two.

"I hope you have fed well and feel better after washing some of that grime off yourselves. You have been through a terrible ordeal, and come out of it with your loyalty to Rome intact. That is commendable and will be rewarded, but first there is one thing you can do for me. I want you to describe in as much detail as possible exactly what happened, how the attackers subdued so many of our cavalry and who was in charge.

"You will be interviewed separately and anyone not co-operating fully will soon be found out. Although, as future citizens of Rome, I am sure that will not be the case." He looked round smiling, seeking reassurance. The slaves nodded fervently.

"I know you will all co-operate and wish to help. Those that do will start new lives as house slaves, which is a far more agreeable prospect than breaking rocks. Then in a matter of a few years, if you continue to show your worth, you could be made citizens of Rome and take your place among us as freemen. Now how does that sound?"

The slaves perked up visibly at this. Being a freeman was so remote a dream as to be completely unimaginable, but being a house slave was something else again, so they were, to a man, willing to show their loyalty to Rome.

Within two hours, the interpreter-interviewers returned with their results.

"So Caratacus himself," mused Marcus Relis. "We will of course send out patrols, but he'll be long gone. Useful intelligence though."

He stared into space for a moment or two. It was his job to find out what warlike intentions the tribes had, and right now Caratacus was beginning to take on all the hallmarks of a war leader again.

After his crushing defeat at Tamesis, Roman considered opinion was that they had seen the last of this troublesome warrior, but against the odds he kept popping up, avoiding set-piece battles in favour of hit and run pin-pricks. In short, he was a complete pain in the arse, but Marcus Relis had to admit that his tactics were sound and Caratacus was becoming a force to be reckoned with. Even if he was a shit general he seemed to be able to command loyalty and gather warriors. The road gang slaves had just added 40-odd more swords to his banner, and there would probably be more before he was stopped.

The guard commander interrupted his train of thought. "We've done with the slaves sir, did you say you would find them house slave work?"

Marcus Relis looked at him incredulously. "Are you mad? We've milked the filthy bastards of everything they know, so their value has gone. Can you seriously imagine any household taking on such worthless, ignorant baggage? Dispose of them quietly and bury them where no-one will find them. Don't let them speak to the other slaves or we may have a riot on our hands. The less this is known about the better."

CHAPTER III

Since becoming an auxiliary, Lenc had seen 15 long years of action across the empire. Years in which he fought in running battles and skirmishes in Mesopotamia, Northern Germany, even his own native Gaul.

So to be detached from his auxiliary squadron, to join a disparate band of engineers posted to Britannia seemed like a dream come true. And until recently, being attached to the XX Valeria in Camulodunum had been the easiest and most rewarding tour he had ever served.

He had arrived at the settlement on the east coast of Britannia to help build a fort, as the Legion was reinforcing its stranglehold on the area. The fort would be massive, eventually home to a complete legion, underwriting the majesty and authority of Rome. It was a structure never before seen in Britannia.

"Watch and learn, boy, watch and learn and one day you may be as good an engineer as me," confided his new boss, Optio Pluvius, with a wink and a confidential tap of the nose. "Nobody knows better than me how to build a road, or a bridge or even a fort."

Optio Pluvius was a man of certainties with almost a lifetime in uniform. He knew that the coming of Rome to these benighted heathens was a good thing, and he knew that carving out a civilisation was to everyone's benefit and could not understand why there would be opposition to that view.

"I just can't fathom these people," he often ranted. "We show them how to build proper houses and roads, how to live a better life. We give them art and sports, and all they want to do is stick a knife in your gizzard as soon as your back is turned. If it was left to me I'd go somewhere I was wanted and let this lot fester and starve in their shit-holes of huts."

Lenc one day suggested mildly that perhaps the locals didn't want to be improved by becoming citizens of Rome. Perhaps all they wanted to do was be left alone, even if it was in a festering hut made of compressed cow shit. Which sent Pluvius off on another rant.

Lenc never had much time for contemplating the bigger issues of what the Legion was doing on the frontiers. He was a soldier and did what he was told, but his service in different far-flung outposts had shown him that not everybody thought the empire was a good thing.

He enjoyed building roads and bridges, particularly the mathematical problems of bridging. It was hard, unrelenting, back-breaking work for all of them, including those like him who were engineers. Everyone had to pitch in, yet still took their place in the shield wall when necessary.

Being detailed to accompany Optio Pluvius onto the road pushing northwards was something Lenc had looked forward to. The work on the new fort was interesting and worthwhile, but building a road was entirely different. Planning, mapping, sighting bridges, aqueducts, and viaducts were new challenges, and he relished them. Could have done without Optio Pluvius constantly moaning, but you can't have everything.

Well he's not moaning any more, thought Lenc regretfully. And he could do without a horde of barbarian rabbits coming out of the ground all round him. He smiled grimly at the memory.

After an interview with the intelligence officer, Lenc rejoined the engineer section working on the fort, but hoped that one day he would be re-assigned to the road teams. In the meantime, he decided to work hard and keep his nose clean, his fervent wish that he could carry on without coming to the attention of any more senior officers.

Then, a few days later, while lost in studying plans for the fort's new southern wall, he got the call to report to headquarters on the double.

What now? he thought. Hurriedly, he strapped on his wide belt holding his gladius, the short stabbing sword of the legion on one side and a dagger on the other. On his head went his helmet, plumed with the red brush of the Valeria, rubbing as much dust off as possible as he hurried to the headquarters building.

He walked into the orderly room without knocking. This was common ground where everyone in the legion came to receive orders. Offices behind were more important, the pay office, Senior Optio's office and most important of all, the hallowed portal of the commanding officer of the legion.

Two clerks sat at desks importantly checking documents.

"What's up," asked Lenc. "I hear someone wants to speak to me."

"Not me mate," said one of the clerks. "It's the Legate no less, who wants a little chat."

The Legate and Commander of the Twentieth, Quintus Equitius tended not to move in the same circles as ordinary soldiers, so Lenc was mystified why the great man wanted to speak to him, especially as his conscience was fairly clear.

The clerk inclined his head and nodded towards one of the doors. "I shouldn't keep him waiting if I was you."

Lenc stood outside the door and swallowed nervously. He had never before been summoned into the presence of such an exalted figure, and only ever registered the great man while standing rigidly to attention on the dusty parade square. Finally he swallowed, straightened his shoulders and knocked on the rough-hewn door. Nervously he waited, realising too late that a line of sweat had appeared on his forehead, just under the leather rim of his helmet. He pushed open the door on hearing enter from within, and once again straightened his shoulders and marched into the room. He threw up a smart salute, his clenched right fist snapping to his heart as he stamped to attention.

"Auxiliary Lenculus, attached to the Engineer Cohort, XX Valeria, reporting as ordered sir."

"Stand easy, Lenculus," said Legate Equitius. He sat at a trestle table stacked with the thin wooden tablets on which the army conducted its administration. A wire-thin man with white hair and a kindly expression, his simple off-white linen tunic was well cut and he wore no badges of rank or decorations. His armour was stacked in a corner, ready to be thrown on at a moment's notice. Lenc knew little about him, save he may be riding a desk now, but his steady rise up the ranks indicated he had commanded men in some of Rome's bloodiest battles.

Quintus Equitius looked at Lenc thoughtfully for what seemed like an age. Lenc wondered, not for the first time, what was coming.

"You had quite a nasty experience out on the road gang, I understand?" queried the Legate finally.

Lenc looked fixedly to his front, unable to say anything. He had no idea what this exalted officer wanted with him. He gulped.

"Come soldier," went on the Legate. "You did well, it's just a tragedy there were no other survivors. I understand my intelligence people have spoken to you and you have given your report?"

Lenc nodded and added warily, "Yes sir."

"Good, good, I have a job for you, which will be dangerous, but may well save a lot of your comrade's lives. It will be something the likes of which you will never have dreamed of. Having said that, I am assured, that if anyone can do this it will be you."

Despite the sinking feeling in his gut Lenc was intrigued. What could he do that would be so important to this high ranking officer?

Equitius stood and moved over to a large hand-drawn map

of Britannia painted onto animal hide stretched over a free-standing frame nearly shoulder high.

Silently he contemplated the map, hands clasped behind his back.

"You see this map, Lenculus," he finally asked, gesturing at the hide. "You will note the fine detail in the parts we have colonised. From Glevum in the west across to Camulodunum and the coast from our channel ports up to Lindum and the route of that infernal road we are building.

"But look at the bits outside. Damn all," he spoke fiercely now. "Hell's teeth, it could be the surface of the moon for all we know." He turned and sat on the edge of the table.

"What I am about to tell you is confidential and must not be repeated to anyone. You understand this?"

"Of course sir," replied a mystified Lenc.

Equitius nodded. "Good, good." He paused dramatically. "The Senate has decreed that we are shirking our duties by failing to subdue this god-forsaken dump and particularly in failing to colonise the west and the north. The gods know we have enough troubles keeping subdued the ground we have supposedly conquered. The latest raid on your road building detail being a case in point."

Lenc nodded sadly.

"Despite our manpower shortages we have, with the greatest reluctance, agreed that in the spring we will mount a campaign from Glevum," continued Equitius. "We will march through Siluria, and the lands of the Demetae and Dobunni, until we have rolled up and conquered the west of the country. Then we will swing north and on the way, take out that poisonous nest of priests on Mona.

"Now I am told your native language from Gaul will give you a working knowledge of their barbaric dialect, enough so you can make yourself understood. I want you to travel to the border into Siluria, mingle with the locals, find out their strengths, what worries them, whether they want a war with us, that sort of thing. But most importantly, make us the most detailed maps possible, so that when we march in six months' time, we will have some idea of what lies in store."

Equitius looked at Lenc keenly. "Do you think you can do it? If you're not sure, say now and we still have a chance to find someone else. But I am assured you are the man for the job."

Lenc knew that turning this mission down was not an option. If he did, he would always be known as a shirker. He would never be able to hold his head up in front of his fellow soldiers. Besides something inside him tingled at the thought. What a career opportunity!

"I'm your man, sir," he heard himself say.

Equitius nodded appreciatively. "Good fellow. Now go and find Tribune Aurelius. He's my senior intelligence officer, just returned from Glevum. Between you, I need you to come up with a working plan that will satisfy the suspicions of these ignorant savages.

"There's also the problem of this fellow, Caratacus. He is getting to be a damned nuisance, and if you hear anything about him, I want you to report in straight away. It's a pity you didn't clap eyes on him at the bridge site, but no matter, I fancy he is heading in the same direction as you so your paths may well cross. If they do, I need to know immediately. Immediately do you hear?"

Lenc swallowed again. "Of course sir," was all he could manage.

Equitius fixed him with gimlet eyes. "I don't need to tell you what will happen if they find you out, so you're going to need to keep your wits about you at all times. If at any time it looks like you've been found out, don't hesitate, just get out quick as you can, and head east. You will run into the army sooner or later. Good luck."

Equitius nodded as Lenc saluted, turned on his heel and marched out. Equitius sighed and wondered if he had done the right thing or sent an enthusiastic and obviously bright soldier to a painful death. Well there's plenty more where he came from, I suppose, he thought dispassionately.

Back in the orderly room, the clerk he'd spoken to earlier told Lenc he was likely to find Tribune Aurelius undergoing officer's sword training in the amphitheatre. "Go all right then, did it?" he asked, dying to know what the great man wanted with a lowly auxiliary. Knowledge was power, and at the very least the clerk valued his importance as the man who knew everything that went on inside the fort.

Lenc snorted. "Yeah, kind of." With that, he stepped out of the orderly room, well aware of the pair of eyes boring into his back. He wouldn't give the nosey bastard the satisfaction.

Outside, in the sunshine, he started to have second thoughts. How the hell do I pull this off? His mind was racing as he crossed the parade square to the fort gate and barely registered the Guard Commander, only just hurriedly saluting in time. "I have a message for Tribune Aurelius," he stammered. "I've been told he's at the amphitheatre."

The guard commander nodded and lost interest.

Lenc pondered his dilemma as he walked the short distance to the amphitheatre. He couldn't just wander into hostile territory and start sketching. Even the Britons might think that a bit unusual. Then there was the language. He had picked up a smattering of the local tribal dialects but knew that the western tribes spoke a completely different tongue. It was akin to his native Gaulish, but even the men of the auxiliary all spoke Latin. He couldn't remember when he had last spoken in his mother tongue.

The amphitheatre was a circular earthwork just outside the main fortress walls and used for a variety of purposes. One day it would be a magnificent arena, but the first priority was the security of a stout wall to protect the garrison. The amphitheatre was work in progress.

Even in its early stages, a crude circle dug into the ground and the spoil thrown up to make a grandstand, it could carry a variety of roles. Lenc settled on one of the lower tiers of hard wooden benches to watch an officer's sword practise, with a big optio taking them through their paces. They were in two teams, facing each other and on the word of command, one team would raise their shields in a defensive position then take a step forward to land a blow on the shield in front, then step back. It was quite entertaining, Lenc decided, to watch officers grunting and sweating, judging by the paunches on some of the swordsmen, most were headquarters officers, going through the sweaty motions.

After about half an hour happily watching the staff officers sweat and listening to the optio's exasperated screams of command, the squad was finally stood down for a break. As the exhausted officers gratefully sank onto the grass and took a slug of water, the drill optio turned to Lenc lounging on his bench and raised a fist.

Oh shit, thought Lenc. The optio pointed at him then crooked his finger, meaning come here soldier. Lenc jumped up and jogged over to the big optio, stamping to attention in front of him.

"Do you have business here?" growled the optio. A livid scar ran across the bridge of his nose and down one cheek.

"Tribune Aurelius, Optio, been sent to speak to him," said Lenc as he stared fixedly over the optio's right shoulder.

The optio grunted and called for Tribune Aurelius, who got up from where he was resting and walked over. He was dusty and breathing heavily after his exercise.

He looked at the auxiliary. "You must be Auxiliary Lenculus?" he asked.

Lenc snapped to attention and saluted, right fist to heart.

Aurelius turned to the optio. "Thank you, that will have to be all for me today, I have urgent business with this man."

The optio also jumped to attention, saluted and trotted back to his other charges.

Aurelius watched him go, a slight smile on his lips. "Well if nothing else you got me out of the clutches of that sadistic brute." He had the dark wavy hair and long aquiline nose of a Sicilian. His skin was dark despite the lack of sun in Britannia, and Lenc's instant appraisal was of a clever and shrewd operator, which pleased him, because one day it could save his life.

"There is a saying, you can fight hard, or you can fight clever," mused Aurelius. "In the legion we usually have to fight hard, because we don't have any other option. We rarely know what we are going to face, so when we attack, we simply form ranks and go, and hope that superior discipline and numbers win the day. We usually have little idea of what we are facing or over what terrain we will be expected to fight.

"Thankfully most of our enemies can be beaten by our iron discipline. But when we are defending sometimes we have no idea who or what is the enemy. These Britons hide in the shadows, they wear no uniform, and you only know they are enemy when they stick a sword in your back."

Lenc nodded in agreement. He had been on too many patrols and lost too many friends to ambushes and booby traps.

"But this time we have a chance to do something about it," continued Aurelius. "We have at least six months before the Valeria marches to Glevum to start the campaign westwards. If you can use that time to draw us maps and provide information on how many fighters they have, and how they are likely to oppose us it could save a lot of lives and effort.

"We have heard something of these Silurians, a nasty lot, and vicious. They've been raiding across the Sabrina for years and are feared locally. You wouldn't want to be caught by them, that's for sure.

"Our general feeling is that these bastards in the west will give us a scrap. Which ones will fight? How hard? How many? Where? Any info has got to be of use."

Lenc nodded thoughtfully. "All well and good sir, but I don't speak their language very well, how can I possibly move among them without being found out?"

"Agreed," said Aurelius. "It would be hopeless to pass you off as a local, but there are Armorican traders sailing from Gaul who roam all over, trading for hides and metals, that's how we'll get you in. We have a man in Armorica who is looking for the right trader. We want someone greedy enough to do it, but frightened enough not to give you away. Being with him will also give you a chance to brush up on your Gaulish, it's not the same dialect the Silures speak, but it's close, and should help your cover.

"So we must leave here as soon as possible, take passage for Gaul and get you down to Armorica. Then we will meet again in Glevum, where you will be selling your wares to the Silures."

CHAPTER IV

Deep within a dense forest of oaks that covered virtually the whole of the central region of Britannia, four days hard march from the growing city of Camulodunum, stood the Great Lodge of Verulamium. The Lodge was surrounded by a timber palisade built from straight lengths of solid trunks. Outside the palisade, the ground had been cleared so that any attackers would have to cross open country, and inside a town was steadily growing as families sought sanctuary not only from the new aggressor, the Roman Army, but also from warring bands of tribesmen looking for easy plunder.

The mood at a packed council meeting was sombre. The king, Cunobelinos, sat on furs on a large, carved tree trunk raised on a plinth made from rough timbers. Slightly behind him were two of his sons, Togodumnus and, affecting to be bored by the whole procedure, Caratacus.

Togodumnus slouched on a smaller throne, leaning to one side to favour the spear wound in his side. His face was chalk white and he was sweating, obviously in pain. He grimaced and shifted, hoping to reduce the torment by moving to an easier position. It wasn't working.

The chamber was a round room, fashioned from rough planks of wood standing on a beaten earth floor. Behind the king's throne were more planks, intricately carved with hunting scenes and high on the wall, the stuffed head of a brown bear, the sacred animal of the Catuvellauni, glared down over the king's shoulder.

The council of 30 leaders of the tribe had just heard the

account of the latest raid, but instead of applauding the beating of the Romans and the destruction of the bridge camp, there was muttering, then an angry outcry at the possible repercussions.

Cunobelinos congratulated his son on the raid, but was also concerned at the possible backlash.

He turned and leaned forward. "Are you sure no-one saw you?"

Caratacus shrugged. "My men killed all the Romans before we rode down. They were all dead, well, except one and he probably perished in the forest."

Nathan, an elderly man with swirling tattoos on his face, adjusted his cloak before asking, "What about the slaves who were building the bridge?"

Caratacus dismissed the question, saying only, "Most joined our band and the rest ran."

"Then the Romans will know who is responsible," replied Nathan flatly.

"Well so what?" sneered a suddenly angry Caratacus. "It's about time those bastards got a bit of what they deserved, and if they know it was Caratacus of the Catuvellauni that did it, then so much the better." He glared belligerently round the room, one hand on his sword. Many of the elders clearly agreed with him but there was more than a sprinkling of head shaking.

Cunobelinos looked regretfully at the beaten earth floor before replying. "By your actions you are putting the Romans in a position where they have no choice but to retaliate, and to find you they will come here and probably destroy us in revenge. They will kill all in front of them, and any that are spared will become slaves. That is our concern."

Caratacus paused for a moment, clearly finding it difficult to hold his temper. Finally he spoke, eyes glittering. "We can accept Roman rule in our own lands and perhaps profit from it like my bastard brother in the south. Or we can fight. Many men have been lost because we do not have the skills in war that the

Romans do. Since the Battle of Tamesis we have been successful with raids which have hurt the Romans, but now we must change our tactics. I intend to visit all the tribes and raise an army so strong it will sweep the Romans back into the sea where they came from.

"We have learned from them and will train our men to attack in a way which will defeat them. I have seen the way they fight, their discipline is something to behold. Our lightning strikes are effective but will never give us full victory.

"So the best plan is for me to leave here so you can tell the Romans I have been banished. That may save you. You can also enlist the help of my brother Adminius who has been a house-dog of the invaders right from the start. At last his treachery may do some good.

"In the meantime I will be free to visit the tribes and raise an army even greater than the one which failed at Tamesis. The difference is that this time we will be ready for the Romans. And we will beat them."

Cunobelinos bowed his head, gathering his thoughts before speaking. "You speak well, my son. Your plan is a good one. While you are gathering your great army, we shall welcome the enemy, break bread with them, and assure them of our loyalty. While they think we are their lap-dogs we shall gather arms and hide your men in the forest, feed them and train them, then when the time is right, the Catuvellauni will take their rightful place at the front of your army, and yes we shall drive the bastards back into the sea."

Caratacus hitched his long cloak and addressed the elders. "My close warriors and family will leave immediately on this great mission and the Romans will not find us. You may say the raiding was nothing to do with you, that the Catuvellauni wish only for peace. Then when the time comes I will call for the whole tribe to join us, so when men talk of this time round the tribal fires they will know the hated invaders were sent packing by a great army led by the Catuvellauni."

As Caratacus sat down again, the group of elders erupted in approval. Cunobelinos waved them to silence and eventually the pandemonium subsided.

Cunobelinos, ever the wily statesman could see the sense in the plan. If they attempted to defend the town, in their present state of readiness the Legion would simply roll over them leaving devastation in their wake. This way they had a chance and the Catuvellauni would be the backbone of the new army, ready to fight when the time was right. Besides what was the point in having a traitor for a son if you didn't make use of him?

Cunobelinos stood once more. "So my son, go with our best wishes and the grace of the gods. We will try and fool the Romans and live to fight again, but we know we may fail and they will kill us all anyway. It will be difficult to keep this momentous plan secret, but keep it we must if we are to survive. I will send for your brother Adminius, so that he is here for whenever the Romans make their move."

Cunobelinos clasped arms with his son and they stood for a moment. Then he muttered, "May the gods be with all of us."

Caratacus strode from the meeting lodge with the stamping of feet from the elders ringing in his ears. Outside, his lieutenants were waiting. There was also an interested knot of townspeople, eager to hear the news. For their benefit, Caratacus stood on a step and shouted, "Cunobelinos, my father, has disowned me. I am no longer of the Catuvellauni and neither is anyone who rides with me. We have a sacred task to fulfil and the destiny of this country is in our hands. I pause only to collect my family and then we leave."

He strode through the throng and swung up onto his horse and clattered away from the meeting lodge. His men looked askance at each other, then Esico, a senior lieutenant, still proudly carrying his long spear with two Roman heads tied to the tip, shrugged and simply said, "We have Romans to kill." And followed his leader.

Caratacus rode hard the short distance to his homestead and as he reined in at the wooden palisade his men surrounded him, impatient for an explanation of the denouncement.

"I bet that came as a surprise," he grinned. "But don't worry, I will explain everything, only inside with my family as well, mainly so I only have to say it once, but also, because other ears may be listening."

They all dismounted and led their horses into the family stockade. The most imposing building, home to Caratacus and his kin, was right in front at the other side of an earth square. It was a single storey house, with a thatched roof, and stone walls. The entrance was a sort of dogleg, so anyone entering had to turn a sharp corner to find the way inside. Either side were servants' quarters, stables, barns and animal pens.

Caratacus threw the reins of his horse to Esico and strode over to his home, where waiting for him on a wooden verandah was his wife Vellibia. She was a striking woman, past the first flush of youth, but with a presence that still turned heads. She stood with her hand on the shoulder of their son Maglos, on the verge of manhood. Her robes were made for royalty, and she wore them proudly, her slim figure ably complementing the fine material and enhancing her beauty. Her flame-red hair was collected into tresses which swept down her back.

Vellibia stood tall and straight but the expression on her face was torn between pleasure to see her husband home unharmed and concern that something disastrous had happened.

"Forgive me," he said consolingly, "I have something momentous to say to you and to these men, I only wish to say it once, and then we must all act."

She sucked in her lower lip and impulsively put her arm through his. He smiled, looking down fondly at Maglos, and ruffled his hair. Then he turned to his men and held up an arm to command attention.

"When the new enemy came across the sea, he brought ways of fighting we had never seen before. At the Medway, we had a good-sized army and by rights should have hurled them back from where they came but they destroyed us."

At this, his head went down and he ostentatiously cuffed back a tear. "Most of you were with me on that terrible day and saw the Romans stand as one, just waiting for us as we dashed ourselves on their shields. I will never forget the brave sacrifice so many of our countrymen made that day, and I swore it would never happen again."

He nodded as he registered the mutterings of agreement from his lieutenants.

"Since then, those of us that were spared slunk away to lick our wounds and then a great thing happened. We did not have the men or horses, or even spears and swords to put up another great battle, so we chose our fights carefully and fought the invaders where we knew we could beat them, and much to our surprise we realised that we were hurting them. Not outright victory, but we were stretching their supply lines, making them double and treble guards. No Roman can sleep easy at night.

"We do not use guile and tricks to win in battle, we use our strong right arms, swords and spears. But sad though I am to say it, we have to learn from these bastards, or we will never be rid of them.

"The strange happenings of today will mark the start of a new campaign where we fight the Romans at their own game. We will lie and cheat and they will believe us, because they want to believe us. Why would these obviously clever people believe us, who paint images on our bodies, who wear fur and cannot read and write?"

He looked at them, daring an answer.

"Because they are on a crusade. They want to reform us, to civilise us, and make us like them. Then when we see all the Roman things that will make our lives better, that's when the shackles go round our necks and we will be their slaves, working for them and sending wealth and goods back to Rome to prop up their corrupt stinking empire."

At this there was a shout of encouragement from his assembled warriors.

Caratacus nodded grimly. "Today my father disowned me and cast me out of the tribe. Word will already have gone to that shit of a brother of mine who is in Rome's pocket. He will be asked to intercede on behalf of the tribe, which wishes for nothing more than peace with Rome. This way, we hope to save the communities of the Catuvellauni, who will seem to be welcoming the Roman bastards.

"While they are doing this, I, and I hope you," he said, looking out at his men, "will be riding the length of this country, raising an army the like of which Rome has never seen. And when we have that army, only then will the Catuvellauni rise up and shake themselves free of this Roman plague."

A great shout rose up at this and again Caratacus raised his arm for silence.

"Some of you will have to stay behind. We have many men already in the forest, and they need training. The freed slaves speak many different languages but they must all be moulded into one army. Here in the great forest you will be safe from the legions and can train hard."

At this he walked forward and gripped his lieutenant by the arms. "Esico I am giving you the responsibility of training our army in the forest. I know you would want to come with me, but the job of raising the army is paramount. I trust no-one else as I trust you to carry out this sacred task."

Esico nodded and looked down at his feet, then finally, "Lord, I will do as you ask. I know it is a great honour, and I thank you for the trust you place in me. But you know that I would rather be at your side killing Romans."

Caratacus put his arm round Esico's shoulders and turned to

his tribesmen. "Men, you see before you one of the great warriors of the Catuvellauni. By the time I return Esico will have built an army, skilled and strong, which will sweep the invaders into the sea." Then with a shout he drew his sword and with a ringing cry, roared, "Between us we shall free our country of this Roman pestilence!"

When the shouting and cheering died down, Caratacus, in a quieter tone added, "As for myself, the last part of the deception in making me look like a castout is that I must take my family and household with me. It will no doubt expose them to hardship that I would never have wanted them to share, but it is necessary.

"Now go, make your preparations and return as soon as possible. We must be gone before people start asking questions."

As the warriors re-mounted their horses and clattered out of the main gate, Caratacus turned to his wife with a look of concern etched on his face. "My wife, I am about to put you in great danger. Any that stay will be seen as traitors and betrayed if we are to keep up the pretence. I have no idea how long we will be travelling but I do know we have hard miles ahead and we must face them with fortitude. When we are far enough away, we may find somewhere I can leave you in safety, but until that time, you and the children will be bandits and raiders just like me."

Vellibia smiled and shook her head ruefully. "Caratacus, I have watched you ride off to war these past ten years and during that time I have never shared with you my fears. When you came home I wanted to enjoy the time with you as much as possible. I wanted you to see your children and have peaceful days with them. This time you are saying that I and the children must go with you, can't you see how much that pleases me? I have only ever wanted to share your hardships and dangers. To be by your side is all I have ever asked for."

He smiled and caressed her cheek. "It will be hard and dangerous, but we will find a safe place for you and the children. I am not saying you will be an encumbrance, but if you are with me and in danger I will be thinking of you instead of killing Romans. I need to know that you are safe."

"No, no," Vellibia protested vehemently as she clutched his arm with both hands, pulling at him to show the strength of her feelings. "I wish to be at your side, to ride with you and fight with you. I know it will be hard, but not as hard as lying through the night in safety, knowing you are in danger."

He smiled uncertainly. "Your words do you credit. Now prepare for your journey. You must look like a princess, but you must travel light, only one pack horse. I need to speak to my men again, hurry now."

He watched her leave and reflected that even after three children she had kept her figure and vitality. She was a handsome woman all right.

Shaking these thoughts from his mind, he went in search of his warriors, returning in ones and twos and waiting near the gate to the homestead. Their horses carried little in extra baggage, but each had two tightly bundled sheaves of fodder in front of the rider's knees, and a bed-roll with food and extra clothing tied to the back of the saddle. A shield and spear hung from each saddle.

An air of excitement filled the air as the household entourage lashed packs to horses and stowed their weapons in their two-horse chariots. Vellibia, now wearing wool-spun trousers and a jacket climbed up onto a magnificent chariot, drawn by matching roan mares. The driver, a muscular warrior with his long hair tied back, shuffled to one side to let her aboard and showed her where to stand. Behind were the children, retainers and slaves, all clutching onto the sides of chariots.

Once again Caratacus addressed his warriors. "The stay-behinds will be chosen by Esico and will find a place in the forest where they can house and train our people, our own tribesmen and the rescued slaves. When I call for you I will expect a disciplined army, which as Catuvellauni will be at the fore of our battle with the Romans. Make Esico proud.

"Remember Medway where a smaller force overwhelmed us with their discipline and tactics. That can never happen again. I intend to ride west then north, to raise the biggest army this country has ever seen and give these Roman bastards the hiding they deserve. Wait for me and be ready."

CHAPTER V

The commander of XX Valeria, Legionary Legate Quintus Equitius was not in a good mood. He had been briefed about the latest ambush and stood facing his senior commanders across a polished wooden table in the Legion's meeting room. He stared impassively at his senior men, his knuckles showing white as he leaned on the table.

"Gentlemen, this Caratacus is being more than a thorn in my backside. He is becoming a figurehead and has to be slapped down."

"Tribune Aurelius, your thoughts please."

The Tribune, the Legion intelligence officer jumped to his feet then paused for a second to collect his thoughts.

"Sir, we gave his tribe and the rest of them a hiding when we routed them on the Tamesis and Medway. But since then his army has grown. His tribe, the Catuvellauni is still ruled by Caratacus' father Cunobelinos, and the older brother Togodumnus would be his successor, but he was severely wounded at Medway and is not expected to recover. Another brother, Adminius is a prince in Cantiaci and controls a very useful harbour and the estuary approach to the Tamesis. He has sworn allegiance to Rome and is under our protection.

"Cunobelinos has his main dwelling at a place we call Verulamium which is about four days march west from here. It's a quite large defended town, surrounded by the great central forest. We have little information as to whether Cunobelinos is encouraging Caratacus to oppose us, but certainly outwardly, he, and Togodumnus are staying neutral.

Legate Equitius motioned for Aurelius to pause.

"So we have a king with at least one son with us, another on the fence, and another who is leading the opposition against us?" he mused.

Aurelius shrugged: "In a nutshell sir. If you are considering military action, I believe that only the strongest force possible will suffice. That forest could hide 10,000 men and the first we would know of it is when they burst upon us."

The Legate pondered. "Maybe that would be the wrong strategy," he mused. "This Cunobelinos is clearly something of a statesman, albeit a crude and savage one. He is probably fully aware of how stretched we are, although I agree that if we were to mount any sort of campaign, it would have to be strong enough to be effective.

"What if an envoy were to go under a truce, as one leader to another and persuade this king to throw in his lot with us? If he gives us Caratacus as a form of guarantee, in return we will not only allow him to live, but will send him and his family to Rome where they will be educated in our ways and see for themselves the advantages of Roman civilisation. Do you think he would agree to that?"

"Sir, its certainly worth trying, we are after all trying to pacify the tribes."

As Equitius mused, his deputy, His Grace Tribunus Laticlavus, Senator Publius Ostorius who also wore the broad purple stripe, and was also of senatorial rank looked at him with alarm. He could see where this was going. Senator Ostorius had grown up in one of the grandest families in Rome, accustomed to status, and fawning servants. Service in Britannia was a bore, but an evil to endure to speed his inevitable passage to the Senate and the power and influence that would go with it.

Equitius was pretty sure that Ostorius was reporting everything that was going wrong in Britannia back to the Senate in Rome.

Ostorius would have to beard the barbarian if commanded, and if his head was cut off so much the better. Accident of war really. And if he succeeded it would bring peace to the region, which he as leader could take credit for.

Equitius had made up his mind. Ostorius was about to become a great envoy of Rome – whether he wanted to or not.

Ostorius could see no way out, outmanoeuvred by a bunch of dumb soldiers, and he was the politician. But, he thought, he would show them. He would negotiate with this British barbarian, bring about peace and accompany Caratacus to Rome in triumph. His special trophy. He tried not to think of the possibility of the barbarians separating his head from his shoulders. No, he was far too important for that.

At first the cavalcade made good progress. The new Roman roads were pushing out from Camulodunum so the four-wheeled litter was pulled along relatively smoothly, although Ostorius was glad of the cushions protecting his generous posterior. His initial feelings of absolute terror had faded away to some extent and he comforted himself at the sight of his escort, 400 Germanic auxiliaries, some of the toughest soldiers in Rome's army.

Their leader, the bushy bearded Decurio Gaius Asmodeus looked a real thug, thought Ostorius. When they stopped at the middle of the day to rest the horses and take some food, Ostorius called the Decurio over. Ostorius thought he had a surly expression on his strong bearded face. I'll soon put a stop to that, he thought smugly.

"Senator", said the Optio as he lifted a grudging salute.

Ostorius pulled himself upright and was about to launch into a blistering diatribe, when the big German leaned forward on his saddle and kicked his horse forward so that it was right up against the side of the litter. He spoke quietly but forcefully so only they could hear. Ostorius was close enough to smell the sweat on the big German, and leaned back hurriedly.

"I am responsible for getting you in and out of this fool's errand and I know that when we get to our destination you are to be treated as a great and important Senator all the way from Rome," Asmodeus said dispassionately. "I have 400 cavalry to protect you, but I have to warn you that if these Britons decide they don't want to hear what you want to say they will be all over us in minutes. My men and I will be grateful for a quick death, but you, I imagine they will take their time with. Knowing them, you will be lucky if your head arrives back at Camulodunum without your cock and balls sewn into your mouth, so until we get back to safety, you will do everything I say and do it at the double. Is that clear?"

Ostorius gaped as he looked at the implacable big German. Eventually his mouth opened then shut again. For once he had nothing to say. Asmodeus nodded and wheeled his horse away.

The second night out on the trail they camped in a small clearing in the forest. Asmodeus set a double guard, with all their precious horses hobbled in the middle. He was surprised and relieved that the night passed without incident as his forward scouts had cut across several lines of track from heavy horses so he was under no illusion that they were being shadowed. As long as that's all they want to do, he thought.

Ostorius was deeply afraid. He started nervously at any small noise from the forest and he finally accepted that his vanity had allowed him to fall into a deadly trap. If I get out of this alive, I shall make damned sure I get all the credit for it. Equitius will be forced to spend the rest of his career trying to keep the peace in this shithole, while I return to Rome in glory, with or without Caratacus. If he thinks he is going to get any credit at all, he's got another think coming. These feverish and panicked thoughts were interrupted by Asmodeus, walking down the column and joining him.

"I shouldn't say it, but I am beginning to think we may get away with this crazy venture after all," he said quietly to the Senator. "If they were going to jump us, I think the critical time would have been when we got well into the forest. There's no merit in letting us get nearer to their town, because that would make it more obvious who had laid any ambush. Even if we are overstretched, Rome's vengeance would be absolute. My scouts have seen plenty of sign that we are being observed closely but they haven't tried to stop us.

"So," he smiled at Ostorius, "I think Senator, you had better start working on your speech."

The next morning, Ostorius gasped with relief when he heard the advance scouts report back that the town was just ahead. Surely that meant that the barbarians wanted to hear what he had to say after all, he thought exultantly. Imperiously he clapped his hands for his servant. "Fetch me my purple stripe robe, clean shoes and water to wash this blasted mud off, I have the destiny of Rome to deliver."

By the great God's balls, thought Asmodeus, shaking his head.

When the column arrived at the settlement, Asmodeus stopped short of the open gate, his horse pawing the hard earth of the track. Behind him Ostorius sat in his litter, trying to look imperious and dignified, but inwardly quaking. He hoped he could keep his lunch down. They waited.

Eventually a single man rode out through the open gates standing in a chariot pulled by two roan horses. He wore a Roman tunic, his hair long and blonde, and tied back. He reined in, in front of Asmodeus. "I welcome you on behalf of my father, Cunobelinos, King of the Catuvellauni," he said. "Rome is always welcome at our home."

Asmodeus studied him keenly. This must be Adminius, the lap-dog brother from the south coast.

"I am pleased to see you here," returned Asmodeus. "We want only to build bridges not destroy them, and to that end, may I introduce Rome's envoy, Senator Publius Ostorius who has much to discuss with your father and you."

As he spoke, he raised his arm and the litter with its senatorial passenger moved forward. Ostorius sat upright as the auxiliary guard moved off the track to let him through. Adminius bowed his head as the litter approached, which Ostorius acknowledged with a gracious curl of his raised hand, without even looking or showing interest.

When the column arrived at the Lodge of the Elders, Adminius motioned to a mounted warrior: "Take the escort to their quarters, while I take the Senator's party to my father's lodge."

Adminius had been in his own kingdom on the south east coast when he received the urgent summons to attend his father who was expecting the imminent arrival of a Roman column. He immediately grasped the danger behind the visit, especially to his own fragile fiefdom built up with the grudging approval of the Roman administration.

It took him four days of hard riding before he arrived at his father's settlement, but it was worth it to arrive in good time before the expected Roman backlash.

He smiled inwardly when the watching scouts waiting for the Roman response reported that a mere 400 cavalry and a fat man in a cart were all that were on the road from Camulodunum. His father, dreading a full scale invasion that would destroy his community turned to him quizzically. "What does this mean, Adminius, do they not wish to destroy us?"

"Oh, I think they would quite happily destroy your town and everyone in it," he replied. "But the army is desperately overstretched. They will try diplomacy first and if that doesn't work, then we will see the savagery of the Legions. But this gives us a chance to convince them we are harmless and perhaps they will leave us alone."

A guard of honour awaited Ostorius as his litter drew up at the King's lodge. They wore clean tunics and wool trousers, their long hair tied back and each man carried a long spear. They lacked the bearing of a Roman honour guard but to Asmodeus they looked tough and ready for anything. Ostorius simply saw a ragtag semblance of militarism and sniffed as he walked disdainfully past and into the Great Lodge.

Inside, Cunobelinos rose from his wooden throne as the Roman envoys walked in. Ostorius looked round and despite himself, was impressed. This was clearly a wealthy gathering. He swept his cloak back and gave a formal bow.

Cunobelinos walked across the large hall, and smiling broadly held out his arm in greeting. "We are honoured that Rome has seen fit to send such an august statesman to us. Your reputation goes before you."

Ostorius acknowledged the compliment gracefully. No more than he deserved, he thought. "One of the mightiest and most influential tribes in Britannia deserves the best that Rome can provide," he said as he firmly grasped Cunobelinos's arm.

Cunobelinos drew him across the great hall and motioned to a seat next to the great throne. "You have met my son Adminius, this is my other son Togodumnus, please forgive him for not rising, he is not very well."

Togodumnus sat, half sprawled in his chair behind the throne. He was pale and sweating and clutched his side. He was clearly in pain, and simply nodded to Ostorius, who nodded back. "I do hope you get better soon," he said carefully. Pity the soldier who stuck him didn't do a better job, he thought vindictively.

"And what of your other son, Caratacus," he continued loudly. "He is not present?"

Cunobelinos sighed and lowered his head. "I only have two sons," he said finally. "After I heard of his trail of destruction and his murderous raids on your work parties, I implored him to stop, saying you were bringing great benefits to us, but he wouldn't listen. He wants nothing of Rome and calls you invaders. I had no choice. I banished him from our lands, his family and retainers too."

Adminius nodded vigorously. "What my father says is correct. Caratacus does not understand the modern way of living together and prospering. He does not understand that Rome is bringing us civilisation, fine buildings, roads and bridges. He would rather die than accept that, so he has been cast out."

Ostorius looked round at the solemn nodding heads of the elders. If this was a deception it was a bloody good one.

"Hmm," he pondered. "I was looking forward to taking him back to Rome as an honoured guest. I wanted to show him the senate, the greatest place of government in the world. His children would have benefited from the best education that Rome could offer, and Caratacus would have taken an honoured place in the seat of government.

"Have you any idea where he may be?"

Cunobelinos shrugged. "I think he has ridden west to the hills of Cambria. When the tribe cast him out, we thought it for the best, so there was no impediment to our relationship with Rome. Of course if we receive news of his whereabouts, we will be sure to let you know."

The two statesmen looked at each other. Both knew the other was lying through his teeth. But both could also claim victory.

"Where are my manners," Cunobelinos suddenly exclaimed. "You must be tired and exhausted after your journey. Come, I will show you to your quarters, there is refreshment there and after you have rested, we will all eat together and talk further."

"At last," thought Ostorius, "Gods balls, but I thought the old goat was never going to offer us a drink." He contented himself with a long nod of his head and followed Cunobelinos, trailed by Asmodeus, his personal bodyguard and servant slaves. They were shown into the royal quarters, another wattle daubed building with a thatched roof. An elderly slave indicated separate bedrooms for the two dignitaries, the bodyguards and slaves would sleep in the corridor.

Ostorius sniffed disdainfully when he saw his room, but perked up when two slave hand-maidens who had been standing against the wall took a step forward and bowed deeply. And one with auburn hair tumbling down almost to her hips was carrying a beaker of something. He hoped it was wine.

Shyly, with downcast eyes she offered the beaker. Ostorius eyed her appreciatively. God's blood, but she's not bad, he thought, and her friend's not far behind. I suppose there are some good points to this god-forsaken shit-hole.

The girl kept her eyes lowered as Ostorius took a tentative sip. It was mead, sweet to his taste but better than nothing and he could taste that it had quite a kick.

"What are your duties here my girl?"

She looked up at him and smiled. "We are here to serve, whatever you want, we will arrange, Lord."

"Would it be too much to ask for hot water, we have been travelling some days?"

"Prince Adminius said you would ask for water and some is being prepared. It will be here shortly when it is warmed," she replied.

"Good, good," he nodded absently and settled himself down on the furs, still holding his beaker of mead. The girls came and sat either side of him. One tentatively reached out and massaged the back of his neck. He moved so that she could use both hands. "Mmmm," he whispered, "that is so good after that long ride." He closed his eyes.

'Ah the responsibilities of state,' he mused dreamily, as his shoulders were pulled and pummelled.

Ostorius was quite happy to be ministered to, and after his bath in a makeshift tub, reluctantly allowed himself to be helped out and towelled down before sitting on his bed with another horn mug of mead. One of the girls was stroking his sparse hair flat when Asmodeus knocked and entered. "All the comforts of home, eh?" he grunted.

Ostorius gave him a condescending smile. "It's quite gratifying that these people recognise a true statesman in their midst. I believe we shall have a satisfactory visit after all, even if we don't bring that swine Caratacus back in chains."

Asmodeus contented himself with a non-commital grunt and sipped the mead handed to him.

A few beakers later, a household slave diffidently asked them to join the King for dinner. Ostorius stood and adjusted his cloak. "Will you be here when I return ladies?" he asked of the two slave girls.

One smiled and looked at him from under long lashes, "Of course, Lord, we look forward to your return."

"What sort of filth do you think they are going to serve us?" Ostorius hissed at Asmodeus. "I have a delicate stomach at the best of times, and all this travelling and the thought that, despite those two lovely little vixens, I could still be wearing my cock and balls in my mouth by the end of the evening has had a very unsettling effect on my digestion.

"I can't even get so drunk I won't taste anything, I have to keep my wits about me if we are to get out alive," he said, nervously twisting the purple tassles on the plaited rope around his ample waist.

They were ushered back into the Great Hall, where tables had been laid in the centre, round the fire in a horseshoe shape. Across the end of the horseshoe was the King's throne with a smaller table of honour and seats either side.

Just inside the entrance, Cunobelinos waited for them and hailed them as long lost friends.

"Into the lion's den" whispered Ostorius before smiling widely at his host. "Your hospitality will be one of my fondest memories when I return to Rome."

Cunobelinos accepted the compliment graciously but Asmodeus noted the look which passed between the two sons. Adminius who stood behind his father and the white faced and sweating Togodumnus, already seated at the table and half leaning into it for support.

He's not long for this life, thought Asmodeus.

The evening passed in a blur for Ostorius. He had not fully appreciated the potency of the mead he had drunk in his quarters with his two new ladyfriends, then when he sat with the king and his sons, he was plied with even more. Eventually, food arrived but without the fastidious attention to detail he was used to. He soon got used to stabbing cuts of beef and other unidentifiable pieces of meat with a dirk and hacking off lumps. Bread, soaked in gravy was put in front of him, which he chewed with the meat. Despite the appalling table manners of the Britons around him, he was quite enjoying himself. Although how much that was due to the mead he had drunk and the pleasurable anticipation of returning to his quarters he wasn't altogether sure.

Asmodeus drank little, but saw that the slave girls were ensuring that the Senator's beaker was constantly full. It made sense to him, and besides he couldn't care less if the pompous arse made a complete fool of himself.

The next morning, Ostorius was awakened roughly by Asmodeus shaking his shoulder. He groaned and squeezed his eyes shut and tried to turn over. His head was splitting, but the swine shaking him just would not stop.

"Rise and shine, Senator, time to go."

Through the pain of his hangover, Ostorius knew he had to respond. "Zeus' balls but my head hurts, what were we drinking last night?"

Then suddenly he shot bolt upright on the trestle bed. "What happened? I was supposed to be negotiating?"

Asmodeus wanted to say: 'You made a complete arse of yourself and cocked everything up. Worst of all these Britons were laughing at you.'

But what he did say was "No no, Senator, it was fine. You came to an agreement that the King would let us know if Caratacus came back and would hold him until we could send a patrol for him. You all agreed that there was no point in chasing after him, then you wanted to return to your room to your ah, new lady friends."

Ostorius winced. He could see through Asmodeus' honeyed words but for now that would have to suffice. He looked round hopefully for the girls but they had beaten a diplomatic retreat when the big soldier burst into the room.

He struggled to get out of the bed, treating Asmodeus to the sight of spindly snow-white legs, and splashed some water on his face. Flashes of the previous night's activities came back to him, some good, some not so good. He vaguely remembered bums and breasts all over him, threshing and writhing under and on top of the furs. Those girls were good fun though, he thought; being carried back to his room by hairy arsed Britons not so good.

Feeling a little clearer, Ostorius turned back to Asmodeus. "Anyway, what's the hurry, I don't see any need for us to rush about," he asked petulantly.

"You forget, Senator, last night you were most adamant that you had to get back to Camulodunum as quickly as possible, so the good news of the friendship brokered by yourself can be announced. You also said you wanted to take the news back to Rome personally."

Ostorius thought for a moment. "Yes I did, didn't I," he said reflectively.

Despite his pounding head, the Senator realised he was in a potentially dangerous position with the big soldier. One word of his indiscretions in the wrong ear and he would be finished. Even the whispered suggestion of wrong doing in front of the leaders of one of the post powerful tribes in Britannia would signal the end of his time in the Senate. And if that snivelling bastard Quintus Equitius gets to hear of it, he would probably see it as a great excuse to part my head from my shoulders, he thought.

"Asmodeus, come a little closer, I need to speak to you man to man." Ostorius managed to stitch on what he thought was an endearing smile, but sufficiently alarmed the soldier who for a second, thought that with the two slave girls gone, he was the next choice.

"We've been through quite a lot on this expedition, and it will be important to convey the right impression when we return. Do you follow?"

Asmodeus gave a careful nod.

"As far as I am concerned, we have done all that can be done here, and I think we can call our trip a great success. True, we have not found Caratacus which is a pity, but following our surprising forging of friendship with the tribe, that may still happen. What we can point to is that the tribe wants to embrace the Roman way and that's a huge step forward isn't it?

Asmodeus was clearly expected to respond, but all he could manage was a non-committal shrug.

"Now I know we haven't exactly seen eye to eye on this trip, but I would be a poor member of the Senate if I didn't recognise that you have had a really tough and dangerous job to do, and you have done it in a way that is a credit to Rome. When we return to Camulodunum I shall be fulsome in my praise of the way you handled things and helped to facilitate the declaration of friendship with the tribe. And then, of course, it would be natural for you to be my escort back to Rome where there will most certainly be promotion from a grateful senate. So you see how important it is that we both say the same thing," whined Ostorius as he tailed off.

'So that's the devious little prick's plan,' thought Asmodeus. 'And why not? This could be my big chance. If I go along with it, chances are it will be my ticket out and back to Rome and promotion. If it does go wrong I can always say I was ordered to lie, but how is anyone going to know? And I'll have this shitty weasel right where I want him.'

Asmodeus pushed himself away from the wall and nodded agreement. "I can see how you can argue that the mission is a success Senator. I see no reason to add a discordant note, because as I am sure you will agree, there will be those who would look for any excuse to ridicule you."

"Er yes," replied Ostorius. "I will certainly ensure that you are properly looked after on our return."

Ostorius followed the big soldier out to the meeting hall where his escort was already saddled up and waiting. Standing on the steps were King Cunobelinos and Adminius, who both smiled when Ostorius stopped in front of them.

"I do hope your other son is well," said a concerned Ostorius.

"As well as can be expected," replied the King, "the cold mornings do not agree with him I'm afraid. We are sorry to see you go so soon, I was looking forward to taking you hunting in our forests, we have some fine sport."

Ostorius bowed: "My Lord, following our long conversation of last night, I feel sure that that this fleeting visit will be the first of many as we cement our relationship. Hunting with you is something that I can anticipate and look forward to on my next visit, which I hope will not be too long."

Not while I've got a hole in my arse, he thought to himself.

The King also had his private thoughts. Smug bastard, perhaps we did the wrong thing after all and we should have sent him back with his head in a sack.

Both men smiled winningingly at each other. Then with an air of regret, Ostorius climbed onto his litter, which immediately started to move as he was arranging himself on the cushions. He waved to the King and Adminius in as gracious a manner as possible and smiled at his new friends. As the Senatorial cart pulled away, flanked by the jingling cavalry, Cunobelinos spoke out of the side of his mouth to his son Adminius. "Do you think it worked? Will we have peace with the Romans?"

Adminius spat contemptuously as they watched the Roman

column leave. "That pompous arse will go back to his people and be loud in his conviction that his statesmanship has advanced the cause of Rome with us peasants. He will be feted, and we will be left alone, at least for the foreseeable future.

"Caratacus may well raise an army and defeat the Romans, but I doubt it. The tribes would just as soon fight each other as the Romans, and while doing so, the invaders will make even more ground. While we stay friendly with them they will leave us alone and we can make wealth from them. But if Caratacus does look like he will succeed, we can still join him on the winning side."

The King nodded sagely as the Roman convoy rode out of sight. "Just so long as I don't have to make polite conversation with fucking idiots like that one too many times."

When the tubby senator arrived back at Camulodunum, he was full of his own importance. He spun such a tale of the magnificent way he had dealt with the Catuvellauni, it sounded as if the whole of Central Britannia was grovelling earnestly at the feet of the great statesman, Publius Ostorius. The Legate, Quintus Equitius did not believe a word of it, but had to accept what the portly statesman was saying. Ostorius waved away the thorny question of why Caratacus was not in chains being dragged in triumph into camp.

"That is a mere nuisance," said Ostorius airily. "My carefully engineered diplomacy with Cunobelinos, King of one of the greatest tribes in Britannia will bear fruit. We'll have no more trouble from them, I can assure you. Now I must hasten to Rome to pass on the momentous news to the Emperor. This is far too important to be written in a despatch, I must tell him face to face."

I bet you will, thought Equitius. This is your ticket out, and as far as I'm concerned, good riddance. And so it was that Ostorius lost no time in arranging his departure for Rome, accompanied by the baleful Asmodius and a troop of horse. Unknown to

Ostorius was the full report by Asmodius on his drunken, carnal activities which he passed to his friend, Primus Pilus Appius, Senior Centurion to Equitius.

"I had to go along with the conniving bastard's explanation, but I didn't have to like it," Asmodius explained uneasily. "I would never forgive myself if soldiers were to die as a result of his actions, but I could never contradict a senator of his standing. I pass this to you my friend in the hope that you will do the right thing with it. At least it's off my conscience."

The Senior Centurion immediately passed the damning report to Equitius, who after having it copied, sent it by courier to a friendly senator in Rome who he knew would get great sport from denouncing the mighty Publius Ostorius. That should sort the fat bastard out, he thought grimly.

CHAPTER VI

Aurelius and Lenc left Camulodunum at first light, the same day that Ostorius set out on his diplomatic mission. Despite being so involved in the planning of the reconciliation bid, Aurelius was relieved to rid himself of the political infighting and relished being out on the open road.

They rode through conquered Britannia and after fording the mighty Tamesis, arrived at Portus Dubris on the south-east coast where they joined a legion transport ship to Caletum on the mainland. From there they drew fresh horses and took the military coast road to Armorica.

Further south on the Armorica peninsula there had been stiff resistance to Roman domination for many years. Rome had inched forward, bribing and coercing, and where that seemed slow, the might, muscle and discipline of the Legion took over. There were plenty of people still prepared to fight the Roman eagle, and it was difficult not to notice the scowling locals who refused to look up when they passed. They were travelling in civilian clothes, but it was hard to disguise their true identity. Even their horses looked military. Besides why would the locals look more fondly on soldiers pretending not to be soldiers?

They usually took shelter in one of the garrison forts along the way, but some nights slept under the stars rather than risk finding lodgings. Always the sea was to their right until they skirted the Gallia Lugdunensis peninsula and took the new straight military road to their destination, Gesoscribate. Eventually they arrived at the outskirts of the busy fishing port, pausing on the top of a hill to look down on the bustling town. Clear on the coast, on a small hill, a short distance from the town was the rising construction of the new fort which would eventually dominate the entrance to the river mouth and harbour.

Lenc studied the building work with interest. He could see that the stone wall containing the main gate was already finished, and workers were building right and left to extend round, replacing earlier timber defences. The fort was taking shape on a rocky outcrop, scoured away by the River Penfeld at its estuary. Like most Roman forts it was a work in progress. Once the stone walls were complete, they would be strengthened and one day would have walls four metres thick with 10 cylindrical towers dominating the sea and land approaches. In the shadow of the growing fortress a fleet of galleys lay at anchor, ready to intercept pirates.

"I think this is where we must part company," said Aurelius. "It wouldn't do for a lowly Gaul to be seen on an army horse in the company of a fairly obvious officer." He pointed to the building work. "That's where I am going, I should have fresh instructions waiting for me there, while you can try your language skills in the town. Good practice for you," he grinned.

Lenc grunted. All his military life, someone had told him what to do and where to go. Even on this adventure, Aurelius had been the officer and made the decisions. Now he was on his own.

They agreed to meet that evening on the approach to the fort where the road met the town so, with nothing more to say, Lenc swung off his horse and handed over the reins. He stood back as the horse skittered, and after a short pause, hunched his bedroll containing his few possessions into a comfortable position on his shoulder and followed Aurelius down the sloping road into the town.

As he walked down the hill, the smell of the sea, and particularly fish, rose to meet him. He paused at a crossroads, the new stone road heading towards the town, crossing an older mud track which headed to the shoreline. He decided to make for the beach and walk into town along the seashore, almost certainly taking him to the harbour.

After a short but pleasant stroll along a golden beach he was stopped by a jetty wall, behind which, he could see the masts of ships. Stone steps climbed from the beach to the top of the wall. He looked round carefully, he was alone.

Quickly, he rolled out his blanket bedroll which was hiding his gladius and a special harness. He pulled his tunic down to his waist and strapped the harness over his shoulders, making a concealed scabbard between his shoulder-blades. Carefully he felt for the top of the scabbard and gently lowered his gladius into it. He had practised the manoeuvre before and was very aware of how careful he needed to be. Wouldn't do to stab myself, before I let the Celts do it, he thought grimly.

When he felt the blade was as snug as it could be, he pulled up his tunic and after a last look round made for the steps up onto the harbour wall.

An old fisherman dangled his feet over the stone wall above the rancid mud of the riverbed. He was mending a net spread out round him, and nodded in a friendly way when Lenc paused to watch him. "It's a nice day," ventured Lenc eventually in unfamiliar Gaulish. The old man agreed. Emboldened, Lenc asked if there was any work to be had in the town.

"You're not from round here, eh," said the old man. It was not a question.

Lenc agreed that he was not from round here, that's why he was looking for work, and also somewhere to stay.

"Where you from then?" asked the old man, "I don't recognise your accent."

"Alesia originally, but that was a while ago, I've been on a merchant ship but we were paid off, so I just started walking."

"Well you've walked a long way, you could have saved yourself the trouble, there's nothing round here, although you could always get a job helping to build that bastard Roman fort," grumbled the old man. "It's shit money, but you get a midday meal and you're not fighting gales trying to catch fish. If you're looking for somewhere to stay, I do know a widow who has a room. It's not much but it'll keep the rain off."

Lenc thanked him and went in search of the lodgings. It was a dump, but an inconspicuous dump that reeked of stale fish. The old crone who owned it took his money, and offered meals for an extra few coins. Looking at her filthy face and hands he declined politely. She shrugged and shuffled off to her private quarters.

That first evening Lenc met Aurelius on the fort-side of town. Dusk was just descending as he described the way to his lodgings and also to a mean fisherman's tavern just beyond and nearer to the harbour. He reported that so far, although there had been a few questions, he seemed to be getting by with the dialect, and quite enjoyed trying out his conversational Gaulish.

"That's good," said Aurelius approvingly. "That'll be a big help when you get back over the other side. You'll need to prove yourself as a Gaul, if they think you're Roman, you'll be very dead."

"Well thank you for those encouraging words, I'll certainly bear them in mind."

Aurelius smiled and shrugged. "I can't say I envy you your task, it's going to be very difficult." Then he clapped Lenc on the shoulder. "If anyone can do it, it will be you. I have every confidence in you."

Marvellous, thought Lenc. Out loud he said: "I can honestly say that makes me feel so much better, sir."

Aurelius looked at him with a slight smile on his lips. "Oh I'm sure it does. I'm sure it does."

From then on, he and Aurelius met after dark in the tavern on the seafront. Like dockside drinking dens anywhere, the tavern encouraged anonymity, not a place to make new friends. It was low ceilinged with a guttering peat fire, pumping gouts of smoke into the room whenever the wind blew from the sea. Those first few days he spoke to as few people as possible, trying to blend into the cosmopolitan nature of the sea-port. Smuggling was too lucrative a profession in this war-torn country for people to seek out a stranger's business, but gradually he felt the confidence to try out the local dialect, and was pleasantly surprised at how quickly the idioms came back.

On the fourth night, Lenc already had a pewter pot of sharp red wine in front of him as he waited for Aurelius to arrive. He signalled to the landlord for another as his officer pushed open the heavy door and shrugged off his heavy cloak.

"What a charming chap," drawled Aurelius as he took a first tentative swig of the wine. He grimaced, and pulled a face, "which is more than I can say about this piss."

"Not exactly officers mess," agreed Lenc with a chuckle.

"Needs must, but otherwise I wouldn't give it to my dogs," grumbled Aurelius. "So how are you getting on with the locals?"

"I have to say, it seems to be getting easier all the time," conceded Lenc, leaning forward on the scarred and wine stained table. "More importantly do you have any news for me?"

Aurelius leaned back and reflected. "There are any number of boats crossing over to the coast of Siluria, getting passage won't be a problem, but it's the weather, a lot of captains won't risk it this time of year because of the storms that come up so suddenly.

"However, Roman gold usually has a way of opening doors and I think I have our trader. He is looking for a ship going to Britannia, but planning to go to the more civilised part. They of course have money to pay for his crap, so we have to persuade him that the Silurians have stuff of value to him."

That night, after Aurelius had slipped back to the garrison, Lenc sat by himself, reflecting on the chances of success of his mission. He would be depending heavily on people he had not yet met and that could be disastrous, he thought.

As the tavern filled up with fishermen and dock workers, he slurped a steaming bowl of fish stew and chewed on hard nutty brown bread. He knew he should leave, it was dangerous to sit too long. The last thing he needed was to draw attention to himself, yet the stew was warming and surprisingly good. Even the sour wine seemed mellow after a cup or two.

Suddenly he was jerked out of his reverie by a rough shaking of his shoulder.

"Are you deaf as well as stupid?" demanded a lank haired fisherman leaning forward across the table. The smell of stale fish was rank from his coarse wool cloak, shining with fish scale and grease.

Lenc just about caught the words in unfamiliar Gaulish, but before he could stop himself, he blurted out "sorry?" Unfortunately, his single utterance was in military Latin.

The fisherman started and looked at him suspiciously. "Foreigner eh? And just where do you come from, what's your business here?"

"Are you a bloody Roman?" demanded the fisherman suspiciously.

Lenc was in a dilemma. He had to shut the fool up quickly as others were taking an interest, a bit of sport was just what they needed after a hard day's work.

Yet he couldn't admit he was Roman because they would probably tear him apart. He knew his neutral accent did not necessarily mark him out as Roman, but he had been away from home for so long, his accent smothered by the many countries he had served in, he no longer sounded like a Gaul. Trouble was he didn't sound particularly from anywhere.

Reluctantly he decided his only defence was attack, and looked up at the fisherman glaring at him. "Get out of my space you bastard or I'll tear your fucking head off," he grated through clenched teeth.

Startled the fisherman forgot all about Romans. "Think you're a hard man do you?" he sneered. "I've eaten bigger than you for breakfast."

Lenc looked down at the table for a moment. If he could get away from this situation he would. At least he had to try. He put his hands flat down on the scarred table and levered himself upright. Without looking at the fisherman he gathered his cloak over his left arm and with one final look at his tormentor made for the door.

The fisherman scented victory and wanted to milk the situation for all its worth.

"Go on, fuck off Roman, you're not wanted here. Never saw a Roman yet who wouldn't piss himself if he had to fight on his own." That nearly stopped Lenc and he half-turned. He swallowed and headed again for the door.

But the fisherman had more. He caught up with Lenc and pushed him hard on the shoulder. "Is it true Romans fuck their sisters because no-one else will have them?" That brought a roar of delight from the appreciative audience.

Lenc finally reached the door. He went to lift the latch but the fisherman put his flat palm on the door, blocking his path.

There was only one way this was going to end.

"You're in my way," Lenc said flatly.

Something in Lenc's eyes finally made the fisherman think he may have made a mistake. There was no fear there, only a calculating appraisal. Too late to go back now.

"What are you going to do about it? Roman," asked the fisherman, almost pleasantly.

Lenc took a step backward, then suddenly lunged his head forward like a striking snake. The surprised fisherman took the blow high on the cheekbone, just under his eye, and went sprawling backwards into a table awash with cider and wine goblets. He lay half on the table shaking his head before gravity took over and he slumped to the floor.

As he pulled the door open, Lenc rubbed his forehead and

leaned down to the dishevelled fisherman lying in a pool of stale cider, wine and sawdust and said quietly, "And for the last time, I'm not a fucking Roman."

CHAPTER VII

As he slammed the door on the warmth and fug of the tavern, and just before he started running, Lenc heard the fisherman roar. Behind him, the tavern door burst open, spilling light onto the cobbled street. At least ten men came boiling out, looking for blood and revenge.

Lenc had a rough idea of the layout of the town, but he needed to be absolutely sure no-one followed him to his lodgings. If he could just reach that sanctuary undetected, he would be safe.

He ran fast and easy, his cloak bunched up under his arm, the steady rain a blessing. After a while the houses started to change, not so much the crude buildings of the seaport, but coming onto shops and taller buildings. No place for someone running from a baying mob, even if the cobbled street was dark and wet, keeping good honest people near their firesides. He looked round and seeing no sign of pursuit, slowed to a walk, pulling his cloak round him, grateful for the anonymity and warmth.

Once he was sure his pursuers had given up, he turned back towards the harbour. With a bit of luck they would have gone back to the tavern, telling each other what they would have done to the stranger had they caught him. His lodgings were a little too close to the hostelry for comfort but he knew he had to go back there or it would excite comment. But it was not to be.

He was in sight of the low-roofed cottage when out from the shadows stepped the fisherman.

"Thought you'd escape me, did you Roman, well no surprises this time, I'm going to gut you like a fish."

The man's eyes glittered in the half-light. He hunched over, in his right hand he gripped an evil looking fisherman's knife with a long blade, point upwards.

Lenc dropped his cloak and put his hands up as if in surrender. His opponent's lips started to curl contemptuously, but his expression changed when Lenc reached over his shoulder and drew out his regulation gladius scabbarded between his shoulder blades. With a metallic scrape, the blade pulled free and glinted in the rain. He hefted it in his right hand, feeling its finely balanced weight. Fashioned from premium tempered iron, it had served him well for many years and the awkwardness of its hiding place now proved its worth.

At last, the discomfort of carrying the blade in its hiding place proved justified, and he thanked Mithras for not having to face his opponent unarmed.

Warily, the two men circled each other on the treacherous cobbles. With his longer blade, Lenc had the advantage, but before long the rest of the mob could arrive, dramatically tipping the balance. He knew well enough the theory of street fighting, any fighting really, get in first with as much shock and aggression as possible. Put your opponent on the back foot quickly and effectively, and then put him on his back and not stop until he's staring sightlessly at the stars.

Lenc lunged forward, as his opponent tensed and raised his blade above his shoulder, poised to stab down, but Lenc was already inside the arc of the swing. He blocked the swipe with his forearm and followed through with a jab to the fisherman's windpipe and a knee to the groin.

Even as the man convulsed at the onslaught, his razor-sharp blade arced down, slicing through Lenc's left forearm. He grunted as he felt the blade scrape bone.

He was prepared to take a slash from his opponent's blade if it meant getting under his guard, but wished he still had his cloak which would have protected his arm. He lunged again, then feinted right. The fisherman jumped back defensively. Lenc knew by the way the man crouched and held his weapon he was no knife fighter. But he still had a sharp blade and this could be his lucky night and he could be reinforced at any time. Besides he was a big bastard.

Lenc cuffed the rain from his eyes as he inched back to the wall, feeling for it with his left hand. He could feel the warmth of blood coursing down his arm, not particularly painful, that would come later, but he knew he was losing blood. His blade was held point upwards as he steadied himself, before crouching in the attack position. Suddenly he sprang forward, his attention focussed on his opponent's knife arm, and with his sword held low, aimed his left fist at the big man's head.

Involuntarily, the man flinched. He had suddenly realised that he was fighting for his life, probably against a man more experienced and better armed. As the blow came in the fisherman flinched and automatically tried to roll his head away from the blow, leaving him wide open.

Lenc lunged forward, sword extended. He caught the big man with a slashing movement which opened his knife arm with a gaping, vicious cut. The man's eyes widened with shock, his upper arm bleeding badly. He took a step backward, and tripped, sprawling helplessly on the wet cobbles. He raised his good arm defensively, the fight was over and he knew it.

Lenc's thoughts raced. His priority was not to get caught, his mission was paramount and the mob would tear him apart if they found him. But who would care if this fisherman turned up dead? Deep down he knew he had no choice, he looked round warily, there was no-one in sight. He looked again at the man on the ground, who was stirring and groaning. Lenc pressed himself against the rough stone wall as the wounded fisherman painfully rolled over and struggled to his feet. He tried to stumble down the narrow lane lurching off the stone walls. In three strides, Lenc caught up and grabbed a handful of lank, greasy hair. He savagely pulled the hair back, exposing a grimy neck. Tightening his grip on his sword, he whispered, "Sorry mate, but you wouldn't leave it alone," he whispered. Then with a swallow he reluctantly raised his sword. The man's eyes rolled with fear as he opened his mouth to plead for his life. But whatever he was going to say was cut off almost immediately to a gurgle as the razor-sharp blade sliced across and through his throat, jarring on the top of his spine.

Lenc let go of the greasy hair and pitched the dead man's head forward, the body remaining slumped against the wall in a kneeling position. And the rain kept falling.

He looked down at the bundle of rags, once a strong, vibrant man. He had little regret at taking a life, it wasn't the first and probably wouldn't be the last. He just wished he had kept well away from trouble.

His first instinct was to run, but where to? His lodgings were close, but he couldn't risk returning there.

He wiped his blade clean on the dead man's soggy wool shirt and hacked a length free to use as a makeshift tourniquet before carefully replacing his sword in the scabbard between his shoulder blades. Slowly, he backed away from the dead man, turned and walked briskly towards the town centre.

As he walked he bound his wound with the musty cloth, using his teeth to tighten the knot. Almost immediately blood seeped through, but it was slower now although throbbing in pain.

Much against his instincts, he realised he would have to contact Aurelius, staying at the fort. That was risky enough, but unless his officer could make the arrangements quickly and he could sail on the tide, the chances were that the big man's mates would want to have a chat with him.

The journey through the silent town was uneventful, a stabbing cold rain keeping the heads down of the few people abroad that night. The climb up the cobbled road to the fort was steep, and he knew the guards on the ramparts would be alert.

"Halt, who goes there," the stentorian challenge from out of the darkness was expected, but still made him start.

"I am alone," he shouted in return. "I have urgent news for one of your officers. Open the gate."

Lenc stood in the rain, his cloak thrown back over his shoulders so the guards could see he carried no weapons. The sword nestling between his shoulder blades would stay hidden. The large double fort gates were solid oak with heavy metal studding. Inset in one was a small door just big enough for a man to squeeze through. From it came a rattling of bolts and the door swung open. Two legionaires stepped warily out, one carrying a guttering torch and both with swords extended. Lenc could sense the archers on the rampart walls with their arrows trained on him.

He stood still, arms outstretched in the crucifix position, which might well be my fate, he thought wryly.

The front legionary, wearing the blue sash of a senior man stepped forward, while the other stepped to the side to keep his sword swing clear and to stay out of the line of sight of the archers above.

"What is your business here," demanded the senior man.

"I am on Rome's business. I need to speak to Tribune Aurelius, staying in the fort on detachment."

Comings and goings in the middle of the night were not common, but did happen. But the fort, being on the edge of civilisation, maintained a constant state of alertness, especially since only the town-facing wall with the oak studded door was anything like finished. Either side the stone met wooden stakes atop a soil bank.

The senior knew better than to dismiss the stranger into the night. He had the look of a soldier and there was blood seeping from a badly damaged arm. The dim light of the torch indicated he'd been in quite a fight.

"Follow him," the senior tersely ordered, motioning to the other guard, who stepped back and through the small door.

Lenc ducked his head and followed. The guard was waiting for him, sword at the ready. Behind came the senior, who re-bolted the entrance then gestured to a door into the guardroom.

Inside, the senior shed his cloak near a warming brazier. "I know of this Aurelius but you will regret it if you are leading us a dance. I am persuaded that there is something about your story, otherwise you would not know this officer." He gestured to the other soldier, "Watch him well, and see if you can find something to bind his arm properly."

The senior man was gone for what seemed like an age. Lenc sank back onto a wooden bench hard up against the cold stone wall. A less than sympathetic legion medic peeled off the bloody cloth sticking to the crusted wound, which flapped open like a fish's mouth.

"I can clean it and bind it and you can get it sorted out later, or I can do a proper job and stitch it, but that's going to hurt. What's it to be?"

Lenc did not hesitate. "Stitch it."

The medic shrugged and reached into his small pack. "This will sting a bit," he warned as he poured a flask of vinegar over the wound and almost tenderly bathed it with a clean cloth. Even although he was prepared, the acidic vinegar on the open wound was still a sudden, searing pain which sent a shock wave up Lenc's arm.

He turned away when he saw the medic prepare his sewing needle, ground from a cat bone, threading it with fine hemp.

"I'll be as quick as I can," said the medic, "I guess it's not the first time you've been through this."

Lenc braced himself as the needle punctured his skin; even so, the sharp pain took him by surprise and he had to fight not to flinch. He told himself it wasn't that bad, he'd had worse, but still it hurt like hell.

Big girl, he accused himself.

The medic was quick and thorough. When he had finished he

leaned back to admire his handiwork. "Not bad at all, pity I don't get paid for it."

The pain eased to a dull throbbing as the medic applied a clean bandage. "You should have a few days bed rest, if that's possible," he warned.

As the medic left the guardroom, he stepped back to allow the guard commander to return. Behind him was Aurelius. He was wearing a short tunic, sandals and his hair was tousled, obviously raised from sleep. He looked at Lenc, took in the pale face, the weary expression and the already staining bandage. He turned to the guard commander, "Leave us alone for a few minutes, would you, he is my man."

The commander jerked his head at the guards and they all left, carefully shutting the heavy oak door behind them.

When the door closed Aurelius swung on the sitting patient. "What the fuck have you been doing? You're supposed to be on a secret mission, keeping a low profile."

Lenc shook his head wearily.

"Sorry boss, I had no choice. If I thought that taking a beating would have ended the matter, I would have taken it gladly. But he would have killed me. The more I backed away from him, the braver he became," he said flatly. "In the end I killed him."

"Oh shit," Aurelius said and sat near to Lenc. He reflected for a moment. "Any witnesses?"

"Not to the actual fight, but plenty of people saw us at the tavern." Lenc quickly described the events and where he had left his victim.

Aurelius stood and paced the small room as he thought hard.

"Right, it's not the end of the world. I can send out a patrol which can just happen on the body. If no-one has found him already, which is quite possible given the hour and the weather, they can dispose of him. That will be that problem solved.

"But it's your mission which concerns me. I found a skipper willing to take you, but the weather at sea is foul right now. He won't sail until it improves. That could be tomorrow or even next week.

"In the meantime you can't stay in town, if they caught you, they would tear you apart if you turned up now and as your cover's blown there's no point anyway. So best case is for you to stay here undercover until you sail. You can get your head down in my room."

Lenc nodded wearily and followed his officer without registering where he was going. He was bone tired now and his arm was throbbing, as Aurelius lit a tallow lamp suffusing the bare limestone walls of the spartan officer's accommodation with a soft flickering glow. Lenc leaned against the wall, eyes closed.

"It's not much, but I wasn't expecting to be entertaining either," said Aurelius with a wry grin.

Two days Lenc stayed in the small room. He slept on a narrow wooden trestle against the wall while Aurelius had a not much bigger wooden bed with a straw stuffed palliase. The room was devoid of decoration. Could be worse, Lenc thought, I could be back in a block with seven hairy arsed legionaries, all farting and wanking, I don't need that.

The throbbing in his arm was intense on that first night. Even after a beaker of local apple brandy, he knew that, mentally exhausted as he was, sleep would not come easily. When it did come, he woke several times as an ill-considered movement brought a sharp pain to his wound, but managed a fitful sleep until the dawn finally touched the small window set high in the wall.

The one highlight was brought by Aurelius who confirmed that the dead fisherman had been found by his patrol and buried in a nearby wood. "Your friend from the other night has been made to disappear," was how Aurelius laconically described it.

During the day, while Aurelius was out, food was brought to the room by orderlies and left outside the door. His toilet needs were catered for by a bucket, which he also left outside the door.

There was nothing to do but stare out of the window, but at least he was safe. For the time being.

CHAPTER VIII

Lenc woke with a start. He had only been dozing, but still failed to hear anyone enter the room.

"So this is where the spy is hiding his bumboy!"

His arm was throbbing and his throat felt like sand. He struggled up onto his good elbow and eyed his visitors resentfully. The speaker was well dressed, obviously an officer from the trappings on his uniform. Flanking him were two of the toughest looking legionaries Lenc had seen. They were dressed for a rough house, without cloak and armour and each held a short cudgel.

"Who the fuck are you?" he croaked.

An expression of distaste played about the officer's mouth. "Afraid you've got it wrong. Around here, I ask the questions, what you do is answer. Now, who the fuck are you?" Satisfied he had made his point, he stood, legs apart and arms folded waiting for an answer.

Lenc studied the officer silently. He was thin, but clearly not from an excess of combat, just naturally thin. He had a long aquiline nose pinching his mouth, which seemed to turn everything he said into a sneer. He looked like a stork wearing a toga.

"Sorry," Lenc hesitated, then decided to add, "sir. Can't tell you that. Any information about me must come from Tribune Aurelius."

"So the bumboy wants to play it the hard way, eh? This is my kingdom and I don't like people keeping secrets from me. Now who are you and what are you doing here?"

"Sorry sir, you'll have to ask Tribune Aurelius."

"No, I think you'll tell me." He smiled grimly and clicked his fingers, and the legionaries stepped forward. The one on the right was tapping his cudgel head into his left palm menacingly, as the officer stepped back with a look of disdain. He seemed afraid that these common soldiers might infect him with something by their close presence.

He gestured to the men. "This toad won't tell me what he is doing in my fort. I need to know, and I want you gentlemen to find out for me."

The two bully boys looked at each other, then stepped towards the trestle bed. Lenc tried to struggle upright.

"He wants to stand men, why don't you help him?"

One of the men, the bigger bruiser with a badly broken nose and cauliflower ear grabbed Lenc by his wounded arm and wrenched it savagely. He had expected them to home in on his bandaged wound but still wasn't prepared for the sudden searing agony.

He fought back the shriek of pain that was bubbling up from his guts and, head bowed, he raised his other arm in supplication. While lying down he could do nothing but take a whacking. Once on the floor it would be a kicking.

By getting to his feet, he might at least manage to inflict some damage on his persecutors. Though he rather doubted it. But, he thought, if he could only get a swing at that sneering officer it would be worth a beating. Nearly.

The two soldiers nodded to each and took a half step back, their victim was clearly no threat so they were happy to oblige. He would be easier to hit standing up, besides there's little satisfaction in giving a beating to someone already on the floor.

Lenc painfully swung his legs onto the floor, staring down, gathering his senses and strength. He was only wearing his under-garment, not even anything on his feet. He put his good hand to his head and groaned, mostly - but not entirely - for the benefit of his tormentors. Who were getting impatient. One of them shuffled a step forward. With his good arm, Lenc felt under the bed, his fingers catching on his piss-pot, which he knew was three-quarters full.

He gripped the top tightly and with a roar stood up and at the same time launched the contents of the rancid pot at the soldiers, who straight away recognised the liquid for what it was and involuntarily jumped back. So did the officer or his two bullies would have crashed into him in the small room.

Lenc knew how this particular brawl was going to end, but before then he was determined to do some damage. Especially to that sneering bastard officer.

His lips curled in a snarl and he let out another roar as he launched himself and managed to dart between the two soldiers, who were more interested in wiping piss from their tunics.

The officer backed away with a look of sheer terror. He found the door with his back and as Lenc charged, was through it with a speed he never knew he had. He turned long enough to scream for his thugs to do something and help, but was stifled as Lenc's forehead connected savagely with his aristocratic Roman nose. Lenc heard the satisfying crunch of broken bone as they both headed floorwards in a tangle.

Lenc risked a look up to see the two soldiers dancing round the melee. They were desperate to get hold of their quarry without, of course, hurting their paymaster, but with limbs flailing, this was proving a bit more difficult than it first looked.

The bigger man hefted his club then indicated to the other to grab a leg or arm….or anything, just separate them. After some ineffective grabs he finally got a hold on a wayward leg and hauled.

Lenc hung onto the shrieking officer with all his might, but eventually his grip started to fade. So far the bully boys dared not use their clubs for fear of clobbering the wrong person. When Lenc did look up again, a fist smashed into his cheek, then as his grip relaxed, so blows started raining down on his arms to separate him from the now sobbing officer.

Lenc rolled away and adopted the foetal position, with his knees drawn up to his chest and arms round his head, trying to protect his vital bits.

As well as the clubs, they were using their feet, shod in nailed military boots, to land a rain of punishing blows. Eventually, after a savage kick which caught him behind the ear, he blacked out. He did not hear Aurelius arrive on the double with the guard commander and four-man escort.

By this time the officer had dragged himself up the wall, and while holding a delicate handkerchief to his streaming nose was adding an enthusiastic, if ineffectual contribution to the kicking Lenc was receiving.

"Stop that at once," roared Aurelius as he strove to take in the scene. The stentorian voice of command was enough for the two thugs who, as one, snapped to attention. Their cudgels disappeared under tunics.

The officer was breathing hard and still trying to stem the flow of blood from his bent nose. He aimed one last kick at Lenc's kidneys as he fought to regain his composure.

"This man struck me. Me," he shrilled. "Me, a senatorial adviser. I will have him crucified for that." His voice was thick and adenoidal, the kerchief muffling the words, but the meaning was plain. "All I did was ask him what his business was in your chambers and he violently attacked me. He wants putting down like a rabid dog."

Aurelius paused. He knew of the man in front of him. He was Senator Maximus, a politician and therefore an important and influential man, there to negotiate with the local authorities and report back to Rome and the Senate. The garrison commander was supposedly the man in charge but as Maximus constantly reminded anyone caring to listen, he had the ear of the Senate, and that made him king of the castle.

Maximus was a schemer. He enjoyed the cut and thrust, the mind play of politics, the delicate nuances of manipulation, usually to his own ends. In this game, knowledge was power. So when the news that an injured stranger had arrived at the gates and was being hidden in an officer's quarters inevitably leaked out within the cramped quarters of the fort, he had to know more. If nothing else he was affronted that he was not consulted and kept informed.

With a curt jerk of his head, Aurelius dismissed the bully boys and motioned to two of the guards to take the still comatose Lenc back into the room.

"Lay him down and get the doctor," he ordered brusquely.

He was seething inside but very aware he was treading on thin ice with this arrogant fool. He smiled warmly and placed his hand on Maximus' forearm. "Now Maximus," he said warmly, "Come and sit down, you have quite an injury. The doctor will see to you and we have a lot to talk about." Maximus allowed himself to be steered towards the single bed. He tried not to look at the inert lump that was Lenc laying still, facing the wall.

When the legion doctor hurried into the room, carrying his medical bag, he registered one patient sitting up and holding a kerchief to his face and a body lying unconscious on the stone floor. Instinctively he went to the prone body, but Aurelius forestalled him and pointed the puzzled doctor towards Maximus, snuffling piteously into a rapidly staining linen kerchief.

"He has by far the most serious injuries."

The doctor raised his eyebrows.

"Really," added Aurelius.

The doctor was no fool. He knew his way round legion politics and who Senator Maximus was, and more importantly knew the ears he had access to.

When Maximus could be coaxed to remove his hands from his face the doctor earnestly examined the throbbing proboscis. He clucked sympathetically. It was more than his job and maybe his life was worth to laugh out loud, but he did manage to quell the shout of laughter that was welling up inside. A doctor in the Legion – even a medical orderly – would never normally be called on to deal with a broken nose. It was almost a rite of passage. The number of soldiers who walked into a fist or club which damaged or disfigured their nose was just not countable. Besides what could you do? It was broken, that's it.

He ostentatiously but very tenderly laid his hands on the swollen article. "Yes, it's broken all right," he said gravely. "And now bending to the right. You were lucky, it will heal but it will always bend I'm afraid. I could try and straighten it, but it will be devilish painful." He made a show of cleaning off the affected area with linen strips soaked with lavender water.

"Is it very bad?" asked Maximus tearfully.

"See for yourself." The doctor held up a piece of polished metal. Maximus examined himself critically. He touched his nose tentatively. His eyes widened. "Zeus on his mountain, it's pointing at my ear. Doctor you must do something."

"Sit down Senator, and I will see what I can do."

"Will this hurt much?" gulped the fearful senator. He was starting to have second thoughts about a field operation. Maybe he should wait till he returned to Rome and have a civilised, more sympathetic, more experienced surgeon treat his injury.

"Let me have a second look," said the doctor thoughtfully. He raised his hands to the swollen nose, which had stopped bleeding and the nostrils were caked in coagulated blood. "I'm afraid that the longer it's left, the more difficult it will be to do anything about it," he said gravely. "Cartilage and bone have a habit of knitting and setting which will need to be re-broken before it can be re-set."

Tenderly he put three fingers on either side of the bent nose. He looked round for Aurelius and gestured for him to stand behind the cringing senator, who had his eyes firmly screwed shut. His shoulders were hunched and he tensed against the coming pain.

Aurelius put his hands on the side of the senator's head, ready to grip tight. Maximus flinched as he felt the hands on his temples.

"What are you going to do?" he asked fearfully.

The medic ignored the question and nodded at Aurelius, who gripped hard. The doctor braced himself and exerted quick pressure on the broken side of the nose.

There was an audible crack and Maximus howled at the pain. A gout of blood shot down both nostrils and streamed down the senator's creased and soiled tunic. He was sobbing with pain as Aurelius and the doctor relaxed their grip.

The doctor squinted at the nose. "Not bad," he said finally. "It's almost straight again, but when the swelling goes down there will be a quite noticeable bump. Now the only thing left is to jam a thin bit of wood up each nostril and hope that will complete the straightening process. There is a slight danger that the wood can go too far and enter the brain, but I haven't heard of that happening in ages."

Aurelius choked as he stifled a laugh, which almost set the doctor off. He fought to control himself.

"Actually, looking at it again, you know I think it could be an improvement. Makes you look like a warrior. People will see that you have been in a real fight and can obviously handle yourself. Here, have a look."

Maximus looked at him suspiciously. The medic seemed to be in earnest. He reached for the small polished metal mirror and examined his re-arranged nose from every possible direction.

"Yes, I can see what you mean," said Maximus slowly and critically as he contorted his face, "A bit drastic but I can see how people will think I'm a warrior."

As he put down the mirror, his expression changed. He glowered at Lenc, who was by now groaning in a heap.

"That bastard should get 500 lashes at least. Or crucified," he brightened. "And crucified. I like the idea of crucified."

Aurelius broke in on this uncomfortable train of thought.

"Senator," he said gravely, "as you can see, this man is going nowhere for now, so why don't I help you to your quarters. You can get cleaned up and I will brief you as much as I can about his mission."

"Well yes," grumbled Maximus, "if you had done that in the first place, we would have avoided all this unpleasantness."

Yes, and if you had kept your nose out of things that don't concern you, you wouldn't have had it broken, Aurelius thought to himself. What he actually said was, "Let's leave the doctor to it, shall we? Some fresh air will do that nose of yours good."

Maximus shot him a suspicious look, but Aurelius was smiling without a hint of guile.

The doctor's snort was quickly stifled and turned into a strangled cough as Maximus spun round to catch him. "Hmmm," he allowed himself.

After Maximus had finally and reluctantly shuffled from the room still tenderly caressing his throbbing nose, Aurelius turned to the doctor. He paused and glanced down the corridor, ensuring that the senator was moving out of earshot.

"Do what you can for this man," he said. "He must be fit for duty as soon as possible. The longer he stays here, the more likely that interfering fool will get in the way again."

The doctor took a quick look at Lenc. One eye was closed, his lip was bruised and bleeding, and swelling rapidly where it had caught on teeth. There were several quite clear bootmarks coming up as impressive purpling.

When Lenc looked conscious enough to respond, the doctor asked,

"What about your ribs. Can you stand?"

Lenc winced. He was in a world of pain. Every part of him seemed to either throb or be on fire. He gingerly flexed his arms and tried to sit up, but a shooting pain in his chest doubled him over. He grunted and felt for the pain.

"Better strap those ribs," the doctor said tersely. "Even if you haven't broken any, they'll benefit from a tight dressing for a day or two."

Lenc nodded, and surreptitiously slid his questing hand down between his legs and sighed with relief as he gently probed his equipment. His instinctive adoption of the foetal position had protected his masculinity from the worst of the assault, although he could feel he took a few kicks close by.

Across his body were the tell-tale signs of nail-shod boots, but in the narrow corridor, his two adversaries had difficulty getting a good swing of their cudgels in.

The doctor silently handed Lenc a horn beaker, filled with apple brandy. He accepted it gratefully but winced as the fiery liquid found the open wounds in his mouth. Even so, the brandy felt good as it lit a fire all the way down to his stomach. He closed his eyes and savoured the warmth as a bandage was wrapped tightly round his chest.

"This will keep the ribs in place while they heal," he explained. "It's important to keep this on for as long as possible. It could be that your ribs are just badly bruised, you don't appear to have done any other damage or you would have known by now. At least you're not coughing up frothy blood which would have been serious."

In the Legion, a medic tended not to take much notice of superficial cuts and bruises, they were part of his stock in trade, but he meticulously checked Lenc over and did what he could to patch up the worst injuries, the rest would heal in their own time.

The doctor looked at him critically, "I must warn you that it's very important you take it easy for a few days. If you disturb those ribs you could be in real serious trouble."

Lenc tried to smile, "I'll do my best doc, and thanks for your help." He pulled on his tunic wincing as the movements pulled at his ribs.

As the doctor packed his medical bag, Aurelius returned and

stood in the doorway. The doctor looked sharply at him. "Tread carefully" he warned. "Maximus may be a pompous fool, but he's an influential pompous fool. You would do well to get him on your side."

Aurelius nodded. "Agreed. You're quite right, I'm going to have to eat that bastard's shit for quite some time."

The doctor paused. "Why not involve him? I don't know what you're cooking here, and don't want to know, but if you had that fool on your side, it may make your mission easier. One thing that scheming bastard needs to learn is that it's in his own interest to be discreet."

Aurelius thought quickly. Maybe that was the answer. Maximus was in a position to completely scupper the mission and probably claim a major victory in thwarting yet another plot against Rome. Plots were seen everywhere, especially in the intelligence community and a paranoid command was always quick to despatch plotters.

"I think you may be right," he said slowly, "but I shall have to give some thought how to go about it."

That evening Lenc, after inadvertently shifting his position on the narrow cot and twisting his ribs, jerked awake from a fitful sleep. The pain coursing up his arm brought an involuntary grunt as he came fully awake and aware of Aurelius watching with a horn mug in his hand.

He offered the mug, half full of brandy. "Do you feel up to a walk outside?" he asked, not unkindly.

Lenc, aching everywhere, shielded his ribs with his forearm and slowly levered his feet round onto the floor as the pain came in waves. He tentatively ran his tongue over his swollen lips as once again the fiery liquid burned the open wounds in his mouth. But still, it tasted good.

"What're the chances of a soak in the baths?" he croaked. "Although I'll have to have these bandages re-tied after."

"Well now you might just be in luck," replied Aurelius. "I've been having a word with your new best friend Senator Maximus and he actually came up with a helpful plan."

Aurelius took a deep breath, "Once we had established that he was god almighty and I was an insignificant piece of shit, I actually had something constructive from him.

"I was careful to give him the absolute minimum, but I think he got the picture that this mission is vital to our success in Britannia. He soon saw the value in being behind that. So when I said we needed a confidential meeting with our trader and the skipper of the boat he couldn't have been more helpful. In a very short time he has worked wonders, we just have to wait and see what the detail of his plan is."

Despite the pain, Lenc lay idly on his cot, listening to the wind howling outside. If it's bad here, who knows what it's like at sea, he thought. Still, right now I'd gladly swap a stormy sea for another day staring at the ceiling of this dump.

These thoughts were wandering idly through his mind when Aurelius bustled in, making a welcome distraction and clearly bursting with news. He carried a bundle wrapped in a regulation red woollen cloak, which fell open when he dropped it on his bed to disclose a set of armour and uniform. "For you," he said with a smile.

"The weather is finally calming and the skipper says it looks like you might be sailing tomorrow. And last of all, I have found the perfect cover for you."

Aurelius sat back with a satisfied smirk on his face.

"Go on then," said Lenc, "are you going to let me into the secret?"

"His name is Anton, Son of Heracles, a Gaul and he trades in Britannia. He takes metal goods, and pots, maybe some wine and cloth and trades them for hides and precious metals.

"He would normally head for the more cultivated, civilised

parts of Britannia, wherever that may be, but I persuaded him there would be richer pickings in the untapped wilder areas, especially as he would have a strong, willing young man to help, and we would of course be contributing to his, ah, expenses."

"When do I meet this fellow?" asked Lenc.

"Well, that's the good bit. It's tonight," said Aurelius briskly. "Senator Maximus is a patron of a very discreet, secure place which I am sure you will like. It's very unlikely that your crew of cutthroats and pirates will venture far from the docks, and they certainly wouldn't get anywhere near this place. Just to be sure, there will be a patrol lurking about as well.

"Maximus wanted to come with us, probably so he could take the credit afterwards, but I managed to persuade him that getting there and back could be dangerous, and he decided he would just wait for a report on our return."

Lenc nodded. Being pleasant to that bastard was probably more than he was capable of. "How's his nose by the way, still sore? Hope so."

"Now then," chided Aurelius gently, "that's no way to talk about a chap going out of his way to help us. Even if it is for the wrong reasons."

Lenc contented himself with a non-committal grunt.

That evening, Lenc needed help to strap himself into his armour. It was the Legion version, lorica segmentata, 'lobster-style' figure-hugging iron bands mounted on a leather frame. As an auxiliary, Lenc wore chain mail, more flexible, but nothing like as effective in stopping a spear or sword thrust. Aurelius helped him into the unfamiliar armour, but even with the straps on their broadest setting, the metal was tight against his bandaged ribs.

When dark fell, the two quietly walked down to the fort's main gate guardroom to meet the town patrol. As the silent soldiers made last minute adjustments to their equipment, tallow lamps cast long shadows on the still firmly bolted oak double gate. The wind was still high and the night overcast, but at least the rain had stopped. Maybe the ship would sail on the morning tide.

The patrol commander, a Decanus, had briefed his men who just shuffled their line to let the newcomers in. They only carried shields and swords, spears were considered too confrontational, and not much use in a built up area anyway. Cloaks were hitched over their shoulders leaving hands free to draw weapons.

The Decanus called the patrol to attention and as one they stiffened.

"Right lads, this is a routine patrol so nothing dramatic. We have some guests with us and we'll be dropping them off in town and we don't draw attention to them. OK? Let's keep it safe and easy."

He then moved to the left of the patrol and quietly gave the command, "Column of two." With the minimum of fuss the patrol shook itself out into two lines, one either side of the gateway. "Keep your concentration, move out."

As the patrol marched down the hill towards the sleeping town, Lenc managed to adjust the unfamiliar armour and get into the swing of the march. At least the pain was more bearable. Without being told, they quietly formed a column along both sides of the new road with at least two arms lengths between each man. Their pace slowed at the same time, so it seemed almost casual. Certainly less threatening.

Out in the open, the wind was gusting hard and the rain started coming down in torrents. It was no night to be out in the elements, and once again Lenc wondered if they would sail the next day. The buildings of the town gave them some shelter, but soon their cloaks were soaked through, cold and heavy.

By now the stone buildings with shop fronts were giving way to more prosperous buildings. High stone walls and solid gates hid the properties within, showing their owner's fears of robbers and terrorists. Eventually they stopped alongside yet another nondescript high wall, yet this one had bright lanterns either side of an iron mounted oak door. On the signal to stop, the patrol flattened against the walls, still watchful and alert, hands on swords.

Aurelius gave a sharp rap on an iron knocker, and almost immediately a small spy hole opened in the door. "Who's there," demanded a truculent voice.

"We are expected," said Aurelius, "courtesy of Senator Maximus." There was a grunt from behind the peep-hole as it dropped shut. A creaking heralded the opening of the door and the guard peered out curiously, all he could see were Aurelius and Lenc and one shadowy figure behind them. The rest of the patrol stayed out of sight, pressed against the wet, dark walls.

Aurelius leaned back to whisper to the patrol commander. "Sorry about this old mate, but I have no idea how long this is going to take. You'll have to give us some time, but I don't want you hanging around outside drawing attention to yourself."

The Decanus smiled, "actually this is quite a plum for us, sir, don't worry we won't be far away and will start to check on you when the town bell rings at midnight. We won't be obvious, but we'll be around."

Aurelius neither knew nor cared where the patrol was going to spend its time, as long as they returned when needed to escort them back to the fort.

The gate guard was fidgeting at the door and gestured to them to hurry. He was carrying a heavy wooden club and looked prepared to use it.

Once through the door, it quickly snapped shut behind them. They were in a well-lit courtyard, a world of difference from the dank street outside. The courtyard boasted several life-size statues, which Lenc appreciated were of nubile ladies, mostly in degrees of undress. Although he considered himself a man of the world, he was still not prepared for this unexpected amount of nudity. He tried not to ogle the life-like statues as he thought, what have I got myself into this time?

CHAPTER IX

As the street door closed, so another door in the main building opened, flooding even more light onto the courtyard.

Framed in the doorway was a young woman, her shining black hair cascading down to her shoulders. She was dressed in a white linen robe fastened at one shoulder, Lenc, fascinated, noted that the light shining from behind her, rendered her dress completely transparent, and she was naked underneath. A tattoo high on her arm, marked her as a slave.

"What is this place?" Lenc eventually managed to stutter.

"Haven't you ever been to a brothel before," smiled Aurelius.

"Yes but soldiers' brothels don't tend to be like this."

"Just enjoy, but remember, you're still on Rome's business. And don't forget to thank Senator Maximus when we get back."

The slave-girl smiled at them and bade them enter, tutting at their heavy armour and sodden cloaks. "Perhaps you would feel better without all this iron," she breathed. She had the dark skin of a Macedonian and an accent to match. They already felt better, and not just because they were out of the rain.

She snapped her fingers imperiously and a bald, wobbling fat man hurried into the reception room, all smiles and bellies. "Help them with their armour," she ordered.

The man bowed, "Yeth ma'am," he lisped respectfully, bowing and nodding, holding his hands together.

"Come along gentlemen, let me help you." He eyed the two tough looking soldiers lasciviously. Lenc wasn't sure he wanted the man helping him. He turned to Aurelius and nodded.

They undid each other's straps as the fat man cooed and tried to help, but they managed to ignore him until they were finally free of the cumbersome metal, which the now pouting fat man carefully stowed in a side room.

The girl slave waited until they were ready, then inclined her head in a bow as the two men walked past her into a second brightly lit room. The walls were covered in paintings and drapes, all revelling in the naked female form. Even the mosaic tiled floor depicted explicit acts of sexual abandon. Lenc gaped as he tried to take in the images laid out before him so unexpectedly.

The slave girl knocked and pushed open another door. "Your friends await you," she murmured with downcast eyes. Aurelius led the way into this inner room. Lit by oil-lamps, around the walls were cushions of a silken cloth in a riot of colours. Lounging in the middle was a fat man in work clothes, with closed eyes and an ecstatic smile on his chubby features. He had a horn beaker of wine in his hand and at his side was a choice array of meats, bread and cheese. A slave girl knelt behind him, kneading his tubby shoulders. This must be their trader, Lenc guessed. Seated apart from him was a man who could only be a sailor. He was also dressed in working clothes, but there was an air of authority about him which suggested a man not used to being taken for granted.

Once disturbed, the fat man reluctantly opened his eyes, but unwilling to let the moment go, closed them again. The smile returned.

"Anton, I think," said Aurelius. The large man negligently waved his free hand. "This doesn't happen to me very often, let me savour it."

Aurelius impatiently clicked his fingers, and gestured to the slave girl to leave. She hurriedly stood and with downcast eyes left the room.

Anton struggled up into a sitting position, about to protest then thought better of it. Mumbling to himself he took a noisy slurp of wine.

"This is your new employee, he will accompany you to Britannia," Aurelius said, introducing Lenc. Anton looked him up and down, noting the bruises, cuts and bandages. "Bit of a fighter is he? Best to keep those fists hidden where we're going, those buggers will chop your balls off as soon as look at you."

"That won't be necessary," said Aurelius smoothly. "If he has to fight, then his mission will be at an end. A clear head and diplomacy are the order of the day."

Aurelius turned to the other man and to Lenc said, "And this is our ship's captain, Lantumaros Morinos, who has agreed to take you and Anton to Britannia." The captain nodded at Lenc.

Aurelius gestured to Lenc to sit. They both arranged themselves, Lenc with difficulty on the cushions. As they did so, two more slave girls entered the room, bearing beakers, a jug of wine and more plates of food. Despite his pain, Lenc realised that he was starving, but even if he wasn't, he would be hard pressed to resist this spread, especially after garrison slop.

He filled his plate and took the offered beaker of wine from one of the girls, who oohed with concern at the spasm of pain that crossed his features as he accepted the drink. As he took a first tentative sip, she moved behind him and gently started to massage his shoulders. He sighed and then grunted when she went over one of his bruises. She pulled her hands back in contrite apology. "No, no, not your fault, don't stop," Lenc said softly.

She glanced at the other men who were watching with differing levels of interest and carefully slipped the neck of Lenc's tunic down, gasping at the blue and brown bruising. Reaching round for his arm, she eased the tunic down, slipping it to his waist, and gasped again at the stained bandage wrapped tightly round his chest and the other bandage on his arm, still seeping blood.

She leaned forward and whispered close to Lenc's ear, "Eat and drink then I will take you next door. We have hot baths, and I will dress your wounds again."

"That would be very nice," Lenc breathed. He dared not think what else might be on offer. "What's your name?"

The girl looked down at her hands in her lap. "Tonia, master," she said demurely.

"If I can have your attention for just a minute, we have things to discuss," said Aurelius impatiently. Anton and the captain were leering appreciatively.

"Sorry boss," replied a grinning Lenc. Aurelius helped himself to a plate of food and sat back reflectively.

"I understand the storm is abating. Can you sail on the morning tide?" he asked, looking at the captain who shrugged then nodded.

"It should be gone by tomorrow, but what will happen out at sea is another matter and out of my hands. I wouldn't normally venture out yet, but as your gold is pretty persuasive, we will go."

"Good," said Aurelius curtly. "I will deliver the passenger to your ship before first light. I want him aboard and out of sight till you leave harbour. Anton, you will make your own way aboard with your cargo, I am sure the captain will find some help to get your kit stowed away."

The captain nodded and took a swig of wine. "I don't need to know the reason for the secrecy, but it wouldn't be to do with a knifing in the port the other night would it?"

Lenc's eyes took in both men.

"Do you have a concern about this?" asked Aurelius softly, leaning forward.

"Not really, just some flotsam hanging round the harbour, neither here nor there. But it would be unfortunate if your man was found." The captain sat back with a condescending smirk on his face.

"If you are fishing for more gold forget it," said Aurelius curtly, his voice full of iron. "You are being well recompensed and the alternative could be crucifixion on the harbour wall as a lesson to all who might think that Rome is an easy touch."

The captain smiled easily. "Not at all," he said smoothly, "just pointing out some obvious facts. I'm sure we shall set sail without any hitches."

Aurelius visibly collected himself and smiled suddenly. "Now that we all know where we stand, and thanks to our senator we can talk some more then relax."

Lenc had been aware of the pungent perfume of the girl behind him studiously making herself as inconspicuous as possible. By the atmosphere in the room she guessed that the serious business was over and leaned forward to fill Lenc's beaker. As she did so, her dress fell open, exposing a perfectly formed small breast. She saw him looking and smiled, raising her eyebrows. He smiled back, shrugged and looked down ruefully at his badly used body. She smiled again and offered him the wine chalice.

This was quite a girl, he thought, maybe if I was very careful and she was very slow we could just about manage to….."Lenc, can you hear me?" He was once again dragged back to the present by the gentle enquiry from Aurelius. All three men were smiling at his confusion.

"You have my attention," he assured them gravely.

"Good," said Aurelius. "What I was saying to you while you were obviously otherwise engaged was there was no real need to detain you, and if you wished to try the healing properties of the warm baths with your new friend, we will come to an agreement on the finer points in your ah, absence."

Lenc smiled, perhaps there were some compensations in a good kicking. He inclined his head in acceptance.

Tonia helped him to his feet and adjusted his tunic. He half-bowed and allowed himself to be led back into the corridor, where they met another slave girl in an equally diaphanous full-length chiton, a toga-like dress, who smiled as they approached.

"This is Sabina, my friend," said Tonia, as they steered him into a small room with a sunken bath in the centre. Steam from the hot water rose in tendrils, he could smell rosewater perfume from the bath and sniffed appreciatively.

"He's gorgeous!" he heard Tonia whisper. The lovely slaves both hid their heads in their hands and giggled. He was about to ask what had been said when Tonia untied the crimson sash belting his waist, then they both carefully started to pull his tunic up and over his shoulders. For once the pain took second place to other feelings.

He stood in his thonged boots and stringed undergarment and as one, both girls kneeled and untied the straps of his heavy boots. The mosaic tiles of the floor were warm beneath his toes.

Tonia stood and critically examined his bandages. She carefully untied the knot holding the chest bandage and slowly unravelled it from his body. It had been tight and was a relief to have the restriction removed. He knew that could be a mistake as it was there to keep his damaged ribs in place.

Then she turned to the stained bandage on his arm. She was even more gentle with this and where the blood had crusted into the bandage she took a small knife and carefully cut it away. Her eyes widened when she saw the savage wound with its crude stitching still seeping a tiny amount of blood.

She turned to a table and took a pot of some type of grease, though there were herbs in there as well. Tenderly she smeared the grease over the wound, not flinching as she went over the black stitches. It was wonderfully cool and somehow calming.

He opened his eyes as she stepped back then both girls did something to the clasp at the shoulder of their chitons. Almost in unison the silken garments fell away to the floor with a gentle rustle to reveal the girls in their beautiful nakedness. He was transfixed by their soft round rumps as they gingerly stepped into the hot bath, and with a giggle stood, water past their knees and beckoned him in.

With one hand, he undid the drawstring of his last remaining garment and could sense his arousal as it slipped down. One of the girls giggled and hid her face in her hands when it caught, trapped on his manhood. He couldn't help but smile. Some things don't change, he thought.

With an impatient tug, he let loose the garment, allowing his member to spring proudly to attention. We'll see if that hot water has any effect on you, he thought. He put a toe in the water. It was very hot. Wonderful.

Carefully he flexed one knee and lowered his foot into the water. The girls watched anxiously. He allowed a long held breath to escape, as the steam curled round his body which already felt better. Carefully he slowly lowered himself into the water, grimacing as the scented infusion stung open cuts.

Finally, he caught his breath as he sank luxuriantly into the hot bath, a naked beauty either side of him. He sighed as he put his head back onto a padded ledge and closed his eyes. He could feel his aches and pains reacting to the heat. After the initial stinging, it felt wonderful.

Sabina looked at him from under her long eyelashes, "Is there any other service we can offer you master?"

"Ladies, you can give me any service you like as long as you don't hurt me." He thought a second, "actually let's live dangerously," he said and stretched out in the bath.

They were careful and considerate but still managed to give Lenc a few twinges as his body responded to their smiling ministrations. Eventually he sighed and leaned back, fully spent. Tonia looked at him and whispered: "Let us give you one last wash-down and then I think it is time for you to go."

"I don't think I can move," said Lenc regretfully. "I certainly don't want to."

The two girls silently soaped him down once again, rinsed him off, like an overgrown puppy and then slowly towelled him down with a wool blanket.

He stood with his arms raised as Tonia carefully wound a fresh bandage round his chest. She frowned at the arm wound.

"I'll put a light bandage on that, although it's already looking better since I put the ointment on it," she said.

She lightly smeared more grease onto the wound and bound it with a strip of linen. They both helped him with his tunic and boots. Finally, he stood in front of them as they pulled their chitons back on and fastened them at the shoulder.

"Ladies, that was wonderful," he said and bowed. "If I can return one day I most certainly will."

They smiled coquettishly and giggled. "That would be lovely, master, and we will certainly look forward to it," said Tonia, "Next time though your body will be better and we can be more adventurous."

Tonia delivered Lenc back to the others but before opening the door, stood on tiptoe to kiss him lightly on the cheek. She smiled shyly and whispered, "Stay safe and come back soon."

"Time to go," said Aurelius. Anton had one last rueful look at the empty plates, the two civilians pulled their cloaks on and went ahead as the two soldiers went to find their armour.

"We'll see you in the morning, then," said Lantumaros. Aurelius paused in his dressing and clasped the swarthy man's arm. "See you then and thanks," he said.

The captain nodded brusquely and turned for the street. Anton looked at the two soldiers and nodded also. "Tomorrow then," he said gruffly.

When they had finally kitted up, Lenc and Aurelius followed the others out into the courtyard. Standing over a brazier with the door guards was the patrol Decanus, who snapped to attention when he saw them approaching.

"I'll call the lads up sir, you'll hear us coming." Aurelius nodded and the Decanus slipped out into the quiet street.

The two took the soldier's place at the brazier, until minutes later they heard the muffled scrape of nailed boots outside. Lenc adjusted his helmet and nodded at the gate guard who opened the door just enough to let them slide through. The patrol was outside and split to let them in, then with hardly a pause, they were off up the dark silent street.

Once back at the fort, Lenc flopped onto his cot with a contented sigh. His mind was full of the memory of his evening and for once he fell off to sleep with a big smile on his face. It seemed like no time at all till he was roused from a deep slumber by the guard instructed to give them a call before sun-up.

Drowsily Lenc swung his legs onto the floor and carefully felt his ribs. They seemed a bit better. Maybe they weren't broken after all. His whole body, in fact, felt a bit better. But by Toutatis's balls he was tired. A nice restful sea voyage will be just the thing, he thought ruefully.

He went to the jug of water on the side table and splashed some on his face. Then shrugging himself into his rank-smelling peasant's clothes, he nudged Aurelius who was still slumbering peacefully.

"Come on boss, time to go," he said softly.

Aurelius grumbled, then came awake sharply. He jumped up, pulling his tunic on.

After a visit to the latrines, the two soldiers slipped out of the fort, quietly followed by four bulky legionaries also muffled in heavy cloaks. Darkness cloaked their movements and a soft persistent rain deterred any casual interest from passers-by.

The docks were already busy. Lenc kept his head down and was content to stay in his officer's shadow as they walked briskly along the dockside. When they found the right ship, a nondescript, down at heel cargo vessel, they went straight on board without pausing.

Two sailors, busy doing whatever sailors do, took no notice as the two cloaked strangers slipped past them, stepping over ropes and boxes, until they found some shelter. Aurelius looked round, taking in the dilapidated state of the ship, and grimaced, then tried to smile. "Well this is it," he said. Lenc smiled ruefully.

"Whatever happens, I've got last night to remember."

They clasped right arms. "Sorry to have been such a nuisance, boss, and please pass my thanks to Senator Maximus."

"Just behave yourself in future," allowed Aurelius with a small smile. Then he turned, and hitching up his sodden cloak hurried back down the gangplank and quickly disappeared into the murk.

CHAPTER X

The small ship made its ponderous way across the Channel and just as the skipper started to think they were home and dry, an Atlantic storm fell on her in a shrieking fury. He barely had time to order the sails down and steer into the wind before the worst that the vengeful sea could throw was on them.

The skipper had known it was a gamble leaving Gesoscribate to sail to Cambria, but the tantalising promise of gold overrode his fears. When they left the safety of harbour, the Atlantic storms were abating and he felt fairly confident they could make a quick and profitable journey there and back. That vanished when, as if to herald the dawn, the seas whipped up again, and the coming daylight obliterated.

Lenc had never encountered sea-sickness like it. He accepted he was no sailor, why should he be, he was a soldier of Rome, but had never felt so helpless, so world-spinningly weak and feeble. He spewed, then spewed again, and spewed some more, until, finally the pain of involuntary dry retching from a drained and strained stomach made him pray for death.

He was lying in his own mess, lashed to a bulwark to keep from pitching into the angry sea. The only relief from the stench of vomit was a freezing wave crashing over the side, drenching him in salt water. All he could do was gasp and shake his head like a dog. Soon he couldn't even be bothered with that. The ship was pitching so badly that he could actually look out on the swirling sea as the prow swooped down curling waves, crash into the valley then heave skywards for the next gargantuan pitch.

He rolled over and dry-heaved again as the icy Atlantic wind whipped the ocean swell into huge waves tossing the small boat in a series of wild bucking gyrations.

The captain recognised the mortal danger they were in as the storm intensified, and turned his wallowing vessel so that it could run in front of the wind. Where they would end up only Neptune knew, but it was their only chance of survival. All that day the small boat was pushed off course out into the inhospitable ocean as the sailors hung on, concentrating only on keeping the shrieking wind at their backs.

She was old, a grain ship that had seen better days. By rights the seas, should have smashed her to pieces, but somehow she survived, a testament to her makers.

The only superstructure was at the stern of the vessel forming a rudimentary bridge, with the tiller, usually manned by two sailors the main method of steering the ship. Underneath the bridge was a shelter which housed Anton's stock, securely lashed down.

The sail had been furled at the first inkling that the unusually high winds were building up to a gale. Throughout the long dark night, three sailors wrestled with the tiller, trying to keep the ship's head into the wind. Then when torrential rain battered into the insignificant vessel carried on a screaming wind, a particularly vicious wave corkscrewed wildly, the tiller was ripped from the sailor's hands, splintered and split close to the raging sea.

Without steerage the poor vessel twisted and turned, creaking and groaning at the whim of the weather. The angry green swell was relentless as she wallowed in the grip of the rollercoaster waves, powering her up mountainous peaks, cresting and rolling down the other side.

Mercifully, as the dawn cast a shadowy light the storm started to blow itself out. The frantic motion of the boat eased and Lenc rolled into a sitting position with his damp, matted hair pressed against the wooden side of the ship. He groaned and licked his tongue over dry and flaking lips. The taste of vomit was in his mouth and nose. He retched. He felt disgusting. As dawn broke, there was no sun, just a weak damp light, making it difficult to see where the slate grey sea ended and the sky started.

He untied himself from his self-imposed prison and looked out onto the scene of devastation on the deck. Even he, a not very experienced sailor, could see the storm damage was significant and would take some repairing.

It was cold and damp in the early morning air and Lenc shivered in his soaking woollen tunic, least I'm alive, he thought.

He was wearing a nondescript grey woollen shift which covered his rangy body to the knees. It was belted at the waist and he wore his army-issue footwear, open-toed boots with strips of leather encircling his legs. They may look like sandals but were tough and thick but also supple and comfortable, with iron nails studded into the soles. They were much mended, veterans of many marching campaigns, and good for many more years to come.

He plucked disapprovingly at his tunic, slimed in his own vomit and decidedly unsavoury. Glancing up he saw the sailors watching him with some amusement.

"Do you have a bucket?" he asked them, "I need to clean myself down."

"You need to clean the deck and your mate too," sneered one of the sailors. He handed Lenc a wooden bucket with a long rope attached to the handle.

"Be careful how you do this or the sea will snatch it from your hands. Here, let me show you."

The sailor, taking care to stay upwind of the malodorous soldier, uncoiled the rope on the bucket as he walked up the deck to the prow. Lenc followed him, marvelling at the way he instinctively anticipated the steady roll and pitch of the boat. The sailor hefted the bucket then threw it forward into the sea. Just before it came abreast of him, he quickly hauled it in, full to the brim with cold sea water.

"Easy when you know how," he grinned.

He seized the bucket and emptied the contents over his head, gasping as the freezing salt water cascaded down his body. Composing himself, he threw the bucket over the side, the way the sailor had showed him. It was heavy, and seemed reluctant to leave the sea when full. With a final pull that seared his balled fist, he finally broke the ocean's grip on the bucket and hauled it inboard. Once again he upended it over his head. His body tingled icily, but he continued with his dowsing several more times until he had cleared the stench from himself.

His hair was cropped short in the way of the Legion and about the same length as the five day stubble on his face, a clue that he was not on official legion business.

Ignoring the biting dawn wind that coiled his body, he grimaced and dropped his woolen shift in the bucket, pummelling and rinsing it thoroughly. The drying salt water prickled on his skin, but at least the activity was warming. He lifted the soaking garment from the bucket, wrung it onto the deck and draped it over a water barrel. It was sodden enough that the wind would not take it. If it started to rain again, he would try and find somewhere dry, a forlorn hope, he thought wryly.

Vomit free once again, and with a rapidly calming, if empty, stomach, he started to take an interest in his surroundings. His fellow passenger was still lying in his own puke under the hides, a bare foot stuck out at an angle. Lenc decided to let his comatose employer alone for the time being.

The sailors had managed to erect a temporary mast and were raising a sail, a heavy cumbersome thing of leather, with jerks on top ropes running to the top of the short mast. Another sailor was re-arranging the stones in the shelter of the bridge, on which would stand the fire to make hot food. If there was any dry fuel left on the boat, thought Lenc.

On the bridge, the skipper, Lantumaros Morinos, stared

fixedly at the horizon. Lenc climbed the short ladder to join him in the face of the fresh wind, the wind was still high, and with the pitching and tossing of the ship, the noise of the sea rushing and gurgling beneath them was deafening.

"Do you know where we are, Captain?" Lenc shouted.

The captain, a heavy bearded man with streaks of grey in his curly black hair shrugged. He squinted into the gale, calculating.

"We left Gesoscribate and were almost in sight of Britannia when the storm struck. We had to run before it, out into the ocean so the gods only know where we are now.

"We sailed before the wind for a day and a night roughly westwards towards Africa. When night comes and if the sky is clear, I can get a fix from the North Star, but until then if we steer west we will definitely hit Africa. Not too much of a problem but it will add a few days to the journey."

Lantumaros looked thoughtful and sucked his cheeks in. "On the other hand, if I am wrong and we are going down the way, parallel to Africa, we may not stop till we tip over the edge."

Lenc looked at him sharply. The skipper was clearly not joking, too many seamen and perfectly seaworthy ships just disappeared so tipping off the edge of the world seemed a distinct possibility.

Lenc clambered down to the deck, where Anton, son of Heracles, the fat Gaul, peeked a bleary eye out from under the hides. He was bald with long hair at the sides of his head which hung lank and vomit stained to his shoulders. He had a look of utter incomprehension on his puffy and blotched face as his fingers twitched nervously at the hide, like a small animal afraid to leave its burrow.

"Come on large one, time to rise and shine and make yourself presentable," shouted Lenc amiably, "besides if you're very lucky there might be some hot food soon."

At this there was an instant transformation in the portly trader. After an unimaginable day and night, puking and wailing, hanging on for dear life, then after hours, not caring whether he lived or died, he suddenly realised he was still alive, if a little frayed round the edges, and wonder of wonders, the sea seemed to be calming down.

He began to realise that not only was his stomach empty, but every bit of nutrition from the nails on his fat feet up had been evacuated until he could only dry heave, contracting his stomach muscles under the voluminous layers of fat, in agony. Some food would definitely be very acceptable.

As his wits returned, he suddenly had another horrific thought. His eyes widened in alarm and his fingers twitched involuntarily. "By Zeus, my stock, my stock."

With a rumbling effort, Anton pushed aside the stinking hide, revealing his rough blanket shift, stained and rucked from the night's adventures. He pulled it down over his chubby thighs to his knees, he was barefoot and shivering uncontrollably.

Lenc grinned as Anton stumbled under the bridge to a canvas-swathed pile about a man's height. This was Anton's whole life. Securely tied down and protected from the elements by canvas soaked in animal oils were his trade goods which he hoped to sell and barter in Britannia. He had collected pottery from Gallica Belgica, bright copperware from Hispania, carpets, bolts of cloth, knives, salt, oil and wine, all luxury goods which he hoped the Britons could only dream of – and of course pay for.

The pile still seemed well protected. Somewhat reassured Anton stood and looked round sniffing the air. An appetizing aroma from the galley cook's cauldron was whipped away by the salty wind but Anton could sniff out food anywhere. And right now, seasickness forgotten, Anton was hungry. Tentatively he picked his way back towards the galley fire, in the lee of the stern shelter. The cook squatted in front of the fire, stirring a blackened pot. He threw a glance at Anton then turned back to his stirring. The heat from the fire was a welcome change from the cold wet wind coming off the sullen sea.

Anton's mouth was watering as he hunkered down next to the

cook, a wildly bearded Vasconian with small sea-shells plaited into his long hair and beard. As a general principle, Anton's sales technique was to be friendly to everyone. It didn't cost anything and you never knew when a friendly word could result in a profitable sale, or in this case a fuller bowl.

He shuffled forward expectantly. "Mmm, that smells good," he sniffed appreciatively, "what is it?"

The cook glanced sideways at him. "Mutton and veg," he eventually replied, "but it's for the crew, they've been up all night trying to keep this tub afloat, while you were fast asleep in the dry."

"I was nothing of the sort," snorted Anton defensively. "I didn't sleep a wink during that infernal storm, and would have loved to help sail the boat but was laid low with seasickness. Not my fault."

The cook turned back to his stirring, "seasick or not, you'll have to wait until the workers have been fed, if there's anything left, you can have some then."

Anton sat back. This wasn't going the right way at all. Time for diplomacy. And that mutton did smell good.

"All right, I take the point," he conceded. "How about if I helped you feed the men would that make amends?" He smiled winningly at the cook.

"How do you mean?" asked the suspicious stirrer.

"Well when you're ready to dish up, I can take the food to the crew, they can't leave their posts now can they?"

The cook thought about this for a moment. "How do I know you won't steal their food?"

Anton looked shocked. "Do I look the sort of man who would steal another man's food?"

"Frankly yes," came the reply.

"Well, I've been accused of some things in my time, but to think I could descend to stealing another man's food is quite beyond reason. I am disappointed in you. Very disappointed."

The fat man leaned back on his heels and slowly shook his head from side to side.

"Very disappointed," he repeated in a chiding voice. "Very....."

"All right, I didn't mean it," interrupted the cook churlishly.

"Tell you what, I'll feed you first, if you take the crew's meals to them. That way you'll be less likely to pinch any, how about that?"

Anton beamed and nodded enthusiastically. He was so hungry and the stew smelled so good he would have agreed to almost anything at that moment.

The cook nodded towards a cupboard lashed to the wall of the shelter.

"You'll find bread in there, one loaf is enough for four men. You can start cutting them up."

Anton could hardly wait to get started. Seizing a large vicious looking knife he sawed the round hard loaves into four, although he couldn't resist stuffing a lump into his own mouth. He moaned in ecstacy as he savoured the dry bread. The crust was hard and crackly. But it was food. The cook grunted, "don't go mad on that bread it has to last a long time. It's all we have."

Anton looked round for something to drink. "My mouth is like a cat's sandpit," he grumbled.

"That barrel there," said the cook, nodding his head towards a wooden barrel lashed to the wall of the shelter.

"What is it?" said Anton suspiciously. "Not water is it?"

"No it's not water, " said the cook peevishly, "it's cider. I'm sure you would rather have some nice Roman red wine, but that's all there is."

"Oh this will do just fine," assured Anton eagerly, "just fine."

He looked round and found a horn beaker which he quickly placed under the wooden tap and twisted it open. He glugged the cider appreciatively, swilling it round his mouth, killing the taste of vomit. The cook ladled the steaming mutton stew into a bowl and handed it over to an eagerly awaiting Anton. He sat in a corner with his cider, bowl, spoon and bread and all of a sudden was as near contentment as he could be. All thought of sea-sickness forgotten and the smell of the stew was more than sufficient for him to ignore the sour odour coming from his body and woollen clothes. Keeping everything from spilling as the ship plunged and rolled was a matter of some dedication, and even although he did not really need it, was further reason to wolf the hot food down.

When he had finished he tenderly rolled his finger round the inside of the bowl and then sucked it noisily, determined that not one morsel would be wasted. He then sat back with his eyes closed for a second.

"Right," said the cook, "you can start making yourself useful by taking the food round. And don't spill it."

He forced himself up, catching the rail on the deck as the ship heaved. He put the wedges of bread in a bag he found and took the pitcher which the cook had filled with stew.

"That's for two men," growled the cook, "empty it into their bowls and then come back for more. Captain first, then the mate, then whoever you can find. They'll see you and won't be left out."

Anton tottered out of the shelter of the galley and climbed the steps up onto the roof where the captain leaned on a rail. The wind was fresher up on the high deck above the small cabin area. Anton sniffed the air like a small dog. Now fed, he was able to look round and appreciate his surroundings. The ship was still pitching and tossing, but in the light of day was far less threatening. Still he had to hang on to the railing for support as he staggered carefully over to the captain.

Captain Lantumaros watched impassively as the fat passenger staggered over to him across the pitching deck. He had been supervising the rigging of a new tiller to replace the one carried away during the storm.

The captain was a Vasconian or Basque, short of stature, with the black curly hair and prominent nose which marked him as a son of Breton. His skin was the colour and texture of leather after a lifetime of salt, spray, sun and wind. Like the rest of the crew, he was sparsely dressed in a tunic shift, belted at the waist, which ended half-way down his thighs. In the belt was a long dagger. He was barefoot.

"Glad to see you're making yourself useful," The captain said eventually, taking the bowl from Anton and watching as the cook's assistant carefully filled it from his pitcher. From his bag Anton took a wedge of the bread which the captain speared with his knife, Anton flinched at the sight of the razor sharp blade. Lantumaros reached into a pocket of his tunic for a wooden spoon which he used to attack the warming food.

The sailors working on the tiller looked up with interest when they saw the food. Anton offered the stew to them, "take this and I'll go back for more," he said. "But I can only carry two at a time."

The captain motioned to the men with his spoon, "half of you go down to the galley, get fed and then bring back food for the others. If we wait for our friend to give waitress service we'll be here all day.

"And you, when you go back down, ask your friend to join me up here."

Anton scurried back down the ladder, he could just fancy seconds so it was important to cement his new-found friendship with the cook.

"Captain wants a word," said Anton brusquely to Lenc, as he went about his self-imposed mission.

Lenc pulled on his soggy tunic and shuddered as the wet fabric slithered down his body, and made for the ladder. The sea seemed calmer and a watery sun filtered through the clouds.

The captain looked at Lenc thoughtfully as he crossed the decking. He put down the empty food bowl before stowing his spoon away in his pocket, and looked out to the horizon.

"I have five seamen who will do as they are told, but not much else, and you and your fat friend as passengers," he said, finally turning to face Lenc.

"No-one foresaw that storm otherwise we would never have left harbour, Roman gold or no. I was expecting a quick passage which is why we carry the minimum of food and water. I don't know where we are, but I think I know the general direction we want to go in. Until I see the North Star, I can't confirm that.

"In the meantime I don't know how long we'll have to make our supplies last so we must conserve and ration until we sight land."

Lenc shrugged, "of course captain, is there anything else we can do to help?"

"There is plenty to do but whether your fat friend will feel the same way remains to be seen, although he does seem to be blending in."

Lenc smiled, "If there's food about, that's where you'll find him. He won't take kindly to rationing, but I am sure I can explain the necessity to him."

The captain chuckled. "Good man, we shipped quite a lot of water last night which we need to be rid of. The only way is by bucket and it's not a very pleasant task, but while you and your friend look after that, the sailors can get on with the necessary repairs."

All that day, Anton and Lenc toiled in the bowels of the ship, scooping up the stinking water in the bilge to throw over the side. Anton was annoyed, constantly muttering under his breath about being a paying passenger and shouldn't have to do manual work.

The ship, crafted from oak from the dense forests of the Basque region was tough and solidly built. She had a wide beam, designed to carry cargo and a planked deck. Beneath the deck, tons of sea water had thundered into her, laying her lower in the water and therefore less manoeuvrable. Towards the end of the storm she wallowed like a saturated sponge.

A hatch in the stern allowed access to the reeking bilge, now virtually full of water. At first Lenc could kneel on the deck and fill the bucket, then as the level dropped he had to climb into the freezing water and pass it up to the grumbling Anton.

"I didn't pay for this, I'm not a slave, I shouldn't have to do this," repeated the fat man in a monosyllabic whisper.

Eventually Lenc snapped; "By all the gods, will you just shut up and get on with it. You didn't pay for your passage, you were actually paid to come, and if you don't stop moaning, I shall make sure you never make a profit again."

Anton recoiled at the angry words, his jowls wobbling at the onslaught. He looked as if he was going to cry. Instead he picked up the bucket slopping with grey sea-water and emptied it over the side with an affronted air of dignity sullied.

Lenc grinned. He had developed an affection for the fat fart since the gods had brought them together in far off Gesoscribate. He thought about the whirlwind course of events which had engulfed him and wondered uneasily how it would all end. His cover was thin to say the least, would it stand up to the scrutiny of suspicious tribesmen and could he rely on Anton not to give the game away? With these depressing thoughts swirling round his tired brain he leaned down once again and filled his bucket with the stinking cold bilge water.

CHAPTER XI

At last the skipper allowed himself a grunt of satisfaction as the mist cleared enough to expose their first sighting of Britannia.

After the battle with the elements out in the middle of the ocean Lantumaros relied on his fix on the North Star to guide them to their destination. In reality he knew that if they steered eastwards they would come on land eventually, but just where and what country was in Neptune's hands. So he was more than gratified to finally sight the familiar southernmost tip of Britannia.

Never had the sight of waves crashing against that hostile headland looked more welcoming. When he was sure they had made the right landfall, the little ship clawed its way slowly round the headland, hugging the coast, north-eastwards, until the skipper, still acting on instinct, turned north across the dangerous tides of the Channel of Sabrina.

Lenc stood in the prow of the ship, coiling a rope when, as if by magic, the mist swirled and cleared and once again the land came into view. The captain wasn't sure just where they were, but it was definitely Cambria. Since then they had witnessed a dramatically changing coastline, towering cliffs gradually changing to a gentler lower line.

"We're getting close to our destination at last," said the captain with some relief. "We'll continue running along the coast, eastwards, and in a day or so will arrive at the mouth of the Sabrina, a great estuary. There is a small settlement there on the bank of another river the Wysg. The people that live there have enough problems of their own to worry too much about you. But that's where your troubles really start," he said.

Lenc shrugged, "As long as there are no Roman military there, it will do me fine."

A light wind shivered the sail more in hope than expectation as they drifted on the tide, which seemed to be taking them in the right direction. As the wind lifted, the mist finally dissolved, although the cold rain, fine as it was, seemed like a mist itself.

"Well, we're about at journey's end for you," the captain said. "You can tell we're close by the smell." Lenc leaned over the side of the ship, eager for a sight of his destination. The land, still some lengths away looked flat and even at this distance, smelled of swamp. He could see miles of reed bed which must be underwater at high tide. Tantalisingly the mist dropped again, cloaking the ship in its own white world.

Unnoticed, Anton joined him at the ship's side. "This is a god-forsaken shithole," he muttered querulously. "Let's hope we find some people with coin, or it'll be a disaster. Surely no-one can live in a place like this. You'd have to have fins or webbed feet to exist. This thrice-damned rain doesn't help, and it's so cold, you can feel it right through to your bones." Finally, the fat trader paused for breath.

"I can tell you're going to like it here," said Lenc with a chuckle.

"I would rather be further up the coast, where at least you know there's less likelihood someone will stick a knife in you, where they have decent food on the table and things to trade. Who knows what this lot get up to? Probably all running round in blue paint, fucking anything with a pulse that will stand still long enough."

Lenc turned and looked at Anton. "Do you know," he said thoughtfully, "I don't think I've heard you say a decent word about anything since I met you."

"Well it's hardly surprising," Anton said with outraged passion. "I get dragged to this shithouse where I'm supposed to trade with savages and smile as they cut my balls off, and for what? I am beginning to think that the pittance I've been paid to come on this absurd adventure is nothing like enough for the danger and hardship I have endured which, let me tell you, I suspect is nothing to what's in store in that dump over there."

Anton was quivering with outrage and sorrow for himself. Lenc moved closer and put an arm round his companion's shoulders, leaning in and in a conciliatory tone quietly read Anton his fortune.

"Now look here old mate," he soothed. "You're being paid well for doing what you do best, which is trading. I have been loaned to you to help and guard you, and you are going where traders rarely go. That has got to mean rich rewards for those men bold enough to want it. And with me at your side, why we're invincible.

"Of course, I don't have to remind you that if you fuck up for one reason or another, there can only be one outcome, can there not? The barbarians may be pretty unpleasant, but they are nothing to what Rome will do to you if you fail your contract."

Anton looked sideways at him. "Do you think it will work, we'll get through this madness?" he said in a small voice.

"Of course we will," said Lenc, squeezing Anton's chubby shoulder.

"You've got me with you, what can possibly go wrong?"

Anton sniffed and looked at the deck. "That's what I'm afraid of," he muttered eventually.

"Now you're being irrational. We are going to sail through this, I shall carry out my task and rejoin my legion covered in glory, and you will return to Gaul with so much profit you won't have to worry where the next meat pie or flagon of good red wine is coming from for many a long year."

Somewhat mollified, Anton visibly cheered up. He sniffed and wiped his nose along a damp sleeve. "It's still a shithouse," he grumbled.

By now, the bleak landscape was cut by low buildings high

above mud flats stretching into the sea, crude wooden affairs with reed-thatched roofs, balanced on stilts in the mud. "It must be a hell of a tide-fall," mused Lenc.

The skipper leaned against the rail and studied the settlement.

"I don't know what this dump is called, but you can get off here without any fuss, they are poor people, and fear everyone," the captain said dismissively. "Why else would they live here, between land and water other than for safety? Long before the Romans came, they were persecuted, tribe-less, friend-less and prey for every marauding band of raiders. They settled here because they could scratch a living, but mainly because no-one else would risk the swamps to attack them."

He turned to Anton, "The tide is going in, so I suggest we get moving. You will have about three hours before high tide when we can berth next to the jetty. That should give you time to find a place to put your goods. Then you will have to find transport."

As the skipper turned away Anton started grumbling again under his breath. "Damn fool errand this is, should never have taken it on. Probably end up food for the fish, probably get tupped by every hairy arsed pagan in Britannia."

"Come on Anton, you have work to do," said Lenc cheerfully, as he slapped the portly trader on the back. "It's time for you to earn your coin, you don't want these pagans to get the better of you now do you?"

Still muttering, the trader pulled his damp cloak about his legs and stomped off in search of something warm and liquid.

Lenc turned back to study the small settlement. He could see that the spot within a wide estuary would be quite sheltered from sea storms, but even so it looked very poor. There was an air of damp, neglect and indifference, and few of the people in sight at the settlement seemed to show any interest in the foreign vessel approaching, which was strange, thought Lenc. It could hardly be a regular event.

There was a smell off the settlement, not the clean tang of the sea, but the rotting putrefaction of a swamp. This was a primeval place and he shuddered at the thought of the desperation of the people who endured this existence between land and water for sanctuary.

As they stood off, waiting for the tide to rise high enough for the ship to tie up, the crew busied themselves, swinging a rowing boat out into the estuary. Two sailors stepped in as it hit the water and freed the oars, one gestured to Lenc to join them.

"Where's your mate," he asked. Lenc shrugged, "knowing him, he's probably stealing your breakfast."

"Well it's up to him, he can fart about all day for all I care, but if he doesn't get a move on, we'll dump all his crap on the quayside and leave you to it."

Whether Anton was listening or not, he suddenly appeared, wiping his mouth with the back of his hand. He exuded importance.

"Right men, come along, we haven't got time to waste, let's get going," he announced.

With some difficulty he struggled over the rail and balancing precariously, managed to get a sandal-hold on the dinghy. Lenc exchanged a grin with the two sailors before Anton, huffing and puffing, managed to find a seat on the now dangerously rocking boat. He carried a leather satchel underneath his cloak, which he made sure was safe on his lap and out of sight before settling.

When Anton was finally still, Lenc sat behind him, facing the prow. For the first time on the voyage he had strapped his legion-issue gladius to his waist. This was time for a show of strength, only it was a small bit of a show, he had to concede.

The journey from the ship to the shore was less than a javelin throw and easily pulled by the two sailors. As they got closer, Lenc saw three men and a woman, dressed in rags, sitting on an open verandah, darning nets, but apart from glancing up to look at the small boat, they showed no interest.

"There's a ladder to that landing place, just to the left," Lenc said quietly to the sailors. One glanced over his shoulder and with a grunt indicated he had seen it. They changed direction slightly and rowed towards the ladder, eventually hitting the piled timber with a soft thud.

One of the sailors reached out to grab the ladder and swing the boat in, while Lenc stood and reached out for the cold and slimy wooden rungs. Carefully he put a foot out and pulled himself up, one step and his head was above the level of the decking. He looked round quickly but could see no immediate threat, the villagers working on their nets seemed engrossed in their work. He pulled himself up and stepped cautiously onto the jetty.

Behind him, Lenc was aware of a grunting and straining as Anton hauled himself up the ladder. His satchel kept slipping round to the front and fouling on the rungs, so he had to precariously push it back with one hand while hanging on with the other before resuming his short journey.

Lenc grinned and leaned down to pull his companion onto dry-ish land.

"I can do it, I can do it," grumbled Anton as he unceremoniously scrabbled onto the jetty on all fours. He stood up, and once again adjusted the satchel. He gestured imperiously at the fishermen. "You there," he said in Gaulish, "I need some help with some goods I am bringing ashore."

They ignored him, concentrating on their nets.

"Now look here," started Anton in a strong tone which bubbled away to a squeak as three men stepped from behind a low building. Two carried clubs and the third a rusty sword, and they all wore knives at their waists. Their clothes were rags, no better than the fishermen's, but they looked fit and capable of handling their weapons. Lenc took a step to one side so he could swing his sword free if necessary.

Finally, the self-appointed leader of the trio spoke, "No, stranger, you look here, we don't take kindly to visitors, and would feel a lot happier if you just turned round and got back on your ship and buggered off."

At this less than friendly reception Anton smiled. At least he could understand the man.

"I'm sorry," said Anton in a wheedling tone. "We seem to have got off on the wrong foot, and for that I apologise. We have come a long way to your village and I can promise we will stay as short a time as possible. It is our intention to take trade goods further inland, so all we want to do is store them here until I can buy a cart and a horse. You will of course be paid for this service."

"So there are just the two of you coming ashore," the villager asked suspiciously. "Of course," reassured Anton. "The skipper will want to be on his way as soon as he can. So will we."

The man grunted, "we will let the elders decide."

The villager stepped aside for Anton to walk past, which he did eagerly. Lenc hung back, still not sure he wanted these men behind him. The lead man noticed and gestured. "Come we will walk together. We do not seek to harm you."

Lenc hesitated then shrugged. If they turned on him there wasn't much he could do about it except go down fighting. He smiled acceptance.

The village seemed to be built on a wooden pier, with driftwood the building material of choice, lashed together to make a lattice-work filled in with mud and wattle. Away from the open sea, the buildings crowded in on each other with a walkway less than four paces wide. The rush thatch of the roofs was so low they had to duck their heads to avoid brushing it, and the few windows and doors just holes in the wall with a rough wool blanket draped across for privacy and warmth. In the centre of the village stood a larger building. Not more imposing, but it was bigger, and its neighbours gave it some breathing room. Once again the thatch came right down to head height, but he could see that it rose to a peak maybe twice that. There were no windows, just a hole for a door, with a ragged blanket drawn back. He hoped it would stay open, the building needed all the air it could get.

He was gestured forward by one of the ragged fishermen, and taking a deep breath, ducked and entered through the small doorway. Inside he almost gagged as he took his first breath. The place smelled of dead fish and rotting bodies. He looked round and through the gloom could see men, squatting on the wooden floor, who stared impassively at him. The fishermen gestured to Lenc and indicated that he should sit with them. He shook his head and pointed to Anton, who had a pained expression on his face and a hand over his nose.

"Come on Anton," he said, "selling time. This is what you're good at."

With those encouraging words, Lenc almost grinned but that would have meant opening his mouth even wider than he had to, so settled for a furtive smirk.

Anton, realising he was now centre stage, pulled his shoulders back, and with an imperious gesture, swept his cloak off, and arranging it on the ground, primly sat down on it, cradling his leather satchel on his lap. "I bring you greetings from Gaul," he started. "We are not here to hurt you or spy on you. On the contrary we wish to trade further inland, and if you have a secure place available for storage it could be mutually beneficial for us to deal together. You seem very secure here."

"What exactly do you want?" came a voice from the middle of the group.

Lenc looked towards the sound. God's blood but this man was old. His skin was wrinkled and he was hunched into his body. He kept a blanket tightly wrapped round him as if freezing. His face was filthy, and his hair, matted and stringy, hung down past his shoulders. When he spoke, he revealed rotting stumps where teeth should have been, but by the way the others deferred to him, he was clearly an elder, presumably possessed of much wisdom. On the other hand, maybe his achievement was simply to attain great years, so everyone thought he was a clever bastard.

Anton was speaking. "We need a place to store our goods, here in your village, and I will need a guide through the swamp to somewhere I can buy a cart and a decent horse."

"What's to stop us knocking you on the head, using you as fish bait, and taking all your stuff?" asked the old man craftily.

"Well that ship out there for a start," replied Anton. "I have a share in it and the men on it have a share in my endeavour. If we don't come back, the first thing they will do is flatten this charming village of yours."

The old man grunted, and conferred quickly with the filthy creatures on either side. He was not to know that once the ship disappeared over the horizon, it would have no further interest in their enterprise.

"What's in it for us if we give you our generous help?"

"Oh, I am sure we can come to some sort of amicable arrangement," said Anton in his best trading voice. He fished in the satchel, and with a flourish, pulled out a bone-handled dagger. "Have you ever seen a better knife than this?" he demanded. "And what about these?" From a pouch he pulled fishing hooks, carefully placing them on the decking in front of him. "These are the best hand-forged barbs in all of Gaul. Just imagine how many more fish you will catch with these. And I have more.

"Now, something for the ladies. Wouldn't she feel special wearing this?" He flourished a cheap, brightly painted necklace with a polished stone as a pendant. He threw it to the old man. "Here you are, make your wife or girlfriend very happy."

The old man snatched it from the air and examined it greedily before tucking it away in his filthy blanket.

"We can be friends, and I see the start of a mutually rewarding relationship, will you agree to find storage for my goods?" finished Anton in his best and oiliest voice.

Lenc realised that the fat fraud had them. Suddenly they were eager to help, if only to see what other wonders would appear from the magic satchel.

"Good," he purred, "Now why don't you lend me some men,

we will wait for the ship to come in and store my goods, then talk further."

The old man nodded eagerly and quickly pointed at the three fishermen, gesturing to them to go with the two strangers. Anton stood and bowed from the neck up. "You have been very helpful, I shall not forget that," The old man's head was bobbing up and down as Anton swept out of the small door, quickly followed by Lenc.

Outside, the air seemed fresh and sweet after the rancid fug of the meeting hall. "My gods," Anton breathed deeply, "please save me from cretins and half-wits, or if I have to deal with them, at least make them clean and fragrant cretins and half-wits."

They followed the three fishermen back to the sea-shore, where one of them indicated an empty hut right on the sea's edge.

"This will have to do," said Anton, "hopefully we won't have to leave the stuff here long."

Lenc glanced out to sea. The tide was coming in quickly and soon their ship would be able to tie up alongside. It was out in the estuary, within hailing distance, and the skipper was standing on the prow, waiting for a sign that he should weigh the boat into shore. Anton waved to him, then pointed both hands down where the ship should berth, the skipper waved in acknowledgement.

Lenc turned to Anton. "How are we going to play this?" he asked. "One of us is going to have to stay here to watch the goods, while the other goes off to find a cart. What's it to be?"

"All things considered, I think you had better go," said Anton, "and I will stay here on guard. But you must get the best price possible for a cart. You must haggle and haggle hard. If you don't, people will know you aren't a trader and get suspicious. Besides I may come this way again and I don't want you setting a high price for transport."

Lenc smiled at this affront to his horse-trading ability. He was no trader, it was true, but he knew horses, and anyway, neither of them had any idea what a horse and a cart should cost in this wild, untamed land.

With high tide approaching, the ship slid alongside the jetty, and the crew lost no time humping the merchandise into the hovel that passed for a warehouse, watched over by a fussing Anton.

The skipper stepped ashore and looked round. "God's teeth but this place stinks. The sooner we're finished, the better. Stay too long and you'll never get the stench out of your skin."

Lenc smiled, "Agreed, but at least it's safe. These people seem to be on their own, at the mercy of any and everyone. If we can keep their co-operation it will be a good start."

"I don't like it," added Anton darkly, "these are the sort that smile to your face then stab you in the back as soon as your guard is down. I for one, will sleep with one eye open."

Towards the horizon through the fading mist another land mass started to appear. "Is that another island?" asked Lenc.

"No," replied the skipper. "It's all part of Britannia, but separated by this huge estuary. There is a fierce tidal race here and treacherous mud flats, enough ways to kill an honest sailor to keep even Neptune satisfied. But some, like this lot, know the waters and make a living here. Not for me though."

When the sailors had finally finished unloading and stowing the cargo, the skipper grasped Lenc's forearm. "We're off now, so god speed, and be careful. Still not sure what you are supposed to be doing here, but I can guess. If the worst happens, just think of yourself. Get out and keep riding east, you'll hit Roman forces eventually. And beware of these fish fuckers. They may look and act stupid, but they've managed to survive somehow, so don't underestimate them."

Lenc felt a pang as he watched the preparations for the ship to slip from the jetty, and his last real contact with safety and civilisation. From now on, he was on his own. Well not completely alone. He turned as he heard Anton's querulous voice inside the warehouse as he frantically searched for something.

Lenc smiled to himself. I still have him, he thought, but whether that's a good or a bad thing remains to be seen.

CHAPTER XII

L enc was quite sure that without a guide he would have wandered into the swamp and drowned. Instead he found himself following a teenage lad, who confidently led him on a completely submerged path.

The surface of the grey water was broken by rush clumps, and he had been warned to stay exactly behind his guide, something he needed no encouragement to do. At times they waded ankle deep in the cold, gloopy water and he could feel his iron-shod boots sinking in, then the strain on his calves as he pulled his feet free of the clinging mud. After about half an hour of wading and walking, the landscape began to change, the dirty brown of the rushes gradually changing to green shrubbery, and underfoot the murky water ebbed away as they approached dry land.

Finally they scrambled up a dry bank of sand and tussocky grass, and Lenc paused to look around. From the security of dry land, he could hardly make out the village, so completely did it blend into the swamp rushes and the grey sea beyond.

To the north and west the purple hills of his destination rose to the horizon, and turning he saw the swamp stretching away in both directions. A keen wind whipped the tops of the rushes and spattered his bare legs with sand. He could just make out the sea in the distance, and there was the estuary leading to the Roman camp, sanctuary for some, but not for him. Wading birds swooped and tumbled on the keen wind, waiting for the tide to go out once again so they could start hunting.

Lenc shivered, it was a grim place all right, a complete contrast to Camulodunum and the flat plains on the other side of the country. His guide was getting impatient, and urgently plucked at his cloak. Clearly the boy felt ill at ease being away from the safety of his swamp home, he wanted to deliver his charge and get back as quickly as possible. Fair enough, thought Lenc, but he was quite sure he would be pleased never to see that stinking, damp dump ever again.

They turned their faces to the north, the lad in the lead, following the bank of the estuary. The path was grassy, indicating little use, meandering through a copse of large beech trees. After the horrors of the swamp village, the contrast could not have been more profound. Lenc was breathing easier and enjoying his surroundings.

Eventually he asked, "Where are we going?" The boy gestured vaguely northwards, thought for a moment, struggling for the right words. He clearly did not meet many strangers. "We need to go towards the hills, to avoid the Romans building forts further up the river."

Lenc agreed. He knew that forts were being built at Burrium and Glevum, strategic outposts in a line of strongholds stretching northwards, all the way to Luguvalium and the current end of Roman ambition. He would give them a wide berth but keep an eye out for patrols.

Overhead, a big blue sky was studded with small clouds, moving quickly inland. Winter was coming but this was an autumn day to be savoured. There was constant noise from small birds in the trees, and he could also hear the plaintive screech of a hunting bird, circling high above them.

"What's wrong with you, are we in danger?" Lenc asked. The boy flinched. Between Lenc's Gaulish and the boy's own strange dialect, they managed to communicate but it wasn't straightforward.

"There is always danger away from the sea, people here don't like us, it is best to be alert at all times."

"Who would want to harm you?"

"They all do, that's why we make it difficult for them to find us. We are surrounded by the Silures. They are farmers, but they are raiders as well. They don't fish, but if they want fish they will take from us. If they can. They take slaves too. We have to walk up the river to get away from the Silures near us. If they knew you carried coin they would slit your throat and take your money. But if we travel a bit further we will find Silures who understand trade. The village of Mynydd-Bach is on the Silurian border. If you want to find a horse and cart it will be there."

These Silures seemed an odd lot, thought Lenc. Farmers, growing crops and rearing animals, yet capable of savagery and raiding.

They walked on in silence. Lenc enjoying the sensation of being on land and walking on soft grass, the lad moving forward furtively, hunched over as if expecting a sword blade between his shoulder blades at any moment.

After walking for some time Lenc called a halt under a large silvery-smooth beech tree. The land here was on a slight rise and they could just see through a sea-haze across the estuary to the flat land on the other side. Lenc rummaged in the bag slung across his shoulder and found some hard bread, from which he broke pieces and threw some to the lad, who instantly started gnawing. Lenc drizzled olive oil onto his bread, then laid a few strips of dried fish on top. The lad watched warily.

While Lenc waited for the oil to soak into the bread, he brought out a small flask of wine, from which he drank appreciatively. The bread was softer now, and the oil made it more or less palatable. The fish was smoked, fairly fresh and tasted good. At least the swamp waders could deal with fish, he thought sourly.

They ate their meal in silence. Lenc still enjoying the rolling view, while the lad, hunched over his bread, chewed quickly, as if afraid someone would snatch it from him. Lenc leaned back on his elbows, feet stretched out comfortably in front of him, and looked at the lad. "Have you always lived in the swamp?" he asked finally.

The lad looked shifty. "For a long time," he answered. "My family was chased here. We came from over there," he gestured vaguely towards the mainland across the estuary. "There was always fighting, we had a smallholding and grew crops, raised some pigs and chickens. But more often than not, come the harvest, we would be raided by one tribe or another and lose what we could not hide. In the end it was move or starve. Now we are left alone to fish, raise some animals, and we have as little contact with anyone as possible. Which is why we want you gone as soon as you can, it is certain sure you will draw attention to us."

"What's your name lad?" asked Lenc.

"My name is Peiskos."

Lenc smiled, "It's a good name for a fisherman."

The lad shrugged, clearly upset and frightened.

Lenc could not conceive how anyone could grow up this intimidated. Impulsively he leaned forward: "I am sorry for your distress, but you must know that eventually you will have unwelcome visitors even in your swamp retreat. You should prepare for that and be ready for them. Right now you are outsiders in a hard world, and people treat you with contempt. You must make them fear the swamp and be afraid to go there."

"We don't care what they think of us as long as they leave us alone," mumbled Peiskos.

"You just think on what I have said," smiled Lenc. "Perhaps a solution will come to you. Now let's get going, I am eager to see this village of yours."

As they walked, the estuary narrowed into a sluggish river, rippling slowly down to the sea. The banks were grey viscous mud, which looked solid enough to walk on, but when he lobbed a large stone, it sank immediately with a glooping sound.

The river did not seem deep as rocks would sometimes appear.

No doubt there were trout and maybe even salmon lurking in its depths. Lenc wished they could stop and try some fishing.

They detoured from the riverbank to avoid a large sweeping turn in its course, at the same time as the track grew wider and muddied from the churning of farm animals.

"This is as far as I go," said Peiskos. "The village is just ahead, you must make for the centre where you will find the blacksmith who is also a farrier. He will have what you need."

"Will you be alright here on your own?" asked a suddenly concerned Lenc.

"Of course," smiled Peiskos, "I shall move back into the trees and wait for you. I don't expect you till tomorrow, but no-one will find me here."

Lenc nodded. "I'll be quick as I can," he promised.

After a hundred paces Lenc turned, Peiskos had vanished.

The path twisted through a small copse of trees and he barely noticed the small hut, set back within their shadow. A fire burned in a brazier near the entrance with a cooking pot boiling away on the top. A burly man with a full ginger beard and wearing rusty chain mail reached for his sword belt when he spied the stranger. Two other men, also wearing chain mail had been dozing on the grass but soon jumped to their feet when Gingerbeard kicked them on the soles of their boots.

By now the other two had found their weapons, and taking their lead from the speaker, stood some paces apart in a loose semi-circle in front of Lenc. He recognised them as mercenaries, hired to protect the village from marauding raiders, though by the look of their vast bellies, their fighting days were long gone.

He smiled. "Good day," he said in Gaulish.

The lead man grunted and his eyes narrowed. "You are a Gaul?"

"I am."

"What are you doing here then?"

"We arrived yesterday by sea and I am looking for a horse and cart so we can trade our goods in the area."

The lead man licked his lips and hitched his sword belt over his ample girth. His eyes narrowed. "So you have coin?"

Lenc nodded happily. His sword was still sheathed between his shoulder blades, and despite the dagger at his waist, he looked for all the world like a simple trader.

"Maybe you would like to share some of that coin with us, in return for a safe passage?"

Lenc pretended to consider this offer. "I don't think so, I am sure I will come to no harm."

"Beware stranger, there are raiders in these parts who would rather slice you in two than talk," added one of the others.

Lenc sighed. He knew a show of strength was the only way to get past these thieving lumps. He smiled again, then quickly reached back over his head, freeing his sword. When it came down, he was holding it with both hands, his legs instinctively flexed into an on guard position.

He smiled again. "I don't think I'll have any trouble, do you?" Gingerbeard, in closest range, took a step backwards. The second man put his hand on the hilt of his sword but made no move to draw.

Out of the corner of his eye, Lenc saw the third edge a pace away to widen the distance between them. He was pulling his sword from its scabbard as Lenc swung his own blade.

"I don't think so. There may be three of you, but I'll cut you down before you can draw iron. I shall be coming back this way with my horse and cart, and it would be better if you do not try to stop me. Next time I shall forget I'm a guest in your country."

The three watched sullenly as he edged past them, walking backwards down the path, until he turned a leafy corner. If they were going to take their revenge it would be now, he decided. He stepped into the foliage just far enough to be hidden from the path. After several minutes went by, he smiled, thinking the pot on the fire was a better bet than robbing a traveller, especially one with a sword he was obviously not afraid to use.

He moved off down the path but decided not to sheath his sword. Not yet. You never knew.

CHAPTER XIII

The village on a rise looked prosperous, if a little short on people. Peiskos had ventured the notion that Mynydd Bach meant Little Hill. Which to Lenc, at first sight, seemed about right.

The houses seemed well maintained, with neat thatched roofs, the only sign of life, chickens and pigs which clucked and grunted, scratching for food.

Lenc headed to the centre of the village following the rhythmic clang of a blacksmith's hammer. Soon he could smell the acrid smoke of the fire, air pumping through it, raising the temperature to twist and shape iron. The smithy was unique in the village in that it had a roof of slate, supported on stout timbers. A spark from the over-heated fire would soon catch in a thatch roof.

The smith was a big man, heavily muscled, with a thick straggly beard almost to his chest. He wore a brown leather apron, and round his forehead, a bright bandanna, stained dark with sweat. Keeping the fire bright was a young boy pumping energetically at bellows made from pigskin.

After a series of blows with a big hammer, the smith dropped a half-formed horseshoe into a blackened bucket of water, which hissed and sizzled. Realising he had an audience, he wiped his forehead with a rag and looking up, he said, "Good day, how can I help you?"

Lenc smiled and replied, "I am told you are the man to see about buying a horse and cart."

"Could be," came the cautious reply.

"My employer would have a cart to carry the goods we have brought from Gaul. We only landed yesterday and he is keen to get going."

"Where did you land? I've not heard of ships coming into the river mouth."

"We landed where the river meets the sea, a sorry place of marsh and swamp and poor fisherfolk."

The smith nodded in understanding. "The marsh dwellers. Some say they have developed gills and can swim like the fish. I'm surprised they allowed you to land."

"They were wary but seemed pleasant enough," conceded Lenc. "Bit smelly, but quite harmless I think."

The smith gave a short bark of laughter. "I have a couple of carts you can look at, and I can find you a horse, but nothing is cheap these days, what with bastard Dobunni raiders and now the Romans wanting the food out of our mouths. But we will see what we can do."

Lenc looked round the small village. "It's very quiet here," he observed.

The smith looked round. "All the men are at work in the fields, and the women are inside, doing what they do. Come let us look at horses."

"What's your name by the way, I am called Gobann." After telling the big blacksmith his name, Lenc followed him past a stable in a sloping field down to a stream where four horses were grazing.

Three carts were lined up with their traces touching the ground. They were differing sizes but only one seemed large enough for Anton's goods.

Gobann eyed him. "You won't get better than these anywhere," he said defensively. Lenc nodded and took a closer look. All three had obviously been worked hard, but they seemed serviceable. He put his hand on the largest one.

"This one looks about the best of a bad lot, how much do you want for it?"

"That's a fine cart and will stand you in good stead. Are we talking Roman coin by any chance?"

Lenc nodded. "Coming from Gaul, it makes sense to have coin that is recognised, even if you don't want to use it. I'm interested if the price is right."

Gobann looked at him shrewdly and smiled: "If we are already at the negotiating stage, perhaps we better find somewhere more comfortable, and something to drink. By the way, did any of the nags take your fancy?"

Lenc looked again at the horses. They were all big draught horses and would plod all day. "They seem all right," he said grudgingly. "How about that brown and white one in the middle?"

"Not a bad choice," conceded the smith. "He will do the work you want."

They returned to the smithy and then on to a wooden building set back with rough wooden tables and benches placed outside. "This is our meeting place," offered the smith. "We make all our own ale and cider and we can talk over a pot."

Lenc looked round at the village on its slight hill. "It's a nice place," he conceded.

"Yes, it's nice enough if we're left alone, but we're on the edge of our tribal area, which makes us a great temptation for our neighbours the Dobunni, who like to raid every now and again."

The blacksmith paused, "Now if those bastard Romans building that fort at Glevum wanted to make themselves useful they could chop a few Dobunni heads off. That would calm the bastards down a bit."

He led the way into the dark interior of the meeting house which, like most of the buildings was made of stout timbers with wattle woven between. There was no light except what found its way through the open door.

"You will try our cider," said Gobann. Lenc wasn't sure whether

132

this was a question or a statement, but contented himself with a nod of appreciation. The smith poured the cloudy apple mix from a barrel into a smaller pot jar and then carefully filled two mugs fashioned from cow horn.

They took the jar and their brimming mugs outside to a trestle table and sat in the autumn sun. Gobann took a deep draught and grunted appreciatively.

Lenc tentatively tasted the cider. He was used to the taste as it was a staple in Gaul, but this was piss. Rough and cloudy, nothing at all like the cider from the mainland.

"It's strong," he managed to concede. Gobann exploded in laughter. "Come on get it down, it's good for you."

Lenc looked down at the brew. He knew he would have to keep his wits about him if he was going to get a decent deal. "So how much do you want for the cart and the nag?" he started.

Gobann wiped his mouth with the back of his hand. "Well that's a particularly strong cart, and the horse came from good stock, it will work all day and as long as it's fed and watered, will never complain.

"I think five gold Roman coins should cover it. You are Roman military aren't you?" he asked slyly.

Lenc gave a start was he that obvious?

"What makes you think that?"

"Everything about you screams military," laughed the big smith. "All you're missing is the uniform."

Lenc conceded the point. "I was military," he agreed. "But no longer, now I run about after a trader, do his messages, look after his back, fetch and carry. It's a lot safer than being a soldier, and it should drop your exorbitant price by at least half."

"Hmm," said the smith, "we'll see. Will you be bringing your goods here to trade?"

"We can do of course, you could be our first port of call," conceded Lenc. "We have plenty of things you might be interested in, pots, jewellery, wine, olive oil, tools, all sorts. Perhaps we could come to some sort of deal over the cart?"

The big man shook his head. "No, I think not, let's get the deal done, and start anew with anything you have that I may be interested in."

"Fair enough," accepted Lenc, "but our generosity will be more than rewarded by yours. And doing good to strangers gets you a lot of new friends."

The smith thought about this. But before he could respond, a piercing scream, quickly followed by thundering hooves shocked them into action. Mugs tipped over as they sprang away from the table. They both looked round frantically trying to identify the new sounds and source of danger.

"Dobunni," gasped the smith. "The bastards have crossed the river again. They know our men are in the fields, so they're raiding for anything they can carry away."

The smith grasped his large hammer, and nodded approvingly as Lenc reached behind his head for his concealed sword. "Said you were a Roman."

They both skirted the meeting house as Gobann, throwing caution to the winds started to run forward. Lenc grabbed him by the shirt and pulled him into the shelter of the building. At first Gobann brushed him off, keen to find out what was going on.

"Calm," said Lenc. Something in his voice made the smith check. He looked questioningly at Lenc.

"We must move slowly and carefully if we are to be of help. There's bound to be a good few of them, even it is a small raiding party. If we go blundering in, we'll be no use to anyone and just get ourselves killed. Take it easy and let's see what's happening." He grinned. "Then we kill them all."

Gobann nodded and walked towards the noise, keeping close to the wall of the meeting house. They cautiously turned the corner to see six horses held by one man. All the traces were in one hand, his sword in the other.

"Where are the rest?" hissed the smith. He was answered by a scream from one of the huts.

"Bastards," he said, his face contorted as he gripped his hammer. "But they'll know there is one man left at least."

"Wait, wait," urged Lenc. "If I go for the one with the horses, there should be a bit of a gap before the others come out, which will give us a better chance. We don't want to raise the alarm and have to face them all together if we can help it, better one at a time."

The smith grunted, he could see the sense in the simple plan.

The two cautiously crept forward. Lenc with his sword, and Gobann with his big hammer. They used the building as a shield and as they got closer to the sentry they identified the huts where the screaming was coming from. Lenc gripped the smith's arm and pointed towards the nearest one. The smith nodded and slipped away towards it. Lenc wiped his sword hand on his tunic, had a quick look round and cautiously stepped towards the sentry.

Clearly the raiders sensed no danger, the sentry was hopping from foot to foot, desperate to get into the action. His attention was completely focussed on the huts and what his comrades were doing. Thinking with his prick was going to get him killed, thought Lenc.

Silently, he skirted the huts so he could come up on the sentry from the road out of the village. He broke cover and ran the short distance to the horses, but before he could get close enough to strike, one of the skittish animals pulled away from the sentry, who almost lost his grip. He looked round and immediately saw Lenc bearing down on him, sword at the killing point. His eyes widened as he dropped the reins and, pulling his sword took a defensive stance. Once freed, the horses scattered in all directions, further confusing the sentry. He jumped to one side to avoid a flying hoof, then tried to focus on his attacker, but too late, Lenc rushed him, sword shoulder high, abandoning all finesse as he gambled on one powerful swipe and came down with all his might, slashing into the raider's collarbone. With a shriek the man went down, dropping his sword and clutching his wound. Lenc stood back and plunged the point of his blade into the man's heart.

Breathing quickly Lenc took a step backwards and warily looked round.

Gobann had not waited to see what was happening. As soon as he saw Lenc charge, he dived into the first hut. He soon re-appeared, but as he was making for the second, a wild-haired man angrily stuck his head out of the door as if enquiring what all the noise was about. The smith let out a wild cry and hit him foursquare on the temple with his hammer. The man fell back into the hut without a sound.

As the smith was looking round for his next target, Lenc went for another hut, still at a crouch. He pulled up short as a naked apparition erupted from the hut, carrying a long sword.

Lenc paused, then went into his attack position, feet firmly fixed on the ground, back slightly bent. "Come on you bastard, I'll cut your prick off and let you bleed to death."

Whether the man could understand the actual words was not obvious, but he recognised the tone. He came forward at the crouch, sword in front, held with both hands. Lenc was aware of the smith behind him, bellowing in rage. He was still using the hammer to good effect.

Lenc concentrated on the man's eyes as he slipped his dirk from its sheath. He pointed the blade upwards then suddenly feinted left, his sword protecting his body. The man moved with him, covering the move, it didn't seem to bother him that he was naked, his now shrivelled manhood waving side to side. This time Lenc came in quickly with an overhead blow, which the man parried, still with his sword in both hands. The big sword rasped down the blade of Lenc's gladius, checked by the cross guard or quillion which saved his clenched fingers.

They stood there, grimly swaying, locked together by their swords. The naked warrior thought he had the advantage by still holding his sword two-handed and was pressing down as hard as he could. Lenc took a pace backward, but as a triumphant grin started to spread over his opponent's features, he stabbed upwards with his dirk, under the ribs. His victim's eyes opened wide in surprise as the blade slid into his body. There was a puzzled look on his face as he registered the knife scraping across a rib and through a lung. He slowly let go of his heavy sword as he slipped to the ground with a sigh. Lenc had to stoop to tug his dirk from the man's body then wipe the blood off on the man's bare arse.

At least four down, he thought to himself. Six horses, so at least two more to deal with, where can they be?

Gobann was still rampaging from hut to hut looking for raiders. He came out of one, blood on his face and arms. He looked at Lenc and shrugged, palms open. He also had counted the horses and knew there were more raiders at large.

Suddenly the missing two appeared in the street. Clearly, they had been looking further afield for booty or women and hurried back when they heard the unexpected sounds of combat. They were running but skidded to a halt when they took in the scene of carnage. One of them, a big man with wild hair down his back and extensive whirls of tattoos on his face and naked shoulders, put his hand out to restrain the other. They stopped and sized up the situation, before the big man raised two fingers to his mouth and let out a piercing whistle. This was the signal for back-up to come to their aid, as with a thundering of hooves four more wild haired raiders came charging down the earth street and swerved to a halt behind the raiders on foot.

"God's blood" said the smith. "More of the bastards."

Lenc moved away from the dead men on the floor. This was going to be difficult and the last thing he wanted was to trip over a corpse. Gobann moved to his side.

"Keep in front of them so the riders can't swing at you and try to concentrate on the horses," Lenc murmured. "A smack between the eyes from that hammer should do it."

The smith swallowed and contented himself with: "right".

The two waited as the big man gave his instructions to the riders. He was clearly ordering a full-on charge. This was not the first time Lenc had faced horses, but in the shield wall, men had the advantage and the horses would usually sheer away when confronted by spears. He had no spear, and no shield and his only ally was a man of unknown quality. It would be the most logical thing to do to turn and run in the face of charging horses. Logical but deadly.

The front horse wheeled as the rider drew his sword, there was a rasp as the others followed. The head rider nudged his horse forward, sword in the air. Suddenly he let out a scream of pain and slid from the saddle to crash to the ground. The others looked uncertainly at him and then around them, their charge checked. The man on the ground pointed his sword at Lenc and Gobann and screamed at the horsemen to charge. They kicked their heels into the ribs of their horses but before they could get momentum, another of the riders threw his arms up and with a cry rolled off his horse, a vicious gash across his temple.

The two standing raiders finally realising they were under attack from an unknown source, stood back to back apprehensively waiting for another strike, but nothing came. The two remaining men on horseback rescued the riderless horses and sat nervously waiting for the next move.

Lenc and Gobann stayed at the crouch, just as mystified as the raiders as to where the attack had come from.

Eventually one of the two on foot gestured to the riders, who brought their horses over. They mounted and one pulled his horse round savagely and glared at Lenc and Gobann.

"I shall remember this, you craven bastards. You do not kill the men of Dobunni and get away with it. We shall be back."

He dug his heels in and the band turned and galloped from the village.

Lenc watched the cloud of dust disappear as he began to relax and gestured at the fallen riders. "Make sure they are dead, and see if you can find out what killed them."

As the sound of hooves receded into the distance, timid faces appeared at the doorways to the huts. One woman, clutching a torn shirt to her breast, stepped out onto the path, her face bruised and an open wound slashed her cheek. The smith ran to her, "Elise, are you all right?"

Shaken the woman nodded. "Yes, you stopped them in time, but it was close."

She registered Lenc and looked up at him. "Who do I have to thank for saving me from violation?" She was older, with a calm air of authority. Her face was lined, both from age and laughter.

Gobann clapped Lenc on the shoulder. "This is an honest trader who came to me to buy a cart, and got himself caught up in our problems," he boomed.

The woman smiled. "We are all grateful, this is not our usual sort of hospitality, but I can assure you, you will always be welcome in our village."

He gratefully sank onto a bench outside one of the houses as his adrenaline ebbed away. Tentatively he felt his ribs, but to his surprise they seemed fine.

He watched as the big smith examined the two fallen Dobunni, the first was quite dead, but the second took another sickening blow from Gobann's hammer. Both lay still as Gobann went through their pouches for anything of value, then he gathered the horses and led them to where they could be tethered.

"Looks like they were hit by a sling-shot," said the smith. "Whoever did it was a fine shot, strong too."

Just then, Lenc spied a small figure peering round a building, grinning shyly. It was Peiskos, his watery guide. Lenc beckoned him, and he came forward twisting a leather thong in his hands.

"I thought you were going to wait outside the village," demanded Lenc.

The boy looked to the ground. He seemed unsure whether he had done the right thing.

"I was," he said nervously. "I hid in a thicket where I could see the path and also those men in the hut you had the argument with. I was asleep when I heard horses, and when I looked up the raiders had fallen on the men in the hut and slit their throats. They were all asleep and saw nothing."

The smith growled at this news. "What the hell did we pay them for?"

The boy continued: "From their markings I recognised them as Dobunni raiders and I just wanted to hide until they went away. Then I thought, I was your guide and should look after you, so I decided to follow. When I saw you fighting, I was afraid. But then when I saw the riders ready to charge I knew I could help.

"I have had a lot of practice with the slingshot," he said proudly.

"You were sent by the gods," said Lenc gravely. "Without you we would be carrion meat by now, and this village would have been levelled before their men came back."

Peiskos said nothing. He scratched a mark in the soil with his bare big toe. Then he looked up, and grinned. "I am glad," he said. "It felt good."

Gobann was occupied ransacking the pouches of the dead men. He was laughing at the naked man, saying that was one way not to get robbed, just go about naked, when the man stirred and groaned on the ground. The smith shook him. "This bugger's still alive," he said in a tone which almost said, 'how dare he!'

The woman who had been the raiders' victim pushed forward, "give him to me," she demanded. The smith said nothing, but stooped and picked up a bone handled knife lying near the man.

"This was his, perhaps you might like to give it back to him?"

The woman nodded, her eyes bright. She grasped the knife and leaned down to the man twitching on the hard-baked mud ground. His eyes rolled in fear as the woman leaned over him.

She shook his shoulder. "Can you see me?" she hissed, spittle foaming round her lips. The man shrieked as the movement stirred his wound which was spilling gouts of blood. "Can you see me?" she demanded again in a shrill tone.

"You were keen to use that thing between your legs on me, weren't you? Weren't you?" she screamed. The raider looked terrified and strangely pathetic, as even in his final moments he tried to cover his manhood with one hand and stem the flow of blood with the other. His matted hair stuck to his face as he whispered for mercy.

"I'll give you the same mercy you were trying to give me," said the woman contemptuously, as she sliced at the man's hands. He screamed once, then louder as she suddenly leaned down and cut through his manhood. His back arched and he tried to scream again, but this time nothing would come out. He slumped back, obviously dead. The woman, screaming with rage, attacked the body with the knife, slashing and hacking, as the villagers stood and watched. Eventually she grew tired and slumped down next to the man, now an unrecognisable lump of meat.

The smith watched her dispassionately. "We must bury them, remove all trace, and we must find out where the rest of their band is. We must call the men in and defend the village until we can be sure these Dobunni bastards have all gone."

Lenc watched the activity for a short while, then wearily walked back to the meeting hall, and with a sigh lowered himself onto a bench, watched by an anxious Peiskos. The cider stood undisturbed on the table, and as he reached for his mug, his young friend hurried to pick up the pot jar and poured the cloudy, golden liquid into it. Lenc nodded his thanks, and lifted the mug. It was warm but still welcome, funny how a fight to the death can even improve the taste of this piss, he thought.

Lenc was glad to just sit and try not to think of the short and unpleasant fight, what was he thinking of, getting involved in someone else's war? It could have ruined his whole mission. What a fool, he thought angrily.

He snapped out of his reverie when Gobann returned, dropping his blood-crusted hammer on the grass by the table. He sat with a sigh and reached for a mug. "We have three Roman forts within spitting distance and a full legion, all bursting to show what great friends they are to us and still we are raided by Dobunni. If they really wanted our friendship they could start with sorting those bastards out."

The big man spat on the ground then drained his mug. He gestured to Peiskos to give him a refill. After another prodigious gulp Gobann wiped his mouth with the back of his hand. "In the old days, before the Romans came, we would gather arms and take the fight back to the Dobunni. We would raid, take cattle, sheep and slaves and anything else we could carry. Then they would come for us and do the same, and so it went on. This time, we will see if the Romans will be any use at all."

Lenc looked at him reflectively. "You are going to enlist the help of the legion?"

"Sure, why not, be good to get some use out of the thieving bastards."

"Well, you better let me get well clear before you do, I don't want to complicate things by meeting Romans."

Gobann studied him carefully, "I fully understand that you have an issue with the Romans, but I can keep you out of it. If you go now you will be well out of the way when they get here, if they decide to come at all.

"As I said, there are three forts locally, all in the process of being built." Gobann reached for a stick, which he used to scratch a rough map in the dirt. "Here is our river, the Wysg, which starts way up in the hills and empties into the sea in the estuary of Sabrina, near where your swamp people live. The Romans are building here at what they call Venta Silurum, their nearest fort to here, at Glevum and again, here at Burrium." He stabbed the ground indicating the line of forts. "When you leave the coast, head straight for the hills, then turn north. It will be bad luck if you run into a patrol, you will just have to do some fast talking. Oh and keep them covered up." He gestured at the military tattoos on Lenc's arms.

"Where exactly are you planning to go?" enquired the blacksmith. "I may be prying, but perhaps I can help. I owe you that much."

Lenc looked at the big man thoughtfully. He decided there was no harm in him knowing the plan, vague as it was.

"We intend to head north for a while where there are villages and towns. My boss understands that there are plenty of people who can buy or trade for his goods but because of the lawlessness of the area, it's not a place where traders tend to go. He thinks, if he can keep his head on his shoulders, he will do well."

Gobann nodded. "You're quite right about the lawlessness. Well you've seen it first-hand. Trouble is, as strangers you will be looked on with suspicion. How do they know you are not a spy here to betray them to the Romans, rather than a deserter?"

Lenc shot him a look, but Gobann was smiling. "Well, you're either a spy or a deserter. I can understand your trader wanting to break new ground, sort of, but I don't think he could pay you enough to accompany him as his bodyguard without some other incentive, and I prefer to believe you are a deserter rather than a spy."

Lenc suddenly realised how farcical his great plan was. If a simple village blacksmith could see through him straight away, what chance could he possibly have? He thanked the gods that at least the blacksmith was on his side. Maybe the fight would turn out to be a blessing after all.

Gobann nodded, "I need to deliver some horse tackle to Gobannion, so how about we travel together, and you can start your trading there, and I can introduce you to the Silurian council of the north of our territory. That way, you may keep your head on your shoulders."

An introduction to the tribal council was too good to pass up, so Lenc made a show of hesitating, then thanked the blacksmith for his offer.

Gobann nodded: "I have things to do here, and I need to go to the fort to report the raid, for all the good it will do, so I will meet you on the road. I will get the lad to put you on the right trail along the edge of the hills. You'll eventually come to a joining of two rivers, make camp and I will meet you there. From there it's only a days travel to Gobannion."

CHAPTER XIV

Anton was still grumbling as they stowed the trade goods in the cart. He had finally conceded that Lenc had struck a good deal for the horse and cart, in gratitude for his help in fighting off the Dobunni, the blacksmith gave him the horse and only accepted a minimal payment for the cart.

"I would give you the raider's horses," Gobann said, "but I'll dispose of them and in return you can have the work horse you fancied. It's the least we can do, and besides they would take a bit of explaining if you ran into those Dobunni again."

On his return to the swamp plain, Lenc sent Peiskos ahead to the village so that Anton could arrange for his goods to be manhandled over the treacherous bog to dry land. While he was waiting, he gathered wood and lit a fire to roast a hare presented by the grateful villagers.

He also had bread and a flask of the potent cider. Which, he decided wasn't that bad when you got used to it.

After skinning and dressing the hare he impaled it on a wet stick and placed it over the embers of the fire on two triangles of branches. Every minute or so, he carefully turned the makeshift spit to cook the animal.

"Zeus's blood," exploded a voice behind him. "I could smell cooking meat from that stinking bog, what have you got there?"

Lenc grinned to himself. Some things don't change.

Anton hurried forward, followed by several villagers all laden down with the precious trade goods. He squatted by the fire and reached out to touch the hare. Peiskos followed and sat next to

Lenc with a big grin on his face. He had clearly made a friend.

"What a pity we haven't got any garlic," offered Anton, his mouth watering. "But never mind, plenty of time for that later."

He turned to Lenc, who was lying under a big oak tree, feet comfortably outstretched with a mug of cider in his hand.

The villagers dumped their loads by the cart then stood around looking aimless. They wanted to get back to the security of the swamp village, feeling vulnerable in the open meadow.

"What are you lot doing standing about with your mouths hanging open," grumbled Anton. "I suppose you want paying do you?" Muttering to himself, he reached into his voluminous cloak and produced a small leather pouch. He fished inside and reluctantly extracted some coins.

"Here," he said grudgingly to one of the men, "and thanks for all your help."

The man looked at the coins and sniffed. "Doesn't seem much for all that humping."

Anton looked incredulous. "What, you want more, for that short stroll? You should be glad of the chance to get back on dry land for once."

The men started muttering at this less than tactful remark and Lenc noted some hands moving to daggers.

He wanted no argument with these peaceful swamp people, "Give them a few more coins," he told Anton. "We've done well with the cart and horse, and they deserve it."

Anton opened his mouth to protest, then shut it again abruptly as he saw the expression on Lenc's face. "All right then," he conceded, and fished into his purse.

Grudgingly he gave the man some more coin, who nodded and turned away without another word. Silently the villagers followed him, disappearing into the rushes at the edge of the swamp.

Anton turned to glare at Peiskos still sitting next to Lenc. "What do you want fish boy? Shouldn't you be going with your people?"

"I'll stay with you till you leave. I can help you load up."

"Yes and load up with some hot meat as well," laughed Lenc. The boy nodded eagerly as he watched the succulent hare sizzling and slowly turning brown.

Anton busied himself checking his stock. "What's that you're drinking?" he finally demanded.

"It's cider," conceded Lenc, "but a bit rougher than you get in Gaul. After a few mouthfuls it's not too bad."

He poured a beaker for Anton who slurped greedily. "Any port in a storm," he conceded.

When the hare was judged ready, Peiskos took it off the makeshift spit and cut generous strips of meat. He handed some to the others then after blowing on it to cool it down greedily crammed a big chunk into his mouth. They all sat back in appreciation of the unexpected feast, and quietly ate. Anton passed round some hard bread, and Lenc drained the flask of cider into their mugs.

Eventually Anton belched loudly and proclaimed, "I was ready for that. My compliments to the provider."

After the last of the trade goods were stowed to Anton's satisfaction, the horse was backed into the traces. He stood impassively, snorting and tossing his head to ward off the gathering flies in the tall grass.

Finally Lenc turned to Peiskos and put his hand on the lad's shoulder. "Well old son, it's time we were off. You had better get back to your people."

Peiskos's head bowed. "I will be sorry to see you go," he said quietly. "I have never met anyone like you. I hardly knew you, and yet I wanted to fight for you."

Lenc squatted down so he could look the lad in the eye. He gripped the boy's shoulder tightly: "I'm sorry you've killed men at such a young age, but that's the way of the world. If you hadn't used your slingshot to such good effect, I wouldn't be here now.

And for that I thank you. Go back to your village and remember, you don't have to be afraid of raiders, you can fight them and protect your people. Tell them of this and be ready always."

Peiskos nodded, still looking at the ground. Suddenly he blurted: "Can't you take me with you? I don't want to stay with my people, they're always afraid. I can be useful to you, help with the horse, make your food."

Lenc smiled. "Your people are afraid because no-one has taught them otherwise. You now know the secret, and as you grow older, you can show them how to defend themselves. You will surely grow into a leader of your people and make them secure and happy, afraid of no man. I think that is your destiny. Can you accept it?"

Peiskos looked up at the man who had changed his life so dramatically. "Yes I do know the secret, and if I have to impart that to others then so be it." Suddenly his face was split by an impish grin, "but I know you are going on adventures and I would rather be with you."

Lenc laughed. "You may also get yourself dead before you can have adventures. But we will meet again, and eat meat together and I will be happy to call you friend."

Peiskos sighed, "So be it, only if we meet again at my village, it's fish we shall probably eat."

Lenc laughed again. "I look forward to it. Farewell and remember that a warrior's duty is to look after his own, especially those who cannot help themselves. Now tell me of the trail, and where we should meet Gobann the blacksmith."

After getting his directions, Lenc joined Anton who was impatiently holding the horse's reins. He turned and waved to the boy, who was watching disconsolately. He was still standing under the big oak tree as the cart slowly meandered from view across the wide meadow.

Replete after his unexpected feed, Anton scrambled up onto

the top of the cart, found a comfortable spot, and was soon snoring gently in the autumn sunshine. The creak and jingle of harness and the wooden groans of the cart as the iron shod wheels slipped and turned on the hard mud of the trail all worked together to foster an air of calm and peace.

Even Lenc, so conscious he must stay on his guard, enjoyed the tranquillity of the journey. The landscape they were travelling through was ideal farming country and he marvelled at the greenness. To their left rose the blue heather clad range of hills, and the gods only knew of the horrors waiting up there, but below was sweet meadow and stands of tall trees. Birds twittered on the branch and every now and again came the shrill call of a hunting bird.

Lenc idly watched a pair of falcons as they circled high on the thermals, patiently watching for prey below to reveal itself.

According to the marsh people, they had to follow the line of the big river Wysg, keeping close to the foothills of the hill range on their left to avoid Burrium, the site of a new Roman fort. They should reach their destination, Gobannion, by midday the following day.

With these simple instructions, Lenc felt quite confident that they would find their destination, a growing township, sitting astride a crucial entry point into the unknown hills of this wild and mysterious land. Yet Lenc could never relax completely. If the raiders were long gone, there was still the Legion to worry about. He knew that the commander of the fledgling fort would throw out cavalry patrols to keep him informed of local activity and to buy or commandeer food. He would have brought stores with him, but would be expected to live off the land, with the local population's approval or not.

Looking ahead, he could see they were approaching a crossroads in a copse of trees. Everything looked peaceful, but for once there was no birdsong, which worried him. He had been walking at the side of the cart, behind the horse's rump, the reins held loosely in his hand. Now he quietly drew his sword and laid it on the floor of the driver's platform.

"Anton," he hissed, "time to take some notice."

"What is it, what's wrong?" came a querulous voice, followed by its tousle haired owner, anxious to know what was happening.

"Don't know," said Lenc tersely. "Only something seems wrong. Take the reins."

Anton reached forward and picked up the reins, holding them slackly. He still lay full length on top of the cart and fearfully looked round at the peaceful scene. The sun was still shining through the trees and everything seemed normal.

"I can't see anything wrong," he said scornfully.

"Well I hope not, just keep your eyes open."

They meandered on to the crossroads, and Lenc let his breath out in a sigh. Maybe he had imagined it after all. As they turned to take the left fork, he smiled up at Anton and shrugged his shoulders.

With the easing of tension, Lenc realised that he had been holding in an exceptionally full bladder. He walked over to the nearby bubbling river, where, with a sigh of relief he let go his own stream into the water. Suddenly he stiffened, someone else was present, he could feel it. He casually tied up his undergarment and dropped the hem of his tunic, then grabbed for the sword hidden between his shoulder-blades. Shit, he'd left damn thing on the cart. He sprang round in a wary crouch, but at first could not see what had caused his feeling of danger. Slowly, he drew his knife and scanned the nearby foliage, when he heard a subdued clicking noise coming from the river bank.

Looking down into the gloom, he made out the shape of a man lying at the base of a large oak with his feet in the water. Lenc had missed him because he was lying so still, head down on his chest, and wearing a long nondescript hooded cloak which blended perfectly with its surroundings.

"Thank the gods for that, I thought you were going to piss on me," said the hiding stranger. "I've been waiting for you."

Warily Lenc raised his dagger to the ready. He moved slowly away from the bank. "Who are you, what do you want?"

The man levered himself up against the tree, he was tall and thin, his face burnt by the sun and weathered by the elements. The hood stayed in place, so little could be seen of his features.

"Show me your forearm," he commanded.

Lenc switched the dagger to his left hand and held out his arm. The man took it, exposing the military tattoos.

"This confirms it. You are Lenculus, of the XXth Valeria, and by the look of those bandages you've made some enemies along the way. We've been expecting you for some days now but had no real idea when you would show up."

"All right," agreed Lenc, "we know who I am, who the fuck are you? And by the way, those are dead enemies."

The man bowed his head slightly. "I am Agrippa, and I lead the XXth Pathfinders. We go ahead and clear the ground for the Legion and try to eliminate the nasty surprises."

This was Lenc's contact, and link with Roman forces. He had heard of the Pathfinders, even seen a few of them in camp. But they did not encourage familiarity and kept themselves to themselves, preferring to live like locals. They were the commander's eyes and ears, the Legion's special forces.

Agrippa motioned to Lenc to sit on the grass, and he went back to his own seat, his back resting against the tree.

He looked at Anton and the cart. "This looks like a good cover," he conceded. "I think you should be accepted, especially if you can make yourself understood, do you speak the local language?"

Lenc confirmed that he could make himself understood in Gaulish, which was pretty close to the other Celtic dialects. He also mentioned Gobann the blacksmith who would vouch for him in the Silurian council.

"Even better," agreed Agrippa, "Did you meet the auxiliary cavalry? They're from the 14th who we are relieving. I stopped them on the track earlier and told them to look out for you, but not to hinder you. They don't know your task or who you are, but just to leave you alone."

Lenc grimaced, "No, not a sign, thank goodness."

Agrippa nodded. "You will be going places we can't possibly get to. But the real value is knowing what these tribespeople are thinking. Will they fight, or will they accept us? Unlikely I know; so let's just say when they fight, how will they do it, what are we going to face?" Agrippa paused and grinned. "Not much to do then. Just get their confidence and get them to tell you their plans. And if you can supply some maps of what's lurking in those hills, so much the better."

All very well, thought Lenc, but it's not you wandering into their camps. If I get caught they'll hang me by the balls.

"One thing I can tell you is that these tribes are at each other's throats," replied Lenc. "After my dust-up yesterday with raiders from the Dobunni, the blacksmith who is a Silurian, thought he would try and make a complaint to the fort. A bit of sympathetic treatment could work wonders."

Agrippa nodded, "Good to know, that could well drive a wedge between the tribes and persuade the Silures towards us. Even one tribe on our side in these badlands would be a blessing.

"Don't worry about reporting in, we'll find you. It may be in the villages, but more likely when you are travelling between them. Don't worry we'll be discreet.

"The first place we really need to know about is a concentration on a hill to the north west of Gobannion. This hill commands virtually all the approaches to the lower end of the line of hills into Silurian country and is an ideal observation point.

"Something else of interest is a raiding party led by a southerner, Caratacus. He got his arse kicked just outside Londinium, then went in for lightning raids, which hurt us a lot. The last we heard he was on his way over here to do a bit of stirring up. Not that this lot need any help, they're looking for a fight all the time. He and his people used to fight from chariots, but after the battle at Medway, they realised how useless they were against a disciplined shield wall.

Lenc nodded. "I know who Caratacus is, I was the only survivor of his last raiding party. Wouldn't mind meeting up with him myself."

Agrippa drilled him with a stern gaze. "Put the thought of revenge out of your mind. You have a mission and killing Caratacus comes a long way second." He gave a short, snorting laugh.

"Right, now that we all feel truly sorry for ourselves, I think you should get back to your friend, he'll be starting to think you've fallen in the river."

Smiling, he added: "Fat boy there is starting to fidget." Lenc look round at Anton, sitting on top of the cart. He looked frightened, almost terrified. He was twisting the reins in his hands, straining to hear what was being said.

"Who is he," he hissed nervously, as Agrippa stepped back into the undergrowth, "what does he want?"

"He's a friend," said Lenc, "that's all you need to know. We may be seeing more of him, but you should be pleased he's in the background."

"What if he's discovered and gives us away," said Anton, "we'll be right in the shit. God's blood, we're already in the shit, he's going to drown us in it."

CHAPTER XV

Though the sun had long slipped behind the range of hills, the day was still bright when they reached the merging of two rivers. "This must be it," said Lenc as he looked round. "Nice spot."

The main river, the Wysg, ran dark and brown and wide. The current, judging by debris on the surface, was minimal until the smaller river tumbled into it, swelling the amount of water in the main channel. The rivers ran through a lush meadow, flanked by lofty oaks, and judging by the burnt earth from cooking fires, a popular place for travellers to rest.

Lenc cast around for firewood and soon amassed a good supply of dry windfalls which would burn well. He dropped some on one of the burnt spots and reached for the flint in his satchel. Kneeling, he arranged a handful of dry straw on the ground, sheltering it from the evening breeze with his body, and vigorously scratched across the flint with a small piece of iron, causing a spark. The straw soon caught and gradually built up to a satisfying fire.

Suddenly he tensed as he heard horses in the distance, and quickly stood, draping his cloak round his shoulders, then retrieved his sword from the cart and slid it into the scabbard on his back. He picked up a water container and made to walk down to the riverbank, idly swinging the leather bucket.

Anton paused in his efforts and glanced up, then round. He sensed something was amiss, gulping when Lenc hissed at him to keep calm and act naturally. So he did exactly the opposite. He hurried after Lenc, eyes wide, thoughts of food forgotten. "What is it, what's wrong?" he demanded querulously.

Lenc paused and whispered. "I can hear horses approaching. Go back to the fire and try and look natural. You have nothing to fear."

Anton's eyes popped. "Nothing to fear? Nothing to fear? By Zeus's nuts, we have everything to fear. The barbarians could take our heads off and not think twice about it. The very people who are supposed to be our protectors are even more likely to murder us. And you say we have nothing to fear," Anton spluttered over his wobbling chins.

Lenc gripped his arm. "You fat fuck!" he spat fiercely. "Go back to the fire and try to act normally. I'm just going to the river and will be back shortly."

Anton stood back and shook his head. He was still frightened, but saw no alternative to doing as he was told. Slowly he turned and glancing furtively left and right, stumbled back to their camp. Lenc watched him go and smiled to himself. He slipped down the bank of the river onto a patch of sand, scooping up a handful of mud to smear over his bare arms, covering his service tattoos. Then he pushed the bucket underwater and watched as the air bubbled out. Behind him, he could hear the horsemen arrive at the camp, he was desperate to turn round and look, but concentrated on the job in hand. It could either be a band of raiding warriors or a Roman patrol. He couldn't decide which would be worse.

Only when the bucket was full did he look round at the horsemen. They were Romans. Shit, he thought and stitched a smile on his face as he walked towards them. It was a full squadron of auxiliary cavalry. As the Decurio, the commanding officer, sat motionless on his white horse in front of Anton, his second in command, the Duplicarius, nudged his horse to the wagon and lifted the securing sheet. He reached inside and withdrew a flask, then suspiciously sniffed the contents and smiled. "Olive oil," he said. He moved back so his horse was next to his officer's and handed the pot flask over. "There's loads of stuff in there, boss, it's like market day in Rome."

"That's what I was about to tell you," gabbled Anton nervously. As he spoke, Anton was ringing his hands, the very picture of a frightened man. "I have come from Gaul with trade goods for these barbarians, all I am looking for is a little profit."

Lenc registered that the horsemen were quietly moving round so the wagon was surrounded, either covering an escape attempt or defending themselves from possible attack. Probably both, but the squadron was certainly alert and ready for anything. He was aware of several sets of eyes on him as the troopers moved their big horses into position.

The Decurio eyed Anton from under his plumed helmet. "Why are you so nervous? You have nothing to fear from me if you are telling the truth. You are telling the truth, aren't you?"

At this Anton almost prostrated himself, he was bowing so low. "Of course, of course, Lord. I am just an honest trader."

The officer then turned to Lenc who was hanging back behind the cowering Anton.

He gestured. "You! Come forward." He spoke in Latin and obviously was talking to Lenc, who shrugged his shoulders and looked puzzled. The officer pointed at him then pointed to the ground in front of him. "Come here you clod so I can see you."

Lenc pointed to himself and raised his eyebrows questioningly, then shuffled forward.

Anton saw where this was going and hurriedly interjected. "He is my servant, I took him on in Gaul, just in case the natives decided not to pay for their goods. He is a bit slow and doesn't understand Latin, like us more worldly people."

The officer grunted and looked carefully at Lenc, protectively wrapped in his cloak.

He turned once again to Anton. "Have you seen anything of a big raiding party with chariots, led by a blonde-haired man?

There would be women with them."

Anton looked puzzled, not sure how he should answer. He shook his head. "No Lord, nothing, although there was a raiding party yesterday in the village where I bought my cart. We managed to miss them, thank the gods, but I was told they were a nearby tribe."

The officer nodded. "Yes, I heard of this incident, I shall be visiting the village to find out what happened. We will leave you to your business." He touched two fingers to his helmet and wheeled his horse back to the path. The squadron silently fell in behind him in two columns and they cantered across the meadow to disappear as quickly as they had come.

"Zeus's bollocks," Anton shrilled through his teeth. "That was close, and they didn't even take a tribute from me. I need a drink, and not that bloody cider either."

As Anton rummaged under the cart sheet for his special bottle of apple brandy, Lenc thanked Mithras, the god of soldiers, for Agrippa's timely intervention. Both the Decurio and the Duplicarius looked like hard bastards and if they had thought he was a deserter there would have been no sympathy.

Then another thought struck him. I've had two lucky escapes, the first in befriending Gobann and the second running into Agrippa. How long can my luck last, especially with this bloody flimsy story you could drive a horse and cart through?

By now Anton was working through his second beaker of brandy, and almost choked when Lenc clapped him on the back and suggested that food was now in order. "I have had more than my share of upsets today," Anton grumbled loftily, "and I don't need you adding to them."

Lenc laughed mostly with relief. "Come on, a big strong warrior like you, afraid of a few auxiliary cavalrymen?"

"I don't mind admitting it, they scared the shit out of me. At the very least I expected them to confiscate half my stock, and I wouldn't have been a bit surprised if they had tried to warm my backside over the fire."

Lenc had to agree, "I can only think they were in a good mood, which is not something you often see in a squadron of cavalry. Let's have something to eat, and be glad they've gone."

Anton grunted and went back to preparing their food, while Lenc poured a beaker of cider and squatted near the fire. Suddenly he was startled from his reverie by the unmistakeable sound of a single horse and cart approaching.

What now? he thought as he stood to greet the new arrival, but yelled with relief when he recognised Gobann the blacksmith waving from the cart.

"We meet again," said Gobann as he gripped Lenc's proffered arm.

"You are a welcome sight and no mistake," said Lenc. He shouted to Anton who was cowering round the other side of the cart. "Come out, he's not going to bite you. He's a friend."

Nervously Anton stepped round the side of the cart. "Is this the blacksmith from the village?" he asked.

"I am indeed, and very pleased to have caught up with you. Have you seen any Romans on the road?"

"Aye we've just had a visitation from a squadron of cavalry, but they didn't seem very interested in us. Hardly stayed to catch their breath."

Gobann looked serious, "I think they have bigger fish to fry. I reported the raid to the fort, but once they confirmed that it was Dobunni, not some fugitive called Caratacus, I realised I was wasting my breath, so I buggered off smartly and here I am."

The big man reached into the footwell in the front of his cart. "Here's my contribution to our evening's dining. Sorry it's not deer, but very acceptable for all that. However someone else can cook it." Anton's eyes gleamed as Gobann held up a substantial pot of cider in one hand and two brace of plucked and dressed woodcock in the other.

"Worry not," said Anton with a smile on his face for the first time that afternoon, "I think I can do those proud."

The next morning saw few signs of human life on the wide, tree-lined track, which was riven with large ruts. But guiding the cart along the smoothest route proved easy work as around them the landscape changed from meadow to trees, rowan, ash, birch, and oak, with outcrops of grey rock poking through the undergrowth. Gobann had taken the lead in his wagon which made sense, he was familiar with the road and was likely to know anyone they encountered.

The countryside started to unfold before them as they broke out from the shelter of the trees. The line of blue-grey hills was still marching along on their left, but up ahead Lenc could make out a gap, and in the distance what looked like a flat-topped cone, reminding him of the extinct volcanoes of Gaul. Nearer, and off to the right was a peculiar-looking outcrop pointing back towards Britannia. It was long and thin and he realised that this must be the feature that worried Agrippa. As a soldier he could understand the concern. An observation point on the top of this hill could warn of approaching armies with plenty of time to prepare. It could also be easily defended.

Lenc was already thinking of his first map, and looking forward to seeing what lay before him in the valley between the high points. The river would be a prominent feature.

When they stopped at midday, Lenc hobbled the horse, while Anton busied himself with unpacking dried meat and bread. He slipped down from the cart, arms full of food and a leather flask of wine. Gobann joined them with bread and cheese and more of the cloudy cider.

"I'm ready for this," Anton smiled happily, carefully lowering his bulk onto the grass.

They ate in silence, sprawled on the grass next to a bubbling stream with a clear view all round. Gobann paused in his chewing and looked at Lenc. "Keep close to me as we approach the settlement. There's a guard and they don't take to strangers. Just follow me and keep calm."

Anton looked a little alarmed at this, but Lenc shrugged and said the guards would see they were peaceable and meant no harm.

"These are troubled times, my friend, and people have learned to be safe rather than sorry. Just stick with me and we'll prevail," said Gobann.

By Toutatis, I hope so, thought Lenc fervently.

By late afternoon the range of hills on their left bent and turned to the west. Lenc noticed the turn came below an imposing hill with a shaped, quite distinct curve at its centre. The view from the top would be useful. As they meandered gently round the big hill, their destination finally came in sight. A green meadow flanked the river, and on the far bank a square wooden fortress crowned a rise, which Lenc studied with interest. Judging by sudden quick movements, they had already been spotted by sentries on the wooden wall, and as they grew closer, a small delegation appeared, following their progress closely.

Lenc wondered how they were to cross the river, which was about 30 paces wide, and curled round the base of the hill fort providing an effective defence. Smoke rose from several different places behind the wall, indicating quite a few family homes inside. They could see no sign of the entrance.

Gobann kept his horse placidly plodding on round the side of the rise, following the bank, onto the flat meadow with the fortified township on one side on its low hill, the river running under its walls, and the towering bowl-shaped hill on the other side. It was a picture of great beauty thought Lenc. He shouted to Gobann on the other wagon. "It's a nice spot, what do you call the hill?"

Gobann looked round and up at the hill looming over the meadow. "That's the Red Mountain. When the sun comes on it in the early morning, the whole hill has a red hue, and in the autumn when the bracken dies off, it goes a deep, dark red."

He jumped down from his cart and tied the reins of the horse to the brake handle, effectively tethering the animal. He walked back to Lenc and Anton then turned to stare up at the hill fort.

"This is as far as we go for now," he said. "There is a ferry across for the carts, but there's no real benefit in breaking our backs trying to get across when we can do just as well staying here in the meadow. Don't worry Anton, when the people see what you have to offer, they will find a way to you."

Lenc looked around at the meadow, spanning both sides of the river. It was a sweet spot, with plenty of grass for the horse, the river nearby and that curious bowl-shaped hill, towering over them. Maybe it would be better to stay out in the meadow, rather than cross the river to the fort, safer probably.

Gobann explained that he would need to get his cart across because he had deliveries to make. "But I can leave that for now."

Lenc turned and with hands on hips surveyed the wooden wall. Under the wall, a rope and plank footbridge was the way across, and next to it a system of ropes and a flat raft which could sway animals and carts across. He still could not see a gate or entrance and assumed there would be a way in further round, where, away from the river, the ground would probably slope more gradually. The defences were made entirely of large tree trunks, about 20 feet high. All right for deterring local raiders, but wouldn't even break the stride of a legion cohort. A small township had sprung up outside the gates as building room inside was used up. Obviously not too bothered about an attack, thought Lenc.

"It's best you come with me, I can introduce you to the town's elders. They may not welcome you with open arms otherwise," said Gobann, breaking into Lenc's reverie.

"Yes, of course," he replied, with an enthusiasm he did not particularly feel.

Gobann nodded. "There's our path."

They walked over the footbridge, then almost immediately started to climb up towards the shadow of the palisade.

It was a crisp afternoon with no hint of walking into a firestorm, no birds fell out of the sky, no strange animals crossed their path and the sun was not suddenly blacked out by the moon. Lenc felt a little disappointed that on this potentially momentous occasion there were no portents at all. Perhaps that was a portent in itself. He brightened at the thought. Surely that must be good, let me be treated with complete indifference and I may live through this yet.

The approach was bare, cleared of trees and undergrowth to provide a field of fire from the parapet round the top of the wall. They ambled on, gradually rising away from the river, arriving at a track cresting the top of the long slope and leading to the settlement.

The track was muddy and pitted with rain-filled holes, and deep ruts showed where a constant stream of carts had ploughed the ground. They danced round the water-filled ruts until they arrived at the open iron-studded double gate. Either side were wooden towers the height of the main wall, joined at the top by an enclosed balcony. He could see only the heads and shoulders of the sentries who looked impassively down on them.

Outside the wall a township of its own with mean wattle buildings clinging together for support had started to spring up. One of the buildings was a tavern with men standing and sitting outside. All conversation stopped as the drinkers paused to take stock of the newcomers. Then the silence was smashed as Gobann roared out a ribald greeting which was met by good-natured waves and jeers. Once again Lenc thanked his luck in befriending the big blacksmith.

The gate was open but as they approached, guards stepped out into the middle of the track. They were wearing swords but so far had not drawn them. Their faces and arms were covered in swirling blue tattoos under forests of matted curly hair. They seemed wary, and ready to react if necessary.

Lenc had already decided this was Gobann's show, best all round to leave it to him.

Gobann paused at the gates, his passage blocked by the guards. He shouted at them to stand aside. They stood still, then one of the guards shouted back: "It's orders, no strangers in the town."

"I'm no fucking stranger, you arse," Gobann shouted. "Let me in."

The guards conceded that Gobann was no stranger, then demanded, "But what about him, who is he?"

Gobann stood back. "Why he is a friend of the Silures," he boomed. "This man was with me when we slew five, no six Dobunni in our village. You won't get friendlier than that."

The guards conferred and eventually came to a decision. "Gobann, of course you can come in, and the stranger can come under your escort. But you must go to the council lodge and they can decide what to do with you."

Gobann twisted and looked at Lenc, who shrugged his assent.

They walked through the gate, and the soldier in Lenc noted with interest how badly designed it was. Up above, the narrow walkway meant the defenders would have difficulty drawing an arrow without exposing themselves to full view. Hard against the wall were low, mean houses with thatched roofs, just inviting fire arrows. Puddles and mud were everywhere, churned up by humans, cattle, dogs and horses and there was a ripe smell of sewage, human and animal.

The town and the people may seem poor, but they did seem well fed and the houses were well maintained. Maybe they had riches in other ways, he thought, cattle, perhaps or horses, although he could see no evidence of them. Maybe there is some trading here after all.

He was content to follow the lead guard as they walked deeper into the mire of the town. He tried not to wrinkle his nose in disgust at the stench, it was no worse than any other town, he admitted, but why can't they live like the Legion? It doesn't take much effort to syphon your shit away from your house. Eventually the path, just wide enough to take a horse and cart widened out into a square with another, but bigger mud and thatch hut in the centre, which must be the chieftain's hall.

Surrounding the larger building within the square were several market stalls, selling produce, meat and fresh vegetables, river fish, beans, bread and beer. The stalls were well stocked and the produce looked wholesome. He thought he knew of at least one fat trader who would be pleased to buy a mountain of food.

One of the guards motioned him to stop while Gobann and an escort went through the open doorway, ducking their heads under the low eave.

Lenc stood at his ease, outwardly without a care in the world, but inwardly surveying the scene, assessing how defendable it would be. His thoughts were arrested by two small boys looking at him gravely. They wore sack-like tunics, down to the knees, and were barefoot and filthy. They looked at him as if he was a strange animal descended from another planet. Which as far as they were concerned, he could well have been. One small boy wiped a line of snot from beneath his nose and said something to Lenc in a language he did not understand. It was obviously a question, in Silurian, he imagined.

Lenc crouched, still smiling, careful not to let the hem of his tunic touch the muddy ground. He pointed to himself. "Lenc," he said.

The two boys shrieked, turned tail and fled. Lenc's escort laughed and spoke in Gaulish. "They think you are a night demon, come to steal them from their beds. Maybe they think worse, maybe they think you're a Roman spy."

"No chance of that," replied Lenc through his stitched-on smile, "I avoid those bastards like the plague."

Before the guard could follow up on this interesting line

of conversation his friend reappeared, followed by two men with brown capes over their shoulders. These two were older, and although wearing makeshift tunics and barefoot, carried themselves with an authority that marked them as village elders. The tattoos on their faces were almost obscured by ingrained dirt and wood fire smoke.

One of the men addressed Lenc in an unfamiliar language. He guessed that he was being asked his business and replied in Gaulish. The man turned to the guard and rapped out a sharp question. The man offered the translation that Lenc was a trader with goods to sell and barter.

The elder grunted and asked another question. The guard pointed vaguely south east, towards the river-meadow. The man grunted again and gestured for Lenc to enter the chamber. Immediately he coughed and his eyes watered, the room although quite big, was thick with smoke from a smouldering fire in the centre of the mud-hammered floor.

Animal skins and antlers decorated the walls and a large dark brown hide provided a suitably regal area for the man sitting in solitary splendour on a roughly carved wooden chair, who studied Lenc with interest. He was quite old, at least 40 and like the others had tangled hair reaching to his shoulders. He had a long beard which failed to hide the blue tribal tattoos adorning his face which disappeared under the neck of his sack-like tunic, and reappeared snaking down naked arms.

Unlike the others, over coarse leggings he wore rudimentary leather shoes laced up to the knees. Behind him stood elders, and guards in dark robes. There were four other men in floor length woollen robes, tied at the waist who somehow managed to keep slightly distant from everyone else. They had the pious look of priests, and seemed a bit cleaner than the tribesmen. Behind them, sitting near the wall were three young women. Lenc spared them a second glance. They were wearing shawls over their heads so he couldn't see their faces, he just wished he was talking to them, rather than these old men.

He joined Gobann near the centre of the room and listened hard, trying to pick up the sense of the Silurian dialect as the blacksmith gave a highly embellished tale of the fight with the raiders. The sense of his story was fairly obvious and Gobann's arm actions gave enough theatre for Lenc to follow his account.

He told how the Dobunni sent a raiding party, killed their mercenary sentries then fell on the village to rape and pillage. He stretched his arms out wide to give emphasis to his tale, as he described how Lenc went for the raider watching the horses, while he went through the huts, caving in heads with his big hammer. His gruesome account of catching a raider about to rape a Silurian woman brought an angry muttering from the throng, which changed to a yell of appreciation as Gobann described, graphically, the mess his big hammer made. "It did a lot more damage than that bastard Dobunni's hammer did," he roared to general appreciation. He described, in great detail, Lenc's skill in fighting the raiders even the part played by the swamp boy came into the tale.

At this the older man leaned forward with his arm raised, dismissing Gobann. "You Gaul, who are you and what do you want here? Our tribesman Gobann the blacksmith, thinks you are friendly, yet you fight like a Roman. You look like a Roman," he said in Gaulish, more of a statement than a question.

Lenc inclined his head. "I am here to trade. My name is Lenc of Alesia and I come from the mainland. Pray tell me who I am speaking to."

The man shrugged his cape about his shoulders. "I am Verico, a chieftain of the Silures, I command our tribe's northern territories, and you are a spy," he asserted forcefully.

"What?" retorted Lenc. "Spy on who, for who? I can assure you that my master and I wish to trade with you, bring you goods and, yes, take goods home with us for the betterment of all. We are certainly not spies, but come with entirely peaceful and honourable intentions."

The chieftain sat back in his carved wooden chair. "You expect me to believe that?" he sneered. "The Romans are busy building their forts not a day's walk from here. And what happens when they have finished? No doubt they will try to enslave us. But they won't find us as easy as the Dobunni. We intend to fight. There, that's a piece of news a spy could take back to his masters."

There was vigorous nodding of heads round the room at this statement. "Perhaps if we sent your head back to the fort on a plate it would show the foreigners that we mean business."

"It would show them nothing," protested Lenc. "They don't even know we are here. We thought that as we don't want to trade in Roman territory, we would avoid them. We came up from the coast without going anywhere near the forts, and we would be more than pleased to keep it that way."

Verico shifted on his seat. "What you say may be the truth, but I doubt it. Why would you avoid the Romans? You would come under their protection."

Lenc looked down at the hard-baked mud floor. He hung his head and said haltingly, "Sometimes, Lord, the Romans with all their pious ways don't really understand that a man has to make a living any way he can, and if he has to pay taxes then that can mean starvation. We avoid the Romans and their taxes as much as possible."

Gobann nodded eagerly. "Lord, my purpose in being here, as well as bringing some ironware, is to tell you how this man saved our village. I was on my own when we were attacked and without him I would be dead, and our womenfolk raped and dead, or taken for slaves."

The elder looked at them keenly. "I understand what you are saying, but I am not convinced. We will see. In the meantime, you may camp in the meadow beneath the town and set out your stall. Now as to the matter of taxes, I am not averse to adopting this Roman practise. It is a good name for something we have always done. Take payment from strangers who cross our lands. How much should I be levying on you, eh?"

Lenc put on an expansive air and spread his arms, opening his hands. "Lord, we understand that we need to pay to be allowed to trade here. Perhaps when we have set up our camp you and your family may wish to come and see our wares, and you will have a better understanding of the good things that we bring to delight you."

There was a general buzz of conversation round the smoky room at this new development, and Lenc could see the payment of a bribe was going to save the day. He was beginning to relax as he watched the elders discussing the strangers and the goods they had brought with them, when there was a commotion at the door opening.

As everyone stopped chattering and turned their gaze to the entrance, Lenc looked round slowly. The opening framed a young man carrying a spear, who had to duck deeply to get into the room. He was obviously a warrior.

Unlike the other tribesmen that Lenc had seen, this one was quite tall. He wore an iron cap on top of his matted hair, which, although as dirty as the others and as curly, seemed lighter in colour. He had the obligatory facial tattoos, was heavily muscled, wore a sword at his waist and looked ready for a fight. He looked round the room, taking in the tableau then addressed Verico. "Lord, why are you talking to this Roman piece of shit. Let me spit him with my spear and we will send him back to his people with his cock in his mouth."

Verico smiled fondly. "Trenos, your zeal does you credit, but I have decreed that they can set up camp in the meadow so we can see their goods. They will want to buy from us as well."

The warrior bristled at this "Why don't we spit him anyway? Then we don't have to buy his goods, just share them out. Silures don't trade with foreigners, we enslave them or kill them."

Verico smiled again. "Maybe that will happen yet, in the

meantime let us welcome these strangers to our land and hear from them about the mainland and the Romans. This one may yet be helpful. I would hear more of this attack by the Dobunni. It sounds as if they have created some unfinished business for us."

Lenc heaved a sigh of relief when Trenos turned and stormed out of the council chamber. He had thought his time was up in that grimy, smoke-filled room, but he was under no illusions. He and the young Silurian would meet again, and blood and iron would likely be involved.

CHAPTER XVI

The meadow camp site was idyllic. Once Anton had stopped moaning about not being allowed into town to trade, he settled down quite happily in a sheltered spot near the river, with the settlement looming on its hillside above them. Gobann decided to join them in the camp after dropping off his ironwork, and parked his empty wagon nearby. It was too late to open their stall that afternoon, so Anton announced that he was looking forward to an early start the next day.

The meadow spanned the Wysg which meandered through, cutting oxbows and in some places, steep banks where the constant action of the river eroded the soil. Lenc could appreciate the strategic advantage of the settlement, with flanking hills either side, a properly fortified stockade dominating the valley, the key to Cambria.

The Red Mountain to the south was the start of the high ground which stretched away, he knew not where. It was a strange looking mound and Lenc noted the angle of the early morning sun, rising directly to the left of the mountain, throwing a distinct shadow, etching out the contour of the curve to the front. He had never seen such an odd-shaped feature. The lower slopes were thickly covered in dense woodland, which stopped abruptly about half-way up. From there, above the tree-line, the hill was russet red, and green, studded with purple heather, bracken and grey protruding rocks. He stopped, entranced to watch a cloud shadow scud across the face of the bowl and marvelled at its speed as it traversed from east to west.

He turned and looked up at the wooden stakes of the hill fort. They thought themselves secure behind their barricade, he supposed, but the Legion could roll through without much of a backward glance. He hoped it never happened.

Anton hummed an obscure tune as he set out his stall. There were woven fabrics in bright colours, warm wools, all manner of cooking utensils and pots, knives and axes, needles made from cat bone, bright trinkets and jewellery, and a selection of herbs, eastern spices and exotic perfumes. There were also small pot containers of the pungent fish sauce, a staple of the Legion's diet, so effective at masking the acrid taste of turned meat.

"Pearls before swine," sniffed Anton disdainfully. He explained to Lenc that the trick was to stock lots of small items, which the locals might wish to have and could be bought at reasonable prices. "I don't expect to get much coin. But they know how much a deer hide or a sheep skin is worth, that's what I want to be taking home. There is worthwhile metal under this benighted place, but unless it's gold or silver, it will be too heavy to carry back in profitable amounts, so I'll just stick with hides."

They had a few visitors that day, enough to make Anton hopeful for the immediate future. Most had come out of curiosity as strangers were in fairly short supply. Some older women came along to feel the fabrics suspiciously and examine the pottery. A couple of men tried the Basque daggers with bronze handles, but it was the young girls of the tribe who raised Lenc's interest, attracted to the colourful trinkets and bright fabrics.

He watched with a smile, as Anton displayed the attractive colours, persuading them to feel the quality of the cloth, holding it against them, making them giggle at the thought of wearing a gown made of such finery.

Lenc was particularly interested in the three girls he had noticed in the council chamber. He recognised them by their clothing, and now that their headscarves were abandoned he was pleased to confirm their fresh, youthful vibrancy. The leading girl was a beauty. The others seemed to defer to her as she teased out the cloth, and discussed its merits with them, while on the sideline Anton smiled ingratiatingly at his prospective customers.

Lenc moved closer, amused at the age-old confrontation between buyer and seller. The girl was now haggling for the cloth. The language barrier seemed to mean nothing against the universal language of trade. Anton asked her how she would like to pay for this sumptuous length of cloth, because, of course, no disrespect, but such a fine piece, woven by highly skilled craftsmen on the finest looms in the Roman empire, naturally comes at quite a price.

The girl clearly did not believe him. She fingered the cloth sceptically while Anton protested its exquisite quality.

In the end the girl took some coins from a pouch hanging on her belt with a 'take it or leave it' attitude. Anton seemed taken aback at the effrontery of this chit of a girl who displayed such a disregard for one of the finer things in life. "At least double," he protested.

"One more and that's it," she replied holding out the extra coin between thumb and forefinger. Anton appeared to be about to protest some more, then reluctantly accepted the handful of coins and handed over the cloth. The others crowded round her, to admire the fabric. As they were doing so, the girl looked up and saw Lenc watching her. He bowed slightly at the recognition. She looked down quickly and returned to her friends as they bustled back towards the town.

"Well you've broken the ice at least," he told Anton.

"Yes not a bad start, " agreed the trader, "not a bad profit, could have been better but she seemed to be someone special by the way her pals spoke to her, so maybe her buying will encourage others."

As the day wore on the number of curious visitors slackened, and Anton decided to pack up the stall for the evening. Suddenly he was more interested in food.

That evening, after a meal of chicken, beans and fresh baked bread, all bought from the market stalls near the council chamber, Anton and Lenc lay on the sweet grass by the river sipping the local cider. Anton made a face of distaste. "It'll never replace a good red wine," he grimaced, "but needs must."

"Oh I don't know," responded Lenc, "it's really starting to grow on me. I'm actually getting to like it. Better than their ale anyway."

They lay there for a while, Anton making plans for setting out his stall in the morning, when Lenc decided it was time to wash the dust of the last few days off his body and clothes. This triggered a nostalgic flash-back to Gesoscribate and cavorting in a steamy bath with two fantastic young ladies. Why that was less than a week ago, he thought incredulously.

Shaking his head and smiling at the memory he wandered upstream through the meadow alive with wild flowers and the hum of bees in the evening light. To his left the Red Mountain towered above the meandering river like a sentinel. The valley climbed and the hills either side seemed to crowd in making them appear even more precipitous. A dark place for an attacking column.

But this evening was no time for sombre thoughts. There was no doubt about it, this was a special place, green and fertile, but more attractive and somehow more welcoming than the terrain he had been used to on the other side of Britannia. Must be the hills, he thought, but even though they were a reminder of home, their green gave them a softness and beauty quite unlike the steeply jagged, rocky hills of Gaul.

It's good country, he thought, all we have to do is sort out the locals and it will be a nice place to live.

A bend in the river with a small beach of sand and pebbles, and some shrub giving an element of privacy, seemed ideal as his open-air bathroom. He unbuckled his wide leather belt and stripped off his tunic. With boots off, he stretched his toes luxuriously in the sand, then untied the string holding up his long undergarment, and, naked, stepped cautiously into the river. The water swirling round his feet was quite fast moving and cold. He gasped as he waded deeper, and the cold crept up his legs. He waded up to his thighs, gasped a mouthful of air and belly-flopped into the water. The shock to his torso soon receded as he tentatively tried a few overarm strokes.

He was surprised that his ribs, apart from a slight twinge seemed to be fine. Then he rolled over, floating on his back, as the current swept him away from his clothes. He put his feet down on the pebbly bottom and pushed himself back against the tide. It was a pleasant sensation and he felt a tingling all over as the cold water flowed and surged round him. After a few minutes swimming against the tide, he waded back to his clothes, and one garment at a time gave them a vigorous scrub in the river. When he had done all he could to remove the grime and sea salt he draped his clothes over a bush and waded back into the river, where he idly lay in the shallows, covered by the water, but deep enough for the current to pull at his legs.

After an invigorating swim out into the centre of the river, he splashed around, like a playful otter, enjoying the feel of the smooth stones under his feet. The water was clean and clear and felt good following the time at sea and the travelling afterward. He carefully removed the bandage on his arm, and tossed it onto the bank. The stitches underneath were red and puckered, but showed no sign of infection, no tell-tale smell of putrefaction. He unwound the constricting bandage holding his ribs tight, and apart from some fairly livid bruising they seemed fine, at least they seemed to be healing. He wondered if it was the sea-water he was soaked in on the boat crossing that cleared his aches and bumps and disinfected the severe knife gash. Or maybe it was those two versatile whores on the other side of the Channel. He smiled at the memory.

Then he flexed, waiting tentatively for pain to remind him that he was simply human, but everything seemed fine. He clambered carefully from the water, watching where he put his feet on the slippery stones. Some were quite large and moved easily under him, the last thing he needed right now was a turned ankle. Still naked, he recovered his sodden bandages and squeezed them out, rubbing sand and grit into the blood stains on the cloth. The stains would not go, but at least they faded and from a distance would not look quite so alarming. He squeezed the water out as best he could and draped them over a bush to dry.

Tentatively he felt his ribs, the bruising had gone down a lot and apart from a few occasions when he had twisted, he felt no pain from them. I'll see how I go without the bandage, he thought, if they start to hurt I can always put it back on again.

To give his wet kit more chance to dry, he decided on one last swim and carefully felt his way on the slippery stones before splashing into the water. After a short, invigorating swim against the tide, he rolled over and was thinking of getting out, when he heard people approaching. The noise was of female voices, laughing.

He looked round desperately, but his clothes were too far away, he would have to get out of the water and scramble over to them. They would be up with him before he could manage that, so did the next best thing and edged down into deeper water. Which was getting distinctly cold.

The voices came round the bush and stopped. He was facing the river but he was aware he was the centre of attention. He did not dare look round, better to pretend he hadn't heard them.

Suddenly one spoke in a sharp tone. "You there, what are you doing?"

He shuffled a bit further into deeper water and turned onto his stomach so that he could see his questioner. He saw two girls, late teens, both strikingly beautiful, wearing loose shifts. He recognised one as the haggler at Anton's stall. She had tattoos of what looked like blue vine leaves twirling up her left arm and disappearing under the sleeve. She didn't seem upset, just curious.

Her hair was dark and curled down beyond her shoulders.

"What are you doing?" she asked again.

"Why I am bathing and washing my clothes," by Mithras she was pretty.

"Why?" she demanded.

"Because I was dirty, and my clothes even more so."

She stopped to think about that. "So when you get dirty you get in the cold river and let the river clean you?"

"Something like that, yes"

"Again, why?"

"Because I feel better clean."

She screwed up her face. "It seems like a lot of effort when you are just going to get dirty again."

"Then I wash again."

She considered this. "Perhaps I should try it." The other girl had been hanging back during this exchange, giggling behind her hand. Now she came forward and in a shocked tone said: "No mistress you cannot."

"Of course I can, there's no harm in it," she replied, imperiously. She was wearing a green sash tied round her waist, which secured a tunic of a fabric woven into coloured patterns. She untied the sash, letting it fall to the riverbank, then pulled her tunic over her shoulders. She was naked underneath.

Hesitantly she stepped over the pebbles and felt the water beneath her toes. "Ooh its cold," she breathed. Her skin was goose bumping and her nipples, small and brown began to wrinkle and harden.

Lenc tried not to look down at the curly brown triangle between her legs. Instead he concentrated on the ivy leaf tattoo, which, now that she was closer, and naked, writhed from the back of her hand up her arm and disappeared over her shoulder and down past her shoulder blade. It was an intricate piece of work in several colours and got thicker and broader as it climbed further.

No, it was no good, even in the cold water, he was becoming aroused. He moved his legs, swishing the stream.

The girl gingerly waded out deeper and when up to her waist splashed in over her head. After some seconds she launched from the bottom and shot up with a whoop of joy. She splashed back and dived again, for a second exposing her delicious rump. He was not quite sure what to do. So best thing, probably, was to just sit back and let events take their course.

The other girl was now sitting on the bank, her legs demurely drawn up under her gown, watching the proceedings with interest.

When the mermaid eventually surfaced, she waded a few steps towards the bank, then rolled over, staring at the blue sky. Her small breasts bobbed tantalisingly on the surface. Again, she rolled over and smiled impishly at him. "What's your name?" she asked. He told her, and added, "what's yours?"

"I am the Princess Veldicca, daughter of Verico. I saw you at the council chamber."

"That's nice," said Lenc cautiously, "I've never met a princess before."

"Well you have now," she returned triumphantly.

"And what is your friend's name?"

"She is not my friend," retorted the Princess Veldicca, "she is my slave, she looks after me and is my chaperone. If you are so interested, her name is Ailid, but she is only an Ordovica."

She levered herself up against the current and stepped carefully past him to the bank. He tried to appear uninterested, as if beautiful naked girls walked past him all the time. She clambered onto the bank and lay down dripping next to her slave, who passed the princesses's gown to her which she slipped on, still dripping. They put their heads together and started giggling about something.

He felt fairly sure the giggling was about him, but there wasn't a lot he could do about it. Besides he was getting a bit chilly.

Looking down, he saw his manhood had tactfully shrivelled in the cold water, so he stood up on the stones with the water lapping his ankles. He stumbled out, striving to maintain his dignity. To slip and go sprawling stark bollock naked in front of these two giggling girls would scar him for life.

He managed the task with some aplomb and casually disentangled his tunic from the bush. It was still wet, but he used it to wipe most of the river water from his body. His underdrawers, too, were still damp, but he pulled them on anyway. Ailid watched as he struggled with the soaking linen, then giggled and put her hand over her mouth. He looked down and saw that the damp material was transparent, fully revealing his thatch of black hair and manhood in the sleeping position. He hurriedly pulled his drawers away from his body, abruptly closing the peepshow.

He sat down on the grass a discreet distance from the girls. "Well I hope you enjoyed the show," he said. "I must say, I'm not used to an audience when I bathe."

The Princess sat up, "Yes, I can see I was quite forward," she conceded, "but I was curious about you. We don't get many strangers here, and the ones we do get, hold little interest for me. You however are different. You are near our age and you know of the outside world, which I would like to hear more about. Besides it must have been quite an experience for you to bathe with a princess of the Silures."

Lenc estimated at least a ten-year gap in ages but he let that go. He realised that the princess would probably report back everything he said, so would have to choose his words with care.

"I am from Gaul, and used to work on a farm. We were very poor and when I was old enough, my father enrolled me in the Legion, but I didn't like that. Marching all over the place, killing innocent people, being shouted at, so, first opportunity, I was off. Then when my fat friend asked me to help him with his venture in the uncolonised parts of Britannia, I thought, why not, it would be something different and certainly a change from before. And not a Roman soldier in sight."

The princess leaned forward: "but why come so far west? Surely there is more profit in the east? They have better farmland, are more prosperous and under the Romans more desirous of the things your friend sells."

Lenc feigned reluctance. "It's the Romans that are the problem," he admitted. "When you join the Legion, you don't get a choice about when you leave, so I deserted, unfortunately if they catch me, they will execute me."

He held out his arms to show his spread-winged stork of the III Gallorum and on the other arm the running boar of the XX. "See, I carry the mark of an auxiliary and the Legion, but I don't have the mark of discharge or the right documents. I dare not get too close to the Romans, so when Anton said he wanted to try his luck ahead of the Roman frontier, I decided I would join him.

"I'm no trader, but I help with the heavy stuff, and if necessary I persuade people to pay rather than steal."

She nodded: "That must be very comforting for him."

Lenc had the feeling this conversation might not be going quite the right way and now was the time to make an exit with whatever dignity he had left. He was pulling on his damp tunic when he looked up and saw a group of warriors striding purposefully toward them. "Oh shit," he breathed.

It was Trenos and a small band of his men and he did not look happy. He stopped at the Princess's side. "What are you doing here Veldicca?" he fumed.

The Princess Veldicca lay on the grass, propped up on one elbow, her companion watching the exchange avidly.

"I would have thought that was perfectly obvious," she replied coolly. "And what business is it of yours?"

Trenos visibly checked himself. "You know full well what business it is of mine. You are promised to me and I do not take kindly to you throwing yourself at every stranger that comes to our town."

She looked at him appraisingly. "I am a Princess from an ancient line and it is true my destiny is mapped out for me, but I don't have to like it. Until we are married I will go where I please, with who I please. Now you are starting to bore me, you had better go. And take your playmates with you."

With that, she rolled over onto her tummy and stared across the meadow, completely ignoring everyone present.

Trenos stood there clenching and unclenching his fists. He spun round to Lenc looking for someone to vent his anger on. "And what are you doing here, Roman? If I had my way you would have been sent back from whence you came, only minus your head."

Lenc smiled. "I came down here to bathe, as is our habit in the civilised world." He laid emphasis on the word civilised. "The lady wandered by and was interested in what I was doing and decided to try it. I believe she enjoyed the experience."

Trenos took a step forward, his hand on the handle of his sword.

"You bastard," he breathed. "Fetch your sword, we'll settle this right now."

Lenc shrugged. He could see no way out of this quandary. If he failed to fight he would be marked as a coward and treated with contempt, that is if they let him live, but he knew that if he accepted the challenge he would either die, or if he looked like winning, the tribesmen would step in and he would still die.

So there was only one course of action, he picked up his sword belt and unsheathed his short sword.

Trenos smiled as he unsheathed his own sword, at least as long again as Lenc's gladius. Suddenly there was a shout from across the meadow and both men turned to see a big man, beard and wild hair flowing in the breeze hurrying towards them.

"Lenc," he shouted, "can't you go anywhere without getting into a fight?"

Lenc stood up from the fighter's crouch and breathed out.

"Gobann," he smiled. "What are you doing here?"

"Looking after you by the look of it," laughed the big man. He turned to Trenos and held out his hand. "There is no danger here, Trenos, this man is a friend. As I told the chief in the meeting house, this stranger stood by my side when we were attacked by bastard Dobunni. Between us we killed a good fistful of them. Without him, our women would all have been raped and we'd all be dead. Put the sword up, he is a friend."

Trenos stood undecided, then Gobann strode across to Lenc and took his arm.

"Come my friend, I was bringing some cider to the town and I think I have made the mistake of leaving a skin or two with your fat friend. Let's go and see if he has left any for us."

He turned to Trenos: "I wish to drink with friends and I count you in that number, you're welcome to share a pot."

Trenos saw he was beaten. Muttering curses, Trenos reluctantly put up his sword, and Gobann beamed. "That's the way, drinking is always better than fighting. Least, it is in my opinion."

The Princess sat up. "Am I included in this invitation," she asked haughtily.

She looked first at Gobann, then Lenc and finally Trenos. Lenc was saying nothing. Gobann took in the scene and looked from Trenos to Veldicca. "My lady, from my point of view I would be honoured, but if your intended feels that we are too rough and ready to share a drink with their betters, that of course is up to him."

With an expansive gesture he attempted a bow, which ended up as an outstretched arm showing the way back to the camp. He took Lenc by the elbow and steered him along the riverbank, as the princess and her companion stood and brushed the grass from their gowns. They followed Gobann and Lenc, leaving a glowering Trenos and his friends to reluctantly bring up the rear.

As they approached the camp, Trenos had a word with his men, who passed the group and walked back to the town.

Trenos caught up and made a point of shouldering his way through to walk at Veldicca's side until they arrived at the camp, where Anton fussed over an open fire. "There you are," he said brightly, "Oh and guests too. Perhaps we should sample that cider now?"

"You mean you haven't got stuck into it already?" asked a surprised Lenc. Anton looked affronted. "Are you suggesting I would have started on my own, without waiting for you? Apart from a small sample, just to ensure it was drinkable you understand, I never touched a drop."

Trenos was quick to sit next to the princess, smiling triumphantly at Lenc as he did so. Innocently she turned and smiled winningly at her betrothed, suggesting that it was hardly fair for visitors to be providing the refreshment perhaps he would like to go to the town and bring some more to drink and some mugs. Lenc hid a smile as Trenos tried to think of a reason why he should stay, but with a face like thunder he eventually stood and did Veldicca's bidding.

Before leaving he flashed a sideways glance at Lenc as if to say, "You dare, you just dare".

Lenc smiled and eased himself down onto the log into the recently vacated place.

Anton fussed and handed out mugs to his guests. "I am afraid you ladies will have to share," he said. "That is my full complement of mugs."

The princess smiled, "No matter, we are quite happy to share until he returns."

With the glowering Trenos gone, the mood of the impromptu picnic lightened considerably. Encouraged, Gobann told a risqué story to Ailid, which she listened to while giggling between her fingers and Anton nearly tripped over a wayward log while also trying to follow the tale, and fuss over some bread and olive oil at the same time.

Lenc turned to the princess. "You will forgive me I hope, but I am keen to learn your ways. I was surprised when you just took your clothes off and joined me in the river. Where I come from a lady would never do such a thing."

She appraised him coolly. "Perhaps in your country, women are a protected species. Here we grow up to fight, learning swordplay with the boys. When my father raids he expects me to be with him, and when eventually he becomes too old I shall lead our people. I would not last five minutes if I was more interested in coloured ribbon and fine clothes than training to be a warrior.

"My body is mine, but as a princess I cannot do with it as I please. I cannot lay with a man until I am wed, then I am expected to carry our ancient line forward with an heir who will one day take over from me as the leader of our people."

He thought about that for a minute, then asked, "So Trenos is your intended?"

"Yes he is," she replied. "He came to us from the south and has proved himself to my father, so when the Bard names an auspicious day, we shall be married."

"Well I can see why he was annoyed when he saw us at the river," replied Lenc. "He must look on me as a real threat."

"You flatter yourself Roman, you are no threat at all. I shall marry Trenos and that will be that. Afterwards when I have provided the tribe with a successor then I will take my partners as I wish."

Lenc tried not to look shocked, but his attempt to appear as a man of the world failed. Veldicca saw straight through him and laughed out loud.

"I think I have shocked you, though I can't see why, we obviously have a different way of living to you."

He thought about that and had to agree.

The princess looked at him with a small, secret smile and continued: "Men of course are for procreation and making babies. My girlfriends and slaves like Ailid are all I need to ensure that I can face the wait to be married and have full sex with a man."

She looked at him from under her long eyelashes and for a moment he was confused. "What, you mean that the company of your girl friends is enough to stop you thinking of sex?"

She laughed again, and Ailid simpered, trying to hide her face with her cloak. "By the great gods, but you have led a sheltered life. We have evenings together and we can pleasure each other. Men, in this respect are an unnecessary encumbrance."

"You mean you…" Both girls collapsed in fits of giggles. "Of course we do, what do your womenfolk do before they are married off? Do it themselves?"

Lenc shrugged. He definitely felt out of his depth. "I don't know," he confessed, "It's not something I ever thought of."

"What's better," asked Veldicca, "that I am pleasured by one of my girlfriends, or I look for a man who is only out for his own gratification and could leave me with an unwelcome stranger in my tummy? Men, especially young men, have no idea or interest in the needs of women. It is for us to learn and enjoy, then when married, pass this knowledge onto our men." She tossed her hair dismissively.

"Men get so excited at the thought of doing it with a woman, they just charge in, sow their seed then roll off, thinking if they had a good time, then their woman must have too, that is if he thinks of it at all. Our sexual needs are taught and taken care of within the sisterhood."

Put like that, Lenc could see the advantages. But it still didn't seem right.

CHAPTER XVII

As dawn broke on a cloudless morning, Lenc was struck by how perfectly in tune the path of the sun seemed to be with the meadow, the river and the Red Mountain that signalled the start of the high ground of southern Cambria. He watched fascinated as the first glint of sun burst silently, from the river downstream to the east, painting the mountain a rustic shade of red. During the day it would complete its arc across the sky, completing its trajectory in the west, upstream sliding back into the river again. "The Red Mountain," he breathed.

This profound thought made him smile as he prepared for his first mapping expedition. He put some bread and cheese in a hessian bag with his wooden writing tablet and a skin of water and set out towards the rising sun. He had decided to use the wax covered tablet for his field expeditions then re-draw his maps onto the more expensive papyrus sheets he had carefully carried from Camulodunum in a leather roll.

From the river meadow, he skirted the town and set off for the hill which had aroused the pathfinder's interest. It was set in rolling fields and forest, running due west to east, a long ridge cloaked in trees almost to the top. But what was especially interesting was its northern end, where a section of the hill had split off, creating another, smaller hill giving a dramatic impression. It hadn't been visible on the way to the town, but now he could see it in all its peculiar glory. Lenc could not imagine what force of nature ripped the great chunk of hill away from the main body, to slip down and away, but still look as if giant hands could come along and press it back together and make it whole again.

As he walked, he became aware he was not alone, and glancing behind saw an older man walking on a path which was about to join his own.

"Greetings," offered Lenc as the man drew level. He was wearing a gown with a hood, gathered at the waist with a twisted rope and round his neck an ornate Celtic charm. It was quite large and obviously heavy, the main design appeared to be of a spreading tree, but looking closer the base of the tree was a human figure and the branches and leaves were growing out of his head. Small brightly coloured stones set into the metal flashed as they caught the sun. He was carrying a thick ash staff and smiled as he returned the greeting in Gaulish.

"I saw you arrive, Lenc isn't it?" he smiled. He looked a kindly man, with silvering hair and skin brown and wrinkled like a nut from too long outdoors. "And I apologise for the distrust shown to you. The people here are set in their ways and afraid of strangers. Their experience is that strangers tend to bring danger to their doors. As a man of faith, I prefer to see the good in people, but I still carry a big stick. I am known as Cainos and I look after the people's spiritual needs," he smiled.

"And where are you going this morning, priest?" enquired Lenc.

"My destination is yonder," he replied, gesturing upwards to the hill.

"In which case we can keep each other company," replied Lenc, "for that's where I am bound. I was keen to see where part of the hill seems to have gone its own way."

"They are called Ysgyryd Fawr, which means shattered mountain. As druids we believe that everything in life has a significance so what is the significance of this hill suddenly shattering? It was a long time ago, but can you imagine the huge forces at work to cause such a terrible split. To us it is a holy place

186

and we come here to pray and contemplate.

"Being on the hill gives an inner peace and you can truly communicate with your ancestors. At the four crossroads of the calendar we light bonfires on top of both the big and small hills. We drive our animals through between them to increase fertility, and of course it works with our newlyweds as well. We have a fine crop of children after the hopeful parents walk between the fires."

They left the small, orderly fields behind as they started to climb the gradually steepening foothills. Within the leafy canopy of the trees, there were paths criss-crossing each other through the vegetation.

"There are deer here, and boar, so plenty of meat, if you can catch it," said Cainos. "There are also our own animals, safely tucked away against marauders."

The forest was cool under the canopy, but the going was easy as rainwater drained quickly from the wide and well-trodden path, and there were plenty of cattle and horse tracks. The sun cut through the canopy to dapple on the leaves, creating a curious half-light, and sound seemed to be dampened among the foliage. Lenc could see how the townspeople would see this as a mystic place.

They continued plodding upwards through the dense forestry, the light improving as they climbed, then at last broke out of the treeline onto the windswept hill.

The path narrowed and zig-zagged, following the easiest route, and as they rounded the hill, Lenc could appreciate what a vantage point this would be. As the vista opened up before them, he could even see the estuary where they landed, far off in the distance.

Here there was only tufty grass and patches of low-lying heather blasted by the wind. Above that nothing but clear blue sky with clouds rolling at speed from the high country before disappearing inland. A metal brazier stood on the edge of a sheer cliff, packed with wood and kindling and covered in a protective leather mat.

Cainos saw him looking at the brazier. "It's a signal fire, if the boys at the other end of the saddle see enemy, one will run here and set fire to the beacon. Then they will run down the hill and help get the stock in, while another runs to the town to report."

Simple but effective thought Lenc.

Finally they cleared the brow and looked along the saddle, studded with rock formations stripped of soil by the ever-present wind. In the distance, he could just make out a small stone building with a conical roof.

"It's a shelter, very welcome to the people who keep watch up here," explained Cainos. "And because this place is so close to being our spiritual home, it is also used for contemplation and prayer."

The going on the top of the saddle was easier and, as they walked along, Lenc could make out where the smaller hill had been part of the bigger hill before it split away. It must have been quite a sight, he thought, to see it happen.

"Do you have any idea what caused the split?" he asked.

Cainos shrugged as if to say, who knows? "For the gods' amusement? Lightning? I have heard of such cataclysmic movements of the earth. Your guess is as good as mine."

Cainos had been recognised by two boys, sheltering in the curious stone building with its bee's nest roof. They greeted him formally and with deference, and replied quickly when asked who was keeping watch.

"Come and see," said one of the urchins and led them round the building, where, poised on the edge of the steep slope was a small stone hide, simply a curved wall, big enough to protect two men at most. It was occupied by a third boy, studiously scanning the terrain into Britannia. Lenc had to admit, it was one hell of an observation post. To the north he could see the line of hills disappearing into the distance, with two odd shapes at the end of his vision, both with an angled flat top but one a steeper angle than the other. Turning east he could see another line of high hills with a valley running between. In front of him, the land fell away to a thick canopy of trees, stretching as far as the eye could see, to the south was the Wysg and the sea away in the distance. The view was breathtaking.

"This is quite a vantage point," he admitted grudgingly.

The priest Cainos nodded. "From here we should be able to see raiders coming in good time to prepare our defences and get our livestock in. I expect we will eventually have to defend ourselves against the Roman invaders, although I think we should get plenty of time when they do come, they move so slowly."

Lenc said nothing, he did not like to contradict the priest or pass on that the might of Rome may be slow in coming but it was inexorable and would crush everything in its path when it did arrive.

Cainos excused himself and went to the shelter to talk to the boys. Lenc stood there, gazing out at the landscape, trying to commit it all to memory. He wondered if he dared risk starting a sketch. Probably not, he thought reluctantly. Better just get it down back at the camp.

He roused himself and noticed a band of rain sweeping in from the western hills. He had no idea how fast it was travelling, but he knew that before long they were going to get caught in a downpour.

He shouted to Cainos, who poked his head out of the shelter. "We're about to get wet," said Lenc pointing to the rapidly approaching rain. "Are you ready to go, or are you staying a bit longer?"

"I will stay here for a while," replied Cainos, "but you go along, I shall wait out the rain and come back down then."

Lenc nodded his assent. "Yes I really should be getting back, my employer frets if I am away too long."

He waved and started back along the saddle. He glanced at the approaching rain and was glad he had thought to bring his cloak, by the looks of things he was in for a soaking. He picked up his pace and pulled up the hood of his cloak. Suddenly the rain was on him, slashing down as the wind threatened to rip his hood off. He held it tightly as he tried to negotiate the steep and now muddy path.

At the end of the saddle, he dropped down the hill, into the cover of the trees, which gave some respite from the elements.

He carefully picked his way down the track through the trees until the path started to level out. Thankfully the downpour eased as he neared the edge of the forest and when he did step out of the treeline, it had just about stopped. He was properly soaked but a strong walk would soon dry him out, he thought.

When he reached the river, he walked round, under the wooden wall of the town to the footbridge and crossed to the meadow. There was a small crowd at the wagon, and Anton was holding forth, extolling the virtues of his stock. Lenc gave him a wide berth but Anton saw him and shouted imperiously, "There you are, better late than never, come and give me a hand with my customers."

Lenc tried to ignore him and gathered his small set of paints and brushes then, with a sigh of exasperation, turned to Anton, "Not now, I've got something to do which can't wait."

Anton opened his mouth to argue, but Lenc was already hurrying out of range. He walked to the riverbank and found a secluded spot to stretch out his precious parchment. Quickly, he marked in the main points he had registered from the high vantage point on the Ysgyryd and when they were on the parchment, selected colours to fill in the salient points. The map soon took form as he remembered details from his walk and the view from the top. In one corner, he jotted details of the numbers of boys acting as look-outs on the top, and the signal beacon on the closer end of the saddle. He also mentioned the hidden corrals of sheep and cattle.

Eventually his furious scribbling came to an end and he paused to check his efforts. He made a few changes, added some detail and then stopped, satisfied with his work.

He had just packed his sketching tools into his bag when he suddenly realised he was not alone. Approaching him along the river was the Princess Veldicca, idly chewing a length of grass.

She acknowledged that she had been spotted and took the grass out of her mouth as she approached, while Lenc casually stowed his bag inside his cloak.

"What are you doing?" she asked..

"Nothing at all," he replied, "just watching the river and contemplating my life."

"Well that won't take long then," she replied, scathingly.

Lenc reflected, "all I know is that things can always be worse, and usually happens when you least expect it, so live for the moment."

Veldicca looked at him steadily. "That is very true, especially for you. My father wishes you to come with us to the high country, to a meeting of the tribe. It will be quite a gathering."

Lenc tried not to show his interest. "And where will this great meeting take place?"

She gestured vaguely behind her. "Up there, on top of the Black Rock. The tribe only comes together for special occasions, or when something momentous is being considered. And there is nothing more momentous than the danger we are facing right now."

"You can tell your father that I would be honoured to accompany you to your council meeting and I look forward to it with great interest."

"Hmm," said Veldicca. "My father does not know whether to trust you or not, so for the time being he will keep you close."

CHAPTER XVIII

A chill mist rose from the river as the tribe filtered into the meadow. The early morning sun was obscured by cloud, making a cold start to what promised to be an even colder day. Lenc was to travel in the chief's entourage, which he didn't mind because hopefully it would mean time with Veldicca, although that would depend on whether Trenos was going to be present.

As well as the warriors, men and women, there were families, with children, some on horseback, but most on foot, but all looking forward to meeting relatives and friends at the tribal gathering. They waited patiently for the royal party, all wrapped tight in their cloaks.

"I wish they would make less noise," grumbled a voice from under the wagon. "A fellow can't sleep with that row going on."

There was an air of anticipation as the travellers called out to friends and exchanged jokes and insults. It gave the day a fair-like quality, which Lenc supposed it was. This was to be a great gathering, so there would be much feasting and drinking, and no doubt some courting as well, definitely something to look forward to.

Eventually there was a stir, as the warriors turned to greet the royal party. Across the meadow, Verico led the cavalcade, some 40 horse, all carefully combed and groomed. The chieftain led his royal party, one hand gripping the reins, the other on his hip, as he gazed imperiously ahead. His wool cloak was arranged over his horse's flank, and he wore his long hair tied back with a short piece of rope. He paused as he arrived at the campsite and motioned to Lenc to fall in behind.

Lenc acknowledged the command and looked around for Veldicca. As he spotted her, he noticed Trenos, bare chested despite the cold, spur forward and pointedly position his horse next to the princess. He glared at Lenc, and defiantly rested his hand on the hilt of his long sword. Lenc nodded in understanding and diplomatically fell in behind.

At first the trail followed the line of the river on a relatively flat extension of the meadow but when the river turned to the north, the column carried on, and almost immediately started to climb a steepening valley. The track wound its way into a thick beech forest, gradually getting narrower, forcing the riders to bunch in.

The path up the Rock was picked out of sheer cliff, and etched in the surface were lines of black coal across the face. Some of these seams were spider's web thin, but others were bigger than a tall man standing. Lenc made a mental note to include this geological gem in his next report, the Legion was always looking for supplies of coal.

They made slow progress as the track climbed away from the valley floor. A narrow but fast running stream crisscrossed the path, crashing over rocks, creating pools and narrow fissures where the water all but disappeared.

There was little light in the forest, even less as the steepening banks closed in on them. The riders let their horses make the pace, trusting them to find their own way.

As they climbed, the trees thinned out, replaced by bare rock, rising sheer above them. The rush of running water became louder as they passed spectacular waterfalls, cascading down the bare face of the hill. In several places, rough planks had been laid to ford the streams as they thundered their way down to the river below. A wild place, thought Lenc, which could swallow a legion without a trace. He wondered, not for the first time, whether the effort to subdue this wilderness and its people was really worth it.

His horse, like the rest, was surefooted enough to be left to plod on by itself. There were few passing places, so he could not even relieve the monotony of gazing at a different horse's arse. How long would the journey take before they broke out into clear mountain air?

Then at last, a diversion and a welcome one. Waiting, backed off the track was Princess Veldicca, sitting demurely on her dappled horse, her long hair blowing in the strengthening breeze. She was wearing a riding cloak, gathered round her to ward off the biting wind, her long sword easy to hand in a scabbard attached to her saddle. She was wearing an impish and secretive half smile, as if she had been caught out doing something naughty.

"Where's Trenos?" asked Lenc.

"He's gone ahead to warn the council of our arrival. I don't suppose we shall see him until we get there." She didn't seem concerned in the least at this.

"Then perhaps you will ride with me, Princess."

"Well thank you, of course I will, and you can tell me all about what the ladies in Rome are wearing."

Now that certainly was something. To be describing the finer points of Roman fashion with such a beauty carrying, and used to using, the three foot of iron hanging from her horse, would be strange enough, but he knew his knowledge of the subject would not suffice for such an imperiously demanding mind as Veldicca's.

"Princess, much as I would like to impress with my knowledge of fashion, I fear you would find me out straight away," he floundered. "This is not a subject I know anything about. I have never been to Rome, and have no idea what even the grand ladies in Camulodunum wear."

Veldicca hid her smile behind her hand. "It is I who should apologise, I am teasing you. I would have been very surprised if you could hold forth on such an insignificant matter, but my friends were agog to know, so I thought I would ask. My biggest fear was that you would drone on for ages about cloths and colours and hair styles, and I know I would have fallen asleep on the back of my horse before too long."

Lenc laughed, mightily relieved. "Then let's continue the journey and you can tell me where we're going and what's going to happen."

It was late afternoon by the time they arrived at the meeting place, a collection of some 20 standing stones, arranged in a circle. Lenc wondered who on earth had taken the trouble to manhandle them to this place, each one at least the height of a man. Quite an achievement, he hoped it was worth it.

The tribesmen who had already arrived from the south hailed the newcomers as they gratefully slid from their mounts. After stretching aching limbs, the work of setting up the camp started with tents being pitched and fires started.

The council would meet the next morning Veldicca said, then seeing that Trenos had rejoined the band, rode on to find her father.

Lenc passed a fitful night. He had no tent, just his bedroll, but thank the gods the rain stayed away. He woke as dawn was breaking and sat near a campfire, chilled to the bone. He chewed on hard bread and some cheese, while the camp gradually came to life. More riders were still coming in, and judging by the way the tribespeople were drifting to the standing stones, the meeting would be starting soon.

The chill wind blew unopposed as two druids dressed in sombre woollen robes made some sort of incantation. Then Verico stepped past them and into the centre of the stones. He looked round at the Silures tribe, now probably more than 2000 warriors, plus families. There was an expectant hush as they pressed in, the better to hear.

"People of the Silures, we have lived in the shadow of danger for as long as we can remember. The tribes around us are sworn enemies, and they will wipe us out if they can. That is if we don't wipe them out first." This brought a shout from the assembled mass, and Verico raised his hand.

"But now, a new threat may well consume us. The Romans are steadily getting closer, the fort at Burrium is proceeding apace, and they are sending out more and more patrols into our land. We either accept them, pay their taxes and tribute, or we fight. Our land is defendable and we know they are not invincible."

There was a general murmur of agreement from round the stones. Then Trenos stood. He looked at Verico as if asking for permission to speak and received a nod of assent.

He was barefoot and carried a spear, with a long sword trailing from his waist, and over his shoulders a heavy fur cloak. His legs were covered in heavy cloth trousers held at the waist with a leather belt and leather straps round the lower legs. Despite being bare-chested, he showed no sign of feeling the cold.

"The Romans are many and we are few," he said, his voice carrying on the wind. "But we can wear them down by sudden raids and ambushes when they least expect it, then retreat back to the high country. They can follow if they like but we will be ready for them. The Romans do not like our way of fighting and will have to answer for it.

"They will only take so much punishment then will slink away to find easier prey. And of course if we catch a few bastard Dobunni along the way, so much the better," he added, grinning wolfishly.

Don't you believe it mate, thought Lenc.

Once again Verico held up his hand to silence the chattering that broke out when Trenos finally sat down. "We have one amongst us who has proved his worth, someone who is familiar with the Romans and the way they fight," he shouted. "He also seems to know why they are here and why they want to conqueror us in the first place. I must confess it's a mystery to me. Will you let him speak?"

At this Trenos and several of the other younger warriors rose angrily to their feet. Trenos, said, "What need have we of this intruder's knowledge. Do we know anything about him? Is he one of us? I hear he was once a Roman soldier and in my mind, once a Roman always a Roman."

Some heads nodded, but more shouted, "Let him speak."

When they had quietened, Verico nodded to Lenc who stepped forward. "Your chieftain is of high birth among the Silures. He wants only what is best for the tribe, and he senses an alternative to fighting the invaders. Yes I have fought as a Roman, but the reason I am here now is that I am no longer a Roman soldier. I cannot go back, or will face certain, painful death. What I can tell you is that they will keep coming."

Verico stopped the ensuing melee of angry voices, and when he had silence motioned to Lenc again. "You mentioned another path that Rome would have us take, can you tell us of that?"

Lenc breathed a sigh of relief. At last he could try and persuade this warrior race to step back from annihilation. "Rome wishes to extend its empire and remove the threat of attack as far as possible. For that reason it has no real reason to enslave you. If you show that you are willing to welcome the Romans, the benefits to you will be great. Rome will bring peace and stability to Britannia and opportunities for trade and enrichment."

"We are not children who need guiding," interrupted Trenos. "We have been running our affairs in ways handed down from father to son for generations. We have no need of them or their laws or their taxes either. I say we fight them as we have always fought. Hit and run raids, small attacks so they never know where we're coming from next, then fade into the high country where they will never find us.

"They will be so afraid and demoralised they will soon decide to give up and find peoples they can defeat. I say fight them and keep fighting until either we are dead or we push them back into the sea and they can sail all the way back to their thrice-damned

Rome."

With this he drew his sword and raised it triumphantly aloft as his followers gave a united roar of approval. Verico caught Lenc's eye and shrugged. He knew there would be no more talk of negotiation with Rome. Lenc knew it too, and for once was afraid. He had grown to like these people in the short time he had been among them. Now he feared they would suffer the fate of all those who defied Rome, death, servitude or slavery. He turned away, despondently, hardly noticing a messenger on a foam-flecked horse riding hard to the gathering.

The messenger sought out Trenos and quickly passed on his news. Trenos nodded sagely, then raised his sword.

"I have news that at this moment a column of Romans is seizing grain and livestock on the plain," he shouted. "They look ready to try their luck in the high country, but can't have any idea of their danger. We will ambush them in strength, take their plunder and kill all of the bastards."

The warriors surged forward, roaring their defiance. Trenos saw Lenc standing at the edge of the stones and called over to him, "Hey, Roman, why don't you come with us and I will show you how we kill your people?"

Lenc looked at him and said carefully, "I will come with you, but I will not raise my sword against the Legion. By the same token I will not raise it against the Silures. For you, however, I could make an exception."

"Brave words, Roman, one day perhaps you may have to live up to that boast. I look forward to it. Today we celebrate with the tribe and tomorrow we ride. It will be a momentous day for the Silures."

Lenc thought feverishly about his dilemma. He could see no clear way out, he knew he was being watched so could not leave the camp, but he must get word to the Pathfinders of the impending attack. He would have to take a risk.

The camp was like a wasps nest with tribesmen bustling from

one family to another. The young warriors were excited about the raid and the older ones were talking to anyone who would listen about raids they had been on. The women were preparing the fires and meeting friends and relatives. When the raiders came back, there would be lamenting because some would be killed or wounded. But that was always the way.

Lenc found Trenos surrounded by his warriors. They were laughing and joking, confident of their skills and abilities.

"So do you have a plan, great general?" asked Lenc. Trenos laughed. He had scored a great victory already today and was inclined to be expansive.

"If I have learned one thing about you Romans, you do not like to be ambushed in your column. About 800 of your troops are, as we speak, marching towards the high country south of here where they have never ventured before. They've already sacked and pillaged on the plain and collected grain and cattle, which will slow them down. Unfortunately there are a lot of obstacles that have suddenly appeared on that road, which will undoubtedly slow them even further. When we have finished with them we will have their plunder as well. Come and be amazed at how simple it is to defeat the Romans."

That afternoon, Lenc sat by a cooking fire and chatted with the tribes-people who would speak to him. The top of the hill was bare, so the Pathfinders would not dare to get too close, although he knew Agrippa would give his eye-teeth to know what was being said. He had no doubt they would be close, so it was up to him to get out of the camp and let them find him.

The light was just starting to fade when he took his chance. He murmured to one of the warriors sitting at the fire that he had an urgent call of nature.

"That mead's powerful stuff," he said apologetically, "I think it's given me the runs." The warrior grimaced, then guffawed, "well don't drop it near me."

Lenc responded with a grunt and strode quickly from the

camp. He headed for a fold in the ground on the way back toward the valley they had ridden up. He was pretty sure the Pathfinders would be somewhere towards the trees, but knew he did not have much time before he was missed.

He scrambled down into the fold which, at the bottom was studded with clumps of grass, standing in brackish water. Almost at once he heard a clicking sound, but in the gloom could not see anyone. He stopped, untied his undergarment and squatted. A disembodied voice said: "I hope that's not loaded."

He cursed under his breath. "I have an urgent message for Agrippa. There's a big patrol out from Burrium, sounds like a cohort. It's heading towards the high country south of here and will be ambushed when it rides into the hills. You don't have much time."

"Got that," came the voice. "You better fuck off smartly, they'll be looking for you."

Lenc agreed and pulled up his drawers.

He hurried back to the camp prepared to take the jokes about his delicate stomach from the warriors. He had done what he could.

CHAPTER XIX

The gathering broke camp before sunrise, the warriors quietly saddling up, ready for the journey to the ambush site. They moved out with a resounding send off from the tribe ringing in their ears, travelling throughout the day, south, down a gently sloping valley. The hills were high above them, steep and forbidding and seemingly bearing down on the column. Small streams tumbled down, running into each other and making bigger and bigger causeways. The line of trees, rowan, oak, beech, only marched so far up the thin soil of the valley slopes before being defeated by wind and cold.

By now there must have been nearly 900 warriors in the raiding party, some on horseback, the majority on foot. The foot soldiers travelled light, just their weapons, a blanket thrown over a shoulder and a small pouch of dry potage their only food. Descending from the high country and plunging back beneath the treeline gave welcome relief from the swirling wind, but it was no warmer under the dense canopy.

Trenos finally called a halt at the top of a steep valley, as both light and temperature were dropping. He called for his lieutenants and quickly sketched a rough map as they crouched in a clearing.

"We are coming down the main valley," he explained, mainly for Lenc's benefit. "And we are joined by two smaller valleys coming in right and left. Our interest is the eastern side, which is where the Romans should be tomorrow. Our forces will be divided into three and will attack on my signal. The first group will be the highest and will cut off the advance party. The second group will hit the middle, while the third will let the rear party pass and attack up the track.

"We will move into position on the north side of the valley, and prepare traps on the south side just inside the trees. We can attack as far as the track, but remember, the traps don't take sides.

"The column will advance up the valley, which starts off quite gently and then gets gradually sheerer, until eventually the track will force them into a maximum of four men, or two horses abreast. My scouts tell me they seem to be very confident and haven't thrown out a proper screen. It also looks as if they don't know the terrain they are advancing into. They'll soon find out," he said, grinning wolfishly.

"They will come to a sharp bend in the track, where the few scouts they do have will be isolated and out of sight for long enough for us to dispose of them."

He looked up at his lieutenants. "We can be hidden in the treeline as they march past, and at the signal we'll fall on them with everything we've got. It should be a complete surprise. Are we all clear what we have to do?"

The plan was simple and, Lenc realised, potentially devastating. If the cohort blundered into this ambush, only iron discipline would save it. But he knew that they would be at a distinct disadvantage trying to fight in an unfamiliar formation, or no formation at all.

Lenc watched Trenos moving among his men, sharing a joke, clasping a shoulder, instinctively encouraging and inspiring. He appreciated that the young warrior had no idea that he was acting as a good officer should, ensuring that his men knew they were part of the team, and were all in it together.

Trenos saw him staring and smiled. "Well, Roman, tomorrow you see how we fight your people. They think they are invincible and they probably are if allowed to fight on their own terms. Unfortunately for them we don't do it that way."

Lenc shrugged. He knew the legion would take casualties, but he also believed they would win in the end. For every legionary slaughtered tomorrow, another ten would take his place.

"Are we bedding down here?" he asked brusquely.

"Yes, we will eat, then try to sleep. We will be in position before first light and we expect the Romans up this valley by mid-morning. They're camped below and already scouted their way forward. It's very handy that they have shown us their intended route."

Lenc managed to stay inscrutable but inwardly he groaned. The cohort must think the track up the valley was clear. He desperately hoped the Pathfinders warning would arrive in time, but that was in the hands of the gods.

He was glad to accept the offer of a bowl of warming stew and a hunk of hard bread from one of the women warriors. From a distance the woman was no different to the men. Her hair just as straggly and unkempt, blue tattoos on her arms and neck, and a rough wool shirt over leggings. She wore a dagger on her hip, but her long sword was carried in a scabbard on a cross-belt which, while she was eating, lay by her side, handy for her right arm. A small embossed shield completed her weaponry.

He noticed one of the male warriors scouring out the stew pot. Clearly the woman's duties did not extend to cleaning. There were no women in the Legion, but he had fought women on several occasions, and very soon learned not to dismiss them. He wondered how good a fighter she was.

She smiled as she realised he was looking at her. "Will you fight tomorrow, Roman?" she asked.

He shook his head. "No I have already told Trenos I would not lift my sword to the Legion, but I told him I would not fight the Silures either. Tomorrow I will be a bystander."

The woman shrugged and stirred her stew. "Do you think we will win?"

"Possibly," he admitted. "It really depends on how alert the column is. They've been out on patrol for several days without any trouble, so may be off their guard. But if they are alert, as they should be, that will be an entirely different matter."

The woman reflected. "No good worrying, we will do our best and hope that is enough. I pray it will. Now I must go and check on the men building traps. They will most certainly be a nasty surprise."

She stood, stowing her bowl and spoon in her bedroll and settled the sword cross-belt on her shoulder. Then with a nod to Lenc, walked through the forest to the track where he could hear the sound of digging. He knew the attack would come from one side of the track, and the column would instinctively fall back into the trees on the other side. In a few short hours, the Silures could create some deadly traps in the undergrowth. He only hoped the cohort held its discipline.

Lenc lay on the hard ground, wrapped in his cloak. Usually he could sleep well enough, even with a battle looming the next day, but after fitfully turning most of the night he was glad to see the first flush of dawn through the trees. A mug of warm honey mead was welcome to take away the chill of the dawn and he sipped gratefully. All around him the warriors were silently preparing themselves for the coming fray. No words needed to be said as they moved out towards the ambush.

Trenos found him and gestured for him to follow. "We will be on the higher ground so we can watch and control, the warriors know what to do and need no more orders."

They climbed the slope of the valley, until they broke out of the treeline. From there they could look down on the steep sides of the slope as far as the bend round which the column was expected. About 900 warriors were concealed in the dense woodland along the track, and although he could not see them, he could feel their presence. He hoped the cohort had the same sense.

A jumble of large stones jutting out of the heather and bracken seemed to be the command post. "This is the place," Trenos confirmed as he spread his fur cloak on a smooth rock and sat down. "Our information is that the column set off at dawn so should be with us by mid-morning. They only had four scouts out on horseback, but that could change as they get further up the valley. We've not troubled them for some time, so hopefully they will think they are safe enough.

"Unfortunately the baggage train has headed back to Burrium, they obviously didn't want to try and bring loaded wagons up the valley," Trenos grinned. "We can concentrate on killing Romans."

During the next few hours, a succession of runners came panting up the hill with progress reports. Everyone was in position and apparently the cohort was proceeding as if on a routine march in Rome. Trenos smiled when one of his scouts reported that there were still only four horsemen scouting ahead of the column.

"Won't be long now," he said cheerfully. Lenc was in turmoil, clenching and unclenching his fists. He tried to look calm and collected but inside was raging. The Pathfinders must have failed to get the message through, what could he do to save the cohort?

Suddenly he realised with a start that Trenos was watching him closely. "So the Roman still cares for his comrades?"

Lenc swallowed. "It's not easy preparing to stand by and see men die."

Trenos laughed, "You don't have to watch if you don't want to."

For the first time since the tribal council, Lenc realised that he had a chance to slip away but what could he do then? The trap was about to be sprung, and he still had his mission to accomplish.

Suddenly Trenos stiffened and pointed down the valley. There on the track, slowly advancing were the four scouts, riding two abreast, completely at ease.

I don't believe it, despaired Lenc, they're deep in hostile country, in a perfect ambush position, riding two abreast and chatting as if on a holiday outing.

He looked sideways at Trenos, who caught the glance and

slowly shook his head while half drawing his sword.

They watched the drama being played out below. Despite himself, Lenc was interested to see how the scouts would be dealt with. The Roman column was still not in sight, but the scouts were disobeying standing orders in that one should have stayed on the curve, with the column in sight, while the others moved on. If they get out of this alive, thought Lenc, I will personally have their hides. But that was not to be.

With a shriek, the tail rider suddenly fell backwards from his horse, blood gushing from his temple from a well aimed sling-shot. The other three looked at him, horror-struck then in panic kicked their horses into action. All three tried to turn, bumping and jostling each other in their eagerness to get away and back to the column.

Suddenly six half-clad warriors burst out of the brush, attacking in pairs. While one man went for a horse's bridle, the other went for the rider. It was over in seconds. The warrior aiming for the rider got in close on the side away from the scout's spear. A quick slash to the man's hamstring and he was effectively rendered useless. From then it was short work to reach up and pull him down from the horse to be finished off before he could draw his sword.

As Lenc watched, sickened by how easy it had all been, the prized legion horses were led away, while the scouts were silently stripped of their armour and weapons.

The column was still not in sight, but as he watched, Trenos dropped his hand, the signal for a warrior standing near to bring a large animal horn to his lips and blow out a mournful note. Not very musical, but audible at a distance.

From their vantage point they could hear shouting as the noise of battle erupted. Suddenly the front ranks of the cohort burst round the bend. They were trying to stay in formation as best they could, being cursed and shouted at by their Optio.

Shields were up and many were peppered with arrows. Lenc

could not see the ambushers, content to stay in the trees and harass the sweating soldiers. He knew the cohort commander would instinctively try to fight through the ambush and re-organise his centuries of 80 men apiece before turning to the attack.

As they turned the corner, still under unrelenting arrow fire, the lead Optio bellowed at his men to make a defensive position. If they could only snatch a small amount of time, it should be enough to get into a disciplined fighting force. As they struggled forward Lenc saw the Optio grab two legionaires and close up shout in their ears. They nodded and started back down the track.

Gone to report, thought Lenc.

The dwindling band of the advance party finally formed up into disciplined ranks of four, but the shower of arrows from the trees kept the Romans crouched under their shields.

The Optio had obviously noticed that the fire was all coming from the northern slope, and although Lenc could not hear him, he could see the man barking his orders. He paused as one of the two messengers returned.

"He can't get through," said Trenos with satisfaction. "We have successfully split their forces. "We will deal with the front of the column and when they have been annihilated, we will turn on the rest."

The beleaguered Romans were backing into the trees, where at least they would have the open track as a barrier. Then Lenc remembered the traps. Almost at once more shrieks came from the denseness of the forest. Lenc could only imagine what foul delights awaited the desperate soldiers. This seemed to be the signal for the spearmen of the Silures to break cover and sprint the short distance across the track to throw themselves at the Roman shields. At last the Silures were taking casualties.

The defending Romans were hampered by the trees and undergrowth, but managed to form a semblance of a line and hack at their attackers, their short swords working well in the dense undergrowth.

Trenos watching the action intently, ordered his trumpeter to blow again. On the signal, at least 100 swordsmen stepped out onto the track. As the spearmen drew back, chests heaving with exertion, so the sword carriers moved forward. All along the line the warriors paused, waiting for the signal. Suddenly a Silurian, shorter than the rest stepped forward, his hair swept back and tied in a ponytail, a long drooping moustache hiding his mouth, and his blue tattoos vibrant as he raised his sword arm. He was shouting and making wild gestures. This small man, sword arm in the air, screamed out his challenge to his enemies to come out and fight, his aggression and fury only too real.

When that failed to get a response, the short warrior pointed his sword at the hated enemy and screamed out the order to attack. He plunged into the foliage, followed closely by his men and the noise of fierce fighting, although muffled by the trees was evidence of a desperate battle.

Trenos motioned to Lenc and his small group of warriors. "Let's go down, this phase will be over soon."

Lenc really did not want to get any closer but knew he had no option. Reluctantly he followed Trenos down the slope where already the sounds of battle were slackening. Trenos reached the track first and walked towards the conflict, head held high and hand on sword, every inch the warrior prince. As they approached the sights, sounds and smells of battle became stronger until they were completely overpowering. Dead and wounded Silurian warriors lay as if in embrace with the Roman soldiers underneath, who had taken such a terrible toll. The narrow track was matted with the dead and dying.

Trenos strode into the forest and reluctantly, Lenc followed. He didn't want to look at what he knew he would find. Under the tree canopy, the light was dimmer, but he could see how fierce the fighting had been. The rear rank of the Roman vanguard had blundered into the series of vicious traps, which as well as being devastating weapons had a crushingly demoralising effect on men already fighting for their lives. Lenc noted the tangle of pits, no more than knee deep, but laced with sharp sticks designed to lacerate feet and legs. From the smell, the tips had been smeared with human shit. Elsewhere soldiers were impaled on sharpened stakes which they had run onto while desperately trying to escape the carnage on the track.

The big Optio, who had done so much to lead his men, lay on the ground, surrounded by dead Silures, still clutching his sword, the cuts and slashes on his body a testament to the fight he had put up.

As Lenc stood with his head bowed, the blood-streaked Optio stirred and muttered something in Latin. An old, livid scar ran across the bridge of his nose, his features almost obscured by a slick of blood. Lenc could not hear and hurriedly went down on one knee. He took water from his flask and tried to bubble it into the man's mouth. As the cool liquid hit his face, the Optio grimaced and opened his mouth to take the water, then lay back. "Thank you stranger. I am not long for this world but that was welcome."

With a shock, Lenc suddenly realised he knew the Optio. The last time he saw him had been in the amphitheatre at Camulodunum when he first met Aurelius the intelligence officer. He must be part of the XX Valeria advance party, if the man recognised him, he was finished. The Optio lay back, an occasional grimace of pain crossing his features. With something approaching relief Lenc realised that the man was slipping away. He shot a glance at Trenos.

"He was a brave man and a good soldier," said Trenos softly. "His path should have led him to be a farmer, providing food, not travelling to other lands to kill people."

"He was a soldier, I expect that's all he knew," Lenc replied.

As he lay in a Celtic forest many hundreds of miles from home, the mortally wounded Roman soldier stirred and looked around. "Not a bad place to die," he said to himself in Latin.

A tribesman knelt over him. The man put his hand on the Optio's shoulder, who found the strength to grasp his arm. Again in Latin, the Optio muttered: "Finish me cleanly, my path is done."

Lenc bowed his head and in the same language, whispered, "I will make sure the Legion knows of the fight that you made and the way you tried to look after your men."

A puzzled look came over the stricken Optio's face as he registered this tribesman was talking to him in his mother tongue. Despite his pain, he concentrated and scanned the man's face. From somewhere came a distant memory of a place far away and an engineer interrupting weapon training. He struggled to hold the memory, and his eyes widened as the memory returned. He was about to speak, as Lenc quietly drew his dagger and leaned over, covering the man's body then stabbed him hard under the chin, up into his brain. The Optio spasmed and was still. Lenc stayed there for a moment, then slowly peeled away, holding the dagger to his chest. He bowed his head again.

Thankfully Trenos had wandered off, bored by the sight of a dying Roman, and Lenc quickly wiped his blade clean and sheathed it.

He continued to kneel by the dead Optio, thinking of his mission, and the dead soldier, who accepted his life in the service of Rome, and equally accepted his death in the same way.

As he sat there, head slumped on his chest, his thoughts were interrupted by a Silurian messenger, the woman from the previous night. She had come to report that they were holding the rear of the column with arrow fire, but the battle had developed into a stalemate. The column could not go forward or back but was well defended within their wall of shields.

Trenos nodded. "We can now release our men from the front and send them into the middle, that should give the Romans something to think about. Come, let's get a better view down the track."

Trenos strode on, followed by his lieutenants, leaving Lenc temporarily alone. He stood reluctantly, and coming to attention, saluted the dead Optio. Then, head bowed he walked after Trenos.

All around him the forest was alive with warriors flitting through the undergrowth, hurrying to their new positions. Cautiously they crept forward to the edge of the treeline. They were higher now, which should have given a better view, but still restricted by the density of the trees to the track.

Trenos studied the scene critically. He could see the standards of the column command group, and although there were many bodies piled up around, they were defended by their wooden carts and holding out well. He could see that the Roman defence was a hive of activity. They were re-grouping and preparing to take the fight to the enemy.

He bit his lip as he thought, knowing he was in danger of letting his great victory slip away. As he hesitated, the woman warrior Lenc had spoken to the previous evening joined them by a mature beech tree they were sheltering behind. "We are all in position," she urged. "If we wait, the Romans will take the initiative and our advantage of the terrain will work against us. If we allow them to fight on equal terms we will lose. We must attack now, before they are ready."

The woman's passion clearly showed through to the listening men. Without realising, she had grasped Trenos's arm, the better to reinforce her words. He carefully prised her fingers from his bare arm and nodded.

"You're right, give the signal, attack with everything we have, the length of the column." She stood back and gestured to the trumpeter, who moistened his lips and blew one single sonorous note which seemed to go on for minutes. He was gasping for breath from the effort when he finally released the horn.

With a rousing cry the warriors, men and women, flung

themselves from the shelter of the trees onto the waiting column. It was a long line to defend, and Roman shields were not designed for this sort of extended close-quarter work. The Romans fought like demons, hacking and thrusting over the top and from the sides of their shields, but were steadily pushed back as the Silurian spearmen swept in, jabbing and slicing.

The battle was going against the Romans, and Lenc could see that the command group had shrunk visibly. It's not often you get to see the utter destruction of a complete cohort of the pride of the Roman army, he thought grimly. He watched as the tattooed warriors, most of them naked from the waist up, launched themselves at the column. They were concentrating on the command group, and although they had no use for the glittering standards the Romans defended so bitterly, they knew this was the head of the snake. Cut it off, and the rest would die.

Suddenly Lenc heard the distinctive sound of the Roman cavalry call to charge. He stood on tiptoe but could not see anything through the trees.

Trenos snapped up. "What the fuck is that?" he demanded.

Lenc kept quiet but inside he exulted.

The woman ran off to find the answer and returned shortly. "It's Roman cavalry," she reported breathlessly. "They caught the rear ambush by surprise and went straight through them. They are coming forward along the track and the soldiers are following our men into the trees. Our men are running."

Trenos nodded and gestured to the trumpeter. "Sound retreat," he ordered. "We have had a great victory this day, but we must save our people."

All along the track the Silurians heard the call to retreat. Most were mystified and shouted their defiance, having no knowledge of the retribution galloping toward them. Some of the Silures helped wounded comrades up and dragged them into the forest, melting away leaving the dead, and the seriously wounded to their fate.

Lenc ran with the rest, through the forest and up to higher ground. At their original vantage point Trenos turned and looked back down the track.

"We have won a great victory this day," he thundered. "Men will talk about it for many years to come, and they will say this is the day we learned to fight and kill Romans, and stay alive to fight another day."

CHAPTER XX

Agrippa the Pathfinder waited for Lenc at their meeting place, a majestic oak on the edge of the forest east of Gobannion. "You did well to get that information to us," he said, as they clasped arms.

"We had to ride hard to Glevum to raise the alarm and managed to scrape up about 300 cavalry, then rode like mad men to catch up with the column. We could hear the battle from a long way off, but the Silures, so sure of victory never thought of keeping a look-out for a relief column, so we formed fours and battered into them. It was difficult in the trees, but we just kept going. It helped they were facing the wrong way, at least at first then they turned and ran."

Ruefully, he opened his cloak to expose a thick bandage covering his sword arm, blood seeping from near the wrist. "That's when I picked this up, but I count it a small price to pay for the damage we did. Mind you, it was a bit strange to be fighting as a proper soldier for once, even a cavalryman. But the lads did well.

"They wanted to follow the bastards up over the hills and hunt them all down but the chance of another ambush was too strong. They knew the ground and we didn't, so reluctantly I pointed this out to the Decurio leading the cavalry. He agreed it would be better to let us track the enemy while his men cremate their dead, look after the wounded and move what supplies and equipment were left back to camp. My men then quietly followed the enemy track onto the top of the hill where it split into different directions.

I bet within a couple of hours they were all safely tucked up in their stinking hovels."

Agrippa gripped the hilt of his sword. "I learned long ago it doesn't pay to get angry, but I made a promise that these bastards won't get away with it. When the time comes I shall happily rejoin the column to wipe away this stain on our honour."

Lenc nodded in sympathy. "I fear you're going to get plenty of chances in the weeks to come. They're triumphant now and know they can beat us. Their tactics are good and if they keep at it they'll give us serious problems. This campaign is not going to be easy."

"I hear you Lenc, but we will prevail," answered the defiant Pathfinder.

Lenc leaned forward. "I'd like to ask a favour, can you get a message back to Glevum? The Optio at the front of the column was a brave man and gave his life dearly. He should be acknowledged."

Agrippa looked at him keenly. "Did you have words with this Optio?"

Lenc looked into the distance. "Yes, I knew him from Camulodunum and spoke to him in Latin, he was about to reply, but Trenos was nearby, so I couldn't take the risk, may the gods forgive me, I had to kill him."

Agrippa leaned over and gripped Lenc's arm. "Put it out of your mind, son," he said vehemently. "From what you said the Optio was on his way out anyway. Now let's leave that and think of the future," Agrippa added, shifting his weight on the ground, wincing as he moved his injured arm.

"The Twentieth is on the move early, so will arrive sooner than expected, and that brigand Caratacus is surely on his way here. We've been pursuing him and his band of cut-throats across the country for weeks. It looks like he's making for Cambria where he can lick his wounds and raise an army.

"Well, we're not going to let him. We're going to keep harrying and pushing till he's found and then we shall remove him. Him and all his followers.

"Once in the high ground he could tie down two legions, and all the time getting stronger." The Pathfinder raised himself up and gripped Lenc with a look of blazing ferocity. "He must be stopped now."

Lenc nodded. "If he comes here, I'll find him, but I'm surprised you fear him so. After seeing what the Silures can do by themselves, I think the threat comes from them. Not some bandit with his tail between his legs on the run for weeks. So what's the priority, me dealing with this Caratacus or my longer term mission?

Agrippa nodded, "Right now, Caratacus has got his arse hanging out of his drawers. He desperately needs fighters, and who better than the Silures? If you stick with the tribal leaders, I fancy Caratacus won't be far behind. You can't compromise your mission by killing him, but you can let us know when he arrives and we'll take it from there."

Later, Lenc was seated by the fire in the meadows camp, idly staring into the flames, wishing he was anywhere else in the empire, when he felt the vibration of many horses approaching. He twisted round to see a band of warriors on horseback and chariots approaching with an imposing figure at their head. His blonde hair, swept back and tied with a band round his forehead, his cloak sweeping back over his horse's rump both spoke of a man used to being obeyed. His beard was also blond and curled, hiding a strong, lean face. By his side, on a chariot steered by a bare-chested warrior, was a startlingly beautiful woman, and clinging on, a boy of about 12 who, Lenc thought, must be the big man's son. Behind them came a retinue of mounted warriors, pack horses and slaves walking.

This must be the great Caratacus thought Lenc. From the cover of their cart, he watched with interest as the warriors dismounted and the slaves started bustling around, pulling tentage from the chariots and setting up a camp.

Caratacus spoke to the woman, then wheeled towards the town, followed by a small band of his lieutenants.

Lenc watched him go and debated whether he should follow, to find out what would be said when Caratacus met Verico but decided it could wait. He would find out soon enough.

That evening a dawdling customer was agog with the news that Caratacus would address the Chieftain's council. Lenc knew this was something he could not afford to miss, and made his way up to the settlement, casually nodding to the gate guards who looked him up and down suspiciously but let him through.

The chamber was packed with the council and senior warriors, and a throng of curious locals drawn by the unusual arrival. Lenc squeezed into the crowd and stood at the back so he could hear and see but not obviously be seen.

Eventually the Chieftain's retinue fussed into the room and as if on a signal, in swept an imperious Caratacus, flanked by personal bodyguards. He was tall and muscled, wearing a cloak but no weapons. His attendants were grim, big men, who took up position behind with their arms folded.

"Welcome to my home," said Verico, "please be seated."

"With pleasure, sir, your reputation goes before you, and you are known in my tribe as a wise counsellor and a fierce warrior."

The chieftain bowed at the compliment so freely given. Caratacus quickly dived into his story by describing the success of his band's hit and run tactics, which led to the ruse of his family forcing him out and claiming he was a traitor to the tribe. Since then he had been harried across the country to the west. Now he was ahead of the invaders with time to raise a great army and take the fight back to the Romans. He wanted to raise the tribes to fight together before the enemy chopped them down tribe by tribe.

"I am sure, Verico, you can see the sense of the tribes uniting in the face of this dangerous threat," he finished.

Verico hesitated and shifted back in his fur-draped chair, but before he could reply, Trenos sprang to his feet, eyes blazing. He looked straight at Caratacus. "You talk of big armies but you have been defeated every time you fought the Romans. We on the other hand damn near destroyed a whole legion, aye, and took much armour and weapons as a result. Our way is to hide and watch, then pounce. We can harry, hurt, kill, drive off their animals then fade away into the hills where they dare not follow. In time they will get tired and find someone else to try and conquer. It may take longer, but believe me Briton, we will defeat them."

"Your success does you credit," replied Caratacus smoothly, "but your way could take decades to achieve success. The Romans are no strangers to a waiting game. Believe me, they will still be here when we are in the ground and just memories around the campfires. But if we raise an army we can sweep down on them and give them such a hiding, they will never come back. Then we will push them back until they eventually disappear again into the sea."

He turned again to the chief: "My Lord, it is true that the Romans have been successful and we have been defeated every time we have faced them. But that is because the legions fight in a way we're not used to. They have discipline and stand on the field as one. This has taken some understanding, and I believe there is no man better than I to turn the tide and beat them.

"If I have your support, I will go north to the Ordovices and petition their help. With both tribes behind me I can then go further. I will send riders to the north even as far as the Picts in Caledonia, yes maybe even the Irish as well. I will unite the whole of the free country behind me, then when we start having successes, the people already conquered will rise up at their backs."

Verico nodded sagely. "There is much to think of here, and you have explained your cause well. Perhaps you will take food with us and tomorrow I will consult with the elders and we will give you a decision."

Caratacus nodded gracefully. "I am grateful Lord, and I look forward to eating with you as much as I look forward to a favourable decision from you."

As Caratacus and his entourage swept from the chamber, a hum of conversation broke out, stopping when Verico stood once again to speak.

"This is a serious business and one which the elders must discuss fully. Now leave us, go back to your homes and you will be told the outcome of our deliberations in good time."

Reluctantly Lenc found himself being swept out of the chamber with everyone else, he would have given a lot to remain listening, but it would draw too much attention to himself.

"Lord, you cannot promise our allegiance to this upstart," cried Trenos passionately. "He has lost every fight he has had with the Romans and now he wants to use our people to fight his wars, as his own have all been killed or cowed. We know how to beat the Romans and our way has been proved to be the right way."

Verico nodded thoughtfully at this outburst. "Trenos you are of course right. Why would we wish to join with the other tribes that we have fought for so long? Yes we will beat the Romans our own way, but what if we were given the opportunity to slaughter the Ordovices? What if we pledged our allegiance to this upstart and used it to infiltrate the camp of the Ordovices? All their warriors would be in one place and off their guard on their own land. In one night we could wipe the bastards out completely."

Trenos looked at him without expression. Then he suddenly let out a guffaw of laughter. "That's priceless. Who else could come up with such a plan? A masterstroke."

"Worry not, we shall take ale and cider, and plenty of food and announce a great feast to celebrate the coming together of the tribes," said Verico. "Our people will keep their heads and encourage the Ordovices to drink their fill. They won't know what hit them."

"Only, we'll have to do it to them before they do it to us."

CHAPTER XXI

That night, safe in his bed, Verico was visited by the dream makers. In his sleep he was aware this was to be an important visit because it followed a soaring eagle, always a portent of significant matters. Then he saw ranks of soldiers, Romans. They moved as one, a disciplined machine. He could feel the noise they made in their purposeful and grim advance as thousands of hobnailed boots crashed to the ground rhythmically. Then he saw a campfire. Round it were his people, wailing women and wounded men. He strove to see faces, but try as he might, could not get close enough.

He woke at dawn, his body bathed in a cold sweat. Dressing hurriedly, he called for his priest, Cainos, who arrived in an agitated state, rubbing the sleep from his eyes.

"What is it Lord, what's wrong, are you ill?" asked the concerned priest.

Verico paced up and down the bedchamber, clearly still agitated.

"I had a dream, many Romans, my people dead and dying, I need to know what it means before I make a great announcement."

He turned to the priest who, now composed, was sitting on a stool. "Tell me everything in your dream," said the priest softly.

Verico reflected, the memory still frighteningly vivid in his mind. He had never experienced a dream so devastating in its reality.

Slowly and carefully he went through it from the beginning, putting in as much detail as he could recall.

"I remember a running boar," he said hesitantly. "The soldiers were marching behind a totem of the boar and they carried this symbol on their shields." He hurriedly scratched XX in the dust. "I could not see their faces because they all wore helmets. Their shields were up and covered most of their bodies as they marched towards and past me. They just kept coming and coming.

"Then I saw a camp of my people. There were dead and dying and women crying, but I couldn't see the faces of the suffering people."

The priest pondered for a few minutes. Eventually he spoke. "This is an important message," he said slowly. "And we must get the interpretation correct. I will take your words to the Druid council, but it seems obvious that you must use great caution. It seems we are about to face confrontation with these Romans, what we do about that is the message in your dream.

"They must be fought, but I would say that the way of Caratacus is wrong. A head-on confrontation will end as your dream ended, and perhaps the tribe wiped out. Perhaps Trenos's way is right. Perhaps we should carry on the hit and run raids and gradually wear the interlopers down. One thing is sure. The people in the east have tried direct resistance and failed. We need a clever way."

Verico nodded. He had come to that conclusion himself, but the priest confirmed that he was on the right path.

"Meeting with the Ordovices in friendship with a view to uniting against the Romans is still a worthy cause," he said thoughtfully. "But I am going to tell Caratacus that we will leave it for a year, until we are stronger and see what the Romans intend. We will still do this but on our terms."

Verico smiled. Suddenly he felt better. A decision had been made and a weight taken off his shoulders. But he would still have the destruction of the Ordovices to savour.

"Call for Caratacus," he ordered the Druid.

Caratacus could hardly believe his ears. After all the positive words the previous night he thought the Chief's decision was a foregone conclusion. Now he was right back at the start.

"I am amazed Lord," he protested. "And disappointed. What has happened to change your mind? I thought you were of the same mind as I, that we would rise up and take the fight to the invaders."

Verico nodded. "I cannot fight the dream people," he said quietly. "If they show me my destiny, I only have one option, which is to protect my tribe. It is not my decision to make, I am just the messenger. I am sorry that it is not what you wish to hear, maybe the Ordovices and those tribes further north will be more forthcoming."

Caratacus looked at the chief, sitting calmly with the balding priest. With a last snort of exasperation, Caratacus turned and swept from the room, swirling his cloak to cover his body.

Outside, his face of thunder was enough to persuade any people he met to give him a wide berth. He mounted his horse and dug his heels into her flanks, surprising the animal enough to make her rear, before trotting on, scattering townsfolk from his path. When he cleared the gate, he kicked again at the horse, who also seemed to want to run. He hauled her back when they arrived at his small camp in the meadow, where Vellibia was waiting anxiously for him. She could see by the expression on his face that the meeting had not gone well.

"What is it husband, what did he say, are we to fight the Romans?"

Caratacus let out an exasperated snort. "The old fool had a dream," he sneered. "And because of that he wants to wait. I think he just wants to let others do the fighting and leave him to pick up the pieces afterwards."

Caratacus paced up and down while Vellibia could only watch anxiously. She knew better than to interrupt.

Suddenly he took a deep breath and smiled. "Sorry my love, I should not take this out on you. I need to ride and think."

He swung back onto his horse and motioned to the leader of his bodyguard. "We are safe here, and I have need of a little solitude. I will ride alone."

"But Lord you know that's not safe, we could be attacked at any time," protested his guard commander.

Caratacus reflected. "Yes, apologies, you are right, but only one man, perhaps yourself?"

"Of course, Lord." All Caratacus wanted was the wind on his face and the chance to think without interruption. Once clear of the camp he jammed his knees into his horse's flanks and let her run. The ride was exhilarating but when she started to flag he reined her in to a walk and patted her neck. He seemed to have a knack for taking out his frustration on others, he thought. He smiled as he said sorry to the horse who flicked her ears at the sound of the familiar voice.

After cantering past the town, the two horsemen rode up a slope to the east toward the oddly split mountain. Caratacus knew it was regarded as a holy place, but all he could think of was what a good view there would be into the hinterland.

They climbed steadily up the track letting their horses pick their own path and as they finally cleared the top of the ridge, paused and gazed silently at the dramatic view. At the end of the saddle was the look-out post, facing toward Britannia. People were sitting on the grass outside, watching their arrival.

"Welcome strangers," said an old man, dressed in a long woollen gown with a rope gathering it in to his waist. He sat, scratching with a stylus on a tablet. He had a kindly look and presented a smile. Caratacus had also noticed two young boys surreptitiously slipping stones into their sling-shots. Not everyone was welcoming, he mused.

He slipped off his horse as the man stood up, saying, "I am Diviciacus, trying to beat some education into these two young miscreants." The boys looked down at the ground and shuffled their bare feet.

"You are a druid?" guessed Caratacus.

"I am, and we come here because this is a holy place, where we find spiritual enlightenment, can you not feel it is special?"

Caratacus shrugged. "And the boys?"

"They are both look-outs and animal herders. From here they can see raiders approaching and can raise the alarm, on the lower slopes are beasts, sheep and cattle, which we keep hidden from view. There are other boys down there keeping them in check."

Caratacus nodded, Diviciacus smiled and offered him a beaker. "This is mead," he explained. "It will keep the cold out. Does your friend want some?"

Caratacus nodded his thanks and sat next to the priest. His bodyguard was still astride his horse, looking round at the impressive view. "I am sure he would."

By now the boys had lost their suspicion and were looking at Caratacus as if he was some kind of a god. They took in his fine clothes and blonde hair, tied back off his face, his curly beard and the long sword and dagger at his waist. When Caratacus saw them looking at his sword, he stood and drew the heavy weapon. The boys shrank back in alarm.

He laughed, brandishing the shining metal. "No lads, if I was going to hurt you, I would have done it already, here." He reversed the sword, and holding the blade offered it to the boys. One came forward hesitantly and grasped the handle, when Caratacus let go, the sword almost fell to the ground. The boy was surprised at the weight of it and hefted it experimentally, shrugging off his friend who was impatient for a go.

Caratacus looked round, savouring the view. The hill was a steep saddle, only marred by the landslip which he knew the druids were convinced had a mystical religious significance. Looking into the heartland of Britannia, he wondered just how far he could see. Further than he could ride in a day, probably.

His reverie was interrupted by the priest, who spoke sharply to the boys. "Put that weapon down and get about your business, the elder is coming."

Caratacus looked again up the track. Sure enough there was a man approaching, leaning on a tall staff. His eyes narrowed. God's blood, it was that interfering old druid Cainos, who had been with Verico. What did he want?

As the druid grew nearer he waved and smiled and the boys quietly made themselves scarce. Caratacus stepped forward. "We meet again," he said frostily. "To what do I owe the pleasure this time?"

The priest smiled and sat on the grass with a sigh. "You have good reason not to thank me for my interference, but there was a reason for it. There was a reason."

Caratacus stared at him, "And what, Priest, might that be?"

The priest shifted his weight on the damp grass. "Verico was very concerned about that dream of his, and he came to his own conclusions about its portent. I could not shake him from that. So I had to go along with it. And I believe it was the right thing to do."

"But we still need to rid ourselves of these damn Romans, while keeping faith with Verico's dream," protested Caratacus. "The way to get rid of them is to raise a great army and fight the bastards, sweep them back into the sea."

Cainos nodded, "But with respect, you tried that and were comprehensively defeated. You are only now picking up the pieces, travelling the country trying to get the tribes behind you. You will fail without some magnificent gesture."

Caratacus narrowed his eyes and asked: "What could be more magnificent than a magnificent victory?"

"Agreed," said Cainos, leaning forward. "But again, you seem to get no further than just getting men onto the battlefield and wading into the enemy. We must come up with something that uses guile, maybe witchcraft, but certainly cleverness. You must beat them with your mind." He leaned back, and sipped thoughtfully from a beaker of mead handed to him by Diviciacus.

"What if we came up with something amazing which, at a stroke, will deal the Romans a severe blow and will have men talking round the tribal fires throughout the whole of the land? Do you think that would unite the tribes against Rome?"

Caratacus looked interested, "Yes, agreed, but what? What could possibly be that amazing?"

Cainos shrugged, "I have an idea, but it needs working on. It may not work which is why I wish to keep the plan secret. Even if it doesn't work completely, it could still be a spectacular victory." The priest leaped to his feet and obviously energised, set off back along the track, shouting over his shoulder to Caratacus. "Leave it with me, and I will make you famous."

Caratacus watched him go. "He's mad, absolutely scrambled."

Shaking his head slowly, he took the reins of his horse from his bodyguard and after a last look round was about to set off, when Diviciacus came out of the stone shelter.

"This high priest of yours, is he all there, or has he been touched by the God of Idiots?" asked Caratacus.

The priest wagged a finger at him. "Have a care before you jest about something beyond your comprehension. Cainos is a clever man, and one of our foremost story-tellers. In the Druid world he has the title of Bard which means he holds the history of our people in his head and is very learned.

"If he has a plan for you, mark him well. To have him on your side is a big advantage by itself. To have him work on a plan for you puts you in a very privileged position indeed."

Caratacus pondered the priest's words as his horse picked its way down the steep hill-side. He let the horse find her own way, he had much to think about.

CHAPTER XXII

When he arrived back at camp, Caratacus tossed the reins of his horse to a waiting slave and dismissed his bodyguard before walking slowly across the meadow to the town. He was anxious to find out more about the priest and quickened his pace as he crossed the footbridge over the swiftly flowing river. He scrambled up to the gates where stalls had been set out and farmers sold their produce.

In the middle of the stalls was an unkempt small tavern and sitting outside were three warriors, nursing pots of beer. They'll do for a start, Caratacus thought addressing them cordially. Their torsos were bare and covered with tattoos and markings which extended from their straggly long hair down to their fingers. All three were carrying swords and daggers. They returned a guarded greeting.

Caratacus called for a pot of ale, "Will you join me men?" he asked with a smile. "Drinking alone is fine, but better with friends."

The three looked at each other. One shrugged and said: "Suit yourself." They made room for him on their bench as he settled with a sigh. "It's a nice place you have here."

Again, the seemingly elected speaker offered: "We like it."

Caratacus quickly decided these three taciturn tribesmen were not worth spending money on. Time to cut his losses he thought.

The three warriors sipped their drinks silently. Caratacus downed his in a few gulps and stood.

"Well it was wonderful meeting you, the conversation was fascinating. Good day."

They looked up as he smiled and left, and one even managed a grunt, before taking another swig.

Caratacus strode through the wooden gates into the town. Two guards leaning against the wooden palisade watched him quietly, but made no attempt to stop him. He walked a few paces further, then turned and went back to the guards. One straightened as he approached and put his hand on his sword-hilt.

Caratacus saw the gesture and smiled, "I mean no harm, but would be grateful for directions. Do your priests have a temple, or somewhere they meet?"

"Temple?" repeated the guard, puzzled. "No, there is no temple. Druids have no need of such a thing. If you keep walking along the side of the hill, after perhaps a 100 paces, you will see a big old oak tree. Underneath it is a shelter, there's usually a couple of them in there."

Caratacus thanked the guard and retraced his steps along the rutted path, running along the top of the hill. It dropped away quite steeply to his left towards the riverbank and the meadow, and on the right sloped more gently to fields of grass and barley. It was a nice day for a stroll.

Before long he saw a magnificent oak tree, in full leaf dominating the skyline. As he drew nearer, he could see that the tree masked the great valley, which seemed to split the hills.

Sure enough, as he drew closer, he could make out a rough shelter in the shade of the huge tree. It was made of sticks, bent and knotted together to form a sort of tent. Between the sticks, thatch gave a waterproof cover. Inside were two priests, sitting on lengths of tree trunk, one, an older man with silver hair seemed to be reciting poetry to the younger man, who was listening intently. They wore long brown robes, gathered and roped at the waist, and both were barefoot.

The older man broke off as he saw Caratacus approach. He

struggled to rise. The younger man gave him an arm to help, and stood himself. The older man smiled and bowed to Caratacus. Seeing this, the younger man bowed as well. "Welcome to our sanctuary I am Dovadonos, druid and teacher."

Caratacus put on his best smile. "I can see I have come to the right place. I would know more of your religion if you have the time and patience to tell me."

Dovadonos smiled: "Your desire for knowledge does you credit, but I have been learning all my life and am still learning. I can however tell you of our beliefs, which may help you to understand. Is that what you want to know?"

Caratacus shrugged and raised his hands. "I am always interested to know what motivates men, do you have gods like the Romans?"

Dovadonos smiled. "That is a fundamental question, and no, we have no gods. Our gods are all around us, if you like. This tree for instance. Do you not sense a great power? It was here long before you came to this earth and will be here long after you have passed from it. Does it not say to you that it is sacred?

"Come, sit and I will try to compress a lifetime's learning into one short lesson." Dovadonos groaned as he lowered himself onto the wooden seat. "As druids, we are taught at our great college on the Isle of Mona, way to the north," he gestured vaguely towards the line of hills.

"We teach that no one system of thought is truer than any other," he said, collecting his thoughts, "so if a Roman worships many gods, that is what he must do. We prefer that the individual follows the path he or she has chosen. We believe in the sacredness of life of all beings, so humanity, in this respect is on the same level of importance as plants and animals. There is an Otherworld, which is a place of existence beyond our physical senses. It is a place we are supposed to go when we die, but can be visited with the help of meditation, certain plants and mushrooms, hypnosis and shamanic trances. This life is an incarnation, and when we die, our soul goes to the Otherworld before returning to this world as either a human, a plant or an animal. Our life is just a part of the journey." He smiled.

Caratacus thought about this. It certainly explained celtic bravery and disdain of death.

"And Cainos," he asked. "Where does he fit into this?"

The druid smiled again. "Cainos is a bard, which means that he has spent his whole life learning our history, which he in turn is passing on. I also am part of that process, passing on my knowledge to this young man."

The younger priest smiled and bowed his head.

"We aspire to wisdom and spend our lives learning, and in turn, teaching," explained the old druid. "For that reason we sit on the right hand of the leaders of the tribes. They listen to our wisdom and we translate the portents, so that they can be successful, either in battle, or trade, or farming. Even choosing a wife."

The druid looked up to see if Caratacus had registered his last remark. Caratacus started. "Oh yes, I see, very good."

"We are not men of violence," continued Dovadonos, "we will always be at the battle if the tribe is fighting, but we are there to record the event, so we can tell of it in years to come, and as necessary, minister to the injured. Cainos has a great gift of telling the adventures of the tribe in poetry, which will be learned and told and retold through the years."

From dismissing the druid Cainos as a harmless old fool, Caratacus now had second thoughts, maybe the old fart did have something worth pursuing. Best to keep an open mind.

After dropping a few coins in the cup proffered by the younger druid, Caratacus wandered thoughtfully back towards his tented camp in the meadow. It was a fine day and the hills round about, for once, seemed to have less of a menacing aura. The colours of bracken and heather sweeping down to the treeline echoed the tranquillity he was feeling after his meeting with the holy men.

He could have walked along the riverbank until he came to the footbridge, but as it was such a fine day, he decided to wade across. It seemed quite wide but not deep, no more than waist high, although he would have to watch the current. He sat on the bank and pulled off his soft deerskin riding boots. He did not care to ruin them in the river, they made a serious statement when most of his men rode barefoot. They said status.

He pulled his short tunic up to his chest, revealing rough-spun drawers down to just above the knee and tied at the waist with string. They would soon dry out.

He stepped down onto the smooth stones of the river-bed, trying to balance, and grip the stones with his toes. He gasped as the cold water lapped over his ankles, he felt very insecure as he stumbled deeper into the water, trying to steady himself by flailing one arm, while holding his tunic and boots out of the water with the other. When he found his balance he carefully edged deeper into the swirling water. At every step he realised that the river was deeper than he thought, and when it started to lap against his chest, he realised he was not going to get across without a soaking.

He let go of his tunic which, once soaked, clung on him like a net. He steadied himself and threw first one then the other boot onto the far bank. Thankfully both landed on dry soil, which made his own crossing, unencumbered by boots and the need to keep his tunic dry, much easier. In fact, now he was used to the temperature, it was actually quite pleasant. He lowered himself into the water so only his head was visible. He should do this more often, he thought, as he lazily lifted his feet from the stony riverbed and felt the strength of the current. He kicked for the shore and swam at an angle otherwise the river flow was going to deposit him further downstream than he intended.

A prickle of alarm shot through him on realising that the current had increased in strength and, although now narrower, the river was definitely moving faster. The white flicks of spray on the surface seemed to be getting higher and stronger. He saw that the bank he was swimming from had shallow placid water which would be safe but turning back wouldn't get him across.

If he had stopped to think, he would have realised that the narrowing of the river and the increase in current meant only one thing. He was heading for deep and probably dangerous water. Ahead he could see that the bank he was aiming for was much higher, and carved out by the action of the river.

He kicked out strongly, and thankfully pulled in under the bank, towering above him, too high to scramble up. He managed to snatch hold of a tree root but could not hold on. This led to a moment of panic as his head went under and he was pulled, coughing and gasping further downstream. By now, the bank was at least three arms lengths higher than him. He looked round and realised he had the choice of battling the current upstream where his boots were – if they hadn't already been stolen by an enterprising villager or trust his luck on the current. He had no choice. He went downstream.

Swirling around in the icy water was exhausting. Several times he scraped against submerged branches, until at last the bank levelled out. Thankfully, he came to a spot where he could scramble out, and exhausted, knelt on the shingle.

Caratacus breathed deeply and coughed the water from his lungs. He suddenly realised just how close to drowning he had come, all the more frightening because he had gone from confident and assertive warlord to drowning victim in the blink of an eye on a serene, sunny afternoon. He shivered, not altogether from the cold.

Lying on the bank idly chewing on a piece of grass was a young man watching him with interest. "You should be careful in that river, it can be dangerous," offered the man amiably.

Caratacus bit back a stinging retort. "Thanks for the advice, I'll remember it in future."

He stripped off his sodden tunic, rung it out onto the sand, then examined his cuts and grazes from the submerged branches. Most had stopped bleeding in the icy water, but they stung. His first priority was his boots, which were, hopefully, still lying on the bank further up-stream.

"You man," he said peremptorily. "Make yourself useful and go upstream to find my boots, they'll be on the bank somewhere."

"Go fuck yourself," replied the man quite pleasantly.

Caratacus was not used to being spoken to like that. Usually his very bearing was enough for the lower orders to know they were in the presence of nobility. But perhaps shivering in his undergarment rather diminished that noble demeanour.

He collected himself. "I am sorry, that was ungracious. But I am concerned about my boots. They are rather expensive and I am going to be a minute or two before I can go looking for them. In that time they could be stolen."

The stranger reclining on the bank with his head on his hand sat up and smiled. "Of course, quite understand" he said. "You try and get yourself dry and I'll go and find your boots."

Caratacus did not often have to say thank you, but managed a grudging grunt while wringing out his tunic.

"To whom am I indebted?" he shouted to the man's retreating back.

"My name is Lenc," the man replied over his shoulder.

Lenc knew very well who the sodden man was. When he saw the well-dressed man on the other side of the river, he could hardly believe his luck as he watched him tug off his boots before wading into the water.

When Caratacus had so obviously got into difficulties, Lenc marvelled at the way the gods had arranged for part of his mission to be fulfilled and by accident! Without getting into even a hint of danger he could watch this royal troublemaker drown and even say that he tried to save him, but failed. Or if Caracatus finally crawled exhausted out of the river, it would have been nothing to push him back in and drown him.

Len was moving forward to carry out his plan when three riders appeared on the far bank. They saw a man in trouble in the water and pointed to attract his attention. Lenc stood and waved and slithered down the bank, obviously about to help the swimmer in trouble. Reassured, the riders moved on, and Lenc had enough time to find his spot and lie down before a badly shaken Caratacus struggled out of the water.

What an opportunity that would have been, thought Lenc as he watched Caratacus crawl up the bank. But killing him would have led to awkward questions from the riders who saw him going to the swimmer's aid.

Now he was looking for the bastard's boots. He walked upstream towards where he had seen Caratacus throw the boots and frowned when he saw one of the boys of the town holding them up and admiring them.

"What have you got there young 'un," he said as the surprised boy whirled round. He clutched the boots to his chest protectively. "They're mine," the boy said defensively. "I found them." He had the pinched face and rough clothes of a lad used to hard work and a frugal diet. His face was screwed up like a determined rat caught with no way out.

"No I'm afraid they're not," replied Lenc, regretfully. "They belong to an important man who is a guest of your chief, and you know how he will feel if he finds out one of his people has stolen from such an important person."

The boy was torn, but still defiant. "He shouldn't go leaving his stuff lying about then. If he really wanted them, he wouldn't have thrown them away." He took a step backwards, as if to turn and run.

"Wait a minute. Nobody is blaming you. Look," he fished in the pouch at his waist and pulled out some coins. "Let's call this a reward for finding them."

The boy's eyes widened. He had been ready to take flight, not just to try and save the boots, but because he expected a good hiding off the stranger anyway. He pretended to consider the offer, then reluctantly held out the boots.

Lenc smiled and tossed him the coins. The boy looked up and nodded, then turned and ran. Lenc watched him go. He could have crept up on the lad, cuffed his ear and just taken the boots and wondered why he hadn't. Oh well.

When he returned to where he had left Caratacus, he found him sitting on the grass, his tunic draped over a bush, drying in the sun.

"There you are," said Caratacus in a friendly tone. "I was beginning to think you'd made off with my boots."

Lenc dropped them on the grass. "Nah, don't fit. Besides I had to bribe a lad who found them, thought that made them his."

Caratacus forced himself to be gracious: "I am very grateful and will repay you, soon as I can."

Lenc squinted at the still wet Caratacus. "You know who I am, who are you?"

"I am Caratacus and until very recently was a prince of the Catuvellauni. Now I am a gypsy doomed to wander this land in search of a home." Caratacus threw wide his arms as he made his extravagant statement and smiled. He lay back on the grass and looked keenly at Lenc. "I have to say I normally find my own circumstances of irresistible interest, but you have me puzzled. What is a Roman bastard doing here in the wilds of Silurian country, and obviously tolerated?"

Lenc stirred. "First I am not a Roman bastard, as you so eloquently put it. I was a Roman soldier, an auxiliary from Gaul, but we parted company. A scrape with raiding bandits proved to these people I bear them no ill-will."

"Hmm, that's as maybe; I suppose that as a guest here myself, I must accept that, but you will understand when I say that I think you are talking absolute bollocks. No offence."

Lenc laughed. "Roman soldier or no, there isn't much I can do about it here. I don't intend to take this lot on single-handed."

Caratacus pondered this. "Maybe not, but maybe you're not here for the Silures, maybe you're here for something else. Me, for example."

Lenc looked at him for a second then snorted with derision. "By Toutatis' nuts, you do fancy yourself, don't you? Why would I be the slightest bit concerned about you?"

Caratacus shrugged. "There are some who say I am the greatest threat to Roman domination of Britannia, and one day I will unite the whole country as king."

Lenc allowed himself a snort: "Well when that day comes, I'll bare my arse and you can paint it blue. In the meantime, I think, great king, you should buy me a drink."

Caratacus laughed easily. "I wouldn't trust you as far as I could throw you, but I will drink with you. Come, let us see what delights the town's taverns can bring."

Caratacus pulled on his damp tunic, gasping as the sodden, icy cold cloth grasped his body. He sat on the grass to pull on his boots, struggling to drag them over cold legs. Eventually, after some cursing, he stood, ready once again for anything.

The pair walked through the meadow, skirting Anton's canvas trade emporium, calling in on Caratacus' camp.

"I have been summoned to meet the council again," said Caratacus to his wife, Vellibia, "back as soon as I can." She stood in front of her husband and his new best friend with suspicion. "I suppose this council meets in a tavern?" She stood in front of her husband, eyes blazing.

Lenc had never seen such arresting red hair, most striking against her pale face and hands. Husband and wife were both in stark contrast to the smaller, darker, curly haired Silures.

Caratacus opened his eyes wide. "What a thing to say, and in front of a Gallic stranger. If I have to have a drink it will be out of courtesy. We are guests here after all."

Vellibia's eyes narrowed. "If you come back pissed you sleep outside," she hissed.

"Of course my dear, but that won't happen."

Caratacus backed away and the two returned to the footbridge over the river. "Why didn't you introduce me?" asked Lenc. "Seemed like a nice lass."

"It was for your benefit," replied Caratacus. "If I get in a state this afternoon, guess whose fault it will be. Better you stay out of it."

Lenc could see the sense of that.

They paused at the tavern Caratacus had sampled just a few hours before. The three surly warriors were still there but one was fast asleep with his head resting on his arms.

Caratacus considered the place. "It's a bit open to the elements, but the ale is acceptable. We could do worse."

Lenc shrugged. He wasn't sure about drinking with this man. He needed to keep his wits about him as one wrong word could be the difference between living or dying. Nevertheless they straddled a pair of benches, either side of a beer-stained table, and almost immediately a young girl came over. She bobbed a sort of curtsey when she took in Caratacus' fine, though still damp clothes.

She was small, with lank dark hair falling over a shift stained with beer dregs and who knew what else. She kept her head lowered as Caratacus ordered a jug of cider.

"So tell me how you came to be here, Roman," demanded Caratacus as he surveyed the stream of people walking in and out of the town gate.

"Well for a start, you can stop calling me Roman. People will get the wrong idea and it could get me killed. At the very least it will stop people buying from us. I am a Gaul."

Caratacus leaned forward. "Maybe, but you seem very touchy about it. Perhaps you do have a dark secret we should know about."

"Bollocks," replied Lenc comfortably. "Do you seriously think that the Romans would have sent me here to spy on this broken-down fleapit? What for? And don't you think I would have been given a better story? If that's all the credit you give the Romans, I suggest you think again. If they want to put a spy among the tribes, they would do it without you knowing. In fact you, Caratacus, are far more likely to be the sort of person they would persuade to come here and do their nasty work for them. You seem to have blended right in."

Caratacus laughed loudly, making the drunk warriors at the next bench look up.

"Point taken," he said as he reached for the newly arrived cider. "I must admit that you are a bit obvious for a spy, but then I never credited Rome with much subtlety."

Not for the first time Lenc blessed the intervention of Gobann, the big blacksmith who had spoken for him at the tribal council. Without him, he would not be sitting in the sunshine, sipping new cider. He reflected on the words of Caratacus. When said like that, it was a bit improbable, his story was certainly transparent.

Oh well, he was safe enough at the present, he thought, and Caratacus seemed like a reasonable sort, even for a prince, exiled or not.

He sipped his drink and watched Caratacus drain his and reach for the jug. When he had re-filled his beaker he offered the jug to Lenc, "Come on you're too slow, get some down you."

Lenc raised his hands laughing. "It's all right for you, you have a stomach full of river water to get rid of. Don't worry about me, I'll catch up."

Several hours later, Lenc could not remember whether it was during their third or fourth jug of cider that two more warriors joined the three at the next bench. As the two sat down, the one asleep finally woke up, and looking round blearily, swept the matted hair from his face.

One of the newcomers made a remark, which neither Caratacus or Lenc could hear, but it was plainly something derogatory about the state of the awakened tribesman, judging by his filthy response and the coarse laughs of the other two.

Caratacus made the mistake of also laughing. Then made it worse by adding: "A nice dip in the river is what he needs. Not only sober him up but clean him off as well."

The table went silent as all five looked over at Caratacus who was still chuckling over his own wit.

Caratacus was of royalty and would normally be able to say anything to anyone without fear of taking a thumping. Unfortunately he was on unfamiliar soil, and for once entirely without his bodyguards. He had no idea what was going to come next, but Lenc could read the signs and knew exactly. He drained his drink and took hold of the pottery jug. It wasn't much of a weapon, but it was all he had. He leaned away from the table and quietly raised his legs over the bench so he could jump up without tangling himself.

Caratacus prepared himself for another bright riposte at the tribesman's expense and failed to register the man slowly standing and stepping away from the table. The dishevelled tribesman put his hand on his dagger and leaned forward on the table, his nose close to Caratacus.

"Who the fucking hell are you to come here in your fancy clothes and take the piss out of me?" he demanded.

Caratacus squinted at him, trying to concentrate. Then he waved a hand in front of his nose. "By all that's holy, you smell worse than a midden. You really should have a dip in the river."

The soldier gave a scream of rage and arced his head back to strike at Caratacus with his forehead. Unfortunately for him, when he shot his whole body forward to gain maximum velocity, he caught his knees on the bench, ending up just grazing Caratacus, who fell backward in astonishment. His mates stood, spoiling to join in the fight. Lenc also stood, holding the jug.

"Now gents, lets not spoil a good afternoon, my friend here meant no harm, he was just saying the same as you fellows had said."

The nearest replied: "Yes but he's our mate, we're allowed to say that. You two arselings are strangers and it's time you learned some manners."

Caratacus was struggling to his feet and at last seemed to realise that things were not quite as friendly as before.

"What's wrong Lenc, have you started an argument?" he slurred innocently.

"No not really, but these gentlemen rather think you have."

"Me?" he said with wide, round eyes, "Me? I never said anything," then he turned to the glowering tribesmen, "Gentlemen, if I have said anything out of turn, I do apologise. Let's shake hands."

As he moved forward with his hand outstretched, he half turned and quietly said to Lenc. "I'll stop the smelly one on the floor, then the two nearest on my side. Can you deal with the other two?"

"I suppose so, on you go then."

Caratacus smiled and walked round the rough wooden table. As he approached the warrior still struggling to stand after skinning his shins on the bench, he suddenly turned and kicked him in the side of his head. He went down as if pole-axed, and with a roar, the other four launched themselves.

Lenc threw the jug at his first target, which burst on his forehead with an explosion of pottery shards and cider. While the soldier shook his head to clear his senses, Lenc eased round him and caught his second target with a swift kick between the legs, which doubled him over, moaning and clutching his balls. He tried to straighten to get back into the fight but was too slow. Lenc stepped in close, and kicked his hands, cradling his balls then turned to crack the first man on the side of the head with his elbow. Both were now well and truly down.

Caratacus was not a street fighter. One of his two opponents had him in a headlock, while the other tried to land punches, though he seemed to clout his mate's arms more than Caratacus's head.

Once again Lenc looked round for a weapon, but failed to find one. He stepped round behind the man who was holding Caratacus and smashed his iron shod sandal into the back of the man's knee. The man squealed in pain as he let go and went down with a crash. His mate immediately lost interest in trying to punch Caratacus, and backed nervously away from Lenc.

Caratacus, with blood seeping down his face, made to go after him.

"Leave him," said Lenc, "he's had enough. Remember we both need friends here."

Caratacus made as if to follow the rapidly retreating tribesman then shrugged and laughed. "More cider I think, but not here, we may just have outstayed our welcome."

As he spoke the crowd that had gathered started to disperse and the waif-like serving girl hurried forward to right the overturned tables and benches and clear up the mess. Lenc helped her with the tables and quietly apologised for their poor behaviour.

The girl kept looking at the ground as she busied herself, "It wasn't the first brawl here and won't be the last. If this lot have no-one from outside to fight, they fight each other."

As Lenc helped the girl to clear the mess, Caratacus, who clearly did not feel it part of his duties to do manual labour, wandered into the low hovel and emerged triumphantly minutes later with a small barrel of cider.

"Come, we will leave these peasants to it, and have a drink in a more convivial place, my camp."

As they approached the tents, Vellibia came marching out. Her body language told both men she was furious. Sight of the cider barrel didn't help.

She stomped towards them, clenching her fists, then as she got nearer saw the blood on her husband's face and her attitude softened completely. She ran forward and tenderly touched the bleeding wound. There were tears in her eyes as she asked, "How did this happen, surely not in the council chamber?"

"Well no, actually," confessed Caratacus, "Um, we were set on by some rascals afterwards, while on our way back here."

Once again the expression changed on his wife's face. She stepped back. "You've been drinking," she accused.

"Only one, in the spirit of friendship," her husband confessed.

"You bastard," she shouted. "We're all in peril of our lives and you spend the afternoon getting pissed and fighting. That's a very regal thing to do."

Lenc said nothing. The last thing he was going to do was come between a man and his wife, especially such a hell-cat. He shifted forward and muttered that he really ought to be getting back to his own tent, Anton would be worried, and besides he had been away for quite a time...

Vellibia turned on him angrily. "Who the hell are you?" she demanded. "Are you the reason he returns in this state?"

Lenc shrugged his shoulders, eyes wide open, protesting his innocence. "Don't blame me lady, it wasn't my fault far from it. Look I'll leave you to it, you obviously have things to talk about."

Caratacus carefully put his barrel down and joined in the protest. "No, no, you can't possibly go, after all you have done. Please come to the tent and we'll broach this barrel."

He took Lenc by the arm and put his other arm round his wife. "Vellibia my dear, this is a new friend and he's an enemy. Actually, he's more a friend than enemy, as he keeps proving. And he can teach us a lot. Please be nice to him and show him some Catuvellaunian hospitality."

Still angry Vellibia pulled away and shouted for her servants. They had obviously been listening with delight from the sanctuary of their tent, because they shot out immediately they were summoned.

"Spread a blanket for these two and find beakers. My husband has the need to entertain his new friend," she ordered peremptorily. "And for the gods' sake find them some food to soak up the rat's piss they've been drinking."

She swept back to her tent, shoulders square and set, hands still clenched.

Caratacus watched her go, as slowly a sly grin spread across his face. "A fine woman that. She'll be all right in a bit."

The servants spread a blanket on the lush grass and as the two settled, Vellibia came out once again with a bowl of water and a flannel. She kneeled down next to Caratacus and gently bathed the cut on his forehead. He winced as the salted water stung.

Lenc watched and considered it must be rather nice to have a woman by your side to minister to your wounds, and of course minister to all those other needs men have, like…

He was interrupted from his reverie by the approaching form of Anton, bristling with indignation.

"Where in Toutatis' name have you been?" he demanded. "I've been working my arse off out here, trying to earn a crust, and you, instead of supposedly helping me are off getting pissed."

"You're just jealous you had to do a bit of work for once, instead of lying back and letting me do it all," responded Lenc calmly.

"Whaaat?" spluttered Anton.

"God's balls, Anton, give it a rest and if you ask nicely, this lovely lady will forgive your bad language and find you a mug so you can join us in a drink."

Instantly mortified, Anton offered his apologies to Vellibia, who had already become one of his best customers, buying some Breton jewellery from him at a very nice profit.

Vellibia tried to hide a smile and motioned for her servant to bring another mug. Anton carefully lowered himself to the ground, reaching greedily for the cider barrel. He almost swooned when a plate of cold meat, bread and cheese appeared. "Oh, this is far more acceptable," he smiled happily.

The early evening passed in a convivial round of drinking and eating, sprawled on the grass in the shadow of the surrounding hills. Lenc was fascinated by the shadow thrown by the sun onto the Red Mountain. He saw that the steep face was a depression, a sort of bowl which caught the sun and shadow streaming across the hill's cloak of tawny red bracken.

"Look out, it's the priest, Cainos, hope he's brought some cider," said Caratacus hauling himself up on one elbow, "Maybe he has news."

Lenc looked up. What news could the priest have for this prince of the Catuvellauni?

Cainos bustled towards them, holding his robe skirts hitched above the thick grass. "Here you are Lord," he said as he arrived at the camp, his chest heaving.

"You have hurried to get here," shouted Caratacus expansively, "Come, sit and take some refreshment."

Cainos looked at him keenly, and kneeled, accepting a mug of cider and some food. "Lord I have great news, which I think I will leave for the morning, when you will be more, ah, receptive. Just be ready to go before the council when I call."

Caratacus leaned forward, "Come on, you can't leave me hanging like that, what's happening?"

The priest stopped chewing and took a mouthful of cider. "This is a bit too complicated to explain now, but tomorrow it will be clearer. Suffice to say that the vanguard of the new Roman legion is at Glevum and we have a chance to deal them a mortal blow. It will combine the tribe's method of fighting with yours, and if we are in luck some magic, which will surely convince Verico that you are a man to follow."

Caratacus smiled lazily. "I shall have to be happy with that then and hold my curiosity till the morning. But tell me this priest, why are you making such efforts on my behalf?"

"A good question Lord. I will speak plainly. You have the courage to take on the Romans and wish to raise a mighty army. At the moment they are picking us off piecemeal, and unless we unite they will soon dominate this whole country. So far you have led disastrously and are the cause of the deaths of many fine

Britons. But you have confronted your mistakes and will learn to fight and win against this skilled, cruel and disciplined invader.

"I have prayed and contemplated your coming and I have decided to support and advise you. All I ask is that you listen to me and take my advice, and let me stay at your right hand. When people see that I and my religion are the strength behind you, they will surely want to follow the true path with me."

"Of course I accept, and thank you for being so honest," replied Caratacus. "I don't mind you god bothering anyone really, but I don't want you preaching to my people. If anyone comes to you and wishes to find out more, that's one thing, but I won't have you preaching cant and confusing my men."

Cainos bowed his head in assent. "I am sure that when you start winning battles Lord, my presence at your side will be all that is needed to persuade men of the true path."

Caratacus grunted. "God's blood, but you've given me spice for the morning. Where's that cider?"

CHAPTER XXIII

A throbbing pain just behind his eyes made a bleary-eyed Lenc squint against the early sun as he rolled out of his robe and blanket to face the new day. He grimaced, rubbed his scalp and squinted across the glistening meadow as the sun's first rays glinted over a low hill to the east, painting his mountain a glowing red. He yawned and struggled to his feet enjoying, despite the trip-hammer in his brain, the feel of the cool, damp grass between his toes.

Completely alone on the river-bank, he savoured the peace and tranquillity. He smiled at the memory of Caratacus flailing about in the deep water the day before. Could have solved a few problems if he had drowned.

But what of the priest's plan? He had to know what it was. Especially as his legion had finally arrived on the border. He would accompany Caratacus to the council, and stay till he was told to leave. With a bit of luck he would hear the whole story first hand.

He walked upstream, away from the town, to his secluded bathing spot, where a patch of sand allowed access into the water, but without prying eyes.

He pulled off his tunic and under-garment and, totally naked, dropped them on the bank. He was used to the chill of the water but wary of the strength of the current but at his chosen spot the river was at least 50 paces wide, slow moving and shallow.

The thumping behind his eyes gradually faded away as he worked his muscles against the river current. He ducked his head under the water and swam hard, enjoying the exhilaration of the mountain fresh water rushing past him, trying to block him and push him down-stream to the sea. He came up for air, gasping and snorting, and found the slippery round stones on the bottom with his feet.

"Hello again," came a female voice. Lenc swirled round to see the Princess Veldicca waving from the far bank. He waved back and carefully pushed himself across to her, aware of his precarious footing. He stopped as the water level started to decrease, very aware he was once again naked. Following their first conversation, he supposed he should be blasé about his nakedness, but it was all right for her, she was used to it.

So he stayed in the water and belatedly wished her a good morning.

"I trust you are well this fine morning, and you are not too hurt after your meeting with our warriors," she teased.

"Not as hurt as them, I'll wager." He was about to kick up and swim on his back, then thought better of it.

She giggled, "That's not what I heard. Our lads had quite a collection of cuts and bruises, but they said they gave better than they got."

Lenc snorted. "They would, wouldn't they? Fear not Lady, I shall heed your advice and fight only men in future. I will leave the boys to their mothers."

She nodded and reclined on the grass bank, her knees tucked under her. Lenc mused at the way the sun caught her long hair and made it glow. She saw him looking and unconsciously twirled a tress of hair. "Come and sit by me for a minute. There is no-one else about to see," she added impishly.

Now this had become a challenge, thought Lenc. On the one hand, he could brazen it out, clamber ashore, sit next her, bollock naked, his cock like a shrivelled husk in the cold, or he could decline with thanks, indicating a far more important task on the meadow.

Oh fuck it, he thought, and clambered carefully out of the water onto a small sand spit, where the grass bank was at waist height. Just downstream was a split in the ground where he could easily walk up, and as nonchalantly as he could, settled himself down next to the princess with one hand carelessly covering his parts. She had that impish look on her face, enjoying his obvious discomfort.

"How did you find me?" he asked finally.

"Are you suggesting I was looking for you? I was just taking a walk on the river bank," she replied, her eyes wide and blue.

Lenc said nothing but the expression on his face was enough.

Veldicca smiled and lay back, looking up at the blue sky. "How long do you mean to stay here?" she asked finally.

The question took Lenc aback. It was the last thing on his mind. "Don't really know," he confessed. "It depends on how long it takes to sell our stuff. Anton seems to think we can buy your animal pelts, which will find a market further inland, so although we won't be right here for much longer, we should stay in the country for a while yet."

She thought about this. "Would you not wish to stay here? You could join my father's bodyguard."

"Why would I want to do that?" he asked cautiously.

She sat up and brushed her hair back from her face. "I will be married soon to Trenos and will have to fulfil my obligations to produce sons, but that doesn't mean we can't spend time together."

Lenc looked at her strangely. "What are you saying? You want me as a secret lover? I should skulk about on the off-chance you might want me to pleasure you?"

She looked down. "Something like that, but the words have come out all wrong. I have feelings for you, but you know we could never marry. My partner has been found by my father and will be for the good of the tribe. I must abide by that but once my duty is done, no-one will mind at all."

"Your husband may have something to say about it," retorted Lenc.

"Well that just shows how much you know," she said fiercely. "Once I have borne him boys no-one will care what I do, least of all my husband. He will be off ploughing anything he fancies, leaving me to worry about whether he brings me back a pox. This is the way."

Lenc leaned back in the grass, deep in thought, completely forgetting his naked condition. As he did so, Veldicca looked down and raised her eyebrows. While he was thinking, his manhood was stirring and waking up. Quickly he tried to hide it, but this time it proved more difficult.

"Well at least someone seems interested in my words. Perhaps it's time to get into the river," she teased.

Abruptly, she stood, pulling off her shift. He watched laying prone on the grass as the naked princess walked carefully down to the river. Slowly she waded out and raised her hands as the cool water lapped up around her white body, as she moved out deeper, ducking under the surface. Lenc cradled his head on his hands as she surfaced and spat out the water she had taken into her mouth. She did this again and then motioned to him to join her.

He crawled over to the split in the bank and climbed down, jumping in as she watched. He waded out to her as she squatted neck deep, and awkwardly took her in his arms.

She looked up at him through damp lashes, her eyes seemed enormous. "I have wanted to … get your attention since we first met. I have never felt like this about a man before. I really don't know what is happening to me."

As the river caressed their shoulders, they stayed entwined, neither wishing to leave but too cold to stay. Tentatively Lenc strayed his hand down to her stomach, then lower. She moaned as he encountered her silky pelt and involuntarily moved to open her legs to his questing fingers.

Her eyes were closed, and then she reached down and stopped his hand. "I am afraid I must go," she said regretfully.

"Surely you can stay a little longer," he pleaded.

"Sadly no, But next time, which will be soon, I will show you how to give me pleasure without consequences and we will talk again about you staying."

With that she slowly untangled herself from his embrace and waded out of the water. He watched as she stood on the grass, her beautiful whiteness, laced with the ivy tattoo, stretching as she lifted the shift dress above her head and pulled it down over her still damp body.

She picked up her belt and waved sadly at him, then turned and was gone. Lenc waded thoughtfully back to the other bank. As he rubbed his chest with his tunic, musing over what had just happened, something very special, he mused, but at the same time unsettling. A jumble of emotions cascaded through his mind, he didn't know what to think, and was elated and frightened at the same time. He pulled on his tunic and was knotting his boots when Anton came bustling and huffing over.

"Thought I would find you here," he wheezed. "You wanted to know when that other lot went for their audience with the chief, well they're making moves now."

Lenc started. He had forgotten his intention to tag along with Caratacus to the meeting. Hurriedly he scrambled up onto the meadow and left Anton behind as he strode past their wagon towards the bigger Catuvellauni camp. Vellibia came up to meet him as he approached. "He is with that priest," she said tersely. "I'm not allowed to be present, but they've been plotting together for some time."

Obviously she didn't think it odd that he was involved, thought Lenc. That was positive anyway. Just have to hope it doesn't occur to anyone else to question his presence.

"It must be magic," she said worriedly. "I never thought it was a good thing to encourage the dark side, you always have to pay in the end. Making pacts with the dark gods is not something I will let him get involved in."

Lenc raised his eyebrows. He had absolutely no idea what she was talking about. Yet he reflected these Britons believed in some pretty strange things. Hobgoblins, spirits, people rising up from the dead. Came from living in such a cold, dark climate he supposed.

He shrugged. "Whatever it is, there will be a reasonable explanation and your man will not have to sell his soul to get what he wants."

Vellibia would not be convinced. "I've seen these people do their work before. We have had healers and people claiming to be able to invoke the underworld, and at the back of it was always treachery and thievery. While I and my children are here, we will have nothing to do with it."

Vellibia was working herself up to go bursting in on her husband, when he and the priest Cainos pushed aside the tent flap and emerged.

Caratacus was dressed in his finery fit to meet the chief, wearing a long simple white robe and over it a tunic threaded in multi colours. Around his forehead was a band of the same colours, which held his long hair back, at his waist his sword belt, holding his longsword on one side and a dagger on the other, looking every inch the imperious nobleman.

Behind him, smiling slightly, followed Cainos, in his usual drab robes, but even so, giving off an aura of a man of importance, someone with a story to tell.

Caratacus looked round at his people waiting for him. He smiled fondly at Vellibia who ran to meet him.

"I know you want to hear what we have been discussing, and believe me, it's an amazing story. If it works, we will unite this country by storm, and even if it only half works, we shall still bind this country together.

"I don't want to reveal it all to you now, because I am still trying to grasp the enormity of it. The priest has given me a vision which I am trying to understand, but I need to describe this vision to Verico, and you must come and listen, and hear what I have to say."

He stopped and looked at Vellibia, smiling, taking her hands. "And let's do it quickly before I forget it all."

Caratacus's retinue fell in behind him, so Lenc hurriedly tucked himself into the centre. He had a feeling he really needed to hear this revelation, it was bound to be something important.

Caratacus steered his wife toward the Chief's hall, closely followed by Cainos. Lenc stayed in the middle as they filed into the council chamber.

Inside, the smoky atmosphere was crackling. Cainos had requested the audience with Verico, and if only from a sense of curiosity, the chamber was packed.

Lenc risked a peep over Caratacus's shoulder as they entered the room. There was Verico, on his wooden throne as before, flanked by his advisors and the senior members of the council. Lenc registered the presence of Trenos, a long cloak draped over his shoulders, naked chest and arms, and long pants held at the waist by his empty sword belt. His lower legs were criss-crossed with straps tethering his shoes.

Verico stood as they entered the room.

"Welcome again, Caratacus, I understand you have exciting news for us?"

Caratacus bowed deeply then almost insolently stared round the room, taking in the ranks of advisers and tribal leaders. Then he settled his eyes on Verico. "Lord, since we last spoke, I have been trying to make sense of your words to me, the portents that came to you and the interpretation of them. Well the priest who interpreted your dream has himself had a portent, and he has chosen to share that with me.

"My goddess of war, Sabrina, who is also the goddess of the river Hafren, has told us to travel quickly to a place in the Great

Forest where the river takes a sharp bend and goes from a narrow stream to a wide river before running into the estuary. There is a local phenomena which, if the tide is right and the currents run right and there is plenty of water in the river, a mighty wave will come crashing upstream, sweeping away anything in its path. Just such a wave is due very soon, and we have the opportunity to catch the Romans in a trap which will set them back generations."

Verico nodded, considering this seemingly wild suggestion. "I have heard of this tide, but never seen it, how do you know when it is coming, and how do you plan to lure the Romans into it?"

"To answer your first question is for the priest, Cainos," replied Caratacus with a sweeping gesture indicating the holy man, who modestly bowed his head. "For the second, leave that to me. My presence will lure them out.

"I shall need as many warriors as you can muster and we must leave straight away, so that all preparations are complete before the wave rises. We have no time to lose."

Caratacus swung round and appealed to the priest: "Cainos, please explain your plan as you explained it to me."

Cainos nodded: "Lord, we have always known of this sudden surge tide which happens on the Hafren. It can be huge and devastating, but is only of use to us if we can predict when it is going to happen, and then persuade the Romans to follow us into an ambush. A fellow druid who has made a study of the river believes he can predict when this next surge will come, and if we are in position, we can lure the Romans into the trap and kill hundreds of them. Even if it doesn't work, we should still be able to deal them a devastating blow."

Verico sat back in his chair and turned to the young warrior Trenos. "What do you think, is it a plan which will kill Romans?"

Trenos considered. He wanted to kill Romans, but did not want to give this upstart outsider any advantage. He had noted the sudden imperiousness of Caratacus's address to the Chief and council. God's teeth, the man was acting as if he was already in charge of a vast army.

"I also have heard of this magical wave, but I did not know that its arrival could be prophesied. If Cainos chooses to support Caratacus, we must assume it is for the good of the tribe. If he can lure Romans to the Hafren, we can be ready for them and slay them anyway. But if the prophesy is wrong and there is no wave, then I think we should say that Caratacus has outstayed his welcome here."

Caratacus nodded, he had half-expected this.

"So be it. If I am wrong, you still have the chance to kill Romans. If I am right you kill even more Romans, but if I am triumphant, will you follow me to treat with the Ordovices?"

Verico considered this for a moment. "It is quite a flight of fancy, but if it works, then we will stand behind you, yes and even be friends with the Ordovices and help you raise an army of all Britannia."

At this there was a great shout and the elders stamped their feet in agreement.

Caratacus nodded in acceptance. All he had to do now was persuade a body of Roman soldiers to follow him across a river and be swept away by a magic wave which the day before he had never even heard of. But if they could pull it off, the destiny of his army, and he as its leader, would be absolute.

Caratacus and his party swept from the council to prepare horses and equipment for the big raid, while Trenos organised his lieutenants: "Bring your bows and swords, gather your equipment and men," he shouted in ringing tones. "We meet on the meadow then ride south. Rally on me there."

Lenc hurried out of the chamber into the bright sunlight. Everywhere was noise and confusion, as men, clutching swords and baskets of arrows looked for their friends or reassured tearful wives. He needed a horse, so headed for the blacksmith's yard.

He spied the farrier leading two horses out of the stable for saddling.

"Trenos has said I can have the same horse as last time," he shouted in the farrier's ear.

"He's out in the paddock, enjoying the sunshine," responded the farrier. "You'll find tack in the stable, take a few carrots and walk down there. He'll soon come to you if you wave the carrots about."

Lenc hefted the saddle and walked down the slope to the paddock. He had to contact the Pathfinders, but how? He would be missed if he slipped away.

In the paddock several warriors were trying to claim their horses. Lenc saw his almost immediately, cropping grass oblivious to the chaos around him. A whistle caught the horse's attention and when he saw the carrots waved enticingly in the air, lost interest in the grass and trotted over. Lenc held one out as the horse nuzzled and snickered it into his mouth. He tethered the horse then swung the saddle over his back and cinched it tight.

Once mounted he steered his horse round under the town wall, following the contour of the hill. It was steep but there was enough room to allow them to comfortably ride round to the footbridge onto the meadow. He passed Caratacus's camp, a hive of activity, as servants, slaves and warriors rushed about, tethering horses, wrapping food and blankets, sharpening swords.

Lenc left them to it and rode on to his own camp, where he found Anton sitting forlornly on the wagon, idly swinging his feet.

"Oh you've come back to join me then?" said Anton piteously. "Can't think why, no-one's come near since the great proclamation. How can I make a profit if no-one is buying?"

"Never mind Anton, a venture, so fantastic as to be ridiculous has won the Chieftain's blessing. The only reason is has been accepted is because that druid, Cainos is behind it. Without his support it would have been laughed out of the council chamber, but the elders are taking it seriously. You will be seeing less of the warriors for a good few days now, we are going south, back to the

Hafren, on what could be a fool's errand."

"Well count me out," said the fat man firmly, "I'll just stay here and wait for you all to return. Failing that, I may just travel east by myself and try my luck further into Britannia. I fancy the further I go, the more civilised and discerning the clientele will be."

"That's up to you," replied Lenc tersely, "but if you see the pathfinders, tell them there is going to be a battle between the Silures and the Twentieth. They are going to be tested good and proper and would be grateful for a warning."

Anton sniffed, "I've just about had it with your pathfinders. Scared the shit out of me. I'll tell them if they find me, but I ain't going looking for them, that's for sure."

Lenc grinned and jumped from his horse. "I'll gather my gear, but could do with some food and drink to take with me. Nobody has said how long we will be gone for, but it's going to be four days at the very least."

"Can't you get food off Caratacus," said Anton aghast. "I can't keep feeding you without you working for it. What do you think I am?"

"Sometimes I think you're an ungrateful swine," replied Lenc evenly. "I keep having to remind you that you've been well paid, and if you play things right, you will do very well from this trip. Now stop moaning and fetch me some food and a skin of cider."

Lenc packed up his bedroll and strapped it behind his saddle, the sack of food, delivered by a muttering Anton, went either side of the saddle pommel. As he mounted his horse, he interrupted the still grumbling Anton. "Don't forget. If the pathfinders come looking, tell them of the danger to the Twentieth. It will be a disaster if their first encounter with the Silures ends badly."

He briefly outlined the incredible plan to an indifferent Anton, who clearly had no interest in anything else but tucking into some cold chicken and perhaps a cup of cider that had been cooling nicely in the river. Lenc hesitated, he wanted to impress the importance of letting the Pathfinders know what Caratacus was planning, but with exasperation, contented himself with, "what's the fucking use?" and wheeled his horse.

He cantered over to the larger Caratacus camp and nearly burst into an argument between the great man and his wife. "Look you're welcome to accompany us, but I don't want you fighting," Caratacus was shouting.

"I thought we were in this together," responded Vellibia, equally loudly. "You said we would stand side by side, together, come what may. Now the first sign of a fight and I have to stay by the fireside waiting for you to come home and patch you up, as usual."

Diplomatically, Lenc reined in his horse at the edge of the camp and studiously examined the shadows dancing across the sun-dappled mountain.

As he waited, more and more warriors rode in to the meadow and centred on a pennant flying from the top of a lance, the raiding party's rallying point. Lenc clicked his tongue and his shaggy horse quietly moved in that direction.

Trenos was talking to his men, but broke off as Lenc came closer.

"Come to see us triumph again, Roman?"

"I confess I do wish to see this magic the priest speaks of."

"It's not magic," replied Trenos scornfully, "it happens often. No magic if you know what to look for, only if you are not expecting it, then it'll make you sorry, although I never knew it could be predicted."

Lenc looked round as Caratacus and his retinue arrived on horseback, the chariots left behind. Vellibia rode at her husband's side but she was scowling, indicating the conversation had not gone her way.

Trenos signalled his warriors for quiet. "For those who don't know, we are heading through the forest to the Hafren. There we will engage the new Romans who have arrived on the other side of the estuary. They are moving into Glevum, Corinium

Dobunnorum and Venta Silurum, and they probably think we are going to sit in our hills waiting for them to be ready to come out of their forts and slaughter us. Well they're wrong.

"We shall take the fight to them as we always have done, and if the plan cooked up by our priest works we will kill many of them. If the plan doesn't work, we shall still kill a lot of them."

A loud yell went up from the eager warriors. "We'll move quickly through the forest and keep ourselves hidden, while our new friend Caratacus takes a party forward to entice the Romans. We shall be waiting for them on the riverbank when they return, and that's when we kill Romans. Join your leaders and prepare to march."

At this the tribesmen let out another cheer, and Trenos motioned to Caratacus to join him at the head of the column. They moved out across the meadow, skirting the line of hills to their right, and the warriors moved in behind. Lenc looked for a way to sidle to the edge and perhaps lose himself when they arrived at the denser trees, but there always seemed to be at least two warriors watching him, their expressions baleful.

He resigned himself to hoping that the Pathfinders would see all the activity and try to investigate. He could see no possibility of warning them before it was too late.

As his predicament swirled around in his head he tried to console himself with the thought that the legion would not blunder into an ambush. But then the head of Caratacus on a lance was a very tempting target and one that might well cause the legion to throw caution to the winds, with dire results.

He did not really believe in the power of this mysterious wave, and until he saw it he could dismiss it as local fantasy. But even so, a body of troops pursuing horses across a river was fraught with danger. If I get any opportunity to contact the Pathfinders I must take it, he thought grimly.

CHAPTER XXIV

There was something of a carnival atmosphere as the warband rode hard, only stopping shortly after dusk. Lenc rolled thankfully in his blankets after a cold meal, then was roused before sun up, and on the trail before the sun warmed the land around them.

Even with so many men and horses around him, Lenc glimpsed deer and even boar come close, as if to find out who was invading their territory. I'll come back here some time and hunt, he promised himself.

At one stage, the priest Cainos reined in beside him, giving Lenc the opportunity to question him further about the mysterious wave.

"It is quite a sight to see," admitted Cainos. "This place is known as the Awre or Noose. Picture the river, wide and slow at low tide, running into the sea. Then the tide turns and the water flows back up the river again. Suddenly there is a bend in the river and from nowhere, all this water is pushed and funnelled into a much smaller space. The very force of all this water creates a wave which can sweep long distances upstream.

"Of course the wave is not always so big or so threatening, but a combination of circumstances, such as less water coming down stream, a powerful wind coming off the sea and a strong high tide can all create the ideal circumstances for a wave of truly frightening proportions. We have seen freak waves as high as eight men standing on each other's shoulders sweep upstream, carrying all before it."

Lenc looked sceptical, so Cainos added: "Of course they are unusual but according to my counterparts who study this phenomena, we are due a particularly high race. It will be interesting to see if the prediction is correct."

Yes I am sure the legion will be fascinated, thought Lenc darkly.

They passed few signs of habitation on their journey, but the scouts stayed alert, as the possibility of a Roman patrol was very real.

Finally, they slowed, as they neared the river. The ground fell away at the river side of the track, and through the trees and low brush Lenc caught tantalising glimpses of the mysterious river with seemingly magical powers. His first thought was one of disappointment, it didn't look any different to any other river.

When a scout came back along the ranks of warriors he put thoughts of river demons to one side. "The front of the column has come to open ground and will go no further," shouted the scout. "They are right above the bend where we want the Romans to come. Dismount here and you will be led to your places of concealment. You will stay there until the ambush starts."

Lenc swung his leg over the saddle and dismounted, stretching stiff joints. He had kept a low profile on the ride, but thought it wise to move up and see what was happening. He tied his horse to a tree, and hitching his sword belt, walked up the muddy track, skirting the horses and riders, gratefully stretching themselves and taking a drink after the long, hard ride.

No-one seemed to pay him any attention as he moved forward, although he did note that his two quiet companions had also dismounted and were following him. He grimaced at the thought of suddenly bursting through the trees, diving into the river and swimming across to warn the garrison. Some chance.

Up ahead, Caratacus and Trenos were watching intently as Cainos drew a crude map in the dust. Another priest stood slightly to one side, and nodded as Lenc sidled closer so he could hear.

"You see how wide the river is here," explained Cainos, scratching the wider section narrowing to less than half its width into the bend. "There is a sandbank there, and from the lower bank on the other side, it looks just like two rivers at low tide. That is what will confuse them. The river is placid and shallow, easy to cross just there and firm underfoot even for horses. We have to time it so that you can get across before the wave catches as many as possible of them mid-stream."

Trenos and Caratacus looked at him in bafflement but it was Caratacus who broke the silence. "You are asking me to rouse the wrath of the Romans, then ride back here, to cross this bloody river at an exact moment, or we won't catch them napping?"

"Just so," nodded Cainos. "My man, Arios here, has studied the river all his life and knows its tricks. He will guide you to the fort and tell you just when to appear and where you can do some damage, and when you have to withdraw. When you get back to the riverbank he will tell you when you can cross and how long you have. You should have ample time before the Romans form up cavalry and infantry to come after you."

"What makes you think they will send a cohort," asked Trenos suspiciously, "that's about 800 men."

"Caratacus must put himself in full view," replied Cainos smoothly. "You may not realise it, but he is a much wanted man. He has proved himself a thorn in the Roman side for a long time, and no doubt his capture is one of the objectives of this legion."

"What if they take too long," said a clearly unconvinced Trenos. "Polishing their armour or finishing their dinner or something?"

"Then you must make them, speed them up," replied an impatient Cainos. "Go back and harass them some more. Taunt them, but get them moving."

Lenc took some heart from this. The plan seemed ridiculous at the start, now it seemed completely unworkable. How could so many factors come together at just the right time?

"And besides," finished Cainos. "We will be praying for you."

Caratacus shook his head doubtfully as he mounted his horse, and his lieutenants moved in closer as he wheeled towards Trenos. "Still keen on this thrice damned adventure?"

Trenos looked up at him and smiled. "Wouldn't miss it for the world."

Caratacus turned again to Cainos. "Is this going to work?"

The priest looked round. "The portents are good, and Arios is convinced that we should have a high tide. The wind is running from the sea and the river is low right now. The tide is higher than these Romans will ever have seen, and when the sea water is forced into a tight space it creates a wave of phenomenal strength.

"I must concentrate my mind and pray."

Caratacus spurred his horse and muttered under his breath. Trenos grinned again and turned his horse, looking for Lenc. "Roman, you stay here with the priest, we don't want you getting too close to your old comrades, might be too much of a temptation."

Lenc shrugged. "I will await your return with interest."

"So will I," retorted Trenos. "So will I."

The small war party, led by Arios, the local priest on a scraggy donkey, picked their way down to the riverbank, which ran placidly, giving no sign of its apparently lethal properties as a weak sun sparkled on the surface.

Arios urged his donkey into the water, but it shied nervously, unused to the smooth stones which shifted under his feet. Swiftly, the priest slipped out of the saddle and let himself into the water. He splashed forward and leading the animal, confidently set off across the river.

Lenc squatted on the bank, watching the band lead their horses across the wide Hafren. It was an idyllic spot and it was hard to take the druid seriously, that in seconds the river could change from a placid millpond to a raging tempest of frothing water deep enough to sweep men away. It just wasn't conceivable.

At least 600 warriors and Caratacus's royal party were left behind on the bank. Quickly they moved back to the forest edge to prepare their positions, while the horses were led further into the forest, but not too far away. If things went wrong, flight would be quick, no-one wanted to be chasing through the forest looking for a horse.

Archers on the river bank emptied their sheaves and stabbed their arrows into the ground in front of them, ready to rain a quick fusillade down on the Romans. Spearmen hefted their weapons and made sure they had plenty of room to swing, while the swordsmen simply lay on the ground talking quietly to each other. If they were needed, they would come out of cover and meet the enemy trying to wade out of the river, tide surge or no.

Lenc looked round. He had nothing to do. He couldn't go anywhere, his watchers would probably run him through. He certainly couldn't get a warning to the garrison, but even so, he could not believe that his old comrades were in the danger that had been painted. They wouldn't be beat by a high tide. Resigned, he knew there was nothing for it but to make the best of things.

Reluctantly he stood up and walked slowly back to the treeline, watched all the time by his two escorts. He walked past the sentries and the lines of men lying on the ground and further into the forest to a small clearing where he found the royal party of the Silurian chieftain.

Verico was seated comfortably on a wool blanket dozing in the weak sunshine. His daughter Veldicca was sitting with Vellibia, wife of Caratacus, their heads close together, probably talking of things only of interest to women. Veldicca looked up as he approached and giggled.

He wondered if they had been talking about him.

Verico opened one eye as Lenc approached and struggled up onto one elbow.

"Well Roman are you looking forward to some druid magic? You will soon see that while we have the druids to do Sabrina's work the Romans have no chance of conquering these lands. Isn't that so, daughter?" He turned to his daughter, waiting for confirmation. She sat demurely, looking down at her hands in her lap.

"It is the goddess's will," she responded quietly, "but I must confess that I find it difficult to believe what Cainos is telling us. And even if there is going to be a big tide, how are Caratacus and his men going to judge it so they get across, and right behind them the Romans will be swept away?"

Verico shrugged. "If Sabrina is with us, she will make it happen. If she is not, and a sizeable number of Romans do chase Caratacus, then we have a strong position here and we will kill as many as we can before disappearing through the forest."

Put like that, Lenc could see that whatever happened, the cohort was going to get a bloody nose. And there was nothing he could do about it.

The band of warriors rode quietly through the open countryside. Caratacus felt exposed and vulnerable knowing he was riding straight into the lion's den, he pulled his cloak tighter round him as he gazed at the rolling countryside. They were crossing a vast plain with little shelter, just isolated hamlets, surrounded by small fields. They skirted the hovels and the few people they saw took good care not to come too close. Armed men never meant anything good.

Caratacus looked sideways at the priest. "How much further?"

The priest shrugged. "Not too far. If it's Romans you're worried about, if we see any it will likely only be a small patrol."

"What if it's a big patrol?"

The priest shrugged again. "In that case we will have achieved our objective."

Caratacus was still far from convinced. "How will you know when to cross the river?"

The priest looked at him. "By the sun, by the wind, by the state of the river. I will know when it's time."

Caratacus was clearly not reassured by this. "You ever been wrong?"

The priest smiled at this lack of faith. "This is not an exact matter you know, we are in Sabrina's hands. I am sure she will make it work."

Wonderful, thought Caratacus. Trenos had been listening to this exchange and shook his head in disapproval.

Caratacus swept the long hair back from his face and gazed ahead. "How far is the Roman fort, Arios?"

"Oh not far, Lord, not far."

Caratacus snorted, he wasn't comfortable relying on the priest in such dangerous country. The column was trotting through bare, open terrain, their only security the screen of scouts thrown out ahead of them. As if on cue, one of them burst out of a copse of trees and skidded to a halt in front of Caratacus, pulling savagely on his horse's bit.

"Romans, Lord, about 50 of them, just ahead of us. Infantry, just one man riding. They are marching this way."

"How long before they are on us?" demanded Caratacus.

The scout looked round, "Lord we have time to set up an ambush in a small wood just ahead. The trail winds past the wood and we can be on them before they know it. They don't have scouts out and I don't think they're anticipating danger at all."

Caratacus swivelled in his saddle to Trenos. "Should we attack them?" he demanded tersely. "It could be our best chance."

Trenos leaned back in his saddle. "We may be a bit premature, but if we take them we need prisoners and when the time is right we can allow some of them to escape and raise the alarm. We're not far from the fort and I think retribution will be swift."

The warrior chief turned to the raiders: "We will spread out in that wood yonder and wait for them. Don't forget this action is to force the Romans to send out a larger force, so we must take prisoners. Hold your men in check until you hear the signal."

The lieutenants nodded grimly and fingered their sword handles. "Don't let any of the bastards get away, we don't want the fort warned before we are ready. Is that clear." He looked grimly at his men. "Good, now take your men into the woods, and for the god's sake keep the noise down."

He watched as the lieutenants swung away and rejoined their men. They clattered past him to take up their positions in the wood, this part at least should go to plan.

The riders were soon swallowed by the wood, and with one last look round, Caratacus's small band followed them. He ducked under the low canopy and immediately felt the coolness under the trees. Noise from the horses was muted instantly by the close, dense foliage, but Caratacus could still make out his men readying themselves.

Trenos had been guided forward by his scouts. "We must move forward so we can watch the Romans come past before I give the signal," he whispered to Caratacus. He turned to Arios: "you can stay here if you like, in fact probably right that you do, we don't want you injured."

Arios, obviously relieved at this advice, nodded sagely.

Carefully, Trenos guided his horse past his waiting men, ducking under the branches. Eventually he came to his forward flank and his leading warriors standing just inside the copse, carefully watching the track about 30 paces away.

They heard him coming through the trees and one motioned him to dismount and come forward. He slid from his horse and, crouching, ran forward to join the front men.

The scout lying on the ground reached out and pulled Trenos down till he was kneeling on the grass. Their eyes were fixed on the path as he leaned in to speak in a hoarse whisper: "Our scouts are all in, Lord, the enemy should be on us pretty soon."

Trenos nodded and put his hand on the scout's shoulder. "You will give the signal. Prepare your men and wait until the last Roman is just past, then fall on the bastards with everything you have got."

"And what is the signal Lord?" asked the puzzled scout.

"The sound of you killing Romans." Trenos grinned. "But don't forget, we need prisoners."

Trenos slipped back to his horse and wheeled her round to take his place in the centre of his attack. He would not have long to wait.

He leaned forward to stroke his horse's neck. He could feel her getting restive, knowing something was about to happen. "Not long now," he murmured, swallowing hard. He hated these last moments before the battle started. It was the time to think about consequences, losing everything, losing a limb, losing the battle, letting his people down.

He grasped the handle of his sword and quietly drew it from the scabbard, making a satisfying metallic scraping sound in the quiet of the woods. He pushed the negative thoughts to the back of his mind and craned his neck to see if he could see the approaching enemy.

In fact, he heard them before he saw them. The jingle of metal against leather, the rhythmic tramp of 50 pairs of feet. Then at last they came into sight.

First was a rotund Roman officer mounted on a shining straw-coloured horse. The Roman officer looked magnificent despite his girth, in glittering armour and a high purple plume sprouting from his shining helmet. He rode with one hand holding the reins, the other, imperiously on his hip. He could be parading before his emperor in Rome, thought Trenos sourly.

Just behind him in the column, two soldiers pulled a four-wheeled handcart containing two large iron-bound boxes. Trenos wondered briefly what they were for.

Every warrior lurking in the trees was holding his breath, terrified that he would be the one to give the game away. Steadily the Roman ranks marched into the ambush. Trenos glanced quickly at Caratacus, who swallowed and pointed forward with his sword and nudged his horse forward, desperate for the off.

Suddenly a screech split the air from the rear of the column, followed by wild cries. The Romans stopped marching and looked round in confusion as the wild warriors burst from the wood bearing their broadswords. They fell on the Roman column grimly hacking into the panicking soldiers before they could rally and set up a defence.

Out of the corner of his eye, Caratacus could see the horse-riding officer staring in horror as his command crumbled before his eyes. He had not even drawn his sword, let alone used it.

Caratacus ploughed through the line, hacking down as the enemy cowered away. He checked and changed direction to attack an optio bellowing hoarsely to his men to get into formation. The optio saw him coming and jammed his spear butt into the ground, his right hand grasping his gladius. The Roman officer snarled and crouched, concentrating on Caratacus and never saw the wild haired, blue-faced Silurian who fought through the Roman line, felling him with a wild slash slicing through his neck between helmet and shoulder armour.

All along the line the Romans were falling back, trying to band together to form a defence. But it was too late. The men who stood and tried to fight were mown down by the sheer weight of the attack. The Romans without orders who turned and ran were pursued and cut down without mercy.

"Prisoners, remember prisoners," shouted Caratacus, but the warriors still had the blood lust and were savagely hacking into the few remaining Romans. He despaired of getting them to stop, then out of the corner of his eye saw the officer abandon his men and gallop away from the fray. Caratacus gestured to one of the archers, "Put an arrow into that horse and don't you dare hit the rider!"

Holding his horse with his knees, the archer pulled back on his bow, and with a twang, the heavily tipped arrow went airborne. Caratacus eagerly followed its track and whooped when he saw it swoop down and take the horse in the rump. It kicked in pain as the arrow sunk in, then stopped and reared, dumping the officer unceremoniously in the dust. As Trenos and Caratacus cantered up, the officer tried to rise. Only then did he attempt to draw his sword. His eyes were wild and he looked terrified as the warriors approached.

Caratacus slowed and looked down at the man. He was now a sorry looking soldier, carrying far too much weight and holding his sword as if for the first time. A rear party man if ever he had seen one, thought Caratacus. Ideal.

Pulling his horse to a halt, Caratacus swung a leg over the saddle and slipped to the ground, still holding his broadsword at the ready. A quick glance behind showed that the dead Romans were being stripped of armour and weapons. He grinned at Trenos, who leaned on his pommel, then turned his attention back to the officer, who was licking his lips nervously and holding his sword out as if ready to repel an attack.

Caratacus took one step forward and with one swipe knocked the sword from the Roman's hand. He jumped back and shrieked.

Caratacus shook his head. What a fool.

In Latin, he told the man to walk back down the track. Caratacus walked behind him, sword at the ready but sure it would not be needed. The tubby officer hung his head in abject defeat, trying not to look as the bodies of his men were looted. Seeing that the attack was successfully ended, Arios finally emerged from the tree line to find Caratacus and his hapless prisoner.

"I thought you warriors were supposed to die with your men," he observed reprovingly in his Celtic tongue.

"Perhaps the Romans have a different ethic," replied Caratacus, "but this sorry specimen should suit our needs if only he can work up the courage to escape."

The Roman officer looked from one to the other, knowing

he was the subject of the conversation but unable to follow the Celtic language.

Again in Latin, Caratacus asked the Roman why he was travelling the road.

"I am a tax collector," was the haughty reply.

"That explains everything," sneered Caratacus.

He motioned to one of his men. "Tie this piece of shit's hands and tether him to my saddle. I want to get a bit nearer to the fort." Turning to Arios, he asked brusquely "How long have we got?"

The priest looked round at the sky and felt the wind.

"We need to be back at the river by noon," he eventually asserted.

Caratacus grunted and looked round for Trenos. "We have to get these bloody Romans really angry, take away their fear of ambush by stoking up the fires of revenge. We want them to throw caution to the wind and come out fighting, desperate to kill every last one of us. I think I know how to do it. Do you mind if I have a go?"

Trenos shrugged his shoulders. "Firstly, I don't speak Latin, and second I am interested in seeing how you intend to make our fat friend co-operate."

"Just watch me," responded Caratacus. "Bring that cart the soldiers were pulling."

A smiling Trenos gestured to his men, and the cart was duly wheeled up. Caratacus asked the quivering officer what the boxes were for. He gulped, then said: "They're empty, we had only just started out, so hadn't collected any taxes at all." He looked ready to pass out with fear. The cart had two wheels and a T-shaped handle so that it could easily be pulled by two men.

Caratacus nodded: "It will do for our purposes."

He turned to the victorious warriors. "Now ditch the boxes and load up with as many Romans as it will take. Then tie this fine specimen to the handles. It's time for him to earn his coin."

The Roman officer looked on fearfully as enough of his nearly naked soldiers were dumped unceremoniously on the cart to fill it. He squealed in fear as he was manhandled to the front and lashed to the handle.

Caratacus stood with his arms folded, watching dispassionately. "I don't think we are going to get this blubbering fool to try and escape, so we'll have to try another way. Right let's go. Let's try and persuade the emperor here to earn his money."

One of the grinning warriors prodded the Roman officer in his ample rear and he squealed as the point of the sword punctured his pale skin. He strained at the handle, but despite prodigious prodding the officer failed to make the cart move. His efforts were not helped by the jeering of the Silure warriors surrounding him.

Losing patience, Caratacus shouted to the warriors to give the Roman a hand and they laughingly started to push the cart with its gruesome cargo along the track.

Caratacus signalled to the bowman who had downed the Roman's horse. "Stick with me and when I tell you, put an arrow in that bastard. Preferably don't kill him, I want him to say what he has seen, but I don't mind if, when he's done, he succumbs to his wounds."

The archer, whose entire upper body bore the customary swirling mass of blue tattoos, nodded and turned to look at the officer. "Just above the arse I think, into his stomach from the back, should live for an hour or so."

They pushed the cart along the track until eventually stopped by the scouts. "The fort is just beyond us, the track goes downhill and then starts to rise to where they are building. If you push the cart to the brow of the hill here, fatty should probably manage to get it at least down to the bottom."

"That'll do," replied Caratacus. "Get the men to lie down near the brow of the hill, and when the cart is halfway down they can stand up and start shouting at the Romans."

He gestured to the bowman, and taking his arm walked him forward to a handy tree near the summit.

"See where the track goes down the hill? Once that cart starts rolling he won't be able to hold it, and he will be pulled along until he either runs out of hill or tips over. Find yourself a good position and when you think it's right, put your arrow into him. Remember now, don't kill him. I want him to warn the garrison."

The archer nodded. "I think I'll stay here, it's a pretty good position."

Caratacus walked back to the wagon, and dropping into Latin again, spoke to the officer. "It's your lucky day," he said. "Not only have you survived an attack from the great Caratacus, but you will live to tell the tale. How do you feel about that?"

The prisoner had a haunted look on his face. On the one hand he was frighteningly relieved not to die, but was in no doubt what his reception would be when he arrived at the fort, roped to a wagon full of his own dead soldiers. His eyes were wild and his mouth opened and closed but he could think of nothing to say, except that he knew he didn't want to stay and equally, he certainly didn't want to go down that hill.

He was still jabbering when Caratacus gestured to the men to set the wagon rolling.

He watched as the warriors pushed it to the brow of the hill then let go as momentum took the cart on. They jeered as it picked up speed and the bodies packed in the back started to jolt up and down. The Roman officer let out a wail as his feet started windmilling, he knew if he tripped he would either fall under a wheel or cause the cart to tip, catapulting him over the handle.

Fear spurred his feet as he fought to stay in front of the careering vehicle. He was dimly aware of Roman voices shouting at him from the fort but was concentrating entirely on keeping upright as the world whizzed past.

The tattooed bowman watched impassively as his target gained speed, running furiously, his feet hardly touching the ground. The bowman shrugged, momentarily amused by his bizarre target, which was screaming loudly as it shot down the hill.

Suddenly a wheel struck a rock buried in the track and sent the cart and contents skyward. The Roman officer shrieked and was flung into the air, as bodies launched out over the sides. The officer crashed to the ground and slid down the hill, carried forward by the momentum, still lashed to the cart.

The bowman nocked his arrow and carefully raised the bow, exerting all his strength to pull back the taut gut. He didn't so much as aim the arrow as feel where it should go. He knew nothing of plotting wind speed, strength of his arm, even trajectory of the arrow flight. Years of practice meant his actions were all instinctive. Unerringly the arrow flew into the sky and with a thud came down and buried itself in the now inert Roman.

Roman soldiers who had been toiling on the fort, building up a soil rampart, threw down their picks and shovels, buckled on sword belts, snatching up spears and shields and hurried into position. When the first section was ready they were doubled down the hill, across the small stream then back up the other side. Despite their discipline there were cries of outrage as the soldiers registered their dead, near naked comrades.

Caratacus watched as the small section reached the cart. Then he turned to his men: "Right boys, give them a volley, then let's fuck off smartly."

In an instant the sky was filled with arrows as the archers targeted the vengeful soldiers. Without waiting to watch their arrows land they turned and ran for their horses. Caratacus was the last to leave the crest but, before doing so, raised his arm in salute. He wanted to ensure the Romans below had a good look at his blonde flowing hair, confirming what he knew the officer would tell them before he died.

He sprinted back to his horse tethered in the trees, and much to his surprise found the bowman holding the reins. Wordlessly, he took them, then swung into the saddle, and the two galloped back up the track following the retreating warriors. Caratacus was in a good mood. Suddenly he didn't really care if the masterplan to drown Romans failed. Whatever happened, they were bound to follow in hot pursuit, and the riverbank was as good a place as any to stop them. He knew the garrison would send out a heavy force, but they would be attacking across the river, then up the bank, with the archers raining iron down on them all the way.

It should make a monumental victory but, he mused, what if the priest was right and they did manage to lure the Romans into a trap? That would show he had the gods on his side, and that was worth its weight in gold.

He looked across at the bowman, who was riding with one hand on his reins, the other holding his bow. His arrows were easy to hand, slung in a quiver on his back.

"What's your name, bowman?" asked Caratacus.

The bowman remained staring forwards. Like most of the Silures, he was a small, curly haired man, but astonishingly wide at the shoulder. Caratacus supposed that was from pulling back a longbow from an early age. His hands were like shovels and biceps bulged under his bare skin.

"I am named Sagito, as was my father and probably his father. We have always been bowmen and always feared by the tribes around us."

Caratacus nodded: "And now the Romans will fear you. If I had a 100 like you, we would soon push the bastards back into the sea."

Sagito did not respond. He knew his worth to the tribe and didn't need to boast.

They were in the open country again with scouts spread out in a screen front and rear. Caratacus was twisting round to catch any sight of pursuit when Sagito prodded him unceremoniously with his bow. "The priest is ahead and seems in a hurry."

Caratacus quickly turned and saw the priest thwacking his knees into his protesting donkey, trying to make it move faster. His feet seemed to be trailing the ground, so small was the animal, which was harrumphing and squealing at this treatment.

The priest was waving his arms about as he tried to coax the donkey into greater speed. Finally he was close enough for the warriors to hear him.

"Where have you been," he screamed, saliva flecking from his mouth. "The river is almost ready, we must hurry."

Caratacus leaned back in the saddle, "I'm afraid that's sort of out of our control. The Romans will be along but I don't think we can ask them to hurry."

"If you don't do something soon you will miss the opportunity," gasped the wild-eyed priest.

Caratacus looked at him for a moment then turned to Sagito. "Get a few of your bowmen mates and join up with the scouts, we need those Roman bastards to forget caution and come after us at speed. Can you do that? The danger is that you may make them even more cautious, so show yourselves but slay only a few."

Sagito nodded and pealed away towards the rear of the column. Suddenly there was a shout and as Caratacus looked up, he saw the scouts galloping over the last hill brow, waving their swords.

"They're right behind us, Lord. Some on horseback, most on foot, but the men on foot are marching faster than I have ever seen."

Caratacus gave a wolfish grin. "Excellent, take the column back to the river, and you, Sagito take your men back down the track, let go a few arrows, then turn and run as if terrified. Don't stop until you join us on the other side of the river."

With that he wheeled his horse and waved the column on.

"Come priest, get a move on or you will be left behind for the Romans."

Arios needed no second telling. Once again he applied his knees to his suffering donkey, who seemed happier to be moving in company with the bigger horses.

The column moved away as the first Roman scouts appeared on the top of the low brow. The first, a sweating optio on horseback, raised his spear to signal he had seen the fleeing enemy. He was still out of arrow range, but Sagito knew that would soon change. He watched as more men joined the optio on the top of the incline. One of them had a fine plume on his shiny helmet. Sagito had no idea what it meant but guessed he was a leader. He gestured to his fellow bowmen. "Aim for the horses," he growled, "but leave the one with the fancy hat to me."

Sagito and his five fellow bowmen quietly nudged their horses back along the track, guiding their animals with their knees as they gripped their nocked bows. When Sagito judged they were in range, he grunted and pulled back his bow. As he let fly, his comrades also shot, releasing their deadly hail onto the Romans who were now fighting to control their horses. The first arrow from Sagito's bow thudded into the hind quarters of the leader's horse making it scream with shock. It jumped and plunged in panic and nearly threw the rider. Then other arrows landed. Two missed the plunging horses altogether, but three found their mark in Roman horsemen. The bowmen yelled in triumph, then quickly turned and galloped after the column, pursued by vengeful horsemen.

After a short gallop, Sagito risked a look round. The Romans had stopped. An element of reason had prevailed and they were waiting for the rest of their column to catch up. But they would not be far behind. As they arrived at the river's edge the rest of the raiding party was climbing the far bank and disappearing into the woods. The river was wide and seemed placid, with an oily, glistening sheen. In the middle was the sandbank surrounded by two channels. Judging by the damp stain up the bank they were at low tide.

The bowmen splashed into the water and quickly crossed to the sandbank. On the other side, Caratacus waved to them to hurry. The Roman column was fast approaching.

Cainos stood by Caratacus, peering anxiously, first at the sky, then at the river. "You must get your men to challenge the Romans," he said firmly. "Insult them, and dare them to come across. You must entice them into the river, and then the river will stop them."

Sagito reined in his horse in the hock-deep river when he saw Caratacus. "They have split their forces, Lord. About 500 cavalry and infantry are hurrying ahead and many more are following."

Caratacus had a wild grin on his face. "Even if Sabrina lets us down, we will cut these eager Romans to pieces, then disappear before the rest of the buggers have time to catch up. To your places and let them hear you."

The archers took their places along the riverbank, lining up with their fellow warriors. The assembled Silurians, capering and cursing at the approaching enemy called down threats of the terrible things they would do to the invaders.

Lenc quietly wandered up to the riverbank when he heard the raiding party return. They were in high spirits and recounted the tale of the fat tax officer roped to his cart and roaring with fear as he shot down the track with bodies bouncing out everywhere. With a bit of luck that could just rebound on you, thought Lenc bitterly. He watched as the last of the warriors splashed across the seemingly placid river, urged on by the priest, Arios, once again leading his donkey.

As the archers struggled up the bank, the Roman cavalry arrived on the far side. Lenc involuntarily stepped back under the tree canopy, but it was highly unlikely that he would be recognised from the far bank.

Nearby, Sagito watched as over three hundred horsemen reined in under the command of the man with the fancy helmet. He had found a new horse, noted the archer. The Romans paused, taking in the unholy din from the Silurian bank. Swords were drawn and lances lowered to the charge position, and within minutes, the Roman infantry, terrible in their remorseless stamping drill, arrived and without pausing, swept down to the river. The officer waved them forward as his cavalry split right and left to flank them.

They waded into the river and, gradually, their discipline disintegrated. It was every man for himself as they surged into the thigh-deep water. "Come on you swivel-eyed bastards," shouted a soaked Centurion. "If those hairy arsed bog-trotters can cross this river, then so can we."

The noise from the far bank intensified as the prancing, dancing warriors hurled insults at the Romans, who, out of breath after their breakneck advance, now had the river-crossing to contend with. The horses of the cavalry fared better than the wading men, though the riders had to struggle to keep in line.

No time for catching breath, they all surged forward and, at last, began to bellow their own challenge. Officers tried to bully their men into some semblance of a disciplined force, but the soldiers were beyond that. They had been humiliated by this bunch of blue painted savages and although exhausted, wanted revenge. But as they waded nearer, the sky was blackened with iron as the Silures shot their heavy arrows. The rain of death fell, and men screamed as the iron heads thudded through plate armour. Even so they did not stop their inexorable march forward.

They were getting closer to the bank and, as their battle cries took on a more exultant note, they could scent victory. Lenc found himself thinking that if he did not want to get caught by the rapidly advancing Romans he ought to make himself scarce, when suddenly, the Romans froze as a strange new noise drowned out the shouting Silurians, a rushing sound like nothing any had heard before. It grew louder as the Silurians stopped their mad ranting and the puzzled soldiers looked round for the source of the noise. The river water had taken on a heavier, slicker sheen, and the sky darkened a second time. Then, with eyes widened and mouth wide open as if trying to scream, a soldier pointed with his sword downstream as a wall of water more than a man's height rushed towards them.

Superstitious solders gulped and muttered incantations to their gods as the wall of water curled above them. At first they stood rooted to the spot, not believing what they were witnessing. Then one man turned and tried to wade for the apparent safety of the sandbank and suddenly the attack was over as the panic-stricken soldiers turned then struggled to reach dry land. But they stood no chance as the wall of water smashed into them while they floundered and were viciously sucked into the vortex of the huge wave. Despairing cries were heard as men, encumbered by heavy armour threw up their arms before going under and were dragged along the river-bed.

Along with the Silures around him, Lenc stood, open mouthed in disbelief. They stopped their chanting and tried to take in the almost contemptuous sweeping away of hundreds of men, doomed to a watery death by the river and their heavy equipment.

Their dry comrades, on the bank shouted encouragement, then fell silent as the wall of water gathered speed and strength, sweeping over the sandbank snatching men and horses and hurling them violently upstream. The surge tide scoured the river, smashing into drowning men, already tired and struggling to stay upright in their heavy armour.

Both the Silurians on one bank and the Romans on the other, fell utterly silent at this awesome manifestation of the power of the gods.

Caratacus stared in awe and disbelief. He had seen it but just could not believe it. How could a river muster such power?

He turned and looked at Cainos the priest, whose head was on his chest as he prayed. On the other bank, also looking dumbfounded was a group of Roman officers, resplendent in their plumed helmets and glittering armour. With them were the standard bearers of the XX Valeria. The central figure of the group looked broken, as if he could not believe that the might of Rome could be deserted so emphatically by the gods.

In the water a few soldiers who survived the onslaught

stumbled back across to the bank. Their faces showed the horror of their ordeal and their surprise that they were in the ranks of the few survivors. Dead bodies, face down, slowly slipped away, carried by the now placid tide, or wedged in the undergrowth.

Reluctantly, when it was obvious there would be no more survivors wading back, the senior decurion finally made a gesture to his troops, then slowly led them from the field.

On his side of the river, Caratacus still could not take in what had just happened. He knew it was fantastic and an amazing opportunity to unite the superstitious tribesmen. When the story spread and spread it would, it would light a fire under the whole country and the tribes would flock to his banner. How could he lose when the gods had given such a clear sign?

"Do you believe now?" yelled an exultant Caratacus. "Who could not believe that we have right, and the gods, on our side?"

At this, the exultant warriors raised their swords and shouted out their war cries. They had annihilated the hated enemy without losing a single man.

Caratacus let out a ringing cry, then mounting his horse again, pointed his sword to the west.

"This is a great victory," he thundered. "We must take the fight to these bastard Romans until we have swept them into the sea. Go now and tell everyone of this incredible day and how the gods helped us. We shall reclaim our land."

Lenc had watched the whole drama unfold from the safety of the bank. He had stayed undercover, not wanting to be spotted by the attacking Romans and was horrified at the scene of carnage he had witnessed. At first he had some twinges of worry when the uncharacteristic rabble of Roman soldiers stormed forward, but thought that the discipline of the optios would surely pull the soldiers into line. Then when the prediction of the druid priest came true he could only watch in horror and confusion as, before his eyes, the best part of half a cohort was swept away in a maelstrom of churning, muddy water.

Could it be true? Could the gods be against them? Did the tribes have the support and approval of the gods?

If that was the case, he might as well pack up and make his way back to the Legion.

With these depressing thoughts he trudged after the warriors, head down and lost in thought behind the exultant victors.

CHAPTER XXV

For all except one, the ride back to Gobbannion was a raucous affair, as the column celebrated a spectacular triumph over the hated enemy. Lenc ambled along at the tail of the column, not responding when riders sought him out to taunt him with their superiority over the Romans. He wrapped himself tightly in his cloak, and stared fixedly at his horse's ears, aware he was endangering his flimsy cover, but so depressed he didn't care, worse, couldn't think what to do next. After a while no-one came to taunt him, he was no fun at all, and was left on his own chewing the dust of the column.

In this black mood, he became aware of another horseman moving up on him from the rear. A straggler or a scout probably. Either way, thought Lenc, if the bastard doesn't just carry on without taking the piss, he might just find out how Romans can really fight.

After a minute or two, the warrior spoke and Lenc started. He knew that voice. Shaking himself from his dark thoughts, he squinted curiously at the man. He was wearing a cloak, and a hood obscured his face, but Lenc knew who he was.

"Agrippa, is that you? Teutatis' balls but you're taking a risk."

"Had to be done," shrugged the Pathfinder. "Anyway, that lot are too busy celebrating to worry about you, and therefore me. I saw that yellow-haired bastard, Caratacus leading the column with the chief and that young warrior Trenos. I had to find out what had happened, then saw you bringing up the rear."

"It's a hell of a story," conceded Lenc. "The priest came up with a plan and it worked beautifully. Caratacus crossed the big river, killed some of our people in the foulest way and the garrison sent what looked like a cohort and cavalry after him. They were in hot pursuit and halfway across the river when a bloody great wave drowned the lot. One minute the pride of Rome was splashing across the river, about knee deep, then the next they were all swept away on a huge tide. I saw it, but I couldn't believe it," he said bitterly.

"How many men lost?" asked Agrippa quietly.

"Best part of a cohort, when you include cavalry. But just as bad, the Silures think that it's a message from the gods, a sign that Caratacus is going to lead them to victory. He's got the druids on his side and this victory could unite the bloody lot of them against us.

"I'm sorry I couldn't get word to you, but they were watching me like a hawk."

Agrippa brushed aside the apology. "It would have been far too dangerous to try and get word out. You did the right thing. Teutatis' balls indeed," he said quietly. They rode on in silence for a while, Lenc descending back into his black mood, his companion thinking furiously.

Eventually Agrippa looked up. "Where does this put Caratacus?" he asked.

Lenc looked up. "Eh? Top of the dung heap I suppose, so what?"

"Come on man, snap out of it and start thinking. We have to figure out what's going to happen next so we can decide what to do about it. What's that devious bastard going to do now?"

Lenc thought for a second or two. "Well, before the priest whispered in Caratacus's ear, Verico had just about agreed to join up with the Ordovices, when he had a dream which saw bad portents and he changed his mind. It was after that the priest suggested this plan to Caratacus." Lenc pondered. "I think it pretty likely that Verico now has no choice because the warriors are with Caratacus and they will almost certainly go north to join with the Ordovices."

Agrippa nodded. "I agree. I'll report back to Legate Quintus Equitius and suggest the legions move north but stay on their side of the river. We'll only come across when we know where the meeting is to be. I will also suggest that the Fourteenth move down from Deva to block them from fleeing. We'll have the bastards yet."

He leaned over and gripped Lenc by the arm. "Hang on soldier," he whispered fiercely. "You've had a bad time, but you've done well. This has been a disaster and will no doubt shake the garrison, but we've had upsets before and come through. This could well be the start of us nailing that bastard's hide to the wall and subduing the whole of this god-forsaken place. Then maybe we can all go home," he ended with a grin. "I'll have a man in the first wood south of the town on the riverbank. He'll be in position every evening until shortly after dusk. Go to him if you need to get a message to me."

Word had gone ahead to Gobannion and it seemed that the whole township had turned out to line the walls and cheer their conquering heroes. As the column approached, townspeople came out to meet them, a great homecoming for returning warriors.

Lenc peeled off and went wearily in search of Anton. He noticed that Caratacus carried on with Verico and Trenos, going to ram home the meeting with the Ordovices, he thought bitterly. No doubt he would find out about it in good time, but right now, he needed some time to himself, perhaps with a decent drink then a good sleep.

As he approached their rudimentary camp, Anton spotted him and stood, quivering with righteous indignation. He even had his hands on his hips as he started to scold Lenc. "Just where do you think you have been?" he demanded, "I have been here, all alone, trying to run…"

"Just leave it," interrupted Lenc as he slid from his horse. "You're not my wife or my boss and right now I am hungry and very tired. So unless you have some food handy, then I suggest you shut that whingeing mouth of yours and keep out of my way."

Anton looked shocked and just this once had nothing to say. Exasperated and angry, he flounced off as Lenc spread his cloak on the ground and flopped onto it. Gratefully he stretched out and looked at the sky. It was good to be off that horse. His eyes started to close just as Anton shuffled back, bearing a plate of food and a mug of cider.

"I don't know why I am doing this," he muttered. "No gratitude, no concern, I could have been attacked by bandits all alone here, and does anyone care? Not a bit of it. I don't know why I bother."

Despite himself Lenc grinned and struggled upright. "Anton, old friend, you have your faults but you can usually be relied upon when it comes to food. You are a lifesaver."

Lenc went for the mug first and gulped down a good mouthful of the sharp tangy cider. Then he turned his attention to the plate of crunchy dark bread, cheese and cold meat, wolfing down handfuls until, eventually coming up for air.

"I was ready for that," he said eventually. Anton's eyes grew rounder and bigger as Lenc recounted the tale of the river wave and the destruction of so many Romans. "Maybe the gods are on the side of the barbarians," he whispered.

"Maybe, maybe not," responded Lenc, "but what it does mean is that if they had any doubts about fighting us, they've all gone now. They think they have the blessing of the gods and that's worth its weight in gold.

"Now I need to get my head down, so why don't you wander up to the town and see if you can find anything out? It'll be a good excuse to try a couple of taverns."

Anton was inclined to accept that suggestion and as he bustled across the meadow, Lenc rolled himself into his cloak and closed his eyes. He slept the sleep of the dead until after three hours, his bladder woke him. He was still reeling from the cataclysmic death and destruction of the sudden killer wave.

The legions will be galvanised, he thought. They will never be able to stand by until the taint of such a severe loss is avenged. This could be just the spur needed to lay waste the tribes and even kill Caratacus. Not even the gods could take on the might of Rome. He wasn't too sure about that last bit, but it sounded good.

He was still thinking such philosophical thoughts when he spied Anton waddling and puffing to get back to camp. He was hurrying, which in itself was a sign that he had juicy news to impart.

When the portly trader finally arrived, he flopped onto a log and wheezed as he tried to catch his breath. After dabbing his forehead with the end of the kerchief knotted round his neck, he finally looked at Lenc.

"Zeus's balls but I'm parched, hand me a mug of that rat's piss will you?"

By now Lenc had lost what little patience he had, and with an exasperated snort hurried to the wagon where the gourd of cider was hanging in the shade and poured out a mugful.

"Come on, fat one, out with it, what have you heard?"

Anton contrived to look offended. "I didn't think that fat people were any good at anything, least that's what you've said in the past."

"No I haven't, I never said that," replied Lenc indignantly.

"Well you probably thought it then," said Anton airily.

Lenc threw his arms up and growled with frustration. "If you don't tell me, I'm going to thump the life out of you."

"That won't be necessary," replied Anton hastily, aware that his teasing wasn't going down well.

He took another swig of cider and grimaced at it. "Bloody horse piss, wish we had some decent wine."

He looked at Lenc standing above him. "Well they've gone

and done it, everyone in the tavern was talking about it. The Silures are joining forces with another mob further north and then they'll take on the Romans together. There's to be a general council this evening."

Lenc digested this. It was the news he had been expecting, but Agrippa would want the detail. He would go to the meeting and then would have to find the pathfinders.

That evening, he joined a stream of men heading for the council chamber. Once inside, he tried to stay at the back of the hall so he could see but not be marked out. He looked round and felt the buzz of excitement in the air, these tribesmen were just dying to take on Rome he realised.

Several of the village elders stood around Verico's ceremonial chair, looking important, but of the main players there was no sign.

Like the rest, Lenc was impatient to hear the news, and there was a collective sigh and rustling when Verico entered the hall, followed by Caratacus, Trenos and Veldicca.

Verico settled himself on his wooden throne and waited impatiently for his followers to find a place to stand or sit. Veldicca scanned the room and smiled when she finally caught sight of Lenc, then quickly looked down demurely.

Verico stood and motioned for silence, surveying the gathering waiting breathlessly for his words. "Fellow Silurians," he started. "Some of you were with me when we witnessed the most incredible sight of an entire Roman army swept away in an instant by our mighty river. If you had told me of this I would have said you were a fanciful storyteller, but I saw it with my own eyes, just as Cainos the druid prophesied.

"It shows that Caratacus was right for us to join the other tribes and take the battle to the invaders. It shows we have the gods with us, so how can we fail? We must spread the word and tell the whole tribe that we march north, and when we meet the Ordovices we shall turn east and drive the invaders from our lands.

"Tonight we celebrate a wondrous victory, and tomorrow we prepare for our march north. The rest of the tribe will join us at Pennocrucium, just over the Ordovician border," continued Verico. "When we have mustered we will then go on to attack Uriconium, the Roman stronghold in the north. When we successfully take that we will drive south, sweeping every accursed Roman out of our way and destroy their forts while we are at it.

"When we ride into battle it will be with the gods at our side."

A great cheer rose up from the assembly, how could they fail, thought Lenc bitterly. The gods are on their side. When the Silurians and Ordovices band together they would become a formidable force.

No doubt they would attract even more support when they marched on Uriconium, still vulnerable as the garrison had only just started replacing timber palisades with stone.

The meeting broke up and gossiping tribesmen spilled out into the muddy walkway full of the momentous news. Those that had not taken part in the raid on the Hafren were demanding the incredible story be told again. It was a lot to take in.

"You still here Roman?" Deep in thought, Lenc had not noticed Trenos push through the throng to confront him.

"There's nothing wrong with your eyesight," replied Lenc. Trenos stood, legs apart and fists on his waist. "I would have thought you would have cleared off after our wondrous victory."

Lenc shrugged, "It matters not to me, we'll be looking for fresh trade pretty soon. With so many people heading for this Pennocrucium, maybe that's where we shall go next."

"Well you better be quick," sneered Trenos, "because you might not find too many Ordovices there to buy your trinkets."

"How so?" asked a puzzled Lenc despite himself.

Trenos laughed triumphantly. "I suppose there's no harm in telling you, Verico has agreed to join the Ordovices precisely so we can get into their stronghold and kill every last one of the thieving bastards. Then when that job is done, never mind Uriconium, we shall come back to our own lands, secure that our northern flank is safe and sort out you bastard Romans ourselves. One after another all our enemies will fall."

"But I thought you were behind Caratacus in uniting to get rid of the Romans altogether?" Asked Lenc, aghast.

Trenos stepped forward, "Just remember, twice now we have shown the Romans how to fight. When we start burning their forts they'll soon find other people to try and invade. You'll see, they'll turn their attention north and leave us alone. Besides if they're foolish enough to try and attack us, we'll do the same thing again and properly kick their arses. Besides we don't need the Ordovices, we can sort out the garlic munchers quite easily by ourselves."

Lenc could only stand and stare at the young warrior leader. The sheer bare-faced lunacy of his idiotic boast took his breath away. In the end he just shrugged and added: "Well you certainly seem to have it all worked out."

"Just watch me," smirked Trenos.

Later that evening Lenc wandered down to the river bank and followed it downstream. He sauntered through the long meadow grass swishing at his legs until out of sight of the settlement, then quickened his pace, pushing on for the safety of the woods.

Immediately he reached the trees the going became more difficult. He had to shove branches and foliage out of the way, not daring to leave the riverbank. He expected that the courier would be waiting, hidden, quite deep in the wood, safe from curious eyes. So he was quite unprepared when he walked into a clearing and found a stranger in a woven cloak and leggings sitting comfortably on the bank, with a pole and line in the river. Could this be him? Lenc knew he mustn't get this wrong.

The fisherman looked round as Lenc approached warily. He

smiled and nodded.

"Come to do some fishing?" he asked in Latin.

"How did you know it was me," asked Lenc suspiciously.

"I saw you when you returned from the Hafren. We were all told to mark you well when you were talking to Agrippa. You might not have seen us but we saw you all right."

Lenc shrugged, at least he had made contact.

"I have some information which must get back to the Tribune. The Silures are meeting the Ordovices at a place called Pennocrucium. It's a hill fort to the north, just over the tribal border. Caratacus and the chief's party will get there first, they're leaving tomorrow at first light and will be joined by the rest of the tribe, who have received the summons to prepare for battle and hurry north. But here's the best bit. The Silures have no intention of joining with the Ordovices, they see it as a heaven-sent opportunity to slaughter the lot of them and secure their northern flank, then they plan to take us on by themselves."

"Well it's ambitious," said the pathfinder after a moment's thought.

"I don't think Verico wants to venture too far into Ordovician territory," conceded Lenc, "but he's also worried about what the Legion will do in revenge for losing so many men on the Hafren."

The pathfinder looked at Lenc steadily. "If you're going with them, I doubt whether we will manage to get in contact again, but keep an eye out for us. I think we are all in the hands of the gods."

Lenc shivered. He had seen what the gods could do, and lately they weren't acting in Rome's favour. He put the thought aside and nodded. "I must go, before they come looking for me." Lenc reached inside his tunic and pulled out his first map. "Here take this, it's probably not much use if the tribe is going north, but it's a map of this area, and I've included as much detail as possible of the observation hill."

He clapped the pathfinder on the back, who threw his

makeshift fishing pole into the river and stood, shaking the damp grass from his cloak. "Be lucky," he said with a grin and faded into the trees.

Lenc turned and walked carefully back along the riverbank. He was relieved that he had managed to pass on his vital information, but was starting to wonder just how much use it was going to be as matters seemed to be coming to a head. Maybe it was time to cut and run.

CHAPTER XXVI

Publius Ostorius Scapula, second governor of Britannia, had been appointed to bring this damp and cloudy island to heel. So far, it was not going to plan, despite the optimistic reports he sent back to Rome at regular intervals. He commanded four legions throughout the conquered part of Britannia and had been forced to move two of them to the west to crush Caratacus once and for all. It should have been a lot easier than this, he reflected, but these damn people never seem to know when they were beaten. His authority came from the right hand of the Emperor himself, the man who ruled the biggest and richest empire in the world. Yet he could not even subdue a few belligerent tribesmen.

Scapula gripped the edge of his map board in silent rage. All his plans, and the ambitions of the 20,000 men under his command were focused on killing just one man. If that meant a bloodbath in the following campaign, then so be it. Better to rule a country empty of people than this turbulent and bloodthirsty lot.

He had moved his command from the relative security of Camulodunum to the other side of the country, where he could give the campaign his undivided attention. Now his command group and the XX Valeria were camped at Durocornovium with another hard day's march to the frontier forts. The Twentieth had marched west to reinforce the II Augustan, which had suffered damaging losses against the Silures. Scapula gave grudging approval of the native tactics, their ambush of a foraging cohort of the Second quickly followed by another disaster ending in the drowning of almost a complete cohort, some of his best troops.

From what little intelligence reports he had gleaned, Caratacus had the co-operation of the Silures, and the guidance of the druids. He refused to believe that the river trap was caused by sorcery, although he knew that was being muttered round the camp fires. He stared at the rough map of the inhospitable and threatening country they were making for and shuddered. He was not a well man and the thought of campaigning in some of the toughest terrains in the empire filled him with revulsion.

He coughed, then coughed again, unable to stop, covering his mouth with a piece of linen. He tried not to look at the contents of the cloth, the bright red bubbly blood that had no business there.

Caius, his personal slave hurried in, concerned at the coughing, knowing what it meant. "Can I get you some warm wine and honey, Lord?" Scapula leaned against the map board, his head touching the leather surface. There was sweat on his brow, but he felt chilled and cold. "Yes please, I would appreciate that. Can you call Legate Quintus Equitius and the Twentieth Command Group, I need to brief them." While the staff officers were summoned, Scapula went into a small side room and lay down. He gratefully took the drink offered by his anxious slave and closed his eyes.

XXth Valeria had marched out of Camulodunum and across country, west to the frontier forts to join their advance party. He, the Governor, had ridden at their head, underlining the seriousness of the coming campaign.

The Twentieth Command Group hurriedly filed into the large briefing tent in the Principia, Scapula's headquarters of the Roman Army of Britannia. The Commander of XX Valeria, Quintus Equitius led his men in, seniors at the front, cascading back to the lower orders, who scrabbled for a seat, or stood around the walls. To one side were the line of scribes, ready to take notes, which would not only go back to Rome, but to the legions spread across conquered Britannia.

Caius dutifully signalled his master. They were waiting for him.

Wearily Scapula struggled to his feet and visibly collecting himself, pulled his shoulders back and head high, strode into the tent, now thick with men. At his appearance, the assembled ranks stood and crashed to attention as he walked to the map table and sat down heavily.

He motioned them to sit, then glanced at the threadbare map behind him.

"Gentlemen, I had hoped that we would have had better maps as we start this campaign, but as usual we shall be drawing them as we progress.

"The setback that Caratacus inflicted on us at the river crossing was heavy. The story is going round that these druids are imbued with magical powers. Tell your men that is not the case. They are priests, yes, but ordinary men. A spear through the guts will kill them just as effectively. But if you allow these stories to fester it will impede the legion's ability to fight, and make no mistake, this campaign will be as hard as any we have embarked on, and one we cannot lose."

Scapula banged his fist on the table "Get this thought out of their minds straight away. I want no more talk of sorcery.

"Once in position we shall advance northwards, skirting the line of the hills then turn inland when we have found the enemy. Your colleagues of the Fourteenth in Deva Victrix will advance south and westwards but give us time to march north. I will send them the signal to march when I judge we are close enough to spring a trap. If necessary, we will drive the bastards into the sea and send every thrice damned druid with them.

"My Pathfinders tell me that the Silures are on the move north and they have Caratacus with them. If he stays true to form, he will want to gather as big an army as possible then face us in open battle. He will, of course lose, and in the bargain we will have stopped the Silures from raiding us.

"Now we need to use all haste in this campaign, as I don't need to remind you, winter is approaching. We have some time yet, but we need Caratacus's head on a pole, and the Silures destroyed as a fighting force, before we can return to winter quarters."

He fixed the officers with a stare. "I will turn you over to the planners, we march on the morrow and our objective is the final annihilation of this upstart. If we take a few druids with him, so much the better," he nodded. "Our gods will prevail."

As he left the tent, his officers got down to the exacting business of preparing the line of march for over 6000 men, with cavalry, artillery, food and supplies, tentage, weapons and the thousand and one details to be confirmed before the expedition could start.

Two battle scarred optios stayed seated, content to let their juniors sort out supplies and passwords. One fingered a small statuette of Mithras, the god of soldiers, which he always carried in his belt pouch. "Got a bad feeling about this one mate. Those Germans were good at witchcraft, but I've never encountered anything like this lot."

His friend smiled uneasily. "We don't have much choice, do we? All we can do is what we always do, rest your head on your chinstrap and get stuck in. First one to bring back a druid's head gets free drinks all night, how about that?"

With all the earth-shattering events of the past few days, Lenc knew he had some hard thinking to do about his future. His relationship with the tribe was as uneasy as ever, but he was duty bound to stay with his mission as long as possible, particularly in the face of the crushing setbacks to the Legion.

He reluctantly accepted that he had to chance his arm once more and ride north to the meeting with the Ordovices. He knew that word of the drowning of so many soldiers on the river was being accepted as absolute proof that the gods approved of Caratacus and his tactics. By Mithras, it certainly looked that way.

He wondered if the stunning victory would change Verico's mind about slaughtering the Ordovice. Probably not, he thought gloomily, that was one war that had been going on for longer than people could remember and wasn't likely to stop just because there was a new threat, even if it was twice as deadly. But wouldn't that work in Rome's favour?

One thing was sure, he could no longer rely on the cover of his trader friend Anton. Where the Silures were trekking was no place for a heavily laden cart. Besides, should the need arise, by himself he would have a better chance of making a break to the east.

He felt a bit better after making such life-changing decisions and smiled as Anton walked across the bridge from Gobannion with a big grin on his face and a large shining salmon in his arms.

"We shall eat well tonight," he beamed. Lenc could only smile and agree to forage for wild herbs and fruits.

After he had devoured a great mound of salmon, stuffed with wild garlic, cabbage and whinberries Lenc had found growing wild on the mountain, Anton sat back with a generous tumbler of cider and prepared to wax philosophic. "You know," he said thoughtfully, patting his replete stomach, "just when you think this god-forsaken country is the arsehole of the world, along comes a magnificent fish and makes you think it's actually not that bad at all."

Lenc grinned at his fat friend. "Why is it that your state of mind is entirely controlled by your stomach? As long as you're well fed you are the happiest of men, yet if you have to go hungry suddenly the world is a terrible place."

"That's not true at all," responded Anton loftily, "it's just that when you appreciate the finer things of life like I do, the opportunity to eat such a magnificent fish is something to savour. All you do is gobble it down because it's just fuel to you, whereas I appreciate good food, and of course, strive to do it justice." With that he sucked his teeth and took a reflective swig of cider.

"Well now that you have sampled some of the nicer things of this place I'm afraid I have some news for you, which you may or may not think is to your advantage."

Anton looked up warily. "Oh yes, what is it now?" he asked anxiously. "Are you expecting me to wander off into the woods looking for ruffians who would as soon stick a knife in me as wish me good day? Because I'm not. Don't even ask." He reclined with an air of finality.

If anything, Anton had just made things easier, thought Lenc with relief.

"No, my friend, I am afraid we have come to the parting of the ways. We have done well so far, you and I, but I must follow the tribe to their meeting with the Ordovices and that trail is not suitable for a horse and cart. You could stay here for a while, or it may be safer to head due east, where you will eventually find a more cultured and certainly less dangerous clientele. If you want to head east, we can start out together and I will set you on the right direction. How's that?"

Anton opened his mouth to say something, then shut it again. He was clearly relieved but tried not to show it, then eventually managed: "Well if you're sure." He seemed hesitant and bit his lip. "I won't say it has been a pleasant experience, and I won't say I'm glad it's over…but I'm glad it's over." Impulsively he struggled upright and embraced a startled Lenc. "Now you take care of yourself."

Lenc still had the horse he had borrowed and figured that no-one would mind very much if he held on to it for a bit longer. After all, he was ostensibly riding as part of the Chieftain's retinue, so needed a horse. Besides, with a bit of luck he would be long gone before the owner caught up with him.

The next day, Lenc, then a yawning Anton, roused from his snoring, were up with the sun, breaking camp and readying the cart for the journey north. Lenc paused as the first finger of sun touched the top of the bowl-shaped mountain, turning it a rustic red. He wondered if he would see it again.

Despite Anton's grumbling, they were soon on the road, as the settlement was starting to stir. Caratacus and his camp were also up and about early, preparing to join the column of warriors which would soon be assembling on the meadow. Lenc waved as they rolled past.

"See you on the road," shouted Caratacus, Lenc knew that the chief's party, including the now venerated Caratacus would forge ahead, eager for the new adventure. The trail would be full of riders, followed by the foot soldiers.

All that morning they plodded along the valley, following the river until Lenc called a halt when he felt the gradual upwards slope to the forbidding hills ahead getting steeper. He looked round and gestured to the east.

"That's your path, Anton. If you follow this line of hills keeping it to your right you will eventually pass into easier country. The nearest Roman fort is well to the south from here, but if you wanted you could head towards it. Sooner or later, you will strike the Wysg river which will lead to the fort and from there if you keep going south-east you will reach the sea. Sell the rest of your goods and get what you can for the horse and cart, and you should end this experience with a good profit."

Anton looked down, fidgeting with the reins. "In a way, I wish I was coming with you, but I expect I'll manage to quell that urge. May the gods be with you, and for my sake be careful. And it might be as well to stay away from that pretty princess, she could well be the death of you."

Lenc smiled at the anxious trader and leaned over in the saddle to grasp his arm.

"Farewell old friend and god speed."

Anton gulped and tried to smile, then flicked the reins and the horse plodded on. Lenc watched as Anton waved for the last time as he rounded a corner and out of view. Anton had been an irritation, but he had his moments, and at least he was on the same side. Sort of.

For the rest of the day, Lenc passed a stream of walking warriors, all headed in the same direction. He started to wonder just how many men Caratacus would muster. From what he could see, the Silures would number at least 4000, with probably the same number of Ordovices and maybe another 2000 of assorted ex-slaves and warriors who just wanted to fight Romans.

Not a bad native army, he thought, but no match for two disciplined legions, druids or no.

The journey was pleasant enough following the meandering river. Through the trees he could see glowering hills on both sides and for the best part of the morning climbed ever upward, his horse ambling along in its own time. They passed through a hamlet and almost immediately the river funnelled into a steep-sided crevasse.

The day was warm and in the trees there was almost no breeze. He dismounted to give his horse a rest and enjoyed the stiff uphill walk, besides, it felt good to stretch his legs.

That night he slept under the stars after a sparse meal of mutton and cheese, and just a few mouthfuls of water. He only had the food he could carry and had to conserve it carefully. At least water was plentiful enough.

Come sun-up, he was out on the trail and made good progress as the steep incline gradually flattened out at the top of a pass. As he started to descend he could see the shine of a river winking in the valley below.

He was on the brow of a mountain pass with more rounded hills seemingly encircling a valley. A vast forest covered the floor of the valley, rising up to a straight cut-off line more than halfway up the range of hills. Above that the tops were dappled in greens and browns. It was majestic but intimidating. He shuddered at the thought of campaigning through this inhospitable terrain.

This will be a hard country to conquer, he thought. Plenty of opportunity for nasty ambushes, and also for attackers to melt away unseen. Not for the first time, he wondered if Rome really needed to flex her muscles in this unforgiving landscape. During the day he passed small bands of men and in turn was passed by horsemen. Some spoke, but most just nodded with suspicion as he greeted them. He had to keep up the pretence of being a friend, but needed to amend his story now he was clearly no longer the employee of an itinerant trader.

The track had at last flattened out, and the going became a lot easier. Ahead he could see two smaller hill courses with the river running through a valley between. A hamlet straddling the river could be the pointer to the hill fort that Caratacus was making for.

Sure enough, the track snaked through the hamlet, and wound up a steep incline, through trees leading out onto open moorland and the hill fort commanding the crown. It seemed solidly built, with a dry-stone rampart running all the way round, at least two men high. There was no gate, instead another wall stood in front of the entrance that anyone entering had to go round before funnelling into the entrance. Primitive, but daunting to an enemy, particularly as they would be attacking uphill.

Pausing at the entrance, Lenc took in the stunning range of hills, dark and forbidding on the western horizon. There was the flat-topped hill he had seen from Gobannion; up closer it had a menacing air in the autumn cloud. Not a place to be caught in a snowstorm.

He dismounted and led his horse into a regular ant-heap of activity. He was momentarily undecided what to do next, when suddenly there was a commotion behind him. He stepped into the shelter of a low, stone-built hut, with his head inside the thatch of the roof, as horses clattered towards him on the narrow pathway. With a start he realised it was Trenos and Verico, followed by

Veldicca and a bodyguard of warriors. They reined in when he stepped out of the shadow.

Veldicca was beaming and obviously pleased to see him, but Trenos scowled, "I would have thought your spying was over, Roman," he growled.

Lenc ignored him as Veldicca slid from her horse and smiled impishly at him. "I didn't think I would ever see you again," she confided. "Yet here you are."

He bowed: "You may not think it lady, but for a person trying to keep away from the Legion, this is about the safest place to be, at least until I can go further west."

Trenos snorted, "You want to stay close to the action so you can report back to your masters."

Lenc turned to the sneering warrior. "You know, I'm getting a bit tired of your constant accusations. I would have thought by now that even a dimwit like you could see that I have no love of Rome."

Suddenly Veldicca stepped forward and, eyes blazing, said: "Enough, the person who is tired round here is me. Tired of you two bickering like children. There is important work to be done while you two preen and spread your feathers like cocks on a dung-heap. You will both have value in the coming struggle, so if you can't reconcile your differences, keep away from each other."

Trenos glowered at her for a few seconds. "I will leave this for now, but one day, soon, I will deal with you, Roman. And as for you Princess, one day you will be my wife, and you will never speak to me like that again."

Lenc let his breath out as Trenos wheeled and led his warriors further into the fort.

"Do you think I've upset him?"

Veldicca snorted a suppressed laugh as she snatched at his sleeve. "You're as bad," she hissed, "goading and taunting him. I can't believe you are a spy, but soon we will be going against the Romans and your knowledge will be useful. I heard my father say this to Caratacus, who agrees. So for all our sakes, keep a rein on that tongue."

He was about to protest that it wasn't his fault, then decided to keep his mouth shut. Teutatis' balls, but she was pretty when she was angry.

Instead he linked his arm in hers and they walked along the track, following the warriors with their horses nodding placidly behind them.

CHAPTER XXVII

That evening the senior members of the Silures and Ordovices gathered in the hill fort in what was declared as a great meeting of reconciliation. When Lenc slipped into the great chamber, he could see Caratacus sitting in the place of honour, but registered that the tribes were separated on two long tables with about 30 warriors seated at each. These would be the leaders of the various factions.

The drinking had already started and, so much for reconciliation, this had all the makings of a first class brawl. Men were drinking steadily, hunched over the long trestles, pausing only to give long hard stares at the opposite table, as they muttered to each other between slugs of beer. At the top of the table Caratacus seemed blissfully unaware of the tension as he talked to the tribal leaders sitting either side of him.

Lenc sat unobtrusively nearby, hoping not to be noticed. He saw Trenos on the top table with Verico and Veldicca on one side of Caratacus, while Alun of Enewydd, leader of the Ordovices, led his contingent on the other. To Alun's left were his two sons, Anarawd and Derfel, two warriors with straggly hair, bold tattoos and each with a silver torque round his neck, proclaiming their exalted rank.

Not exactly a convivial gathering.

Both tribes were pouring ale and cider down their necks, and when slaves eventually appeared carrying plates of steaming meat and bread there was a roar of appreciation as daggers came out, ready to start tearing at the meat.

At least they can agree on one thing, decided Lenc.

He managed to grab a chicken leg and some bread soaked in gravy and sat silently chewing, watching the warriors round him. Heads were close together and men were whispering, looking conspiratorially across the room at the other tribe. This was going to end in tears.

Lenc looked up as Trenos pushed back his chair to step behind Caratacus and through an opening covered in animal skins. The two Ordovician brothers simply drained their own mugs, muttered something to their father and headed down the long room for the front door.

Lenc narrowed his eyes. So Trenos nips out the back for a piss, and these two make for the front. Very convenient.

As the two passed him, he quietly put the remains of his bread on the end of the table and followed. Outside, the two brothers broke into a run, pulling their long swords from the scabbards.

Rain drizzled from a heavy night sky devoid of stars and moon, and sudden movement was treacherous on the slick cobbles of the hill fort.

Lenc shrank back into the shadows as he watched the two Ordovices skid to a halt when they came on Trenos, just finishing peeing against a tree. He jumped back, alarmed when he heard the two brothers, hurriedly dropping his shirt and reaching for his long sword.

Without a thought, Lenc lunged forward, passing the two brothers and stood at Trenos's shoulder. "I think we can put our differences to one side for a bit, don't you?" he asked Trenos, who laughed and swung his sword at the two brothers. "More than welcome Roman, at least we'll find out what you're worth."

The two crouched and faced the Ordovices, who hesitated now that the odds were even. Suddenly a gang of warriors ran from the front of the hall and took up their positions behind the brothers. More Ordovices. Anarawd smirked, "What now, you streak of Silurian piss?"

Lenc and Trenos hefted their swords, ready to face the expected onslaught. Trenos yelled: "Surely 20 against two is good odds, even for you pig-shagging turds?"

Under his breath Trenos whispered, "You go left and I'll go right, let's see how many of these bastards we can take before help arrives. My men will be out soon enough."

With a wild yell he raised his long sword and ran forward, swinging his iron and forcing the three nearest warriors to step back, this was supposed to be an easy assassination, not a fight with madmen. Before his opponents could clear their fuddled brains of beer, first Trenos then Lenc were among them, cutting and slashing.

Lenc sprang forward, taking a swing at the nearest warrior grunting as his raking blow sliced into a shoulder. The tattooed warrior screamed as the razor-sharp blade sank into bone, then scraped back again. His eyes glazed as he slowly sagged to the muddy ground, effectively tripping two others who were about to join the fray.

Then suddenly a gang of Silurians, led by Veldicca, her dagger out in front and eyes blazing, came boiling out of the meeting room to join the fight. A Silurian wearing a grubby sheepskin ran to Trenos. "Apologies Lord, they tried to keep us inside, it was only when the Princess started on them, we got past."

"Are you prepared for the next world, Silurian bastard?" grated Anarawd as he inched forward, his long sword extended in front of him. His brother stood back, as so far there seemed no need for him to get his weapon dirty. Suddenly Trenos snarled a roar, raised his fearsome longsword, and holding it two handed above his head, ran at Anarawd. His opponent went down on one knee and held his own sword up, blocking the powerful swing. There was a clash as the two swords met, then Trenos kicked out, catching Anarawd in the chest, sending him sprawling. At this Derfel realised he was going to be needed after all, and jumped forward trying to swing and slice at Trenos.

Behind him, Lenc could see that if he didn't join in, Trenos would not be long for this world. He came up behind Derwel and thwacked him on the back of the head with the flat of his sword, knocking him down on one knee. He was dazed, clearly not expecting this attack from the rear.

Anarawd looked round uncertainly, and Trenos took his chance.

"Put your sword up you bastard, or you'll both be dead."

Anarawd looked first at his brother, then at Lenc. He shrugged, then his shoulders slumped and he nodded at Trenos. At that moment, Caratacus and the tribal leaders burst out of the side door.

"What the fuck is going on?" shouted Caratacus. "Are you mad? We're here to kill Romans, not each other."

Trenos placed the point of his sword on the ground and leaned on it. "We could have told you about the honour of the Ordovices," he said to Caratacus, "but thought it best to let you find out yourself.

"All they want to do is kill us, they don't care about Romans or you. Their aim is to wipe us out or make us slaves and take our land. If my friend here had not followed me, your plan to beat the Romans would have been over."

Lenc smiled inwardly at the irony of Trenos playing the innocent. He also noted the use of the word 'friend'. If the tables had been turned, Trenos would have been the first to slit a few Ordovician throats. Now he was playing the aggrieved victim.

"As far as this shower of shit is concerned, we are the enemy."

Lenc had to admire his gall. If Trenos had got in first it would have been the Silurians out for murder.

Caratacus gestured angrily. "No more of this. We have real work to do and it will take all of us to do it. Put your differences aside and let's take on the Romans properly. When we've sorted them out you can return to fighting over your tribal differences. Now let's go back inside and drink together in friendship."

As the tribesmen drifted back into the meeting hall, Lenc glanced over his shoulder to where the wounded lay groaning in the mud, their injuries being tended to by their women.

He wiped his sword as Veldicca sidled up to him. Her eyes were still bright in the torchlight but her fighting rage had slipped back.

"So you and Trenos are friends now?"

He shrugged, "looks like it, for now anyway. But this is no way to go into battle, afraid the men at your side may turn out to be the enemy as well."

The next morning Caratacus called a gathering on the open ground in front of the meeting hall.

Caratacus looked visibly angry as the tribesmen arrived. His sword was sheathed but he kept his fist on the handle as he surveyed the gathering leaders of the tribes.

Lenc once again sidled in, intending to stay at the back, but was spotted by Trenos, and pulled forward to stand at the lieutenant's side.

For a fleeting second, Lenc thought he had been better off being treated with suspicion. Now he was one of the boys, his betrayal would be even worse.

"The whole of the defence of our country depends on us all working together," shouted Caratacus. "We can have no more of this tribal rivalry while the Romans are at our door. We need to fight together or they will win. It's as simple as that.

"We know there is an army blocking us further north, and another army coming from Glevum to pin us in from the south. After much thought we, the tribal leaders and myself, have agreed that this is not the right place to meet the Romans. We must go further into the hills where life will be difficult for the invaders and we can meet them on our terms. We need a place to stand, to defend, make them come to us. Where we can use the terrain to our advantage and confound the Romans."

"This is bollocks," whispered Trenos. "We should be doing what we always do. Raid and harry, then disappear. A toe to toe slugging match is just what the Romans want."

Lenc was inclined to agree, but ventured that Caratacus was blind to the different way the tribes fought.

"He'll do for us all," whispered Trenos darkly.

At the front of the gathering an Ordovician put up his hand. "Lord, I know of a place. Levobrinta is but two days march from here and is a sheer ridge, with a swamp in front of it. It will be a killer for men in armour and their horses."

Caratacus looked keenly at the man. He nodded and turned to Alun, the war leader of the Ordovice. "Alun, do you know this place? Will it suit our purpose?"

Alun pondered. "I know it, we can occupy the ridge while they have to fight their way through a swamp and then climb the face. It's as good as anywhere else."

"Good," returned Caratacus, "then that is where we kill Romans. We mustn't keep those bastards waiting."

Immediately after his staff meeting, Scapula dictated his orders for the commander of Legio XIV in Uriconium. They were hurriedly transcribed onto three tablets, and given to three couriers waiting outside with their horses, each aware of their responsibility and the dangers of hard riding through hostile territory. They would take different routes and change horses at Roman waystations, depending on speed to keep out of trouble. As they trotted beyond the gates of the camp and safety, they paused, and before separating, briefly grasped each other by the forearm. Eyes locked and grim-faced until one grinned, and said, "last to Uriconium buys the drinks."

The other two nodded and for a moment pushing the enormity of their task to the backs of their minds, one added: "Agreed, I'm already looking forward to getting pissed thanks to one of you two."

"Don't bank on it," he heard over his shoulder as they galloped in different directions.

Four nights later a bored sentry above the main gate at the northern fort of Uriconium at the far-flung edge of the Roman empire, was trying to shelter from the biting wind coming straight off the ocean. Suddenly he was jerked fully alert by drumming hooves on the road outside. A glance over the parapet showed a moonlit rider, low over his horse, with four other horsemen in hot pursuit. He hurriedly jangled a triangle of metal hanging from a frame and hefted his spear.

"What is it lad?" demanded the Principalis, or guard commander, buckling his breastplate. "Rider coming sir, and there's others behind him, I think they're chasing him."

The guard commander took in the scene. "You did well lad, now ring that triangle again, and call out the guard. Then go down to the gate and be ready to open up, but on my signal, not before."

The young legionary stiffened, then clattered down the stone steps to his new position. As the guard commander watched the galloping horseman approaching, he saw one of the pursuers draw a bow and fire an arrow. The arrow went wide, but even so it helped him make his mind up. "Archers," he roared. "Get some arrows into those bastards in pursuit, get them to sheer off." The bowmen, led by a broad shouldered, bare-headed soldier, stepped up to the parapet. "Nock your bows," he ordered. "On my command aim for the pursuers." He watched tersely as the riders galloped into range. Then with the now exhausted front rider finally approaching the outer ditch, he yelled "SHOOT!"

The arrows with their heavy iron heads sang into the air, then arced and fell, slashing cruelly into the pursuing riders. One went down immediately, an arrow square in his chest. The second was catapulted over the head of his horse, which took an arrow in the neck. The other two skidded to a halt as they savagely reined in their beasts. They stared for a second, then turned and galloped away.

The guard commander bellowed down to open one gate. "But keep your swords up, until we find out who this bastard is."

The rider walked his mount wearily through the gate after it was finally creaked open enough to admit him. He had a bandage on one arm, and his horse, streaked with sweat, had a long bloody slash along its rump. The rider patted his horse fondly, then at the approach of the guard commander, turned. "I have despatches from Governor Publius Ostorius Scapula for Legate Sabinianus."

The guard commander ushered him into the guard-room and the courier gratefully sank onto a bench before a flickering peat fire. The guard commander took one look at the tablet in a leather satchel sealed with the red imprint of the Senate, and said: "I'll have this delivered straight away." He gestured to one of his men and added: "find him some wine and something warm to eat, and see to his horse." The rider nodded in thanks, and through dust-caked lips asked, "Am I the first?"

"First what?" asked the Principalis.

"First messenger to arrive, there were three of us."

"Yes," came the reply, heavily, "You're the first."

As the rider slumped on the bench, head resting on the stone wall, he fought sleep, knowing that at last he was finally safe. The guard commander hurried across to the headquarters building to find the Legion Chief of Staff, right hand man to the most powerful man in his world, Titus Flavius Sabinianus, Legate of Legio XIV, Germanica.

"This better be good," growled Legate Sabinianus as he was roused from his slumbers by his Chief of Staff, Senator Quintus Gallianus. The good senator fidgeted with the tablet, his head down as he tried not to notice the naked male slave trying to look inconspicuous next to the tousle haired Legate.

"Sir," said the Tribune beseechingly.

"Give me strength," muttered the Legate as he gestured to the grateful slave to leave his bed. As he scuttled away, clutching his clothes and sandals, the Senator visibly collected himself and offered the tablet. "We have just received this from Governor Scapula, and I took the liberty of breaking the seal and reading it to make sure it was important enough to disturb you, sir, I think it is."

Impatiently the Legate snatched the tablet and held it near a guttering candle.

"Well, well," he said eventually, "looks like we are going to get a crack at this bastard Caratacus after all."

He sat on the edge of the bed, deep in thought, quite oblivious to the fact he was naked. "Call a staff meeting for first light, I want the legion ready to march as soon as possible. At last we have a chance to destroy this resistance once and for all."

Tribunus Gallianus stiffened to attention and turned to go, but Sabinianus called him back. "Would you send my slave back in," he said matter of factly, "I will need help with my uniform."

The Tribune bowed low and whispered softly, "Of course, sir."

The next morning there was a speculative murmur of voices around the command group meeting waiting for the Legate to appear. Rumour control had been rife since the exhausted messenger had galloped in, and every staff officer was agog to know what it would mean. They would soon find out.

The officers all stood suddenly as an optio, his badge of office a polished vine staff pushed firmly under his arm, strode into the room.

"Gentlemen, Senator Titus Flavius Sabinianus, Legate Legio XIV Germania." He stepped to one side as the great man bustled in, followed by a retinue of purple striped officers.

Sabinianus mounted the steps to a podium and smiled at the assembled officers. He paused for a second, looking out at them. "Gentlemen, at last the time has come to grind these rebels into the ground. We have just had word that Caratacus has an army of tribesmen and is currently heading our way.

"We are to march out and confront him. My instructions from Governor Scapula are quite clear, we are to block him until the XX Valeria arrive. Send messengers to recall the cohorts at Deva and Mediolanum and when we are at full strength the Legion will march. Of course if we find ourselves in a position to take on this upstart Caratacus and defeat him before the Valeria arrive, why that will be to the glory of Rome." He allowed himself a triumphant smirk.

"The glory of Sabinianus more like," growled a veteran optio.

Senator Sabinianus stood, gathering his cloak around him, as he adopted a martial pose and looked into the distance: "Prepare yourselves, gentlemen," he proclaimed. "We are going to make history."

Far to the south, a rider galloped down the line of marching men of the XX Valeria towards the glittering standards held high in the middle of the column. Scapula eased himself on his saddle as the dusty rider approached and saluted, his horse covered in a fine sweat.

The rider handed over his message and stiffened. "From the Legate, Titus Flavius Sabinianus of Legio XIV Germania, sir."

Scapula nodded and took the wax tablet, breaking the seal of the Legio XIV. He hurriedly scanned the brief message, which confirmed that an advance party of the XIV were in a marching camp below Mediolanum awaiting the arrival of the northern cohorts to bring them up to full strength. A screen of patrols working along the river Sabrina had so far seen no sign of Caratacus or the Celtic army.

"Excellent," exulted Scapula. "Only a day's march from the bastard's bolt-hole."

He motioned to his secretary for a fresh tablet and dictated a short reply.

"We do not yet know where Caratacus has decided to make a stand, but we must pursue and harry until we can force him

313

to stand and fight. If you come up," He gestured impatiently. "No, when you come up with him, do not engage. I repeat, do not engage but block his movement further west and await our arrival."

The secretary hurriedly finished the message and imprinted Scapula's personal seal before handing the tablet to the courier.

"At last I feel we are making progress," he said, before doubling up with a coughing fit. His concerned slave ran forward with a large piece of linen and a flask of honeyed wine as Scapula tried to hide the spots of blood he coughed up. The slave retrieved the cloth as Scapula took a long draught of wine, before re-mounting his horse.

As the legion's march started again, he signalled Quintus Equitius, in command of the Valeria to join him. "Bravonium marching camp will be our forward base," he said. "From there you can send out scouts and find the best way forward to meet Caratacus."

Shaking a complete legion out into its order of march was an exercise in confusion and sheer bloody-mindedness. If something could go wrong, it would. But inevitably the day was finally saved by sweating and puce red screaming optios not afraid to use their vine sticks to bludgeon recalcitrant soldiers and animals into their rightful places.

So when Sabinianus was finally invited to lead the Legio XIV Germanica, he swelled with pride at the sight of his legion, quiet and disciplined, ready to march. He mounted a snow white horse held by a slave and took his place in the centre of the column, behind the standards.

Looking round he nodded appreciatively. A full legion was quite a sight. Before and behind him stretched 10 cohorts of 500 men apiece, augmented by auxiliary cavalry and bowmen and with his command group which also protected the precious standards, amounting to about 6000 men. Then there were the baggage train and siege weapons bringing up the rear, way back in the distance. He gathered the reins and licked his lips in anticipation. This campaign could be his ticket back to Rome. It must be done properly.

His train of thought was interrupted by his Chief of Staff, Senator Gallianus, who rode up and touched his helmet with two fingers. "Whenever you are ready, sir."

Sabinianus nodded. "Scouts are out?"

Gallianus nodded. "We have a screen operating well forward, and they know not to let themselves be seen."

"Very good, then let us proceed." Sabinianus motioned to his primus pilus, his senior centurion, who quietly gave the word of command to a trumpeter, who blew one loud note on his cornu, a g-shaped trumpet, the signal for nearly 5000 infantry to step out on their left foot.

The long column marched for several hours before a dusty rider galloped back to report to Sibinianus. The rider saluted as he skidded to a halt next to the headquarter group. "Sir we have cut the enemy's trail. We found track of at least a thousand men and horses. They can't be much more than a day ahead of us."

Sabinianus was elated. "Describe the terrain."

The rider paused to reflect. "Up ahead is easy going until we reach the mountains. That's where things get difficult. We will have trouble getting the wagons through because the hills get steeper and the valleys narrower. But so far they are passable."

Sabinianus nodded. "Good, we shall make Cornoviorum in good time to establish a marching camp, then tomorrow we will deploy into our attacking formations.

"However, we need to move fast. Send a message to the baggage train and siege engines that we need to make time and they can follow us up. Don't suppose we will need the bolt throwers anyway, and the men can lie on the ground for a couple of nights. Do them good."

CHAPTER XXVIII

Caratacus brokered an uneasy truce between Trenos and the two Ordovician brothers, who grudgingly agreed to put their differences to one side – for the time being at least. But of more concern to Lenc was his new position as Trenos's trusted friend, knowing that at some stage the warrior was going to discover he had been right about him all along.

The hard ride to Levobrinta took all that day, and the next, but the bruising ordeal was somewhat compensated for by some of the most captivating scenery Lenc had seen yet. There were steep hills rising from lush meadows, and thick stands of forest which he imagined contained all manner of wildlife. Almost everywhere was the sound of water cascading off hills tumbling down to deep green meadows.

Then at last they came through another valley, flanked by steep and forbidding hills, to see ahead of them a ridge running north and south, with a bare rock face, beneath it a wide sward of suspiciously brilliant green.

"The marsh," said Alun of the Ordovice. "There is a ford, but we have to take care, this place is no respecter of heavy horse."

They worked further round to the north, where, waiting for them was the warrior who had suggested this place for their stand, at the ford marked by a knee-high cairn of stones. When the horses stepped gingerly onto the swamp, their hooves sank in slightly, but as they kept moving, the grass sprang back up as if nothing had ever disturbed it.

"Why doesn't it get muddy and churned up?" Lenc asked

Alun.

The Ordovician warrior pulled his sheepskin cloak round him: "The grass is growing in the marsh," he explained. "Think of it as a mighty river but instead of flowing deep and quick, it's on flat ground so finds its own route, that's why it's so wide. It can be a treacherous place right enough. Unless you know, you could spend hours looking for a safe place to cross."

They rode slowly across the ford until the ridge loomed above. Lenc craned his neck, leaning back against his saddle to get a look at the fearsome rock face. It was sheer, right enough, the grey rock only punctuated by the odd sapling growing from a fissure. He estimated the cliff to be about an actus, or 40 metres high, and although there were some cracks and likely footholds, he shuddered at the thought of attempting to climb it in full armour, particularly if the locals were dropping rocks on you.

Even so, he thought, there has to be another way, there's usually a backdoor somewhere, all I have to do is find it.

The face of the cliff was smooth and unrelenting, until they rounded a small bend, and there was a break which seemed to climb steadily to the top, easily capable of taking three horses abreast.

Alun rode up to Caratacus's side. "We climb here, and when we're on the top will build a trap of tree-trunks and stones which will give the Romans a serious headache."

Caratacus looked along the length of the ridge and the fissure. He nodded agreement. "How far does this ridge stretch?" he asked.

"The ridge is an island which splits the river. We are at the steeper face, but on the other side, the going becomes even more treacherous, where the marsh stops there are steep hills rising right from the river, it's deep and fast. We know it as the Hafren, what the Romans call the Sabrina."

"Really?" queried Caratacus. " Well the gods must certainly be on our side, because this river was very good to us, a long way from here. Let's hope she is still on our side."

Cainos who had scarcely left Caratacus's side since the fight at the river, nodded sagely. "We must stop them here," he said. "From here on, the Romans will have two adversaries. Us and our country. We're used to living and fighting in these hills, but the Romans are not. They will find the combination too much, especially with winter coming on."

Once clear of the marsh, the riders dismounted and walked their horses up the fissure, carefully avoiding the stones that had fallen. The pathway was cool and damp and the rock face seemed to press in on the column. They found it hard not to keep glancing up for fear of falling rocks.

"At least we'll see them coming," said Caratacus.

Swiftly he gave his orders. "We can't do much before the rest of the army joins us, but when they do get here, the gorge will be our centre. Silures to the right, Ordovices to the left. Alun, you will be responsible for the gorge trap, and use men from both tribes to build it. Our camp will be behind us on that hill." They turned and looked at the hill covered in trees looming behind them, "and we can keep ourselves occupied gathering rock and stones to drop on the bastards. There's plenty to do."

Lenc walked his horse to the camp area, where already warriors were marking out places for their few tents to go. He dropped his bedroll on the ground and hobbled his horse so that it could graze near him without wandering off and sat down on the grass wondering what his plan should be.

He knew what his duty was, and that was to get back to the legion, quick as possible, and brief them on the position Caratacus had chosen. And yet, he hesitated. He was feeling a pull from another direction. He reflected for a few moments at the growing enormity of his predicament. It wasn't just Veldicca but, to his surprise, he realised that he liked being with the tribe. They were simple and down to earth people, but honest, and for the first time since he had joined the legion he had been among families living together.

He sighed, he knew where his duty lay.

"You look like you're going to burst into tears, what's wrong?" He hadn't noticed Veldicca walking up the hill, leading her horse. Her long sword swung in its scabbard, looped round the saddle pommel. She sat down beside him, and let the reins trail through her fingers.

"I suppose I am just not really looking forward to the coming killing. At the end of it, a lot of people will be dead and what will be the result? If the Romans lose they'll retreat, lick their wounds and come back, better and stronger. If the tribes lose, they will become lackeys of Rome. Like it or not, over a few generations you will all look and act like Romans. It's all so damn pointless." He stabbed morosely at the turf with his dagger.

Veldicca nudged him fiercely in the ribs. "Ow," he complained, rolling on his side.

"You're going to get yourself killed with this kind of talk. You're one of us now, and you must help us beat the enemy. If you feel sorry for them, you will be a prime target. You must focus on winning as you always have done. Otherwise you will be dead."

Lenc grimaced. "Yes, I have been between two stools for too long. I can no longer take the high ground and say I will not kill a Roman and also will not kill a Silurian. You are right, that's the way to get dead yourself." He smiled at her.

"That's better, now come on, let's see how the defences are going."

By now the footsoldiers were drifting in and were quickly put to work rolling big stones to the gorge.

Lenc drifted from the camp to the ridge top. His careless attitude belied his concern because he had to find a workable route out to the legion and give Scapula as much information as possible. He needed that backdoor if he could find it. He wondered if he was still being watched, but doubted it, Trenos's friendship seemed genuine enough. Something else for his conscience, he sighed.

He walked slowly to the top of the hill, where two guards had panoramic views of the rolling hills beyond, and confirmed Alun's description of the strange feature. Where the swamp lapped against the hill, there was erosion, creating the ridge, which the Celts thought would defend them against Rome. But there would be a way, Lenc knew, there always was.

The severest erosion was where the hill split the river, creating a fast and deep channel on one side and the swamp on the other. But instead of washing away downstream, the rock had fallen and over the years crumbled, creating a beach, catching debris travelling downstream and carving a slope. It was still steep, but eminently passable, Lenc saw, excited despite his gloomy thoughts. This was the backdoor!

Knowing he would be returning in the dead of night, he had to find a safe path down to the beach. A sheep track looked promising so he carefully followed its narrow meandering path taking him to just above his destination. Looking down he felt fairly sure he could manage to jump down onto the beach, even in the dark.

That evening when the fires died down, he readied his bedroll as if for sleep, and sat on it, as, around him, others were doing the same.

He had to travel light, just his cloak and sword, and his precious drawing instruments to make a map. He needed to leave as soon as the camp was quiet, but even then, would still have to get past the sentries.

At last the camp settled down, save for a quiet snicker from the hobbled horse lines. Campfires were dying, drawing in the curtain of darkness.

Slowly he rolled out of his blanket and stood. The first bit would be easy. If challenged he would blame a full bladder. He crept out of the lines of sleeping men and headed for the ridge. The last thing he needed to do was fall over the edge.

He paused as he neared the cliff face. To his left he caught the outline of a sentry, leaning on his spear. He edged more to the right, along the ridgeline, padding stealthily as he left the sentry behind. He was looking for the spot where he had turned off the ridge hours earlier.

Finally, he stumbled over the sheep track, when the grass underfoot changed to greasy mud. After a last look round, he crept forward, carefully pushing back the brush and followed the path in a snaking meander along and hopefully down the ridge. The path certainly seemed to be going down, but in places was dangerous for two-legged animals as it all but petered out against the sheer face. This can't be the right path, he thought desperately. I don't remember this cliff face. He inched forward along the track, desperately gripping onto the rough wall. A tricky walk in daylight, but treacherous and deadly in the dark of night. He would have to make this path work. If he fell from here that would be it.

Inch by inch he edged forward, until at last the track widened out again then stopped. He leaned forward to look over the edge, a rock fall had cut the path completely. No going back now. Gingerly, he got down on his knees and tried to feel for handholds, which certainly seemed to be plentiful in the newly cut face.

Carefully he swung a leg over the edge, searching for a foothold. When he found one, he cautiously put his weight on it and moved his other foot down. Slowly he picked his way down. The night was dark and any moon in the sky hidden by dense cloud.

Then it started to rain.

Zeus's balls, what next?

He got his answer. With no idea how far he was from the bottom, his iron-shod boot slipped off the glistening rock, the jerk causing his hands to lose their grip completely. For a terrifying but thankfully short distance he slid down the side of the cliff face, before thumping into a large boulder at the bottom of the rock fall.

He lay still for a second or two, convinced that someone at the top must have heard. But the only sound was the wind howling through the trees, blanketed by the slashing rain. He sucked some air into empty lungs, and cautiously felt his knees and arms. Stinging sensations told him he was covered in scrapes and grazes, and there was a bump on the side of his head, but miraculously nothing major. He tried to stand, and although hurting like hell, was relieved that nothing seemed broken.

He had a rough idea of his bearings and decided he should follow the ridge westwards, before striking off north east across the swamp. He considered going east to the safe ford, but that would be tempting fate too much. There was no sense in continuing to try to find where the river split, his preferred crossing place.

Carefully he crept along the bottom of the ridge. It was unlikely there would be sentries along the bottom, but he had to stay vigilant. He stepped out onto the lush surface of the marsh and to his surprise did not sink, there seemed enough tussocky grass to take his weight, but he doubted whether it would be like that all the way across.

As he pushed further out, he sensed his feet sinking deeper into the cloying mud. Before long he was floundering, up to his knees as the clinging mud sought to suck him down, making progress exhausting. He paused to slip off his cloak and tunic, rolling them into a ball round the satchel containing his precious papyrus parchment and fastened them on his back with his sword belt. Then carefully he lowered himself full length into the freezing, muddy water.

He gasped as the cold hit him. Once lying full stretch he tried to swim a breast stroke, keeping his legs straight out behind him. That didn't work too well, but when he kept his buoyancy and tried to walk himself forward with his hands in the cold sludge, that was more effective. In this fashion he kept working his way forward until finally with the morning dawn touching the sky at last he found firmer ground.

Looking round, he risked standing up and started to make more progress. With the dawn breaking, the priority was to get away from the swamp and onto higher ground, away from warriors hurrying to join Caratacus. He splashed on, pushing against the water and mud, exhausted but knowing he had to keep going.

Thank the gods, he thought as he finally came to steeper and drier ground. Quickly he pulled on his still damp tunic and cloak.

He knew that by walking south he would eventually cross the path of the legion scout screen, and from there could report to headquarters. He had no idea how far away they were, but was confident he would find them eventually.

By mid-morning he was walking on a sheep track alongside a chuckling brook, when he heard the jingling of harness. At last, he thought with relief, scouts. Then an alarming new thought, what if it's Celts?

He was dressed as a local, and carrying a sword. A threat to both sides. Either could get the wrong idea and run him through before he could explain.

He slipped behind a beech tree as he heard the horsemen coming nearer. Then when they finally appeared through the brush and trees, he saw to his relief they were Romans and nervously stepped out, arms in the air.

He spoke in Latin, but the lead scout still aimed his spear at Lenc.

"Who the fuck are you?" he demanded.

"I am an auxiliary with the Valeria," Lenc replied loudly, "I have been on a special mission and need to get to headquarters."

The senior scout, distinguished by a coloured sash, gestured to three riders to carry on up the path. "See if he's got any mates skulking up there. Don't go too far." One nodded and they carefully walked their horses past Lenc who moved back against a tree.

The scout dismounted and drew his sword while the rest of the patrol circled him. Lenc stretched out his arms at his sides. "Search him," the senior ordered. A soldier came in from the side so as not to mask the patrol's weapons, and undid Lenc's sword belt. It fell to the ground and the scout handed it to the senior. He patted Lenc down, finding the precious parchment, and was about to unroll it, when Lenc intervened. "If you fuck that up, you'll be with me on that crucifix, I promise you." The scout looked at him undecided then reluctantly gave it back.

"I have been with the Silures for some time now and have just come from their camp," he explained in a rush. "They have joined with the Ordovices under the leadership of Caratacus. I need to get back to report and describe their defensive camp. Many men will be lost if the assault isn't planned right."

The soldier weighed him up thoughtfully. "You're Valeria you say, where have they come from?"

"When I left them to come here, they were in Camulodunum on the other side of the country. Before that Germania. I was a building engineer working on the road north. One last thing," slowly, so as not to alarm the scout, Lenc pulled back his cloak to reveal the running boar tattoo on his forearm.

"I need to report either to the Chief of Staff, Tribunus Marcus Pluvalus, or the Intelligence Officer, Tribune Aurelius."

"You know all the right names, I'll give you that," conceded the scout reluctantly. "You'll go back under escort, and I'm warning you, my lads will cut you down at the slightest hint of trouble."

He walked his horse off the path to allow Lenc through and gestured to two of his men to follow. "Keep a close eye on him," he warned, "and if he tries anything smart, show him what your swords are for. Permanently."

"Lovely," said Lenc to his guards. "Sliced by a Roman sword after all this. Keep a cool head, lads."

Before long Lenc and his two mounted escorts walked into the covering force, the heavily armed unit marching six abreast that would be the first troops into contact and would take the brunt of any ambush. They received some curious stares from the formation as it marched briskly past.

Following the covering force on the trail were the advance units of the legion, pioneers and engineers who would ensure that the following cohorts were not held up by obstacles, and then, in roughly the middle of the column, headquarters, including the Governor of Britannia himself, commander of the XX Valeria, his staff officers and the many officers of the administration.

As they approached, Lenc spotted Aurelius, the intelligence officer and waved to catch his attention. One of his escorts growled and moved forward menacingly, sword at the ready. Luckily, Aurelius saw him and cantered over to him at the side of the track.

"Lenc," he said quizzically. "To what do we owe this honour?"

"Boss, I think you'll believe me when I say you're a sight for sore eyes. But first will you tell these two I'm genuine, before they spit me?"

"Of course," he looked up at the escorts, "Gentlemen, I can confirm this man is known to me. You may return to your duties."

The two stiffened in their saddles. One touched his helmet with two fingers and nodded, the other handed Lenc back his sword belt and they both turned their mounts and cantered back up the trail to rejoin the outrider screen.

"Quickly Lenc, what have you got," hissed Aurelius.

"I know where the tribes are making their stand, and I know where the backdoor is." He was about to give his account of his adventures when he was cut off.

"We must report to the Governor," said Aurelius. "No point in wasting time by telling me everything then having to repeat it."

He mounted his horse again, gesturing to Lenc to follow. They passed the sacred Legion standards and behind them, surrounded by his personal bodyguard, the Governor of Britannia, Scapula, riding with his Chief of Staff Marcus Pluvalus, and Commander of the XXth, Legate Quintus Equitius, who gave out a small cry of recognition when he saw Lenc. Pluvalus leaned over to Scapula: "Sir, this is my man who has been with the Silures."

Scapula looked at Lenc keenly, "You have news for me?" he asked.

"Yes sir, I have just come from Caratacus's camp. He has upwards of 7000 spears with him in a strong position about half a day's march away."

Scapula's eyes glittered, his inner strength showing through his pale, waxy skin. "You have done well," he said. "We will be at Bravonium marching camp soon. When we get there, draw me as detailed a map as you can for a briefing after the evening meal. All of my staff will be there, but don't be awed. If you are asked a question and you don't know the answer, say so. Better that than you guessing or telling us what you think we want to hear. Understood?"

"Yes sir," snapped Lenc.

"Stay close to the command group," warned Aurelius.

They marched on for several hours, eventually arriving at Bravonium where the pioneers were busily laying out markers for ditches and tentage.

He followed the command group, whose tents were already up and quickly being stocked with tables and benches for the officers. Apart from the perimeter guard, the universal first task was to dig a ditch all the way round the camp, throwing the spoil onto the bank, making a defensive wall. Only when the digging was finished would the soldiers get to erect their own tents and eat.

Lenc quickly drew the main features of the salient, showing the treacherous marsh and the way the river split to make an island. There was the cairn of stones allowing safe passage through to the rock face, the fissure which allowed access to the top, and an indication of how it was to be boobytrapped. After studying his handiwork he sketched in more detail of the surrounding countryside and as features came to mind he included them as well, not pausing when the clerk brought him a cup of wine and a wooden plate of bread, meat and cheese.

Eventually he sat back looking thoughtfully at the map and took a reflective sip of wine. He went to stand as Aurelius wandered up. "No sit please, Lenc, I just wanted a private look at your map."

Carefully he studied Lenc's efforts. "God's blood, couldn't they have found somewhere a bit more challenging," he exclaimed. "This is going be some undertaking."

Lenc looked at his map: "Sir, these tribesmen are hard fighters and they will fight to the death. Their priests have convinced them that this life is part of a cycle and when they die, they will go on from here to another life. They are happy to die for their tribe. But they are not soldiers." He indicated the map. "The Silures are drawn up to the west of the fissure, and the Ordovices to the east. There is no-one guarding the rear, because they are convinced their back is impregnable. But there's always a backdoor.

"If we cross the river higher up, where the ridge starts, we can be up onto the high ground and attack them from the rear. Once across the river it's straightforward."

"Hmm," said Aurelius, stroking his chain. "But how do we cross the river without them knowing?"

"That sir, is why we have engineers. I don't think they will have any difficulty. The river's not at all deep, but there is swamp which a horse would sink into. I crossed it by stretching out, and while floating on the surface pushed myself with my hands in the mud. It wasn't easy, but if you can float, you can cross."

Later, as night fell, Lenc found himself the reluctant star attraction at the commander's briefing. He was introduced by Scapula and found himself being listened to with rapt attention by the officer corps of the legion, a bizarre situation, he had to concede.

He explained the map and went through the salient points, showing where the camp was and how the tribes had prepared a barrier of rock and timber at the top of the fissure, which would be released onto attacking troops. He also mentioned the piles of heavy stones on the edge of the cliff, ready to drop down on assaulting soldiers.

He described how he managed to swim across the swamp by stretching out and paddling with his hands in the mud. "I'm not suggesting that's how we return, but there is mud and grass root at about knee depth, so if somehow weight can be distributed it will be workable."

Scapula looked across the tent at a grizzled officer sitting with his legs spread wide and leather skirt hanging between. "Marcus Petronius, do you have an engineer solution?"

Marcus grimaced: "How much time do I have, sir?"

Scapula did not hesitate. "I would like to put troops on that hill tomorrow night, what do you think?"

"Well sir, it can be done, but it will be rough and ready. Not suitable for horses or anything heavy, but we have plenty of what we need hereabouts, and if I can have some men, I will build you a bridge."

"Excellent, Auxiliary Lenculus will mark the position on the ground for you, tell me how do you propose to build this bridge?"

Petronius paused, "We collect branches with leaves, and tie them in rolls, about so round." He stood and circled his arms, fingers touching. Then we bind them together and lay cut timber on top, thus making a raft. The brushwood will sit on the mud and spread the weight, so we put one in, then attach the next to it and push out till we are across. That way we can prepare everything under cover, then bring it to the swamp as night falls. With everything prepared it will take no time at all to throw the rafts across."

Scapula nodded. "You will have everything you need. If we go in the backdoor while the Fourteenth keep them occupied at the front, we should roll them up with the minimum butcher's bill."

He gestured for a clerk to take down a message. "This is for Legate Sabinianus of the Legio XIV. Give him the description of where the enemy is entrenching and tell him that he is to deploy his legion in front of the ridge. He may send out fighting patrols, but on no account is to attempt an assault. We will be in position and ready to attack by tomorrow evening."

CHAPTER XXIX

Sabinianus, Legate of the XIV, was feeling triumphant as he nursed a beaker of wine. He was in his command tent in the Cornoviorum marching camp just north and east of the Celtic position. At his foot sat a slim boy slave, from the north of Germania, who smiled as the older man ran his fingers through the boy's blond curly hair. Earlier, Sabinianus had been taken forward by the Valeria pathfinders and shown the enemy's defences. He grimaced as he appreciated how difficult it was going to be to dislodge Caratacus from such an impregnable position.

He had received specific orders from Governor Scapula, that on no account was he to mount a frontal assault, but, he reasoned, it was his duty to use his initiative, and if he judged that he could strike immediately and succeed, then that would be vindication enough. But even for a man of his towering ambition, it was a daunting proposition.

Agrippa pointed out the dark green swamp river, licking up to the base of the cliff face and the fissure, which seemed to be the only point of assault up to the top. "I fear sir, that we should be looking for another way up rather than a frontal assault. They can sit on the top and throw rocks down on us all day long."

Sabinianus tended to agree, but he was on fire to claim the victory quickly. He was not going to be a diversion and lose the glory of defeating the Britannic leader. He appreciated the death toll would be high but the thought he would not be in the assault comforted him.

"No, we have no choice," he said grimly. "At first light we must be in position, speed and strength will take us through, we must succeed."

Agrippa looked at him, but said nothing. It was not his place to argue with such a senior officer, and if he wanted to destroy a legion just for his own self-glory, there was fuck all he could do about it.

Later that evening when Sabinianus outlined his plan to his command group, he pretended not to notice the barely concealed mutterings from his officers. Eventually Praefectus Castrorum Gallianus could contain himself no longer. He stood and waited for his commander to acknowledge him.

"Praefectus," Sabinianus said impatiently.

"Sir, forgive me, your plan is brave and bold, and has the merit of being simple, but with all due respect I can see that we are going to lose many fine soldiers before we succeed, if we succeed. Surely we can find another way to get up there rather than exposing our men to such terrible danger?"

There was an increased murmuring round the room. Gallianus was clearly not alone with his fears. Sabinianus looked at him with a sombre expression.

"This Caratacus has managed to stay out of our clutches, and now we have the opportunity and the will to put a stop to him for good. Yes we could set up camp, dig in, have a look round, investigate other ways to attack, but in the meantime he will see what we are doing and escape once again, and once again make fools of us. No gentlemen, this is our chance and we must take it."

Gallianus again stood, knowing he was on difficult ground and his expression said everything. "But sir," he implored, "can we at least wait until the siege engines are with us?"

"We don't have time, the siege train is at least half a day behind. No more arguments. Get your men prepared for a dawn assault. That is all."

"May Mithras watch over us," said Gallianus under his breath.

That night few men of the XIV slept. They had been told their duties and where to go, and all agreed that this was going to be a bad one. Most tried to get rest, but few succeeded. Finally, in that unreal time before dawn, they were roused and formed into their cohorts. One optio tried to jolly his men along, "Come on lads, plenty of time to eat when we've sorted this lot out. I bet there's plenty of wine and beer up on that hill, all we have to do is get up there and take it."

"I'd go teetotal if it meant I didn't have to try and take that fucking hill," was one whispered retort.

As dawn finally broke over the green hills, the full, jagged fury of the ridge could be seen. Despite themselves the legionaries spoke quietly to each other in alarm.

"Silence in the ranks," came an urgent and furious response from the optios.

Sabinianus was mounted on his white horse just clear of the tree line. Hidden in the trees were the assault cohorts, 3200 Roman soldiers. Sabinianus raised his arm, pointing towards the ridge, then turned to the tree line, his eyes blazing. At once trumpets sounded the advance and the cohorts strode out of the trees and formed themselves into their line of advance. On the command, they marched down the hill toward the placid river.

Above them the waiting warriors shouted insults at the advancing legionaries, getting louder as they entered the water and almost immediately got into difficulties as their heavy armour sucked them into the mud. Discipline disappeared as the soldiers floundered and struggled against this natural enemy. Then a whoosh as a hail of arrows was released from the ridgeline.

"Shields" shouted an optio desperately as the arrows thudded and splashed into his men in the water. "Come on you bastards," he shouted desperately, "heads up, keep your shields up and keep going."

Sabinianus watched as his men valiantly tried to cross the

river; and some did make it, crawling exhaustedly up the narrow shingle bed, hoping for shelter at the base of the sheer cliff. The optios rallied their men and when enough were on dry land, headed for the fissure and their way up the cliff face.

Watching from the summit, Caratacus smiled. "Wait until they are nearly at the top before releasing the main trap. Let's see if we can stop them with the stones."

His warriors crept to the cliff edge and started pushing rocks over onto the enemy. Their efforts were rewarded by the screams of the Romans below, caught in a merciless avalanche. Despite the shouting and threats of the optios, the legionaries edged backwards, fear on their faces as they tried to avoid the tons of stone falling on them.

When the cohort was seen to be retreating, the tribesmen lined the top of the ridge, jeering at their defeated foes. One legionary looked up at them and licked his lips. "By Mithras, there's thousands of the bastards."

At the bottom of the cliff, an optio, a vivid gash on his sword arm rallied his men, seeking temporary shelter under an overhang. "How many have we got here," he demanded.

He looked round and saw that the warriors had stopped dropping rocks on them, expecting them to retreat. Indeed, more and more men were slipping, sliding and wading back across the river. The optio caught his breath as one of his men tied a rough bandage round his arm.

"OK lads, things are different now. We're over the river and there are enough of us to sort these bastards out."

He hefted his sword and crept to the edge of the fissure and looked up. Right at the top he could just make out the barrier of felled trees, apparently lashed together to make a defence. He raised his sword. "There's our target," he screamed. "Let's go."

A wild exultation filled him as he ran and scrambled up the pathway. He could hear his men yelling and screaming behind him as in their determination to get to the top, they ignored the avalanche of rocks that thundered down on them.

Once again Caratacus peered over the edge at the attacking soldiers. There were at least a hundred crowded into the narrow fissure and they were getting closer to the top. He gave a grudging nod of admiration at the bravery of the men below him and then raised his arm. "Let go the barrier," he roared.

Immediately four men jumped forward with axes and sliced through the ropes holding the tree trunks. With a deep rumble, the trunks took off down the slope releasing the tons of stone stacked up behind.

Caratacus and his men watched in awe as the timber and rock crashed into struggling soldiers who went down like mown hay. Almost immediately it was over, the fissure a sea of dead and dying Romans lying in amongst the rocks. Caratacus peered over the edge. "Send men down there and put them out of their misery," he said quietly.

On the safe side of the river, Sabinianus watched, appalled. He had a ring-side seat as he watched the heroic but futile assault and then the crushing defeat as the wall of wood and rock crashed into his men. Even he could see that his legion would have no heart for another attempt on the cliff face. Slowly he turned his horse away and back to the marching camp, leaving others to deal with the dead and the dying.

CHAPTER XXX

The pathfinders crept stealthily forward in the dark night. They were in the trees, having just crossed the marsh, the rafts moving and creaking in the cloying mud. The blindingly simple makeshift bridge worked, and Lenc was confident it would take the weight of the following cohorts. After that, it wouldn't matter.

By Lenc's side, Agrippa motioned the pathfinders to move in closer. "From here on we're the guides for the attacking party," he whispered hoarsely. He touched one man on the shoulder. "Crispus, this is your position on the edge of the wood. Come with us until I give out the next position, then you return here and wait for the cohort and guide them to the next position, hand them over then return for the next lot. Our mission is to guide the cohorts forward and deal with the sentries. All clear?"

His men nodded grimly. "Right let's go."

Silently they eased out into single file, each man gripping the cloak of the man in front. The forest was still and for once the night was clear. Lenc was sure that outlying sentries would hear the crackling of leaves and dry twigs underfoot. To his tense mind each sound was like the crack of overhead thunder.

Agrippa turned to Lenc and grinned, teeth showing starkly: "We'll have you for a pathfinder yet."

Lenc grunted. Back at the Legate's tent, after briefing Scapula on the layout of the tribe's defences and the rear camp, he had asked for the honour of going in with the guides: "To finish the job."

"It's the least I can do," agreed Scapula approvingly.

But Lenc had other plans. He had agonised over his betrayal of the Silures, particularly Veldicca. If there was one thing he could do, it was to try and keep her safe. It was a slim chance but one he knew he had to take.

"Let's hope you don't run into that hairy bastard Trenos," Agrippa had said when he outlined his wild plan. "I should think the chances are he could be quite upset with you."

Typical soldier's understatement thought Lenc wryly. There was little chance of running into the Silures who should be manning the ridge waiting for another assault from the XIV. At least he hoped so.

The news of the abortive assault had reached the Valeria, and word had got out that Scapula flew into a rage when he heard that his orders had been ignored. "What possessed him to make a frontal assault?" he demanded furiously of his Chief of Staff. "Is he that desperate for his own glory he will sacrifice four whole cohorts?

"I won't send him back to Rome in disgrace because he'll weasel out of it. No doubt come up with some half-arsed story that will put the blame on everyone else and thwarting him, the master tactician. No, he can spend the rest of his time in Britannia defending the north. See how he likes the Picts."

The night was quiet and moonless dark as the pathfinders cautiously felt their way through the trees up the hill, before breaking out of the tree line and sinking to the ground.

Agrippa cautiously studied the bare hill, concentrating on the skyline. "Can't see any movement, but they must have sentries out. Go very carefully from here."

Without waiting for orders, the pathfinders fanned out and crept silently up the hill.

Agrippa gripped Lenc's arm fiercely. "My men will identify the sentries and take them out just before dawn. Until then you're going to have to evade them and get into the camp without raising the alarm if you must persist in this damn fool enterprise. If you fuck up you could ruin the whole attack."

Lenc nodded. "I know and thanks. This is something I need to do."

Hours earlier Lenc had laid out his fears to Agrippa and admitted he wanted to get into the camp and somehow save Veldicca. "You want to do what?" shouted the Pathfinder incredulously.

"You could jeopardise the entire assault, put hundreds of lives at risk."

"Look I know the land, I know where she'll be at her father's camp, once I get in, I can find her and get her out of the way."

"You're fucking crazy," was Agrippa's considered reply.

"Has to be done," said Lenc quietly.

"Well I suppose I owe you that much."

The two men gripped arms in the dark. "For fuck's sake be careful," warned the pathfinder.

Lenc smiled at the memory of the exchange and quietly stole away, working his way laterally up the hill. He knew there would be a picket at the top and other sentries round the brow. Steadily he worked his way round and upwards before quietly sinking to the ground. Ahead, outlined against the sky, stood a sentry in a sheep-skin cloak, his back to a tree. Lenc could make out the man's breath frosting in the chill night air.

Hardly daring to breath, he carefully skirted the sentry, then when he was sure he was well past, stood up. He was reasonably sure that from here on he would be taken for a tribesman, it would be seriously bad luck if he bumped into someone who recognised him before he made it to the royal tent.

He pulled the hood of his cloak over his head and held the front closed with his left hand. His right firmly gripped his sword.

He tried to affect the air of a man disturbed from sleep by the need to empty his bladder and was now returning to his warm blankets. He had no idea whether he looked convincing, but if he just kept moving, hopefully he wouldn't be challenged.

He sauntered round the side of the hill then almost immediately saw the fires along the ridgeline, not just to keep the warriors warm but to guard against a surprise attack.

The camp, laid out in a circle with the horses in the centre was covered in a damp mist which clung to the side of the hill, cooking fires still smouldered late into the night. Lenc spotted Caratacus's pennant, hanging outside the tent he knew from the Gobannion meadow.

A short distance away a leather tent seemed the obvious place for the older Chieftain, Verico, and if Veldicca was in camp that was where she would be. He swallowed nervously.

Still gripping his sword concealed under his cloak, he crept forward. He was aware of more sentries wandering around fairly close but they ignored him as he moved closer to the leather tent. He stopped at the entrance and after a quick glance round stepped through the tent flap.

He paused on the threshold, hardly daring to breath and let the door cover drop. Inside a single candle guttered feebly, throwing off a dull light, but it was enough to see four slaves lying stretched out fast asleep. Beyond was another chamber, where he thought Veldicca would sleep, and beyond that, Verico. He tiptoed quietly past the sleeping slaves and slowly pushed aside the hanging door cover. He froze as one of the slaves mumbled in his sleep, then turned over and lay still.

Lenc let out his breath and stepped into the inner chamber. There was only one person there, lying under furs and fast asleep. He crept up to the still body, and kneeling down carefully moved the fur away from her face. Even in the dark he knew it was Veldicca.

As she came awake, she started and her eyes opened in fear as he clamped his hand over her mouth. "Shhh, don't move, it's me. I'm going to take my hand away, but don't say anything," he hissed.

Her eyes opened wide and she sat up. "What are you doing here? I thought you'd run back to your Roman friends."

"I had, but I needed to come back and help you. There's going to be another attack and this time it will succeed. You will all either be dead or slaves unless you escape now."

She looked at him with horror: "Do you seriously expect me to betray my family and my tribe just to save myself? I'm prepared to die and if that happens, it's my fate. But I won't run away."

Lenc expected this reaction. "If you won't come voluntarily, I shall have to make you." With that he lunged forward, straddling her body, and before she could cry out clamped a rag over her mouth, crossing it behind her head and tying it roughly at the front. She made mewing sounds through the gag and struggled violently under his weight.

Lenc was concentrating on keeping his captive subdued while at the same time trying to tie her wrists, when suddenly there was a loud metallic sound and instant pain at the back of his head, before he lost consciousness and fell onto Veldicca.

Standing there, wondering if he had done the right thing was a male slave with a large cooking pot in his hand.

He dropped the pot and rolled the inert Lenc off his mistress. She tore off the gag as Verico stumbled from his chamber, scratching his belly and still half asleep. The older man's silver hair was wispy and stood out like a bird's nest, as he struggled to take in the scene. The slave lit more candles as Verico tried to understand what was going on.

"Father, he came back to warn me, there is going to be an attack. He was going to kidnap me to save my life."

"But why, my dear?" asked the old man querulously.

"He is attracted to me, and I to him, but I would never betray the tribe." Her chin stuck out defiantly as she waited for her father to speak. Suddenly shouts and screams erupted from outside.

Verico looked round, "It's started, fetch my clothes and sword."

The slave ran into his master's bedchamber closely followed by Verico.

Veldicca had slept in tunic and wool trousers, and pausing only to pull on boots and strap her sword round her waist, ran for the entrance, but paused and put her hand on the slave's arm.

"I didn't thank you, but I will." She nodded at the unconscious Lenc. "Tie him up and make sure he can't escape. I'll deal with him later."

With that she ran out into the camp as dawn was breaking over a scene of carnage.

The advance cohort had crept up to the brow of the hill undetected after the pathfinders eliminated the sentries. Only then did the wary soldiers creep forward and over the top of the hill. Then they calmly lay down again, their discipline strong as they waited for the dawn to herald the signal to attack.

Sword handles and spears were gripped as the cohort waited in dry-mouthed anticipation, their job simple. This would be the long-awaited chance to really stick it to these pagans, who never seemed to know when they were beat. Their mission was straightforward, overrun the camp, set up a defensive shield wall between the camp and the defenders on the ridge, who would surely attack and try to sweep them off the hill before the rest of the legion arrived.

One century of 80 men had specific orders to make straight for Caratacus's tent and hopefully capture him, but if he was not there, as was likely, then at least arrest his family.

"Remember lads, we want the leaders alive," warned the optio in charge.

Then, as the fingers of dawn touched the top of the hill a horn blared, releasing the cohort. As one, they stood and with a yell, ran downhill into the sleeping camp.

The surprised opposition stood no chance as warriors scrabbled for their weapons then flung themselves at the enemy, which marched inexorably forward, contemptuously sweeping aside the few who dared to take on their might.

The cohort fought through the camp, knocking tents down and scattering fires before eventually coming to a crashing halt in sight of the trees above the ridge hiding the Celtic army. Instantly they regrouped into a shield wall, ready for the expected counter-attack from the ridge.

Veldicca herself raised the alarm with the men on the ridge. Her father helped her up onto her unsaddled horse then turned to face the enemy. She turned and saw her father slash down with his sword at a helmeted Roman, who simply lifted his shield, allowing the man next to him to lunge forward with his sword, taking the older man under his arm into his heart. She watched in horror as her father sagged to the ground and disappeared under the tread of tramping Roman boots. Then she wheeled her horse and galloped towards the woods and the tribe.

She had just reached the trees when she saw Trenos and his men running towards her. "They've taken the camp," she blurted. "We have to act quickly before more follow. We must sweep them off the hill before it's too late."

"Right" said Trenos uncertainly. He drew his sword, unsure what to do. They could not leave the ridgeline unmanned or the XIV would soon exploit their advantage. But he knew that sweeping the Romans from the hill was the priority.

He called his lieutenant over. "Run back to the ridge, find the Ordovices and tell them we are being attacked from the rear. They must hold the ridge while we take back the camp and the hill. Pull our men from the ridge and bring them here."

He gripped the man's tunic and pulled him close: "Hurry, we must attack as soon as possible."

As the warrior sped off on his mission, Caratacus arrived with his retinue, paling when he saw the Roman shield wall. Trenos quickly outlined his plan and Caratacus nodded. "You did well, Trenos. We all thought the marsh would protect our backs, but they obviously found a way through. As soon as your men arrive we must attack. I would bet that more of the bastards are on their way. We must defeat this lot and be ready for the rest."

Caratacus looked at the destroyed camp with bitter eyes. He knew that his family were already either dead or captured. "Maybe we can save the day yet."

As the Silures hurriedly left the ridge, Alun of the Ordovices spread his men to cover the newly exposed positions. Then he joined Caratacus at the forest edge and stared at the implacable wall of Roman shields.

"The longer we wait, the more there'll be," said a grim Caratacus.

Alun turned to him: "I give you fair warning. If your attack fails, we withdraw. With the Romans behind us our position is impossible. We will be watching, and if the fight goes against you the Ordovices will run and live to fight again."

Caratacus bowed his head, "So be it, I understand."

Suddenly Alun lost control and blurted: "This is all your fault. We should never have allowed ourselves to fight on their terms. I hope you've learned your lesson, even if it is with other men's lives. Never come near the Ordovices again." Then he turned and ran back into the forest to join his men.

Caratacus shrugged and signalled to one of his bodyguards. "Get the Silures ready. When they are all in position sound the attack. But stay back, I don't want you in the vanguard. Oh, and saddle our horses and bring them here, but keep them in the trees." They understood.

As they spoke, the Silures had been steadily filing up the path, then spreading out along the treeline in front of the Romans.

Trenos found Caratacus and confirmed that his men were all in position.

Caratacus gripped his arm: "We have but one chance to redeem this," he said fiercely. "We outnumber them about three to one and if we can once retake the top of the hill we can hold off the rest of them, but we have to do it now. Be bold and strike hard."

Trenos nodded, turned and as he looked at the implacable Roman shield line, his resolve slipped away. He had never faced such an enemy before, but he had listened to tales told by his fellow countrymen who had tried to batter through a shield wall and failed. Now he was facing this awesome military machine.

As he looked, he was joined by Veldicca who had found a shield from somewhere, which she hefted on her left arm.

"No," protested Trenos, "You cannot join the attack, it's going to be a slaughter."

Veldicca drew herself up to her full height and looked at him imperiously. "They have killed my father, so now I am the Chieftain Veldicca and I must be seen to lead."

With a determined air, she lifted her sword and strode out from the forest edge.

"Silures," she shouted fiercely. Almost as one the warriors stepped out. They made a strong line and were encouraged by their numbers, even if they knew they would be running uphill onto the swords and spears of the most disciplined army in the known world.

When the cohort saw the warriors breaking cover, the legionaries started banging their swords on their shields. The rhythmic noise was terrifying in its inexorable power.

A white faced Veldicca stood next to Trenos, then once more raised her sword. With a snarl of rage she started running towards the shield wall. Trenos yelled a war cry and also started running, closely followed by the yelling Silures.

At the rear of the shield wall, a muscular optio watched the warriors running toward them. "Spears ready," he shouted. "Loose spears." Suddenly the air was thick with spears thrown at the advancing warriors. As they arced and headed earthwards, more spears were passed forward to the front rank, and before the first volley had reached their targets the second was in the air.

Agonised screams confirmed the spears were finding targets. Veldicca looked round as her men started to fall. She knew they had no choice. "Keep going," she shouted desperately, "kill the bastards."

Trenos overtook her, using his bulk as a shield from the spears, but she moved to one side and tried to run past him, so they both arrived at the shield wall together, closely followed by the wave of Silures which crashed into the solid wall.

The shield line stood firm despite their lack of numbers. They were trained not to worry about the enemy standing directly in front but go for the man to the right, flicking their swords out and lunging, knowing that their comrade on the left was doing the same. They picked their targets with disciplined ease.

In desperation the Silures threw themselves at the wall. Trenos let out a roar of triumph as he sliced his sword into and through a Roman helmet. The soldier slid sightlessly to the ground, but before he could push through, the gap was plugged by another soldier coming up from the second rank. Undaunted, he let out a roar and hammered again at the raised shields. In despair he sensed his warriors were tiring, they had battered at the wall but made no progress.

The optio at the back was shouting encouragement at his soldiers, whose discipline was standing them in such good stead. He sensed the turn in the battle as the Silures started to flag, and suddenly roared, "One pace forward, march!" The wall crashed forward a pace.

Taken by surprise the Silures had no choice but to step back.

Again the optio shouted, "One pace forward, march!" Again the line paced forward and again the Silures stepped back, looking at each other in fear and dismay. Veldicca tried to rally them and threw herself at the wall once more. She was joined by Trenos, who suddenly reeled back from a glancing blow, opening up a long, wicked gash across his forehead. He shook his head and used his cloak clear the blood from his eyes, then started back in to protect Veldicca. The pair of them fought like demons but could make no impression on the wall. As their strength visibly flagged, a group of warriors fought their way to the two leaders and physically pulled them backwards out of the fray. "Lord, it's hopeless, we are just losing men and gaining nothing, we must retreat."

Veldicca struggled with two Silures, who would not let her rejoin the fight. Fighting back a despairing sob, Trenos reached out to her and put his blood-stained hand on her shoulder. "Come Veldicca, they are right, we will never beat them like this. Come."

He kept hold of her and pulled her away as the light of battle gradually faded from her eyes. She clutched at a long sword wound on her arm, trying to pinch it to stop the flow of blood. Trenos and Veldicca trudged from the field, protected by a screen of Silures who walked backwards, grim-faced and determined their leaders would not be attacked.

When they reached the tree-line, the remaining Silures filtered in and stood waiting for further orders, trying not to listen to the triumphant calls from the Roman line. Trenos leaned against a tree as Veldicca tried to bind a cloth over his gaping head wound.

"We can't do that again," he said listlessly. Caratacus watched him pitilessly. He was unscathed and had made sure he never came close to the shield line. He was about to start haranguing Trenos for leaving the field, when the wounded warrior looked up and focussed on him.

"It's your bastard fault, I saw where you were hiding. You should have been up with us, it would have been better if you died leading your men, rather than skulking in the rear."

Caratacus quickly looked round, only his men and Veldicca were in earshot, the Silures were some way away, most slumped exhausted on the ground.

"You just don't understand, do you boy?" said a smiling Caratacus. "I am the leader who will rid us of our enemies and unite the whole country as my kingdom. This is another setback, but I will prevail."

Trenos's eyes glazed. "You're a fucking madman who will kill us all to get what you want. I think you'd better fuck off back where you came from before my men see you and do what I should have done when I first met you."

Caratacus was still smiling. "It's a shame you still don't understand. You could have been very useful to me."

He put an arm round Trenos's shoulders and moved in so he was shielded from the Silures, as his bodyguard stepped in closer. Caratacus slipped a long dagger from his belt and suddenly stabbed Trenos through his chain mail, the razor sharp blade slipping between his ribs and into his heart.

Treno convulsed as his eyes opened wide in surprise, then bulged in shock as the pain hit him. He had time to squint fleetingly at the still smiling Caratacus and managed, "you bast…" before slumping to the floor.

Veldicca watched, horrified as Caratacus wiped the blood off his dagger on the dead man's tunic.

"Put her on a horse," snarled Caratacus. "Tie her on if needs be."

Veldicca fought back the tears. "What do you want of me?" she managed to ask.

"That's simple. I have lost my family. You are royal blood and will bear fine children. If I am going to be king of this nation, I will need strong sons."

She glared at him. "You bastard, I will never go with you. When I get the chance I will kill you as surely as you murdered my betrothed."

He looked at her, and without changing expression slapped her viciously across the face. She reeled from the blow and held her reddening cheek. She glared at him with murder in her eyes.

"You will obey and you will like it. One day you will be my queen and a great personage. Get used to it, it's your destiny."

With a triumphant gesture he shouted: "Mount up, we have a long way to go."

Lenc came to when a bucket of cold water cascaded over him. He focussed and looked up at the sympathetic face of Agrippa.

"They're running," he said simply. "The day is ours."

Lenc gingerly rubbed the bump on his head.

"What of Veldicca?"

"From what I can gather, Caratacus killed her husband to be and took her, tied to her horse. We have his family though."

Lenc slumped, wild thoughts teeming through his mind. Then he looked up.

"I must follow her, she must be saved."

Agrippa grasped him by the arm. "You're back in the army now. You can't desert. After what you've done, you have a great future with the Legion. I might even take you on as a Pathfinder!"

"That's good of you Agrippa, but my destiny is elsewhere. Will you tell them I died in the assault? I must follow her."

Agrippa nodded in acceptance. "I can do that but how will you find her?

Lenc shrugged. "I don't know, but I have a good idea where Caratacus is headed and by myself I can follow.

"I will kill him and take her." He smiled, "so maybe I am still doing the Legion's duty."

Lenc gripped his friend's arm and pulled himself upright.

"Thanks for your help," he said, as he swung himself up onto a horse that had survived the battle, and with a last small wave turned and steered towards the northern hills.

Agrippa watched as horse and rider gradually disappeared into the morning mist. He did not have the heart to tell his friend that Governor Scapula had personally sought him out and charged him with persuading Lenc to follow Caratacus if he managed to escape. So in theory he was still in the Legion, even if he didn't know it.

He shielded his eyes for a last look. "Be safe and look after yourself," he said softly. "You're going to need all the luck you can get."

Printed in Great Britain
by Amazon